The Best-Kept
Secret

Also by Les Roberts

✿ ✿ ✿ ✿ ✿ ✿ ✿

A SHOOT IN CLEVELAND
THE CLEVELAND LOCAL
COLLISION BEND
THE DUKE OF CLEVELAND
THE LAKE EFFECT
THE CLEVELAND CONNECTION
DEEP SHAKER
FULL CLEVELAND
PEPPER PIKE

Saxon Mysteries

✿ ✿ ✿ ✿ ✿ ✿ ✿

THE LEMON CHICKEN JONES
SEEING THE ELEPHANT
SNAKE OIL
A CARROT FOR THE DONKEY
NOT ENOUGH HORSES
AN INFINITE NUMBER OF MONKEYS

The Best-Kept Secret

❖ ❖ ❖ ❖ ❖ ❖ ❖ ❖ ❖

A Milan Jacovich Mystery

❖ ❖ ❖ ❖ ❖ ❖ ❖ ❖ ❖

LES ROBERTS

THOMAS
DUNNE
BOOKS

St. Martin's Press
New York

❧

THOMAS DUNNE BOOKS.
An imprint of St. Martin's Press.

Library of Congress Cataloging-in-Publication Data

Roberts, Les.
    The best-kept secret : a Milan Jacovich mystery / Les Roberts. —
1st ed.
        p.   cm.
    "Thomas Dunne books"—T.p. verso.
    ISBN 0-312-20499-X
    I. Title.
PS3568.O23894B47   1999
813'.54—dc21   99-22962
                                                                CIP

First Edition: July 1999

10 9 8 7 6 5 4 3 2 1

✿   ✿   ✿   ✿   ✿   ✿   ✿

ACKNOWLEDGMENTS

✿   ✿   ✿   ✿   ✿   ✿   ✿

The author wishes to thank Lieutenant Lucie Duvall of the Cleveland Police Department (ret.), and Catherine Albers of Case Western Reserve University, for patiently answering all my questions.

Appreciation to Suzanne Welsh and Melissa Collignon for rescuing me, and this novel, from "computer hell."

My love and thanks, as ever, to Dr. Milan Yakovich and Diana Yakovich Montagino.

And a real bend of the knee to Ruth Cavin, the best mystery editor in New York, who has guided me with a wise, firm and loving hand; to Nora Cavin, my copy editor these last thirteen books, who keeps me honest, and *almost* politically correct; and to Dominick Abel, my agent and my friend. You've all stayed a long course with me, and in the process become part of my life.

The characters in this book, as well as Sherman College and the city of Sherman, Ohio, are fictional, and any resemblance to real places or persons living or dead is purely coincidental.

CHAPTER ONE

Where do people come up with their agendas, their causes, their passionate advocacies? They don't tell you what your responsibilities are when you're born. They don't give you a job description and a list of your duties. You have to figure it out yourself.

I make my living as a private investigator and security specialist, a job which fulfills and enriches me as well as paying the bills. Still, I'm not presumptuous enough to say exactly why I was put here on earth, because I don't know. And when I meet somebody who does, who tells me they're absolutely certain they were created to save the whales, spread the Gospel of Jesus Christ, revive the American theater, kill everyone who isn't a white Protestant, convince gay people to change their wicked ways, rail against the evils of demon rum, or bitch at other poor bastards about their sexual habits, their choice of reading material, or their cigarette smoking, they are either purely full of baloney or possessed of the most astonishing hubris.

What's right for me isn't necessarily right for somebody else, and I take great umbrage at those who try to force the rest of us to do it their way.

I think our main job is to find out who we are and what's the right thing to do for ourselves individually, and then shut up about it and go do it.

Reggie Parker never had an agenda.

Dr. Reginald Parker, as in Ph.D., is the principal of St. Clair High School, my alma mater, from which my older son, Milan Junior, had just been graduated. His calling, although he'd never refer to it as such, is to educate kids in ethics and living, as well as academics, and to point them in the right direction so they can live productive and happy lives. He doesn't yammer or proselytize; he doesn't even make much of a big deal about it. It's his job, and he does it well.

He's also a tough ex–Green Beret who'd seen enough action in Vietnam to fuel several Schwarzenegger movies, and a ringing voice of decency and reason in the black community on Cleveland's east side, a civil-rights activist, and a two-handicap golfer. And he's my friend.

That's the most important, the friend part.

Reginald Parker loomed large in my office chair.

It wasn't that he was any bigger than I am—actually, not quite as big. At six feet or so, around two hundred pounds, he was a middle-aged, pleasant-looking light-skinned black man with freckles across the bridge of his bespectacled nose. He wore a brown tweed suit with a tan knit tie knotted under the collar of a white shirt—so the mere sight of him wasn't going to send anyone running for cover.

His mild-mannered mien camouflages awesome toughness of spirit. Once, several years ago, he saved my life. Not in Southeast Asia, where we'd both put in a couple of bloody tours in-country without our paths ever crossing—but in a boarded-up crack house on the east side of Cleveland, and at great personal risk to himself, to his life, and to his career as an educator.

So for me, few loom much larger than Reggie Parker.

He'd called me at home the day before, a Sunday, and said he had a friend who could use my help; from Reggie that's all I needed to hear. We set the appointment for four-thirty the next afternoon, Monday. People tend to take care of unpleasant things, such as going to the dentist or calling the exterminator or consulting a private investigator like me, toward the beginning of the week, almost as if they'd spent the whole weekend fighting with themselves over whether or not to do it.

It was a calendar-art crisp fall day, and if I could have seen a tree from my window, it would have been gala with the joyful colors of autumn. The kind of day that makes you glad you live in northeast Ohio.

The public-relations people often refer to Cleveland as "The Best-Kept Secret," because it offers a terrific quality of life that's completely at odds with the sad-sack, Rust Belt image it long ago outgrew. It's just that the television comedians who make Cleveland jokes don't know that yet, and as far as I'm concerned, they don't have to. None of us who live here are anxious to have a million escapees from New York or Los Angeles descend on us, pollute our air, crowd our freeways, and put us on the "cutting edge." We like our town the way it is. That's the charm of it.

My office is in a ninety-year-old red-brick building that used to be a small manufacturing plant, down in The Flats, an old industrial area where the Cuyahoga takes a hairpin curve known as Collision Bend, just across from downtown and so close to the riverbank that if I flicked a lighted cigarette out my second-floor window, it would go *pssh* in the water.

The sun was shining and the thermometer was flirting with the middle fifties—too chilly for keeping my big windows open; but the window cleaner had been there a few days earlier and had left no city grime to block the view of the Cuyahoga's sluggish pilgrimage to Lake Erie or the spectacle of the gulls wheeling and cawing over the sun-dappled current. Across the river, Tower City and the home of the Indians, Jacobs Field, seemed to coruscate in the light.

With one ankle crossed over the other knee, Reggie sat easy in the chair and enjoyed the view; we were friends, after all, go-out-to-dinner-every-other-month friends for several years now. But I could tell he was tense and troubled, and that troubled me, When you've survived hand-to-hand combat in the jungle the way he had, it takes a lot to make you tense.

"How's Milan Junior doing at Kent?" he said, just to get things started. "He wrote me a note about three weeks ago, but that was when he'd just finished settling in. He still hadn't discovered where the biology department is." He smiled tightly. "I guess he's already figured out how to get to football practice."

"He's fine, I guess—we only talk about once a week. He's on the scrub squad, and chafing at the bit for varsity playing time. I keep telling him that four years is a long haul, that he'll get his chance."

"I know he will. I hope he pays as much attention to his grades as to his pass-catching."

"In the meantime, it's a great excuse for me to goof off on a Saturday and drive down to see the games." I pointed a finger at him. "Why don't you come with me sometime? He'd love it."

"I'd like that," Reggie said. "I wish we were just getting together today to do some grave damage to a couple of porterhouse steaks, have a beer or two, and watch a ball game."

"I figured from your call it was more important than that."

"It is." He sighed. "You know I get pretty involved with some of the kids that come through my school," he said. "Especially the good kids, the ones with promise. And sometimes even the bad actors who I think have a chance of making it through with a little help. And I keep track of them after they leave." He ran a hand through his hair, receding like mine to give him a high forehead. "One of my St. Clair boys—he graduated with Milan Junior last spring—has gotten himself into some trouble."

"What kind of trouble?"

"A real bad kind."

"As opposed to the good kind of trouble."

Reggie didn't laugh. "He's a freshman at Sherman College."

I knew Sherman, or at least knew of it—a small, private liberal-arts college in a far western suburb where the atmosphere drips midwest and the student body gets more passionate over saving the rain forests and studying obscure minority writers and painters and composers, than yelling for their football team or throwing toga parties on a Saturday night. Expensive, probably too much so for a neighborhood youngster who'd attended St. Clair High.

"He's there on a partial scholarship," Reggie said, and I grinned. Reggie was always pretty good at reading my thoughts and answering my questions before I asked them. "But this isn't pro bono or anything. I don't want you working for nothing. I'll pay for your time."

"You've already bought me a lot of time," I said, shaking my head. "Your money stinks in this office."

"Well, we'll see after you hear the problem."

I took a yellow legal pad from my top drawer and put it in front of me, ready to take notes.

"I'd like you to look at this," Reggie said, and produced an eight-by-ten piece of bright red paper from his breast pocket. At the top and bottom of the page were jagged holes, as if the paper had been posted somewhere with nails through it, and in the upper-right-hand corner was an eye-catching graphic, a menacing silhouette of a hulking, long-armed, gorillalike man that I imagine had come from some computer clip-art software package.

"These appeared on every telephone pole and bulletin board and blank wall on the campus a week ago, all on bright-colored paper," Reggie explained. "Red like this, bright turquoise, lemon yellow . . . If you're at all involved with Sherman College, you'd have to be living in the bottom of a mine shaft not to have seen it." He unfolded it and smoothed it out on the desk so I could read it.

The top line shouted in bold black letters: YOUR CAMPUS RAPIST OF THE MONTH IS JASON CROWELL.

I looked up at Reggie. Behind his glasses he was frowning deeply. "Read the rest of it, Milan."

I did.

Three weeks ago Saturday, freshman Jason Crowell invited a woman out for coffee. At the end of the evening, instead of driving her back to her residence, he made his way to a secluded area just off campus, parked his car, and forced himself on her sexually.

The woman had been a virgin.

She was afraid to go to the police or the college authorities. And ashamed. She didn't want the publicity, didn't want everyone pointing at her, pitying her, or in the case of some male assholes on this campus, snickering. And she didn't think it would do any good, anyway, because white male establishment types always stick together.

So she came to us. Out of fear and desperation and a self-loathing she sure as hell doesn't deserve.

Rape is not a sexual crime, folks—it's a crime of violence, a pitiful attempt by some pencil-dicked loser to prove his power over someone weaker than he is, and to convince himself he's a Real Man.

We're damned sick of date rape! We believe Jason Crowell and pigs like him should have to pay for preying on women! We believe all right-thinking people on this campus should express their outrage in no uncertain terms. We believe there is no place at Sherman College— or anywhere else in the world—for bastards like Jason Crowell. And if we can't—or won't—punish him legally without doing terrible emotional damage to his victim, the least we can do is let everyone know what kind of a cowardly, scum-sucking son of a bitch he is!

<u>Jason Crowell</u>—and men all over this campus—we're on to you, and you're not going to get away with it anymore!!

At the bottom of the page was typed, *Women Warriors, Sherman College.*

I fingered the flyer thoughtfully. "Bastard, pencil-dick, scum-sucking son of a bitch, huh?"

Reggie laughed, but it was that polite kind of laugh that let you know his heart wasn't in it. "My guess is, it wasn't written by an English major."

"Jason Crowell is your grad?"

He nodded. "Comes from a very nice family. His father is a professional fund-raiser and his mother is a housewife who does volunteer work for the homeless. He's got two sisters, both younger. He had a three-point-five grade average in high school, was the senior-class vice president, and never got into the slightest bit of trouble, with girls or otherwise. A real nice kid."

"I suppose he's claiming innocence."

Reggie shook his head. "He's not claiming it, Milan, he *is* innocent. I'd bet the farm on it."

I was somewhat skeptical; in my years on the Cleveland PD, it had been my experience in accusations of rape or other sexual transgression that there was usually a dollop of truth in there somewhere. But I didn't say that to my friend Reggie.

"And you want me to help him prove it?"

"No," he said. "Not exactly." He frowned deeply, and put his fingertips together to make a cathedral, his head bowed for a minute.

I lit up a Winston and waited uneasily, wishing he hadn't come. This wasn't my kind of case.

"The problem is," he said, raising his chin off his chest, "no one seems to know who it is Jason is supposed to have raped."

"You wouldn't expect them to plaster her name all over the campus."

"No. But no one will even tell Jason."

"What do you mean, nobody will tell him? Why doesn't he just ask 'Women Warriors'?"

"He can't find them. Campus organizations and clubs are supposed to register with the college. But there is no record anywhere of a group called Women Warriors. Most organizations like that have some sort of official status—they even have faculty advisors. But no one knows who's behind Women Warriors or where they come from. Nobody seems to have ever heard of them before. They're completely anonymous."

"Maybe you could check with the various print shops around Sherman and see if you can trace the flyers," I suggested.

He waved a hand around the office, at my PC, fax machine, elaborate telephone answering machine and all the high-tech goodies I'd been suckered into buying when I moved my office from my living room in Cleveland Heights to this colorful old building on the riverbank. "With all your bells and whistles," he said, "you're still operating with a quill-pen-and-parchment mentality." He laughed. "This stuff was done on a laser printer, off a computer. It's virtually untraceable."

"Same with the paper?"

"Every office-supply house in the state sells reams of it every week."

I took a deep drag on my cigarette and held in the smoke for a few seconds before exhaling. Alarms and excursions were going off inside my head; I didn't want the best part of this situation. Frankly, it gave me the creeps.

"That isn't exactly the American way," Reggie went on. "Jason or anyone else is presumed innocent unless proven guilty. And he ought to be able to face his accusers and defend himself. He can't do that unless he knows who they are."

I did a few paradiddles on the edge of the desk with my

pencil. "This doesn't sound like my usual kind of thing, Reggie."

"Yes, but put yourself in the boy's place. It'd be like if you woke up some morning and saw a poster plastered all over town saying, 'Milan Jacovich is a pedophile,' and had no idea who was behind it. Even though you were innocent, you'd still spend the rest of your life having to deny it."

"That kind of stinks."

"The big stink," he agreed. "And now Jason's become a campus pariah. He's already been on the carpet in the dean's office two or three times over this, and the faculty member in charge of sexual harassment cases is doing some harassment of her own. Both the *Plain Dealer* and two of the local TV news stations have been hounding him, and the campus newspaper is all over him. He hasn't talked to them, of course. I told him not to."

"He doesn't need a private investigator, sounds like. He needs a lawyer. A good lawyer."

"His folks can't easily afford one. It's caused an enormous amount of damage to his reputation, something he might never overcome, even four years from now when he's out of school and looking for a job."

"That's stretching it, Reggie."

"Is it?" He uncrossed his legs and leaned forward over my desk. "We don't know if these attacks are going to continue. If some anonymous loonies can plaster an accusation like this all over Sherman, they might have decided to make Jason a lifetime hobby. For all we know, this'll be a *New York Times* headline next week." He rubbed a hand over his face, then readjusted his glasses. "He's talking about getting into therapy because of this. God knows how long he'll need it."

He uncrossed his ankle from his knee and smoothed out the crease in his pants. "Find out who it is Jason is supposed to have raped. Find Women Warriors, Milan, and whoever is behind it. And find out the reason they're trying to pin this on him."

I doodled on the yellow pad—a gallows with an empty noose. I've been doodling that since I was a teenager. Don't ask me why—my mother used to tell me it was morbid. "This is the kind of thing, once it gets out, that's going to make the papers, the six o'clock news. I've talked to the media before, and I didn't like it much."

"I remember well," he said. "It startled the hell out of me when I was sitting watching TV last summer and there they were, talking about you on a national tabloid news show."

"That's what I mean, Reggie. Besides, even though it's a damn sneaky and cowardly thing to do, no one would have put out that flyer if there wasn't any truth in it. I know you feel a responsibility for this kid, but frankly, I agree with the flyer about rape being the action of a coward. Everything in me is saying no."

He took off his glasses and put them in his handkerchief pocket. I knew from experience that when Reggie takes off his glasses he's going to get serious. "Milan, I've never said this to you before. I hoped I'd never have to. But . . ."

He left the rest of it unspoken. I didn't.

"But I owe you?" I said.

He looked down, plainly discomfited, and then met my gaze with a fierce one of his own. I put down the pencil, knowing when I was licked.

"Right," I said.

Reggie left me with two pages of notes and some very conflicted feelings. If this Jason Crowell kid was guilty of what Women Warriors accused him of, he deserved whatever he got.

But the anonymous smear campaign was something else again; I like to see who's taking jabs at me, and I imagined Jason Crowell felt the same way. And accusing someone of that kind of crime anonymously is pretty cowardly itself.

The trouble with the last decade of the twentieth century is that most people consider an accusation tantamount to the truth and are ready to step in and condemn with howls of righteous moral indignation.

The assignment wasn't exactly outside my job description. My main occupation is as a security specialist and private investigator. Milan Security is my company; I contract out certain things, like the technicals and electronics that come with installing a security or alarm system, and some of the more complicated computer stuff. And I have a cleaning crew come in three times a week in the evenings, although I'm not averse to dusting and vacuuming the place myself in between times.

Otherwise I'm a one-man band. I do all the record-keeping, all the marketing—what there is of it—and virtually all the investigative work. My company is named after me—my first name, that is. It's Milan, with a long *i*. Not like the city in Italy, Mi-LAHN, and not MEE-lahn. I figured my last name was too much of a mouthful to stick on my business as well. It's Jacovich, with the *j* sounding like a *y*. And the last syllable rhymes with *rich*, which is its own irony. MY-lan YOCK-o-vich. It's Slovenian, of which I'm inordinately proud.

Most of my work is done for companies wanting better security, investigation of workmen's-comp cases, preventing or identifying industrial espionage, and catching out employees who help themselves to company funds and supplies. But every once in a while I get a missing-persons case, or some lawyer in town engages me to help prove a client innocent. I'm often asked to find things that other people want to keep secret. So searching for Women Warriors didn't really seem outside my normal working area.

Mainly, I couldn't refuse Reggie Parker anything. If not for him, my two sons, Milan Junior and Stephen, would be visiting my grave every other Sunday.

One of the main imperatives incumbent upon all of us, I think, is to back up our friends, to be there when we're needed, without expecting any sort of reciprocity. Reggie did it for me once and came out okay. My best and oldest friend, Lieutenant Marko Meglich, late of the Cleveland Police Department's homicide division, hadn't been so lucky. We'd gone through grade school, high school, and college together, plus my short-lived stint in the department, before he'd gambled his life for me on a rainy night in the Flats, and lost.

So I owed Reggie. For him, and for Marko.

I'd probably always owe for Marko.

Nevertheless, I couldn't help feeling a little bit emotionally blackmailed. I couldn't remember any other case in my professional life about which I was so completely conflicted.

After Reggie left, I went to the little waist-high refrigerator in the corner of my office; it's designed to look like a nineteenth-century safe, and I keep beer and pop in there, mainly for clients. This one was for me, though; I jacked open a cold Stroh's, leaned my butt on the edge of the refrigerator, and drank my beer, trying to formulate a battle plan while I watched the sky darken over the river.

Rape. It made me feel creepy just thinking about it, because I agreed with the poster there. It had nothing to do with sex. It was all about power and control. I felt sorry for the young woman, whoever she was.

Then I thought of my own son, Milan Junior, a freshman at Kent State, and what his life would be like if someone decided to libel him the way that flyer had done to Jason; he had absolutely no shot at defending himself because he had no idea from what direction the missiles were coming.

Young Jason Crowell needed someone who would either try to clear his name and find out who was spreading lies about him, or convince him to turn himself in, face the music, and get help for his problems.

And I like to think of myself as being in the help business.

I guess that's why I went private rather than staying on the Cleveland Police Department. Granted, it's not quite as noble as joining the Peace Corps or teaching in a debt-ridden inner-city school where the plaster is falling down and the rain comes in the broken windows and virtually every kid carries a concealed knife or a sap or a Saturday night special. But one does what one can.

When it was good and dark outside and the homeward-bound traffic had thinned to a trickle, I locked up the office and drove up out of the Flats, to my apartment, where Cedar Avenue and Fairmount Boulevard come together at a point near the western boundary of the suburb of Cleveland Heights. I haven't lived in a house since my divorce, and I suppose I could have bought myself one with the money my late Auntie Branka left me instead of buying the building where I keep my office, but apartment living seems to suit me.

I retrieved my mail, and when I got upstairs I sorted through it quickly, putting the bills in a drawer and throwing the junk ads and catalogs into the trash unexamined. There were no personal letters—there hardly ever are in these times of inexpensive long-distance calling, e-mail and faxes. I carried a beer from the refrigerator into the bathroom, setting it on the edge of the sink while I stripped off my clothes, stood under a nice hot shower, and washed away the caprices of the day.

I was expecting a visitor.

Connie Haley and I had been keeping company, as she so charmingly puts it, since the middle of the summer. The daughter of an ex-Marine–turned–west-side restaurateur, she was strong-willed, funny, volatile, and sexy, with blond hair she usually wore in one single thick braid, and a pair of dimples you could hide golf balls in. She was just over five feet tall, and at six-three I feel like a large building when I'm with her.

I like her a lot, but sad experience and innate caution keep me maintaining a certain, safe distance. I've been in several relationships since my divorce from my ex-wife, Lila, and I've been burned so often that I've learned not to put too much faith in them.

I'm not so sure how Connie's Irish Catholic father and two strapping brothers, also ex-Marines, like the idea of her spending nights in my apartment. They live on the west side, and in Cleveland west-siders and east-siders mix about as well as Serbians and Croatians. And, my knowledge of things Gaelic goes no further than attending the Irish Festival at the Berea Fair Grounds every summer or listening to the New Barleycorn singers when they appear from time to time at Nighttown, just down the street from my apartment.

All four Haleys share a big sprawling Tudor in Lakewood, but no matter how big the house, it's too small for me to spend the night with Connie.

The Haley men seemed to accept me all right, though, and one of the upsides of dating Connie is an occasional free dinner at Leo Haley's restaurant, the White Magnolia, although I think it's really so he and his sons, Sean, who is the executive chef, and Kevin, the bartender, can keep an eye on me.

I put on a pair of clean khakis and a J. Crew sweater, a fashion that's a bit too prep-school for my personal taste; a man as big as I am can't look preppy even if he tries. I felt like a grizzly in a tutu. But Connie had bought me the sweater to celebrate our two-month anniversary and I felt obliged to wear it, especially since I hadn't bought her anything in return. Most men, even the sensitive and enlightened ones who faithfully observe birthdays and Valentine's Day (and not by presenting their significant others with a waffle iron or a washing machine, either), just don't think of buying gifts for small occasions like two-month anniversaries.

Connie arrived at about eight o'clock, bearing a tray of cold cuts and cheese from the White Magnolia. She puts in so much time working in the restaurant—doing the accounts, paying the vendors, and keeping a gimlet eye on the bottom line—that most evenings we spend together we eat in, either my cooking, her brother's, or take-out from one of the many ethnic restaurants of Cleveland Heights—the food spread across my coffee table, since I hadn't gotten around to buying dining-room furniture yet after moving my office from my apartment to the Flats.

Blue eyes sparkling a hello, she brushed past me with a toss of her blond pigtail and took the tray into the kitchen before coming into my arms for a welcoming kiss. It was worth the wait.

Finally she broke away and backed up, grinning, one hand firmly against my chest. "Whoa, Nellie," she said, laughing a little breathlessly. "Or we'll never get to the cold cuts."

"And wouldn't that be a tragedy?"

"Animal," she whispered.

One of the great things about Connie is her attitude about sex. There's no game-playing with her, not a hint of the arch or coy. She's frankly passionate and inventive, and as open about it as she would be about her taste in music. I've had to make a few adjustments to that, but I've done so with much joy.

We went back into the living room and I slipped a Sarah McLachlan CD into the player, one of Connie's favorite singers, whose appeal is frankly lost on me. I can't get too excited about any of today's "hot" vocalists. Maybe it's generational— I loved jazz and swing and the big-band stuff until it morphed into the rock-and-roll years, and my idea of one hell of a singer is Peggy Lee or Sarah Vaughn. Or maybe it's just a guy thing.

We set up a picnic on the sofa, white wine for her, Stroh's for me, and a space cleared for the snack tray.

She brushed an errant wisp of hair from her forehead. "I

needed this," she said in that low, musical voice that makes me crazy, and clinked her wineglass against my beer bottle. "I spent four hours this afternoon screaming at vendors."

"Vendors" is one of those fairly new, businessspeak terms that amuses me. When *I* think of a vendor, he's climbing up and down the stairs at Jacobs Field, hawking hot dogs or beer.

"Just so long as you don't scream at me," I grinned.

"Why? Did you have a bad day, too?"

"Mine was—troubling," I said. I told her about Reggie Parker's visit, and filled her in about our personal history. I spared her the part where I'd had about three minutes to live when he busted into that crack house and saved my bacon. Even though she shared a house with three former leathernecks, Connie was never completely comfortable with the fact that occasionally my work turns dark and dangerous.

Few women in my life have been, including my ex-wife. Lila left me years ago, claiming my job was interfering in our lives, opting for a wimp we'd known in high school, Joe Bradac, whose ownership of a small machine shop rarely puts him in mortal danger. Since the divorce I only get to see my sons every other weekend except for special occasions. My profession has cost me dearly.

When I started telling Connie about Jason Crowell and Women Warriors, her neck seemed to stiffen and her eyes got smaller and glittered. I finished the story and looked at her.

"What's wrong?" I said.

"Nothing."

"You look funny."

She gave me a smile, but I could tell she was forcing it. Her dimples don't deepen when she forces her smiles. "Funny ha-ha, or funny peculiar?"

"Just—funny."

She shook her head and the pigtail swayed provocatively. "This is a pretty ugly story."

I nodded agreement.

"Are you actually going to try and help this little rapist?"

"He says he's not a rapist."

She drew in her chin. "You believe him?"

"I believe my friend Reggie."

"Reggie doesn't really know," she said, waving a hand in front of her for emphasis. "He's operating on faith and hope."

"Then I'll have to add the charity. I'll talk to the kid tomorrow."

"This is lose-lose, Milan," she said impatiently. "It's more than the problems of some college kid. This is the kind of thing that makes national headlines, and you're going to be right in the middle of it."

"Been there, done that," I said. A few months before, a national tabloid TV news program had laid me out in lavender, and for a couple of weeks I had been a bona fide media celebrity in Cleveland. I had hated it.

"Then don't do it again," Connie urged. "Walk away."

"How do I walk away from somebody who saved my life?"

"It's not Reggie Parker's problem. It's this Crowell kid's."

"The principle remains," I said a little stiffly. "Besides, I think if someone's going to make an accusation like that, they should have the stones to sign their name to it. Don't you?"

She shook her head. "I'm afraid you're making a bad decision."

"Is that the polite way of saying I'm being a stupid asshole?"

She didn't deny it, which made me nervous. I got up and went over to the bookshelf that I'd built into the wall when I'd used my apartment as an office; now I actually use it for books. It's also where I keep my cigarettes. I shook one from the pack and lit it. I hadn't wanted this damn case in the first place, and now it was causing me trouble before I'd even started. "This is the kind of thing I do for a living," I told her, waving away the smoke from my initial exhale. "I frequently work for people

I don't care for or whose causes I don't believe in. It's part of the job description."

"This isn't a job," she reminded me. "You're not getting paid."

"Reggie Parker didn't get paid when he blasted into a house full of killers to save my sorry ass."

Her eyes got very big. "He did?"

"He did."

"You never told me that."

"I imagine we could fill a large book with the things we haven't told each other," I said.

She took some time to think about that, but it didn't seem to change her mind any. "Well, you aren't saving Reggie's sorry ass, you're doing it for some punk rapist."

"Alleged punk rapist. You ever hear of that old concept of American justice—that a person is innocent until proven guilty?"

She snorted derisively, which is Connie's way of avoiding an uncomfortable situation.

"If Jason Crowell raped anybody," I continued, "I'll drop him in his tracks. But first someone will have to prove to me that he did it."

She started to say something, but I cut her off.

"That's the way it works, Connie. It's the way *I* work."

Her forehead crinkled. She took a big swallow of her wine, and what she said next made a hummingbird of uneasiness bang its fluttery wings against my rib cage, because I'd heard the same thing from my former wife, Lila, and from nearly every woman I've been serious about since. "This is a hell of a lousy business you're in, Milan."

"It keeps me off the streets," I said.

CHAPTER TWO

In the morning Connie went home a little before seven, leaving the sheets warm and scented. I stayed in bed a few more minutes after she was gone and thought about her, about the way the evening had gone. Our differing viewpoints of the Jason Crowell situation hadn't kept us from making love, but ultimately it had been unsatisfying—for both of us, I think. It had been more like going through the motions than really having a good time. Sex should be a magical adventure, a wild ride, a candidate for the highlight film, not a habit or a duty. But every couple has nights like that, I suppose, so I chose not to dwell on it.

I got up, halfheartedly made the bed, and fixed a pot of coffee, letting it drip while I took my shower. I toasted a bagel and read the *Plain Dealer*, then dressed in a pair of khakis, a dark blue blazer, and a shirt of light blue plaid, complemented by a blue knit tie. I surveyed the effect in my full-length mirror. Still kind of preppy for a six-foot-three, 220-pound man, I thought with some regret, but better than last night's sweater.

Down Cedar Hill I drove, unencumbered by the westbound traffic that had thinned out just after nine, hopped on the inner belt at the Carnegie Avenue on-ramp and headed west on I-90, finally crossing the Lorain county line where the urban sprawl of greater Cleveland becomes "the country." The car radio was tuned to Majic 105, where drive-time champs John

Lanigan and Jimmy Malone were interviewing an author who'd written a book about how the federal government fucks you every day and all the ways you have of fucking them back. Lanigan was having a picnic baiting the guy. I waited for the news on the half hour, then listened to the sports report, and switched the radio off. Sometimes quiet was nice.

Northeast Ohio's fall leaf color was about a week past its peak, but the drive was beautiful nonetheless. I'm always glad to see autumn come around—bracing cold air, carved pumpkins on the front porches, Halloween ghosts and ghoulies and cardboard black cats decorating front yards and doorways, the smell of nice clean smoke, and, of course, football.

I'm not a big fan of summers anyway. When it's cold out you can always get warm, but when it's over ninety, you suffer regardless. Besides, in hot weather you can't wear bulky clothing to hide that extra ten pounds or the roll of suet developing around your middle.

I got off the freeway, following a two-lane road south past the farms that were really the lifeblood of the state. The rolling hills east of the Cuyahoga, the foothills of the Alleghenies, gave way here to flat, open prairie, with surprising copses of silver maple or birch scattered around just to keep things interesting. The occasional buildings that broke the monotony of the roadside were auto-body shops, farms, Dairy Queens, and old Victorian houses that had been turned into antique stores and had nineteenth-century wagon wheels in their front yards.

The campus of Sherman College, hugging the eastern end of the village it was named for, was mostly redbrick Georgian. Tall old oaks, sugar maples, and open greenswards separated the sedate buildings, a few statues of famous Americans broke up the long stretches of lawns covered by the fallen leaves of October, and there was a white gazebo in the center of the quadrangle. Graceful Asian zelkova trees had been planted with geometric precision every forty feet or so on either side of the walkways. The whole campus was quaint, and reserved Midwestern down to its toes.

Except, that is, for the Day-Glo flyers that were nailed, stapled, or taped to almost every light pole and flat surface, all of them the same as the one Reggie Parker had brought to my office. I could see in some spots that the flyers had been torn down, leaving just a scrap of brightly colored paper. The ones that were intact were ugly, not only because they clashed with the stately beauty of the college, but because of the mean-spiritedness of their message.

Just off campus, in what passed for Sherman's downtown strip, were several beer joints, a dozen pizzerias of varying degrees of sleaziness, a Wendy's, a McDonald's, a Taco Bell, a tearoom with lace curtains and white wicker furniture, and two bookstores, one of which sold a wide array of T-shirts, coffee mugs, and sweatsuits bearing the college's logo.

Jason Crowell's apartment was on the top floor of a clapboard house on a side street running perpendicular to the main drag. It had once been a nice, single-family home, but now the former attic had been transformed into a small living suite, and was showing the wear and tear visited upon it by several decades of transient students.

On the steps going up to the porch sat a young man with longish blond hair and the remnants of an adolescent acne condition. He was wearing a windbreaker over a T-shirt and blue jeans with artfully placed holes in the knees and one in the back that was not quite below his underwear line. Wound around his neck and trailing down his back was a red wool scarf at least six feet long, and on his head was a jarringly anachronistic gray top hat, with a garish black-and-white necktie wrapped around it as a hatband. The bizarre ensemble made him look vaguely like Ebenezer Scrooge's nephew, Fred.

"Are you Jason?" I said, hoping not.

He shook his head. "Third floor."

"Thanks," I said, and came up onto the porch.

He had beady little pig eyes, this kid, a faded brown color that was almost beige, and he squinted them against the smoke from a cigarette that hung out of his mouth like a toddler's binky. "Are you another cop?"

"No. What do you mean, *another* cop'?"

"They're crawling all over the place here. You look like a cop." I don't think he meant it as a compliment. "What are you, then? A reporter?"

"A better question," I said, "is who are *you*, to be asking?"

He removed the cigarette from his mouth only half-smoked, and flipped it away with his thumb and third finger. It made a long arc, over the lawn and into the street where it gave off a shower of hot sparks. "My mother owns this house," he said, his scrawny chest puffing with self-importance. "So when I see a stranger hanging around, I ask."

"I'm not hanging around. I'm here to see Jason Crowell."

He snickered. "Jason the Stud?" He dug another cigarette out of a crumpled pack and lit it with a plastic drugstore lighter. If he smoked at that pace all the time, he probably had a five-pack-per-day habit.

He lost interest in me as I pushed the buzzer under the handwritten strip that said *Yagemann-Crowell*, and stared out toward the street intently, as if there were a parade going by. After fifteen seconds I heard a youthful voice yell down to me to come on up.

Jason Crowell stood at the head of the stairs, wearing sweat-pants and a Sherman College T-shirt, and was barefoot. About five-nine, he was compactly built, with slightly curly brown hair and an open baby-face. He didn't appear to be even thirty seconds older than his eighteen years, despite a haunted glaze to his eyes that made him look like Bambi in a staring contest with the headlights of an onrushing eighteen-wheeler.

"Mr. Jacovich?" he said. "Thanks for coming."

His handshake was damp, and not as firm as it might have been, but everything about Jason Crowell seemed a little tentative, almost wary. I couldn't blame him; he was going through quite an ordeal.

"I knew Milan Junior at St. Clair High," he said. "Knew who he was, anyway. He was a jock—I didn't hang around with them much."

"He's at Kent State now," I said. "Still a jock."

He turned and led me into the tiny apartment. It would never make *Good Housekeeping*, but it wasn't as messy as the digs of most college boys. There were no beer cans, pizza boxes, or dirty white socks strewn around, but there were books and sketchpads everywhere, a painter's easel, and a team poster of the 1997 Cleveland Indians—the ones that couldn't quite get those last two outs against the Florida Marlins in the World Series—affixed to the cheap wallboard with yellow-headed thumbtacks. Over in one corner was a midrange sound system with an ugly plastic CD tower, and on a desk in another corner was a personal computer displaying fireworks on its screensaver.

The kitchen, built along one wall in a style that forty years ago was called Pullman, took up one side of the room. Against the opposite wall, beneath the sharp angle of a canted roof, was a plaid sleeper sofa, the kind people bought in the fifties and eventually dumped off in a thrift shop because they were as uncomfortable as a park bench and twice as ugly. I chose instead a rattan mama-san chair in the center of the room so I wouldn't bang my head on the angled ceiling.

One door revealed a tiny bathroom with a stall shower; the other, also left open, led to a bedroom almost as big as the front room. On the two twin beds inside were matching chenille spreads, conscientiously smoothed over the mattresses. There were no posters, pictures or pennants on the wall, and the top of the small student desk against the wall was clean.

"Who's your friend downstairs?" I asked. "The one who looks like Charles Dickens wrote him."

"Oh," he said, "that's Derrick. Derrick Coombes. He's the landlady's son."

"Tough guy, huh?"

Jason averted his eyes. "He'd like to think so."

"Does he go to school here too?"

"No. He's a local. He doesn't do much of anything, I don't think. You want a pop or something?" he said, eager to be a good host.

"Kind of early in the morning for pop, Jason."

He looked uncertain. "I could make you some coffee."

I shuddered to think of what Jason's coffee might be like. I knew I was prejudging his domestic skills, unfairly, but I'm pretty picky about my coffee and preferred not to take the chance. "That's all right," I said. "Let's just talk."

He bobbed his head in assent and sort of collapsed onto the sofa, a listless marionette whose strings someone had carelessly dropped. He didn't seem to have much spunk left in him.

"You're an art major?" I said.

"Uh-huh. I was accepted to the Cleveland Institute of Art, but my father wouldn't let me go. He said I needed a regular education, something to fall back on if the art didn't work out. So I came here instead."

"Mr. Parker thinks very highly of you," I told him.

"Mr. Parker's a good guy."

"I know. That's why I'm here. He told me what's going on in general, but I'd like to get a little more specific."

"Okay," he said. His face radiated choirboy innocence and vulnerability, and I couldn't help wondering if it masked the feral cunning of a sexual predator.

"I can't work with you unless you're completely straight with me, Jason," I said. "So first off, I want you to tell me if there's any validity to that flyer."

He shook his head resolutely. "No, sir. I don't know where it came from. I didn't do anything wrong. I certainly didn't rape anybody. Honest to God." He held up three fingers in a Boy Scout salute, which I found annoyingly ingenuous.

"Jason, you've got to know that if I find out you're lying to me, I'm going to make you sorry for it."

His eyes got bigger and bluer and more frightened, and his voice was wavery. "Don't you believe me?"

"I've got no reason not to," I said. "I just wanted you to know where I stand."

Disappointment dragged down the corners of his mouth. Evidently I was not the white knight he'd been hoping for.

I took out a pen and my notebook, and he stared at them as if they might be medieval instruments of torture. "Now," I said, "when did these flyers first start appearing?"

He didn't have to think about it. "Last Monday. A week ago yesterday. Or probably Sunday night, because they were already up in the morning when everyone was on their way to class."

"They just started sprouting around the campus?"

He nodded. "All over. The first one I saw was on the bulletin board in front of the men's gym. You know how something with your name on it kind of jumps out at you?"

I nodded.

"You can imagine how I felt."

"How did you feel?"

His hands were spread on his thighs, his fingers playing an invisible piano. "I was kind of shocked at first—like it really didn't sink in for a while. And then I got angry and frustrated. Finally I was scared as hell."

"That you were going to get into trouble?"

"Well, yeah, that," he said. "But what's really scary is that somebody out there hates me enough to spread lies abut me, and I don't even know who it is."

"No idea? Not even a small clue?"

He shook his head adamantly. "I've only been here three weeks. That doesn't seem long enough to make that kind of an enemy."

It was plenty long enough, I thought. In my more snarky moods, I can make a deadly enemy out of a perfect stranger within five minutes. "Not even someone you've gone to bed with?"

He flushed.

"I'm not talking about rape now, Jason, I'm talking about anyone you've had sexual relations with on this campus."

"No one," he said, almost breathless.

"No dates at all?"

He shook his head.

"Here you are, eighteen, on your own for the first time, and you haven't even been out on a date yet?"

He looked down at his feet. "I've been too busy getting myself organized to even go out on a date," he said, letting his head loll to one side. "They don't tell you how hard it is to get adjusted to college. It's a little overwhelming."

"What about other relationships with women on the campus? Is there any particular woman you've had arguments with, or who you think doesn't like you?"

"I haven't argued with anyone."

"Anyone holding a grudge?"

"I don't think so," he said. "Not that I can remember. I'm basically just a quiet guy."

"How about in class?"

"What do you mean?"

"Do you raise your hand a lot in your classes? Are you pretty vocal?"

"Not really. What does that have to do with it?"

"A lot of women feel that men get a disproportionate amount of attention from teachers—from kindergarten on—and they resent it. Maybe somebody perceives you as a loudmouthed attention pig and wants to shut you up."

His laugh was weak but genuine. "I try to keep my head down so the teachers won't notice me. That way I can't put my foot in my mouth."

I laughed along with him. "I pretty much did the same thing at Kent State. Do you get along with your roommate? What's the name I saw on the bell? Yagemann?"

Jason frowned. "Terry Yagemann. He moved out Friday."

"You have a fight?"

"Not a fight. He just didn't want to be rooming with me after the flyers came out. He said everybody was looking at him, pointing at him, that it was bad for his reputation." He ran a hand through his hair. "I can't blame him. I'd probably feel the same way if our situations were reversed."

"That must have been a bite in the ass, though."

"It's okay. I mean, it's not like we were friends or anything. We just met at orientation and decided to get a place together."

"And now you're stuck with the whole rent?"

"I don't see any way around that. No one would want to move in here with me now," he said sadly. "I'm looking for a part-time job on campus to make up the money. But I'll bet nobody's going to hire me." His eyes flashed. "Under the circumstances, would you?"

"Probably not," I admitted. "Look, Jason, you've got to give me something, someplace to start. I can't stop every female on this campus and ask her if she's with Women Warriors."

He slumped lower into the sofa. If it had been the least bit soft, he might have disappeared into the cushions. "I can't think of anybody," he said, and then he squirmed into a more appropriate position and sat up a little. "I've tried to ask around myself, but nobody even wants to be seen talking to me."

I couldn't help feeling sorry for the kid, walking around with a clanking leper's bell around his neck. "Who can I see about this officially?" I said. "From the school? That's at least a start."

"There's a special office on the campus that takes care of all the sexual-harassment problems." He scowled. "Room 207 in the ad building. I know it well, I've already been on the carpet in there. But if anyone knows who or what Women Warriors is, it's probably Dorothy Strassky."

"Why didn't you ask her?"

"I did. She wouldn't tell me."

"What makes you think she'll tell *me*?" I said.

He shrugged, slumping down into the sofa cushions again. "Nobody's accused you of rape."

The administration building was newer than most of the other edifices on the Sherman campus, redbrick like everything else, but built with less care and imagination.

The halls smelled like pulpy, raw paper.

I climbed the stairs to the second floor and since the building was constructed as a large T and the room numbering made no sense to anyone except whoever designed it, I had to wander around a bit until I found room 207. There was no lettering on the opaque glass door panel except the number to identify the office, and there were no lights on inside, but I could see the vague shadow of someone moving around, an indistinct shape silhouetted against the illumination from the windows. I cleared my throat and rapped on the glass pane with my knuckles.

The shadow grew larger, and then the door was opened by a woman in her early thirties, yanked open, really, in the manner of a person who has been bothered one time too many by solicitors, salespeople, and Jehovah's Witnesses. With blunt-cut, straight black hair sporting a cowlick that fell across her forehead, and quick, dark eyes, she was just tall enough to come to my sternum, built chunky, square, and close to the ground. She was wearing shapeless jeans faded by too many washings, and seemed to be one of those people who was born with an angry cause. Whatever warmth might have been in her eyes, disappeared as soon as she saw me.

"Yes?" she said.

"Ms. Strassky?"

She didn't seem to like me very much—surprising considering she'd never laid eyes on me before. "Who are you?"

I told her, handing her my business card. She examined it carefully, then jammed it into her pocket. "Private investigator, huh? So what's this visit about? The Crowell kid?"

"That's right," I said. "What made you think so?"

Her lids dropped down to half cover her eyes. "Lucky guess. Are you representing him?"

"I'm making inquiries on his behalf."

She cocked a fist on her hip, using her bulk to block the door like the guardian of a sultan's harem. "Then tell me one good reason why I should give you the time of day."

"Tell me one good reason why you shouldn't."

Her staccato burst of laughter was contemptuous.

"Come on," I said. "You're working on behalf of all the students here, aren't you? Not just the women."

She seemed to relent a little. Not much, but a little. "All right, then. But I've got a lot of things to do this morning."

"Me too," I told her.

She turned and walked into the office with a rolling John Wayne gait; I followed. The decor wasn't exactly spartan, but there were few frills. The standard institutional metal desk and chairs, a filing cabinet with a coffeemaker atop it, and on the walls, several large framed art posters done in art deco style, all featuring women as their central figures. The only illumination came from the windows, and on such a gray fall morning the gloom in the office was palpable. My old eyes would have found any attempt at reading in that light pretty heavy going.

Dorothy Strassky installed herself in the chair behind the

desk and folded her arms across her chest. I found her instant hostility difficult to understand.

"Jason tells me he's been in to see you," I began. She hadn't extended an invitation for me to sit down, so I didn't.

"That's right," she said. "I investigate all charges of harassment or other sexual misconduct on this campus."

"Who said Jason Crowell was guilty of that?"

She jerked open her desk drawer, brought out one of the flyers, this one a glowing green, and thrust it at me. "Read it for yourself."

"I have read it. And it doesn't answer my question. *Who said* Jason Crowell raped anybody?"

She slapped the flyer with her hand. "Women Warriors."

"And who are they?"

Gently, almost as if it was a love letter, she put the paper back in the drawer. "That doesn't make any difference."

"I think it makes a lot of difference to Jason Crowell."

"Listen, Mr. Jacobin," she said, pronouncing the *J* even as she mangled the rest of my name. "I never heard of a rape or sexual-harassment charge that wasn't true, or at least partially true. So I don't give much of a goddamn what's important to Jason Crowell or not."

"Doesn't he even get to know who he's supposed to have raped?"

She glared up at me. "He knows."

"He says he doesn't."

"And you believe him, right?" She radiated contempt, or disgust—I couldn't tell which. "Because you boys have to stick together."

That stopped me for a moment to ponder the question. Why did I believe Jason Crowell? Was it because we shared a gender? I didn't think so—more men have lied to me over the years than women. No, it was because I believed Reginald Parker. Because I wanted to.

"You said it's your job to investigate all charges of sexual misconduct," I said. "Have you?"

"What?"

"Investigated."

"The Crowell boy must have told you himself that I had him in here."

I was quite sure that had I referred to an adult female as a "girl" she would have eviscerated me. But she leaned heavily on the word "boy," so I assumed it was deliberate.

"To accuse him," I said.

"That's already been done."

"What else?"

"What else do you want?"

"There are two sides to every story, but we usually like to know who's telling them before we make a judgment."

Her nose crinkled as if she was smelling something rotten. "By 'we,' I assume you mean men."

"By 'we,' I mean reasonable, fair-minded people."

"And you think that's you?"

"I'd like to think it, yes."

She glowered up at me. "Well, tough noogies, Mr. Jacobin, I'm not going to tell you a goddamn thing."

"Why not?"

"Because you're working on behalf of a little shit who thinks forcing his dick into a woman's body makes him a big man. I frankly don't know who Women Warriors is, or who's behind them. But it doesn't matter. When a woman is raped, especially date-raped, the finger always gets pointed at her, and the man is usually let off with a wrist slap—if that—and not a damn thing is done to him or his reputation. Whoever is accusing Jason Crowell of rape wants to make sure he gets what's coming to him."

"And so do you, don't you, Ms. Starsky?"

"It's Strassky," she corrected me, putting her considerable weight behind the word.

"It's Jacovich," I said, with equal emphasis.

Her swarthy olive complexion went a few shades darker. "Look, we're wasting time here. I have things to do—"

"I thought that handling sexual misconduct at this institution is what you have to do."

"I'm doing it," she said, "by throwing your ass out of here."

"Has it occurred to you, even once in an unguarded moment, that Jason Crowell might not have anything coming to him? That he didn't do anything wrong?"

She stood up, ending the interview, and aimed her chin at me like an artillery piece. "Not even once, Mr. Jacobin," she said evenly.

CHAPTER THREE

Consulting a campus map I'd picked up from the the crusty old security guard at the visitor kiosk in the middle of the main quadrangle, I discovered the dean's office was on the first floor of the administration building, and as I walked down the stairs I hoped for a more sympathetic hearing, or at least one that was more fair. It was always difficult dealing with a passionate agenda like Dorothy Strassky's, which could be bent to embrace any situation. Perhaps Dean Arthur Lilly had a more open mind.

Not much more, as I discovered five minutes into our meeting.

Occupying a large office which smelled pleasantly of books and leather, with a large picture window looking out onto the quad, Dean Lilly was about sixty years old, seeming every inch the dean I remembered as played by Charles Coburn or Gene Lockhart in dozens of black-and-white college movies of the 1940s. His mane of white hair was combed straight back and tamed by a generous application of hair spray. I judged him to be just under five foot eight. His dignified paunch was draped in a dark brown three-piece suit, with a gold watch chain stretched across the front of the vest, and suspenders kept his trousers about an inch above his waist. He looked as if he was waiting impatiently for someone to paint his full-length portrait in oils.

"This is naturally very disturbing to all of us, Mr. Jacovich," he assured me. Apparently he was better with names than his employee up on the second floor. "This school's reputation has always been good, and right now it's at risk." He spoke in an earnest, clipped style designed to make a listener believe that his every word was important and pithy. He leaned so far back in his chair that I thought he was about to take a quick nap. Instead he just studied the vaulted ceiling. "We don't want parents afraid to send their daughters here for an education."

"Or their sons, either, I assume."

He blinked. "Of course."

"It would seem to me, then, that the first order of business is to get some other names into the mix besides Jason Crowell's."

His dark eyebrows, in such rich contrast to his white hair, knitted in dismay. "I don't understand."

"To find out who the alleged victim is, and to identify the person or persons behind Women Warriors."

"Alleged?"

"There's no evidence that a rape actually occurred—just an anonymous flyer."

It was a concept obviously new to him, and he ran it through the calculator in his mind. "It's being investigated as we speak."

"I know how it's being investigated," I said, "I just came from Ms. Strassky's office."

His smile might have been sympathetic; I couldn't tell. "Mr. Jacovich. You obviously have a job to do, and I respect that. I hope you will respect mine. The integrity of this institution is not going to be compromised for any reason. Not on my watch, it isn't."

"Then we have to assume Jason Crowell has done nothing wrong."

"How can we?"

"Because the presumption of innocence has been the cornerstone of American justice for more than two hundred years."

"Well, yes . . ." he said, leaving off on an upward inflection. The "but" was implied.

"Is there a problem with that?"

"The problem is only that this isn't a courtroom, it's a college. A private school, as you know, which is largely supported by endowments from philanthropists and alumni. We can't let anything remotely resembling a scandal threaten that, or this school will sink beneath the waves."

"Waves?"

Dean Lilly's right hand made a tight fist and then relaxed. "The waves of public opinion. And public perception."

"You're not thinking of punishing Jason Crowell without a trial?"

He looked vaguely discomfited, vigorously rubbing his thumb and first finger together, as if he were field-stripping a cigarette. "There's a lot of flak about this incident, a lot of pressure."

"Pressure from where?"

"From the alumni association. From the faculty. From some of the parents." He gently put his hands on either side of his stomach as if he were checking to make sure it was still there. "Innocent or guilty, there's no question that at this time Jason Crowell's presence on campus is a huge distraction. *Huge.* Everyone is talking about him, about the incident, and women are afraid to walk around on campus alone. I see that as a very real problem. A threat to the college."

"So?" I said, the hair on the backs of my hands standing up straight.

"An ad hoc committee has been formed to deal with this as best we can. It's meeting Thursday night."

"That sounds more like a kangaroo court."

"I don't think that's fair," he said, flushing.

"Perhaps not. Is Dorothy Strassky part of that committee?"

Now he folded his hands over his paunch. "As the person in charge of sexual-harassment cases on this campus, she naturally—"

"If she had her way," I interrupted, "Dorothy Strassky would have Jason Crowell stoned to death in the middle of the quad. Surely someone with a little more objectivity—"

"I have the good of the school to think of, Mr. Jacovich. That is what I get paid for. And it's damn well what I'm going to do."

"And you think the good of the school would be served by suspending Jason Crowell without even a hearing?"

"I don't know what we're going to do yet. Whatever measures will be temporary, until we can learn the complete truth." He took his hands off his stomach and placed them on the desk, ready to push himself up out of the chair. They were small, almost feminine hands, with short, well-manicured fingers. "And now I'm afraid I must get on with my work," he said, with an insincere smile.

"And I'll get on with mine. Thanks for your time, Dean Lilly," I said. I hoped my smile was every bit as phony as his.

I stopped back at my office and made some notes on the computer disk I'd labeled JASON CROWELL that morning. I was finally getting used to the computer and all the things it could do, but I still clung to the habit of filling out three-by-five index cards with information on my cases. That way I could spread them out on the table and move them around until they began making sense.

With a black felt pen I made one with Jason Crowell's name on it, another with Dorothy Strassky's, a third I just labeled Women Warriors, with a question mark. Then I did one for Dean Lilly, and for Terry Yagemann as well, and stuffed them all into an old-fashioned file folder. I switched off the computer, locked down the office, and headed east to keep my cocktails appointment with Ed Stahl.

Somewhere back in the Pleistocene epoch, Ed Stahl had won a Pulitzer for investigative reporting. He'd parlayed that into a sinecure with the Cleveland *Plain Dealer* writing a five-times-a-week column on whatever caught his fancy or, as was often the case, what ignited his curmudgeonly ire. There wasn't a single politician or power broker in the greater Cleveland area who had not felt the sting of his words, and while they all feared him, they respected him, too. He was a dying breed, the crusty reporter of fearless integrity, and we had been friends since my days as a rookie in the police department.

Tall and gaunt, with basset-hound jowls and horn-rimmed glasses that had gone out of style with Clark Kent, he smoked his malodorous pipe everywhere he wasn't supposed to, including at his desk in the otherwise smoke-free newsroom. He had an ulcer he continually dosed with draughts of Jim Beam on the rocks, but his drinking never interfered with his job. There was little that went on in greater Cleveland that escaped Ed's falcon eye, and he was my most valuable source of information as well as my sounding board.

And now that Marko Meglich was gone, Ed was probably my best friend.

We met late that afternoon at the well-worn bar of Nighttown, an Irish pub and restaurant which has been a Cleveland Heights fixture at the top of Cedar Hill for more than thirty years. It's a few blocks from my roomy apartment across the street from Russo's Stop 'N' Shop, and only a few blocks farther from Ed's huge old house on Coventry Road, so we frequently plan our meetings there.

We were down where the end of the bar curves and wraps around into the next room, closest to the door and farthest from the small TV set. Ed was on his second Jim Beam and I was attacking my first Stroh's of the day.

"I know Sherman College," he said, sending puffs of blue smoke up toward Nighttown's ceiling. "I spoke there once, to their journalism students, about three or four years ago. Pretty campus. It's one of the few colleges left around here that offers a real education, not just vocational training. Fine arts, classics, languages. I suppose they teach computer science, too." He sighed deeply and bit down on his pipe stem. "Oh, well, nobody's perfect."

He looked up, deep in thought. "That's the last line from some famous film, isn't it? 'Nobody's perfect.' What was that picture, Milan?"

"*Some Like It Hot*," I said. "Joe E. Brown says it to Jack Lemmon in drag when he finds out Lemmon is really a man."

"Yeah, that was it." He picked up his glass and swirled it around so the ice cubes clinked, but didn't drink any of it. "That film was prescient—hardly anything is what it seems to be anymore, is it?"

I knew the signs. Late in the day, and after a few drinks, Ed tends to wax philosophic. "Sherman College," I reminded him.

He blinked. "Right. Well, they're about as liberal and as politically correct as UC/Berkeley or the University of Colorado at Boulder. It's a lousy place to do anything that smacks of sexism, or racism or whatever other '-ism' it's fashionable to go after these days."

"Yes, but to anonymously accuse somebody of rape?"

"That's kind of rough, I admit," he said. "But there's always the possibility that this kid did it."

"I just have his word he didn't. And Reggie Parker's. I mean, how the hell do you prove you didn't rape someone when you don't even know who it is you're supposed to have raped?"

"I seem to remember something like that happening at Sherman before—like a few years ago." He frowned in concentration, his horn-rims slipping down over his nose. "I can't quite get it into focus."

"Can you check on it at the paper?"

"I can, sure." His eyes narrowed and he tucked his chin in and pointed the stem of his pipe at me. "What's in it for me?"

"I'll pay for the drinks," I said.

"Not good enough. If there's a story, I want it."

I reached into my pocket and gave him one of the Women Warriors flyers I'd ripped off a light pole in downtown Sherman that morning. "Here it is."

He read it, frowning. Shaking his head, he read it again, sucking on the pipe and creating a disgusting gurgling sound. Then he put the flyer into his own pocket, took off his glasses, and polished them with the cocktail napkin. "This isn't enough for a column. It'd just hurt the Crowell kid and his family even more, and it wouldn't solve a damn thing." He looked at me over the rims of his glasses. "And the PC police would be yapping at my heels."

"Since when do you worry about things like that?"

"Since being a middle-aged white guy became a hanging offense." He patted the pocket where he'd stashed the flyer. "I'll keep this for a while. If anything develops, it might be worth a column. In the meantime, I'd say you have a long road to travel. Have another beer to lubricate your thought processes." He leaned into me and winked. "It's on my expense account."

I did have another beer before I left and walked the block and a half to my apartment building. Down in the vestibule I collected my mail, and riffled through it on my way up the stairs to the second floor. By the time I got in my apartment, I took it directly to the kitchen and threw it all into the trash unopened. Ads, fund-raising solicitations, an invitation to join the Dessert-of-the-Month Club, and the plague that comes with each autumnal equinox, several catalogs featuring gaudy holiday merchandise that no one in their right mind would buy for themselves. I wish sometimes that someone would actually sit down and write me a personal letter.

I called Reggie Parker at home and told him about my visit to Sherman College. "It was a real dead end," I told him. "The sexual-harassment counselor is ready to whip the horse out from under Jason Crowell, and the dean wants to hush things up and take the easy way out."

"What easy way out?" Reggie said.

"My guess would be suspending the kid. Temporarily, anyway. That'd get the dean off the hook quite nicely, I'd say."

"And it'd drive a stake right through Jason's heart."

I didn't remind him that a stake through the heart was the preferred method of killing a vampire, a creature who stalks the night and preys on the innocent, which was also a pretty accurate description of a rapist. "I'd like to talk to the parents. Is that possible?"

"I can set it up right now," he said. "Is tonight all right?"

"That's pretty short notice. You think they'll be free?"

"I don't think they're doing much socializing these days. Stay loose for a few minutes and I'll call you back."

After I hung up I went into the bedroom and changed from my sports jacket and tie back into the J. Crew sweater. If I was going to meet the Crowell family, the casual look might put them more at ease than something formal. Checking the mirror, I still thought I looked like I was on my way to a sock hop.

I moved back into the den and aimed the remote at the TV set, and the local newscast filled the screen, Channel 12, anchored by Vivian Truscott. A stately, elegant blond, she was the undisputed queen of Cleveland television, much beloved by the viewers. I'd had dealings with her before, on two separate cases, and was probably one of the few people in town who knew that, before coming to Cleveland, she'd been much beloved in Las Vegas as well, mostly by wealthy male tourists who paid as much as a thousand dollars a night for the privilege.

That was Vivian Truscott's best-kept secret.

Everybody has secrets, I thought as I watched her report on

a factory fire down in the Slavic Village area. Maybe Jason Crowell had one, too, and whoever was behind Women Warriors was spilling his beans.

I shook my head to dispel the thought. If I was going to work on Jason's behalf, I had to believe him innocent, for my own well-being; otherwise, when I went into the bathroom to shave in the mornings, nothing would look back at me from the mirror but the reflection of a weasel.

If he really was guilty as charged, he'd have no help from me, Reggie Parker or no Reggie Parker. I operate under my own particular rules, and giving aid and succor to a rapist was well outside the lines.

So I was hoping he was innocent and that I was on the side of right.

Toward the end of the newscast, when the stories had slipped from the hard-news category to the features about pets and shopping, the phone rang.

Reggie.

"The Crowells will expect us about eight o'clock," he rumbled. He had a low voice, and it dropped into the very bottom register when he spoke on the telephone. "I'll come by your place about seven-thirty."

"Good."

"Milan, they're fragile. Nice middle-class family, nothing like this ever happened to them before."

"Life is full of things that only happen to other people," I said.

"Maybe so. But they aren't handling it very well. They're hurting. You need to be gentle."

"I'm always gentle," I reminded him. "You're the bad-ass Green Beret, not me."

"Just keep an open mind, that's all."

I was going to ask him what he meant by that, but I figured

he would've told me if he wanted to. I had a feeling I was going to find out that evening.

Keep an open mind. It seems like I was the only one involved with Jason Crowell and Women Warriors who was doing just that.

At seven twenty-five, I was down on the sidewalk, looking across the street at the Baskin-Robbins store, hunching my shoulders against the icy November wind that whipped off Lake Erie and wondering who in their right mind would want to eat ice cream on a night like this. Two minutes later, Reggie Parker's red Camry glided to a stop in front of me.

I slid in next to him. "You're prompt."

"It's a habit. The school bell rings at eight o'clock every morning. There's no leeway."

"There never is."

We started down Cedar Hill. The illuminated crown of Key Tower down on Public Square dominated the dark sky in front of us.

"Tell me about the Crowells," I said.

"You don't really need an address," he said, "just follow the smell of Wonder Bread. Jim is a fund-raiser, free-lance. Makes a mid five-figure living at it. His wife, Nola, doesn't work, except as a volunteer at Rainbow Babies' and Children's Hospital."

I had to smile, remembering when I'd driven an out-of-town visitor past the hospital and she'd turned to ask me, "What are Rainbow Babies?"

"The Crowells are very community-oriented," Reggie continued. "Jim pitches in on the March of Dimes campaign every year, stuffing envelopes or something. Two daughters, fifteen and twelve, along with Jason. Two cars, a mortgage, and a little fluffy dog. They're right out of a Frank Capra movie."

I didn't bother reminding him that most Frank Capra movies are about ordinary, seemingly helpless people who eventually rebel against the system and oppressive, greedy bankers or businessmen played by actors like Lionel Barrymore and Edward Arnold, and eventually triumph because of the basic goodness of humankind—witness *Meet John Doe* and *It's a Wonderful Life.*

The Crowell family lived in an old three-story Cape Cod colonial painted butternut gray, not too far from the lake, its porch light glowing a welcome in the darkness. On the neatly trimmed front lawn, a scattering of unraked leaves carpeted the grass, and a flowering dogwood tree waited to drop its autumn-red foliage for winter; the bushes flanking either side of the front door were rhododendrons. Behind the house, looming over it like a brooding colossus, was a giant oak that had lost most of its leaves already. The "little fluffy dog" Reggie had spoken of was yipping unseen behind a fence in the backyard.

Nola Crowell opened the door for us. Plain-pretty and in her early forties, the shadows under her eyes and the lines that formed parentheses at the corners of her mouth showed the strain she'd been under for the past week. She wore low heels and a pale green shirtwaist dress, with a matching barrette holding back her soft brown hair, reminding me of Harriet Nelson.

Her husband was no Ozzie, though; he was large and robust like a high-school athlete who'd let himself go, with a receding hairline and a florid complexion, wearing a tieless white shirt he'd obviously had on all day, and the pleated pants to a brown suit. His voice was hearty, almost booming, but there was a defeated slump to his shoulders. He looked like the kind of man who carries around a subcutaneous anger about the fact that he wasn't more handsome and successful and powerful—and Nola Crowell was the woman he'd married when he was very young.

In the living room were the two Crowell girls. The older,

still encumbered with baby fat, seemed bored and resentful; the younger, more animated and well on her way to becoming a stunning beauty, with ash-blond hair and deep-green eyes.

"Don't you guys have homework?" Jim Crowell said, and made it an accusation.

"Did it," the older girl replied. She was at that age when she was unwilling to spend any more than the minimum amount of words on her parents. Her mother had introduced her as Cherie.

"Well, go on up to your room and watch TV, then."

"Why can't we stay?" the younger daughter, Yvonne, asked. It wasn't whiny or sullen at all, just a straightforward question. "Jason's our brother, too."

"Just get upstairs," Jim Crowell ordered, with an edge that left little room for negotiation.

The two girls stood up, Cherie accompanying her move with great, exaggerated rolls of her eyes, and climbed the stairs. After a few moments the muffled sound of a TV set from up on the second floor came through the living-room ceiling.

Someone had built an excellent fire in the hearth, and the pleasant fall smell of woodsmoke permeated the living room. Jim and Nola Crowell sat in wingback chairs flanking the fireplace; Reggie and I were on a sofa directly facing it. Mrs. Crowell had offered us coffee and when we declined, her husband had suggested a drink. But this wasn't a social occasion and I didn't want to make it seem like one.

"Mr. Jacovich," Nola Crowell said, "Mr. Parker says you can help Jason."

"I can try," I said. "Right now I don't have much to go on."

"Jason is very hurt by this. And confused. He's even talking about—leaving school."

"That would be a mistake," I told her. "Almost sure to be perceived as an admission of guilt. But I talked to Dean Lilly this morning, and I wouldn't be surprised if they suspended Jason. Temporarily."

"Goddamn it, they can't do that!" Crowell exploded. "Even with the scholarship, I'm paying a fortune for him to go to that lousy school!"

"They can do it—I think. It would be a good idea for you to contact a lawyer before it happens."

"A lawyer . . ." Nola breathed.

"More goddamn expense!" her husband said.

"I think a lawyer would be more helpful in that situation than either Mr. Jacovich or myself," Reggie put in.

"What I can do is try to find out exactly who is making these accusations," I said. "Otherwise, it's almost impossible to fight a phantom."

"What can we do?" Nola asked.

"Let's just talk a while and see what surfaces." I glanced at Reggie, who gave me a brusque nod. "What do you know about the people Jason met in his first few weeks at Sherman?"

Nola Crowell ran her hand along the side of her cheek, pulling down the corner of her mouth. "I can't remember. You know how kids ramble on about things sometimes. I didn't even pay attention. I didn't know it would be important . . ."

Mistake number one, I thought. Parents who don't listen to their children often live to regret it.

"What about his roommate? Terry Yagemann?"

"I never met the kid," Jim Crowell said.

"But Jason talked about him?"

"Some—not much. They weren't close pals or anything. They were both looking for a cheap place to live and figured if they shared an apartment it would cut down expenses for both of them. Then the little bastard moved out at the first sign of Jason's troubles."

"Did Jason ever mention any women?"

Crowell flushed darkly. "He didn't have time for women. I'm

not paying ten grand a year just so he can go out and get laid."
His wife flinched. "He knew damn well he'd have to buckle
down on his studies or he'd wind up at some second-rate inner-
city college, washing dishes for his keep."

"I'm not necessarily talking about a girlfriend. But surely in
three weeks he must have met some woman he liked—just to
talk to."

Crowell sniffed and shook his head.

"There was a girl he mentioned once or twice on the phone,"
Nola said, picking at a loose piece of skin beside her thumbnail.
She obviously did that a lot, because the flesh was red and sore-
looking.

"What was her name, Mrs. Crowell?"

"It's an unusual name—Marika something. She's in his English lit class, I think. He said they had coffee a few times."

"No last name?"

"I can't remember."

"Mr. Crowell?"

"I never heard anything about any Marika," he almost
growled.

I wrote the name in my notebook. "What about his teachers,
his professors? Did he get along well with them?"

"As far as I know," Nola said. "He's kind of a quiet kid. I
can't imagine him having a run-in with one of his teachers."

"Look," Crowell said, "we're wasting a lot of time here with
useless crap. Whether or not Jason's teachers like him is completely irrelevant. What I want is to get him off the hook so he
can get on with his life."

"Off the hook?"

He leveled a finger at me, swiveled it around to include Reggie, and then back to me. His face was red and he was
breathing hard, as if he'd been exercising heavily. "Whatever
went on, Jason doesn't deserve this, this sneak attack. It's got
to stop."

"Whether or not it stops, Mr. Crowell, it's not going to go away," Reggie said.

"Then I want him exonerated! I want him to concentrate on his schoolwork so he can make something of himself. Is that so much for a father to ask? Jesus, this could ruin his whole life."

"It could," I agreed. "That's why anything you can tell me, anyone he mentioned, anything out of the ordinary that happened, would be really helpful."

"If I knew anything," Crowell said, with more than a hint of menace, "I'd take care of it myself."

I believed he would, at that. "Not a good idea, sir. You're better off leaving it to the professionals. Here's my card," I said, handing it to Mrs. Crowell; I was afraid that in his present frame of mind, her husband might eat it. "If you think of anything Jason said—anything at all, even if it doesn't seem important—give me a call. And get in touch with an attorney. You're going to need one, I think."

"I'm sure Mr. Parker has told you," Jim Crowell said, "that I can't afford to pay you for any of this."

"And I'm sure he told you that isn't a problem."

He glowered. "Just so we understand each other."

"I think I understand you perfectly, Mr. Crowell," I said, and his head jerked a little. Good, I thought; he got it.

We talked for a few minutes more, but no one offered anything that seemed helpful to Jason's cause, and Crowell just got redder in the face thinking about what a lawyer was going to cost him. Eventually Reggie and I made our good-byes. Crowell hadn't softened his aggressiveness much, but his handshake was less warm and more wimpy than when we'd come in—a dead carp, just like his son's. Mrs. Crowell simply nodded a mute farewell; she was too busy wringing her own hands to do anything else with them.

We went down the sidewalk to Reggie's car, and I could feel Jim Crowell's gaze eating a hole in my back. Neither of us said anything until Reggie started the engine and steered the car back toward Cleveland Heights.

"What do you think, Milan?"

I shook my head. "Mrs. Crowell seems like a nice person who doesn't deserve this kind of aggravation. The trouble is, her husband thinks he's a tough guy. At least that's how he acts."

"You probably would, too, if you were in his position," Reggie said in that low, rumbling voice of his.

"He acts like he doesn't like his son very much. As a father, I find that pretty hard to swallow."

"He's under a lot of stress."

"More than you might imagine."

He took his eyes off the road for a second and glanced over at me. "What's that supposed to mean?"

"Forget it."

"That'll be hard. What are you getting at?"

I shook my head. "I shouldn't have said anything. It's just a hunch. Let's not even go there."

"This is no time to shut me out of the loop, Milan."

"You don't want to hear conjecture," I said. "It's not fair."

"The hell it's not," he said mildly. "Jason Crowell was one of my special projects. I like him, I believe in him, and if it wasn't for me, you'd be sitting home by yourself watching *Friends* on TV."

"First of all, *Friends* isn't on on Tuesday," I reminded him. "And secondly, I wouldn't be watching it even if it was. Whiny twenty-somethings with sexual hangups aren't my idea of good companions, even on TV."

"It's a good show, you should watch," he said. "I do."

"What can I do to get you to stop, then, Reggie? Friends don't let friends watch *Friends*."

He chuckled, then turned serious. "I mean it, Milan. What is it you don't want to conjecture about?"

I propped my elbow on the armrest in the door and sank my chin down on my hand. Reggie was tenacious as a Doberman sometimes, and he was not going to be denied. "All right, then. I can't be sure," I said. "But my guess is that Jim Crowell thinks his son is guilty."

CHAPTER FOUR

Early the next morning I drove back out to Sherman, but the trip was less pleasant than the day before. The brisk wind coming across the lake from Canada blew the promise of winter ahead of it. The temperature had dropped overnight and stayed in the low forties, and the sunless sky was no color at all.

Jason wasn't at his apartment, so I ducked into the little tea shop on the main street just across from the edge of the campus. This was not an upscale, baby-boomer, latte-and-cappuccino kind of coffeehouse, mind you, but a genuine tearoom where they trimmed the crusts off the bread on your cucumber sandwiches. Nevertheless, I had a cup of coffee, which I augmented with a buttered croissant in lieu of breakfast. I'm not a great admirer of croissants—bagels with cream cheese, or glazed donuts are more to my liking. But when on alien ground, one makes do.

I sat by a window so I could watch the pedestrian traffic, most of which seemed to be Sherman students. They moved with purpose, on their way, probably, to class. They were mostly white or Asian, with a few black faces thrown in, mostly intense, mostly caught in that fumblingly awkward stage between adolescence and adulthood where everything seems possible.

After I finished the croissant, I walked across the street to the campus proper, diagonally bisected the quadrangle, and stopped off in the main office of the administration building to go through a student directory. Terry Yagemann was listed, but at his old address, the one he shared with Jason. I browsed several pages to see if I could spot a Marika, but there were more than thirty-five hundred students enrolled at Sherman, and I quickly abandoned my search.

My watch told me it was almost ten-thirty, and I retraced my steps across campus to Jason's apartment. This time he was home.

"Hey, Mr. Jacovich," he said, giving a halfhearted wave. He was dressed in rumpled chinos and a plaid shirt. New-looking Reeboks peeked out from the cuffs of his pants. A medium-weight jacket had been tossed onto the mama-san chair, and on the sofa were two books, open facedown, a sketchpad, and several sharpened pencils. "I didn't expect to see you again so soon."

'I know you're studying, Jason, so I won't take up too much of your time. I just have a couple of questions."

He didn't look happy about it, but he squared his shoulders and set himself for whatever was coming. "Shoot," he said. He was a gamer, Jason.

"Okay. I need Terry Yagemann's new address."

He became guarded. "What for?"

"I just want to talk to him."

"Why?"

"I don't know why, yet. If I knew the answers, I wouldn't need to ask questions."

He stood immobile for a moment, not even breathing, his face like a death mask. Then, with dragging feet he moved to the sofa, jotted something down on a notebook page, and ripped it out and handed it to me.

"This is where he moved to. It's about four blocks east of here," he said.

"East?" I pointed out the window, but he smiled tolerantly

and pointed toward the opposite wall. Get me out of Cleveland and I have no sense of direction.

"I don't know what you want to talk to Terry for."

"He's one of the only names I have," I said. "Now I need another one from you."

He raised his eyebrows in expectation.

"You have a friend named Marika."

Jason's face darkened, his brows lowered, and his head wagged from side to side like an angry camel. "Uh-uh, no way," he said, more assertive than I'd seen him before. "No fucking way."

"Why not, Jason?"

"Just no way."

"Look," I said, "I'm trying to get your good name back, keep you in school, and maybe even out of jail. The only way I can do it is to track down every lead. At this point there aren't any. I've talked to Dorothy Strassky, to Dean Lilly, and now I'm going to talk to Terry Yagemann. After that I'm plumb out of names. Maybe your friend Marika can help—if only for a character reference."

"No way," he said again, like a mantra.

We stood there in the middle of his little living room as he glared at me, his jaw jutting out at a pugnacious angle. Finally I broke the staring contest.

"Fine," I said. "I can't help you if you won't help me do it. I'm not getting paid anyway. I'll just get out of your face and you can fend for yourself." I turned away from him and moved toward the door. "I wish you luck. You're going to need it."

I had my hand on the knob before he said, "Wait a minute."

I stopped, turned. His face was stricken.

"Please," he said, and then licked his lips. "Please don't run out on me, Mr. Jacovich. I need all the help I can get."

I didn't say anything.

"Look, Marika's my friend. She's a really nice person. I don't want her getting involved in all this shit."

"I'm not going to involve her, I'm just going to talk to her."

"Promise?"

I gave him the three-fingered Boy Scout salute he'd given me the day before. It made him smile, the first time he'd done so in my presence, and his shoulders relaxed a little. "Her name is Marika Rollins," he said at last.

He went back over to the sofa and fished a small black address book from the clutter on the coffee table and thumbed through it until he found the page he wanted, then handed it over to me. "She lives in student housing on campus."

I copied down the address and phone number in my own notebook. "I talked to your family last night," I said as I wrote.

Jason went on full alert. "Oh?"

"Nice people." I put the notebook back in my pocket. "You get along with them okay?"

"Why?" he bristled.

"Just asking."

He shoved his hands into the pockets of his chinos. "They're all right."

His lack of enthusiasm wasn't unusual; most kids his age think their parents are terminally clueless. But I had to probe a little more. "Just all right?"

His mouth tightened. "They're fine."

"I know parents and kids find it hard to communicate."

"I communicate fine," he said, without any real conviction.

"Sometimes, especially, fathers and sons . . ."

"Look, Mr. Jacovich, my father's okay." His voice quavered a little. "He can be a pain in the ass sometimes, that's all."

I nodded.

He kept hunching and unhunching his shoulders as he paced around the small room. "I mean, his job is a pressure cooker, and he's under a lot of extra strain right now, with all this going on."

"Uh-huh. Your mom, too."

He looked startled, as if this were a new concept. "Yeah."

"Is your dad blaming you?"

He looked down at his shoes. "He says he didn't pay all this money for me to come here so I could screw up."

Something twisted in my gut. The kid needed all the allies he could muster, and apparently he wasn't finding them within the bosom of his own family.

"And he did. Pay a lot of money, I mean. Even with the partial scholarship." Jason wet his lips again. "So, uh—I guess he's acting a little pissy right now. I hope he didn't give you a bad time or anything."

"No problem," I assured him, all the while hoping Jim Crowell wasn't giving *him* too bad a time. I moved away from him. "I'll talk to you later, okay?"

"Uh . . ."

Once more I stopped at the door and turned back.

"When you talk to Marika . . ."

"Yes?"

He screwed up his face as if he'd bitten into a lemon. "Nothing," he said.

"You sure?"

He hunched his shoulders again, took one hand out of his pocket and gave me a small, sad good-bye wave. "I'm sure."

But he wasn't, I thought, as I went out and down the narrow stairway. I wondered exactly what was going on between him and Marika Rollins.

Derrick Coombes, the landlady's son, was leaning against a gleaming new Ford Probe that probably wasn't his, parked at the curb. He was talking to two young black men and a white kid his own age. Now minus the Dickensian top hat, this time Derrick was honing his James Dean impression, complete with a cigarette held in the O between his thumb and forefinger; his companions were all smoking, too, but minus the attitude. When I came down the porch steps they stopped talking and looked at me with the supreme insolence of the very young.

"Look, it's the not-a-cop," Derrick told his friends. They bobbed their heads in understanding; maybe he'd mentioned me. I wondered why.

I nodded toward Derrick and crossed the street to my car. As I was getting in, I heard them laugh as derisively as only teenagers can. I guess they were laughing at me, and what they found funny, apparently, was my not being eighteen.

I hesitated for a moment, stung. I don't like being laughed at, and was seriously considering going back across the street to tell them so.

I rethought it and got into my car without looking back at them. Sure, I'll just go over there and slap around a couple of kids; it'll make me feel better. I shook my head, stifling the urge. It's no wonder we talk about a generation gap.

Terry Yagemann looked a lot like his former roommate, except he had very dark hair, a little bit longer and more unruly than Jason's, and deeper-blue eyes. Several inches under six feet, squarely and solidly built, he carried himself with an easy confidence Jason Crowell had not yet found.

Terry, Jason had told me, was from a Cincinnati family. His father was an executive at a local TV station, his mother was in middle management at Procter and Gamble, and they lived in a house on Mt. Adams overlooking the city.

The Yagemann kid's present digs were on the third floor of a building that, unlike most in Sherman, had originally been constructed for apartment dwelling, although his living room was even smaller than the one he'd shared with Jason. His kitchen was in a separate room, but it was so tiny that any two people not enjoying an intimate physical relationship who attempted to prepare a meal in there would probably opt to eat out.

Terry Yagemann had strewn the place with cardboard cartons he'd cadged from liquor stores, still not unpacked. The furniture, which had obviously come with the apartment, was not anywhere near new, screamed "discount store," and was more utilitarian than decorative. The ubiquitous computer was on a stand in the corner. The sofa he invited me to sit on was rump-sprung, and the coffee table in front of it was the boomerang shape favored in the late, lamented sixties, mounted on shaky-looking metal legs. There were a couple of beer cans strewn around. And brimming ashtrays everywhere I looked, the stale smoke adding to the smell of old sneakers and a garbage can that needed emptying.

I hadn't phoned ahead to warn him I was coming, so I had to explain who I was and why I was there. He nodded, but he didn't seem too thrilled at the prospect of talking to me.

"I don't know anything about Jason or what he did," he said. "I hardly know the kid, all right?"

"You lived with him for three weeks. You had to get to know him a little bit."

"Not really," he said reasonably. "We're different kinds of guys. He's a real straight-edge, studies all the time."

"Isn't that what you come to college for?"

"Sure," he said. "I study. But I'm more . . ." A boastful smile split his well-formed mouth. "I'm more of a party animal."

"So you and Jason didn't get along?"

"We weren't best buds, but we got along okay."

"Then why did you move out?"

He looked at me as if I were a not-too-bright child. "Are you kidding me? With all the shit that's gone down about him around here? I had to move out. I had my own reputation to consider. Would you want to room with a rapist?"

"Nobody proved he's raped anybody."

"It's just the idea of it," he explained, looking everywhere except at me. "I mean, my father always says you're judged by the company you keep."

I guess my expression showed my distaste, because he quickly amended his statement. "It was more than that, though. It was a distraction. I mean, Jason was all bent out of shape about that flyer, pissing and moaning all the time. And people were always calling, campus cops coming over in the evening and asking him all sorts of questions when I was trying to study. How the hell am I s'posed to study with all that going on?"

"I thought you said you were a party animal."

He grinned again. "Well, yeah, I am. But I've got to keep my grades up. I don't want to flunk out of *this* school. My father would kill me."

Curious emphasis, I thought. "Did you flunk out of another school before this?"

He nodded glumly. "Kenyon. Last year. I had a D average. My old man almost went into labor."

Another heavy father in the wings, I thought. I wondered how I'd react if Milan flunked out of Kent State. I don't think I'd start having birth contractions—but I wouldn't be too happy about it, either.

Then Terry Yagemann's expression brightened. "I learned my lesson, though. I still party, but my classes come first." He announced it as if there was some sort of nobility in it. "Will it bother you if I smoke?"

"No," I said. "We'll both smoke." I took out my cigarettes and gave him one, then lit both of them. "Tell me about the three weeks you roomed with Jason."

He frowned slightly. "There's nothing to tell. I hardly spent any time with him. He's all right. Kind of a geek, though."

"In what way?"

"You know—just a geek." His confident smile returned. "He hasn't got great social skills."

"You mean with women?"

"Well, yeah."

"Not like you."

He shrugged his shoulders eloquently. "I do okay."

"He didn't have any women friends?"

"No. Well, this one girl. Marika. But she wasn't like his old lady. I mean, they weren't doing the nasty or anything." He sucked at the cigarette and then expelled the smoke noisily, as if someone were watching him do it and grading him on it.

"Marika Rollins?"

"I never knew her last name. I only saw her a few times."

"And you weren't interested?"

He shook his head with vehemence. "She's kind of a geek, too, if you know what I mean."

Terry Yagemann was only nineteen years old, and I was trying hard to like him, but he wasn't giving me much encouragement. I pressed on. "Jason and Marika never had a fight, did they?"

"Not that I know of," he said. "I didn't see them have one, and he never said anything like that. But like I told you, I didn't hang around with them. Neither one of them was a whole lot of fun. Marika doesn't drink, and Jason does, but not very much; at night all they wanted to do was either hit the books, or sit around some geeky coffeehouse and talk."

"Wha did they talk about?"

"Leonardo da Vinci, probably. Who knows what geeks have to say?" His contempt and intolerance hung in the air of the small apartment, an essence no less noxious than the smoke and food odors.

"Let me ask you something, Terry. Do you think Jason is capable of doing what they're accusing him of?"

He didn't give it much thought. "I really couldn't say. He doesn't seem the type. But that's probably the only way he could get laid. No hot babe was going to give it up to him voluntarily. Except maybe Marika, and I don't think that was happening."

"Is getting laid that important?"

"Not to him, I don't think."

"But to you?"

The smarmy smile widened, showing off the skills of an orthodontist. "You tell me one thing that's more fun, I'll go do that instead."

I wondered if he'd think it was fun if I dangled him out the window by his ankles the way I wanted to. "When you moved out of the apartment last week—wasn't that kind of deserting a friend when he was down?"

"If we'd been friends, I suppose it would've been. But I don't owe him anything." He jerked his thumb toward his own chest. "And you've got to look out for number one, because nobody else is gonna."

CHAPTER FIVE

After my meager croissant break-
fast, I craved a substantial lunch—pasta at Piccolo Mondo's
downtown, or roast pork at Ewa's Family Restaurant in Slavic
Village, or even, more simply, a couple of brats from Frank's
Bratwurst Stand at the West Side Market, eaten standing up in
the aisles and followed up by a pastry from Kim's Strudel Bakery
nearby.

But that was in Cleveland, a good forty-five-minute drive
from Sherman, so here I was back in the tea shop again, because when I'd phoned Marika Rollins, that's where she'd said
she'd meet me. The waitress, who was old enough to be my
mother, gave me a funny look, probably because even though
I don't look like a tearoom kind of guy, here I was for the
second time that day, at the same table by the window, watching as a stiff breeze took the leaves that had fallen on the lawn
of the quadrangle and swirled them around in Technicolor vor-
texes.

Five minutes after the appointed meeting time, I saw a
young woman I assumed was Marika Rollins as she came across
the street from the direction of the campus. She was pretty in
the way some women are pretty who don't give a damn, clad
in a nondescript gray sweater and a plaid skirt, and she wore
a black canvas fanny-pack, not on her fanny but in front of her
at the waist. Her shoes were Doc Martens knockoffs. Dressed

for practicality, with knit gray leggings covering black tights, she had long, frizzy brown hair in hysterical flight all around her head. She looked as if she'd made a conscious decision to be aggressively plain.

I stood up when she entered the tearoom, and kind of waved at her. She checked me out first, just to convince herself I was who she thought I was. She didn't smile, but she had a pleasant, open face that now looked a little worried. She finally nodded at me and came over.

"Marika?"

"Yes, hi," she said. Her cheeks were devoid of makeup, and pink from the cold. I held out a chair for her, which seemed to startle her; I guess young men of her generation don't much observe the social niceties with which I grew up.

"Thanks for agreeing to see me," I said, after she was seated.

She shrugged. "That's okay—if it'll help Jason."

"It might." I gave her my business card, and she regarded it curiously.

"I've never met a private detective before."

"Did you think I'd look like Humphrey Bogart?"

She laughed politely, in the way people do who aren't really amused and who don't laugh often anyway.

"Or maybe Robert Mitchum?"

"Who?" she said.

I'd pushed my luck. I sighed.

The waitress came over with pad and pencil at the ready, and Marika ordered a pot of herbal tea and a scone. The only thing on the menu that looked robust enough to silence the rumbling in my stomach was a sliced turkey sandwich—on a croissant. At least they wouldn't cut the crusts off. I also ordered a bag of potato chips and another coffee.

We settled in at the small table and engaged in small talk for a while, the way people do when they first meet and are feeling one another out. I discovered she was a music-theory major.

"This is all so horrible for Jason," Marika said, when she was finally ready to get down to the business of our meeting, lowering her voice so the people around us, who were mostly older women I assumed to be faculty or support staff at the college, couldn't hear. Her eyes were big and sorrowful, perhaps about Jason's situation or else because of some secret sadness of her own. "It's like one of those nightmares people have and then they find they can't wake up." She put a hand over her heart. "I'd do anything to help him."

"I want to help him, too," I said. I could see she was skeptical. "You're going to have to trust me, though, Marika."

"That's what Jason told me on the phone." She worried her lower lip with her front teeth. Then she said, "I don't know where to start."

"Let's just start by talking, and see where we get to."

She nodded quickly.

"Let's go back to the beginning, okay? How did you and Jason meet?"

She paused as if trying to remember, although I knew it hadn't been that long ago. "It was during registration. Everybody was milling around, especially the freshmen. We didn't quite know where to go or what to do. We were both looking a little lost, I guess, and we started talking. Then after we'd registered, we ran into each other again and went out for coffee."

"Instant friendship?"

"Well, sort of." She toyed with her water glass. "Didn't you ever meet anyone and within two minutes you knew they were going to be your best friend?"

I understood more than she knew, remembering that the first time I'd ever seen my best friend, Marko Meglich, we were ten years old and in the fifth grade and we'd bloodied each other's noses in the schoolyard.

"How often did you see him after that?"

"Almost every day. We'd meet for coffee or pizza or something. Some nights we'd study together."

"Where?"

"Pardon?"

"Where would you study together?"

"Sometimes in the library, or else at my place. Sometimes we'd even come in here, because it's pretty quiet late in the afternoon."

"You mean like dates?"

"Hardly," she said.

"You wouldn't call him your boyfriend, then?"

She flushed deeply. "No. At first . . ." She stopped, frowning until whatever she was thinking went away. "No."

"I'm sorry I have to get so personal," I added.

She shook her head sharply as though a gnat were flying around her nose. "That's okay. But Jason isn't my boyfriend. I mean, we weren't . . ." She stopped and took a breath. "It wasn't all romantic or sexy or anything."

"Does he have a girlfriend, then?"

"No," she said.

"Or anybody he dated? Even once or twice?"

"Jason doesn't date. Neither do I." I guess that sent my eyebrows up, and she rushed on. "A lot of people don't, you know. At school. It's hard enough just trying to get through your freshman year and keep up with your studies. It's just—sometimes dating is just too much trouble."

I could relate to that. Until I'd met Connie Haley, for a long while it had always proved too much trouble for me, too. Frankly I'd rather stick pins in my eyes than go out on the dating market again.

Our conversation stopped when the waitress brought our

lunches, and I waited until she'd gone away. "But he saw you all the time. For coffee and study dates."

"That was different. It wasn't dates." She compressed her lips for a moment. "It was . . . We're friends. That's all."

I couldn't help wondering whether Marika Rollins would like it to be more than that. If so, I had to phrase the next question carefully. "Are there any other women he was friends with, then?"

"Not that I know of," she said. "He's pretty shy. I mean, I've seen him talk to other women, like in class and stuff, but I don't think you could count any of them as his friends."

"Marika, you've seen those flyers . . ."

She shuddered, looking frightened. "It's ridiculous. Jason would never do anything like that."

"Well, we can't help him get out from under this unless we find out who's accusing him."

"He didn't rape anybody," she said firmly.

"You believe he didn't?"

"I know he didn't." She took a very small bite of her scone, and nibbled at it tentatively, like a rabbit with a carrot.

"Then we have to find her—the woman who's saying he did. Or else find out who's behind Women Warriors."

She just shrugged.

"Okay," I said. "Are there any really militant feminist groups on campus you know of?"

"It's almost the twenty-first century. Most of the women on campus are some kind of feminist."

"How about you?"

She colored again, not as deeply as before. "More or less. Women have been getting screwed over for hundreds of years, and maybe our generation will be the first one to do something about it. But I'm not what you'd call militant."

"Who is?"

"What do you mean?"

"Who on campus is militant? Maybe they'll be able to tell me about Women Warriors."

"I don't know. I guess I don't travel in those circles."

"Who would know, then?"

She chewed some more on her scone and then took a sip of her tea to wash it down. "There's a woman here who handles all the sexual-harassment cases on campus. You might ask her."

"You mean Dorothy Strassky?"

She nodded. "She'd probably know."

Disappointment reared back and kicked me in the stomach. "If she does," I said, "she sure as hell isn't going to tell me."

I drove back to Cleveland, not knowing much more than I had when I'd first opened my eyes that morning. I knew Marika was keeping something from me; she'd spoken haltingly and carefully, as if she'd been inspecting each word and discarding the ones she thought were inappropriate or fraught with danger. I wondered if one of those study dates had gotten out of hand and she had been the rape victim herself, and after the flyer had appeared, perhaps without her knowledge or consent, had gotten cold feet and decided to drop the whole thing.

She did not, however, sound like an angry woman—more like a sad and frightened one, suffering the pangs of unrequited love and thinking that perhaps if she helped Jason out of his current predicament, there might be a chance he'd finally notice the adoration in her eyes.

Either that, or she was a good enough actress to make the world forget about Emma Thompson and Dame Judi Dench.

I went to my office and did some paperwork, made out another three-by-five card, for Marika Rollins, and locked up early enough to beat the traffic out of downtown heading east, one of the privileges of owning my own business. I got home at twenty minutes to five, more than enough time to get ready for Connie's visit at seven—we'd planned to see an Italian movie at the Cedar Lee in Cleveland Heights—and turned on the TV set in the den just in time to see the last fistfight of the day on *The Jerry Springer Show*.

Halfway through the five o'clock news, the telephone rang.

"Milan Jacovich?" came a female voice that was not quite familiar enough to place.

"Yes?"

"This is Dorothy Strassky calling. Remember me? From Sherman?" Sometime in the last thirty-six hours she'd learned how to pronounce my name.

"Of course I remember you, Ms. Strassky. How are you?"

"Look," she said, in the same no-nonsense voice she'd used to summarily dismiss me the day before, "I've found something out that will interest you."

"What's that?"

"I don't want to discuss it over the phone. Can you come to my office tomorrow morning? Say ten o'clock? Because I've got a meeting with the dean at noon."

I didn't relish still another drive out to Sherman, but Strassky was talking like an ally now instead of an enemy, which was a quantum leap from the first time I'd met her. "Sure," I said.

"Thanks." Then she hesitated. "I guess I was kind of hostile to you the first time we saw each other. I'm sorry about that. It's just my way."

"That's okay, Ms. Strassky. As long as we can get this business cleared up. One way or another."

After I hung up, I pointed the remote at the television and silenced it. I wanted to bask in relief a little bit. I wasn't sure what I was supposed to be relieved about, but I guessed that Strassky had discovered something either proving Jason Crowell's innocence or cementing his guilt. I hoped she was going to clear him, but either way, it would be over with and I could get on with the rest of my business, my debt to Reggie Parker partially paid.

So I stepped into the shower with a light heart, lathering on shampoo that smelled like coconuts and hoping not too much of my hair would fall out before I was finished; Slovenian men tend to lose their hair early, and I was no exception.

My ebullient spirits lasted until Connie arrived, wearing black slacks and an aging green sweater. Her eyes didn't sparkle the way they usually did, her dimples were hardly showing at all, and there were tight, tired lines around her mouth. She gave me a perfunctory kiss at the door and moved past me into the apartment, bringing with her a strange kind of tension that was almost visible in the air. I wasn't sure what was wrong, but I had a suspicion it was a carryover from what had been bothering her the last time.

"Do we have time for a quick glass of wine before the movie?" I said, trying to lighten the mood again.

She plopped down onto the far end of the sofa with a notable lack of enthusiasm. "I'm not much in the mood for a movie tonight, Milan. I hear this film is depressing, and I don't feel like being depressed. I could use a drink, though."

"I have a Chardonnay chilling."

"Not tonight. You have any vodka?"

"Sure," I said. I'd never known Connie to drink anything but wine before. "With tonic? Cranberry juice?"

"Straight, no ice."

For a social wine drinker, straight vodka bodes ill. I went into the kitchen and took the bottle of Stolichnaya from the freezer where I keep it, poured two fingers into an old-fashioned glass, grabbed a Stroh's for myself, and brought the drinks back into the living room.

I sat down on the other end of the sofa. There was space for one large adult or two children to sit between us, but I got the definite sense that she didn't want me any closer. "I thought you were really hot to see that film."

"Not tonight. Do you mind?"

"I'm just glad you're here, Connie. I don't care what we do."

She gulped down half the near-freezing vodka, gasping as it hit that tender spot on the roof of the mouth that causes great pain behind the eye when cold stuff touches it. "Are you still on that case?" she asked, an unfamiliar edge in her voice.

"I'll probably have it wrapped up tomorrow."

She nodded grimly. "Are you getting the rapist off?"

"I don't know yet," I said. "And nobody's proved he's a rapist yet."

"Uh-huh," she said darkly.

"In the morning I have a meeting with the sexual-harassment counselor at Sherman. She said she had some information."

She finished the rest of her drink in two swallows, then held out the glass to me, her eyes bouncing from the unaccustomed alcohol. "You have any more of this stuff?"

I hadn't even had time to get comfortable on the sofa. "Almost a whole bottle," I said, and went back into the kitchen. It didn't take a rocket scientist to discern that something was amiss. I refilled her glass and brought it out to her.

I'm always loath to ask someone what's wrong before they volunteer it, mainly because I hate it when people ask me that; frequently there's nothing wrong except with their perceptions and I find myself on the defensive—not my favorite position. But things just didn't feel right. "Is something bothering you, Connie?"

"Not really," she said, and then she reconsidered. "I just don't like rapists, that's all.

"Neither do I."

"Then why are you helping the little prick?"

"Is that what's the matter? He says he's innocent."

"Sure," she almost snarled. "What else is he going to say?"

"Besides, I don't think it's fair that he doesn't even know who's accusing him so he can defend himself. That's what I'm trying to find out."

She didn't say anything, but her next gulp of vodka was taken as if she was biting into an apple.

"You want to clue me in on what's upsetting you specifically?" I said. "Then we can both know."

She thought it over for a moment, not looking at me. Then: "I told you, I don't like rapists. And it frosts me that you're working for one."

I wanted to say again that Jason Crowell was innocent until proven guilty, that I was on the case because of Reggie Parker and for no other reason, but the words died before I was able to get them out. I've spent enough time talking to brick walls to know how fruitless it can be, so I kept my mouth shut. Instead I sat down and toyed with the neck of my beer bottle, squirming in the empty cacophony of no sound.

Finally Connie sucked in a lungful of air. "Here's a truth for you. . . ." And then she waited.

So did I, almost fearfully. I didn't want to talk, didn't want to rattle a moment I sensed was as destructible as a single strand of fine silk.

"I was raped once," she finally said.

All at once the skin on my back felt crawly, as if it had just been brushed by a swarm of many-legged insects. I put out my hand to touch her and then pulled it back.

"When I was a sophomore at Baldwin-Wallace," she continued. "There was this guy in my trig class. We went out to dinner and a concert, and when he dropped me home—I was living in a small apartment in Berea while I was going to school—he asked if he could come up and use the bathroom."

I didn't say anything—I hardly breathed.

"When we got inside, it turned out it was me he wanted to use. He was a lot bigger than I am, and he got a little rough." She dropped her eyes, studying her lap. "I was too scared to say no."

I ached for her, even though it had happened fifteen years

ago. I wanted to take her in my arms, but I didn't think it was what she wanted. I tried to cough away the lump that was forming in my throat. "Did you call the police?"

"I was afraid to. He hadn't pulled a knife on me or anything, or even hit me. I had no proof. It would be just my word against his, and in cases like that, the woman usually loses." She shot the rest of the drink, tossing it down her throat.

"I didn't tell anyone," she continued in a tight voice. "Until later when I went to see a psychologist about it. I didn't go out on a date for almost two years after that."

"You didn't tell your family?"

She shook her head vehemently. "If my brothers and my father had found out, they would have killed the guy. Literally. I couldn't risk that."

I finally worked up the guts to reach out and put my hand over hers, which was clenched into a small fist on her lap. "Connie, I'm so sorry."

She blinked her eyes rapidly and pulled herself together, relaxing at last against the sofa cushions. "It was a long time ago, Milan. I got over it. I mean, it didn't turn me off sex or anything—and I don't hate men." She finally looked at me and a smile flickered. "Obviously."

I squeezed her hand.

"But I don't like rapists," she said once more, and her tone was steely again. "And I guess I'm pissed off at you because you're working for one."

"What happens," I said, still hanging on to her hand, "if Jason Crowell really is innocent and gets blamed anyway? What happens if he gets kicked out of school, maybe even sent to prison, for something he didn't do?"

She didn't answer me.

"And maybe, even worse, what if there really was a rape and the guy who did it gets away with it? Would you want that?"

"No."

"Neither would I. That's why I'm working. But I got a phone call earlier—and I think that by tomorrow morning there'll be something definite, one way or the other."

"And if this Jason really did it?"

"I'll make sure he goes down for it. But if he didn't . . ."

She raised an eyebrow.

"Well, that's my job," I said.

We never got to the concert. We stayed on the sofa and talked for most of the evening, Connie finally switching from straight chilled Stoli to Diet Pepsi. She spent the night, but we didn't make love. We just held each other until she fell asleep with her head nestled between my shoulder and neck. I stayed awake for quite a while after that, staring up at the ceiling in my bedroom, memorizing the crack in the plaster that looked like the shape of Brazil.

Early in the morning, in better spirits after a good, long talk and a good night's sleep, Connie cuddled with me in an affectionate but definitely nonsexual way for almost half an hour before she left, giving me a warm kiss on her way out to let me know things were okay again.

I stayed in bed until eight, listening to Lanigan and Malone on Majic 105 and chuckling. Then I made a pot of coffee, poured myself a bowl of Cheerios, and dressed for the drive to Sherman.

I hoped like hell that Dorothy Strassky would have good news for me, news that would clear Jason of the charge that had been mysteriously leveled against him. It would defuse some of the tension in the Crowell family, it would make Reggie Parker happy, and it would make me feel better. It sure as hell would make Connie feel better, too, and that was important to me.

When I arrived at five minutes before ten, Strassky's office was dark behind the glass and there was no answer to my knock. At the end of the corridor I found a wooden bench that must have been designed by Torquemada, and sat there waiting until twenty after. Then I walked down to the main office.

On my way past the double front doors I looked out through the glass and noticed a Cleveland police cruiser parked at the curb. That was curious, I thought—Sherman was a long way out of the Cleveland PD's jurisdiction.

The two women at desks in the administration office were white-lipped and red-eyed, and when I entered they looked at me almost fearfully.

"I'm sorry to bother you," I said, "but I had a ten o'clock appointment with Dorothy Strassky in her office and she hasn't shown up yet. I wondered if she might have called to say she was going to be late."

The older of the two women drew her shoulders back, and her chin quivered. "Dorothy Strassky is dead," she announced in a hollow voice. "She's been murdered."

CHAPTER SIX

Later that afternoon I found myself in the old Third District police headquarters on Payne Avenue and East Twenty-first Street where I'd once worked in uniform and harness, sitting across from Lieutenant Florence McHargue. She had just been named to run the homicide division of the Cleveland PD, replacing Detective Bob Matusen who had served as acting head right after Marko Meglich's death, until they could appoint a ranking officer to take over.

It was strange and sad being in that office for the first time without Marko on the other side of the desk sipping industrial-strength station-house coffee from his custom-made coffee mug emblazoned with his name and a facsimile of his shield, which he'd ordered made because of his firm belief that foam or cardboard cups caused cancer. I had that mug in my office now, and drank my coffee out of nothing else.

That was another change that weighed on my heart. Where Marko had once kept his coffeemaker, on top of the file cabinet, McHargue had a hot plate with a carafe of hot water, and replacing Marko's ever-present can of gourmet coffee was a box of Constant Comment tea bags.

There was also a pair of sunglasses with blue lenses at one side of the desk. Marko would have been boiled in oil before he'd have worn sunglasses anywhere but out on the lake on a bright, balmy August afternoon. Most Clevelanders consider sunglasses an affectation, especially in any other season but summer.

The changes, while jarring, were probably good for me; they made me a little less nostalgic and morose sitting in what had been my best friend's office. A little less sad. Even though the desk and chair were the same, everything else was different; it was somehow easier to let go of the pain.

I didn't know Lieutenant McHargue well at all; I'd only met her once before, several months earlier, while she was heading up the sex-crimes unit. A solidly built woman with skin the color of coffee with just a little cream, she had a childishly pug nose, gray-green eyes, a take-no-prisoners attitude, and a powerful work ethic that had marked her as a "comer" in the department as soon as she'd matriculated from the police academy. She had a reputation for cold, hard efficiency as an administrator and a scorched-earth policy toward wrongdoers, and I had the feeling she didn't have much use for private operatives like me, either.

She let me sit there for almost two minutes without saying anything; to fill the time she toyed with a plastic evidence bag on the desk in front of her. I could see my business card was inside it.

"So, Jacovich," she said severely. I hate being called by my last name without a "Mr." in front of it—I think it's disrespectful—but didn't think it a good idea to tell her so.

"So, Lieutenant."

"You have a knack for turning up when people get dead," she observed, tapping the evidence bag. "Why is that, do you suppose?"

"Slovenian luck, I guess." I looked around for the heavy glass ashtray that had always served Marko so well, but it was nowhere in sight; the new homicide honcho was evidently a nonsmoker. I could have used a cigarette, if only to have something to do with my hands.

I hadn't expected to be called in on Dorothy Strassky's killing. I'd thought of her as a Sherman person; I hadn't known that she'd commuted there from Cleveland. But her home in Cleveland is where she died, so her paperwork ended up on the desk of Florence McHargue.

"Your Slovenian luck is all bad, I'd say," McHargue observed dryly. "Your business card was found tucked into the top drawer of her desk."

"I left it with her a few days ago," I said. "I'd visited her office at Sherman College."

"Just what was your connection to her?"

I sketched out the Jason Crowell rape accusation and my one meeting with Dorothy Strassky.

She rolled her eyes toward the stamped-tin ceiling in apparent disgust. "Christ on a crutch!" she said. "Not another sex crime! I spent the last four years trying to get *out* of sex crimes."

"It supposedly happened in Sherman, which isn't even in this county. This sex crime isn't yours," I reminded her.

"But Dorothy Strassky's murder is." She straightened the blotter so it was parallel with the edge of the desk. Marko had never had a blotter. "You think there might be a connection?"

"I don't think anything. I only met the woman once."

"From what you told me about her, you didn't like her much." It was a statement, not a question. I'd heard somewhere that Florence McHargue had a law degree; she would have made a first-rate prosecutor.

"I thought she was antagonistic and rude," I said. "But if bad manners was a motive for murder, this would be a ghost town."

"Well, *somebody* didn't like her. The crime scene wasn't pretty."

"They never are, are they? What was the cause of death?"

Her eyebrows became twin arches of disapproval. "Did I miss something here?" Sarcasm sprayed like a Rainbird on an

August lawn. "Are you back on the job and nobody told me? Did you re-up? Are you carrying a badge again?"

"No, ma'am."

What I could see of her slitted eyes glittered unpleasantly; her tone turned harsh and rasping. "Well I am, so I'll ask the goddamn questions here, all right?"

"Yes, ma'am."

She lowered her head like a bull about to charge the tormenting matador. "What time was it when she called you last night?"

"I can't pinpoint it. But I remember the news was on Channel 12, and they weren't doing their lead stories anymore, so I'd say it was somewhere around half past five."

"And she said exactly what?"

"That she had some information she thought might interest me and could I meet her at her office at ten o'clock this morning."

"That's all? Nothing more specific?"

"That was the extent of the conversation."

"I find that a little peculiar," McHargue said. "Don't you?"

"Not necessarily. It wasn't something she wanted to discuss on the phone. I'm pretty sure it had something to do with Jason Crowell, since that was our only connection."

"Something that proved his guilt in the rape case?"

"Or his innocence."

She made an unpleasant sound through her nose. "I ran vice and sex crimes in this department for longer than I care to remember," she said. "In all that time there was only one guy who was accused of rape that was actually innocent."

"And all the rest?"

She turned her hands over, palms upward, and shrugged rather elaborately. "Where there's smoke, et cetera."

"So you think maybe she found out Jason was the phantom rapist?" I said.

"I wouldn't be surprised."

"And you believe he might have killed her to shut her up about it."

"If you were still a real policeman instead of a rent-a-cop, wouldn't that thought occur to you?" She smiled with her mouth; her eyes said otherwise. "Sure it would. It just did."

"What would also occur to me," I said, "is that the real rapist—if there even was a rape, and we don't know that for sure—might have done the same thing."

"Thanks for telling me how to do my job, Jacovich," she said. "Of course, I'm brand-new at this, and I'm just a woman, so I need all the help I can get."

"Come on, Lieutenant," I said, shifting miserably in my chair and trying to bite back my irritation; I'd never wanted a cigarette so badly in my life. "I've shown you nothing but respect and courtesy since I walked into this office. There's no need for attitude."

"I'll damn well decide what there's a need for!" she exploded, rocking forward in her chair and leaning across the desk. She aimed a long finger at me, and I noticed her nails were polished a dark, brownish red. "Listen. I know all about you. I know that in the past you had a lot of access to this department, to official police files, because of your friendship with Lieutenant Meglich. Well, sad to say he's not here anymore, and I'm the new stud duck around here. So consider your free ticket punched."

She sat back, pleased with herself but not quite finished. "Now, you stay the hell out of my way unless I call you, understand? I don't want you hanging around under my feet while I'm trying to crack a murder case. This Strassky business is none of yours! Are you following me?"

"Yes, ma'am." I stood up, feeling like I weighed four hundred pounds. "Is it all right if I go ahead and try to clear my client of rape?"

"I don't give a sorry damn what you do as long as you're not interfering with me," she said.

I started for the door.

"Jacovich?"

I turned around to look at her.

"I'm not a nun, all right? And I'm not eighty years old. If you call me ma'am just once more, I'm going to rip off your face."

I walked out of the office and closed the door so gently there was only the sound of a soft snick instead of the massive slam that was inside me clamoring to get out.

I went downstairs at a half-trot, madder than hell. As I was going out the front entrance, I ran into Jason Crowell and his parents on the way in. They all looked grim, and Mrs. Crowell had apparently been crying, because her eyes were inflamed and swollen and her nose was red. Her husband was frowning darkly and chewing on the inside of his cheek, and Jason, white-faced and moving like an extra in *Night of the Living Dead*, looked simply scared to death.

"What the hell is all this about, Mr. Jacovich?" Crowell demanded, as if running into me in the police station was the most natural thing in the world. "We got a call from a Lieutenant McHargue to bring Jason down here to talk to her. He doesn't know a goddamn thing about this Strassky woman. What's going on?"

"There's been a murder, Mr. Crowell, and Jason knew the victim. I imagine it's just routine," I said, secretly wishing that I could be so sure.

"Could you go back in there with us?" Mrs. Crowell said, almost pleading. "I'd feel a lot better."

"I doubt if the lieutenant would permit that," I said. "But remember, Jason, you don't have to answer any questions without a lawyer present. And I'd advise you get one—just to be on the safe side."

"Shit," Crowell murmured. He looked drawn and haggard, and ten years older than when I'd last seen him.

"Just tell the truth," I said to Jason. "Even the smallest lie catches up to you, and then that casts doubt on everything else."

He nodded, almost paralyzed with fright. "I will," he said.

I shook his hand and wished him good luck, then watched as the three of them approached the sergeant's desk in the lobby, feeling impotent that I couldn't do anything to get him through what surely would be an ordeal—Florence McHargue was waiting up in her office, loaded for bear.

I stood on the front steps for a moment, pulled a cigarette from my somewhat crumpled pack, and lit up, inhaling deeply.

I needed that. I needed a drink, too, even more. But it was a little early in the day—even for me.

By the time I got back to my office, my mind was working at warp speed. There are a lot of reasons people get killed in our crazy world—robbery, revenge, a personal vendetta, a lovers' quarrel . . . I wondered which one had reared its head to bite Dorothy Strassky.

It might not have anything to do with Jason, but I wasn't sure. I was completely in the dark, since I didn't even know the cause of her death. I decided to find out.

I pulled out the telephone directory and turned to the S's. It didn't take me too long to find Strassky, D. and J.

I didn't know who J. might be. But I dialed the number anyway.

The call resulted in an appointment that evening with J. Strassky, who turned out to be Dorothy's younger sister, Jane. They lived just on the west side of the Cuyahoga in a storied neighborhood known as Duck Island.

It's just a few blocks from the West Side Market, and isn't really an island at all, but a small enclave sandwiched between a steep ravine leading down to the west bank of the Flats, and the Lorain-Carnegie Bridge. Cleveland's city fathers renamed the bridge the Hope Memorial a few years ago, in honor of the father of native son Bob Hope, but virtually no one calls it that.

Duck Island is almost all residential, except for the little gingerbread cottage housing the venerable Haab's Bakery on West Nineteenth Street. Most of the householders work in the nearby industrial plants and machine shops in the belly of the Flats, and have done so for generations. The houses are built close to the sidewalks, enclosed behind waist-high chain-link fences that keep the family dogs in. Many of the properties had obviously been remodeled and added onto; several of the additions stretched far into the backyards and were painted a different color than the original house, giving them a peculiar barrackslike look. A few of the postage-stamp lawns were decorated with pink flamingos, and in front of one house, under a tree, was one of those ubiquitous, annoying, life-sized black silhouettes of a man smoking a pipe. Some of the lots, right on the edge of a cliff overlooking the river, have a dazzling view of downtown—but it's a working-class neighborhood down to its grass roots.

There are no ducks in Duck Island; I don't think there ever have been. In a neighborhood known for its blue-collar, tough-guy image, old-timers will tell you that beer-guzzling local kids used to "duck" when the cops swung by, but the island has mellowed of late, as the residents aged and matured and started planting flowers instead of raising hell.

The glow from downtown's lights just across the water smudged the sky pink as I drove through the short, narrow streets looking for the house number. A clowder of cats, some tattered and battle-scarred, trotted right in front of my car, fearless. I stepped on the brakes and yielded the right-of-way to them; it was, after all, their turf and not mine.

The Strassky sisters lived in a tall, thin worker's cottage on

West Eighteenth Street, painted a cheery yellow that was in need of a touch-up. Planted all along its front perimeter were now-dormant pansies and marigolds. I went through the gate in the fence, walked the two steps up to the door, and pushed the bell. Jane Strassky took more than a minute to answer my ring.

The familial resemblance between the Strassky sisters was remarkable, except Jane was about ten years younger, putting her in her twenties. There was the same dark hair, stocky build, and intense brown eyes, and recent grief was cruelly etched on her face. She offered me a chilly hand.

I trailed after her into a narrow living room that ran the entire length of the house. A small dining alcove was dominated by a bay window obviously installed after the house was built, looking out on an unlovely backyard and unattached two-car garage. The furniture in the vintage house was of good quality, especially the polished mahogany tables and breakfront, but decades old, and there were ornately framed family photos, mostly black-and-white, on every flat surface. The room seemed to exhale its history in stale breaths.

I seated myself on a rose-colored sofa covered with a white wool afghan, hoping the fibers wouldn't come off on my black corduroy jacket. "I'm sorry to intrude on you at such a difficult time," I said.

She bowed her head in my direction.

"I appreciate your agreeing to see me tonight. I only met your sister once, but I know what it's like to lose someone you've known all your life."

Jane Strassky remained standing, one hand on the back of a leather recliner, perhaps for support. "Dorothy was my best friend, too, not just my sister," she said, her mouth an arch of tragedy. "We were both born in this house. And now Dorothy died in it. God!"

"Do your parents live here too?"

"My mother died right after I was born, and my father about six years ago. I'm just grateful they didn't live to see this. It would have destroyed them." She ran her fingers through her short hair, massaging her scalp. "It's destroying me."

"Can you tell me how it happened?"

Her eyes opened wide in surprise. "Don't you know?"

I shook my head. "As I said on the phone, your sister called me last night and asked me to meet her in her office this morning. When I got there they told me what happened—the people at the school. I talked to Lieutenant McHargue of the police department this afternoon, but she wasn't very forthcoming."

Jane inhaled through her nose and squared her shoulders, preparing for what certainly would be a difficult and painful retelling. She told the story as if reciting a memorized piece for elocution class. "I was the one who found her. She was in the backyard, halfway between the house and the garage, so she must have just gotten back from work. She usually came home about six-thirty or so, depending on the traffic. I went to dinner with some friends, and I didn't get home until a little after ten o'clock." Guilty tears filled her eyes, and her lower lip shook as if from palsy. "If I hadn't gone out—if I'd been here— it never would have happened!"

"You can't blame yourself, Ms. Strassky," I said, as gently as I could. Survivors of murder victims so often played the "what if" game and ate themselves up inside.

"Oh, God, she'd been lying there for hours!" She stumbled into the chair, covered her face with her hands, and tried to regain control of the soft keening noise issuing from her throat.

Whatever I might have said wouldn't have helped, so I stayed quiet. I suppose if I had been sitting closer to her I would have taken her hand or something. Instead I just felt useless.

Finally she reached blindly for a box of tissues on the drum table next to her chair. "She must have been so scared," she wailed, and blew her nose twice.

I didn't quite know how to phrase my next question, but she saved me the necessity.

"There's a woodpile out there," she said haltingly. "Whoever it was—hit her with one of the logs. Many times." She shuddered. "She was a good person, Mr. Jacovich. She believed in her work, in what she was doing. Who would want to do something like that to her?" She began to sob again, painful, wracking breaths as if there were an obstruction in her esophagus.

I waited until her crying wound down to quiet, sad sniffling. "Was it a robbery?" I finally asked.

"I don't know. The police didn't seem to think so. Her briefcase was lying open near the back gate, and her papers were scattered all over. But I don't know if they took anything or not."

"What about her purse?"

"It was on the ground next to her. She only had thirty-three dollars in her wallet, and that was still there." Her eyes turned inward, bitter and angry. "I guess it wasn't enough to bother with."

The open briefcase got me to thinking, but I didn't share my conjectures with Jane Strassky. I also wanted to know whether her sister had been sexually assaulted, but I couldn't bear to ask. Instead I said, "Do you have any idea why Dorothy wanted to see me this morning?"

"No." Her fingers idly twisted the short hairs at the nape of her neck. "She didn't much talk about her work. She always said it was too ugly. Sometimes she'd bring papers home, and spend the evening in her little study working, but she never discussed it with me."

"Have you looked through her study?"

She turned the black holes of her eyes on me. "I couldn't bear it just yet."

"So you didn't know about the Women Warriors situation?"

"Not very much, no. Dorothy mentioned it about a week ago. But she didn't go into any details, and I didn't ask. All she said was that she was glad some punk rapist was getting outed."

"Outed?"

"That's the word she used, yes."

"So she believed Jason Crowell was a rapist?"

She nodded, dabbing at her nose and eyes with a fresh tissue. "So often college women are raped by their dates and they're too embarrassed to come forward, or they figure no one will do anything about it. She was the only one at Sherman that rape or harassment victims could come to. She was a caring, giving . . ." She couldn't quite finish the sentence. I suppose I'd come to see her too soon; had I waited a few days, she might have been better able to communicate with me.

But I wasn't sure Jason Crowell had a few more days.

"As I understood it, Ms. Strassky, nobody came to Dorothy about a rape. She said she didn't know who was behind Women Warriors."

"No—but when those flyers appeared, she naturally got involved. That was her job." Her face turned dark and angry. "Dorothy was raped when she was eighteen, when she was a freshman in college. It really imprinted her. So she decided she'd do whatever she could to help other women in the same situation."

Another rape, I thought. Dorothy Strassky, Connie Haley, and now some young woman at Sherman College who was too terrorized to come forward. I wondered for a moment if we've raised a generation of young undergraduate men to be wild animals.

"I'm sorry," I said. I seemed to be apologizing a lot. "Most men aren't like that."

"You couldn't tell it by me," she said angrily. Then her features melted into grief again and she chewed nervously on a blunt fingernail, trying to make some sense out of the tragedy of her sister's death. "You think there's a connection between this rape you're investigating and what happened to her?"

"I don't know," I said. "That's the police department's area, not mine. I'm just trying to help my client, and I thought you might know what she wanted to tell me."

She closed her eyes. "I don't know much of anything right now." She got to her feet, her knees wobbling like a newborn colt's. "I just can't talk anymore, Mr. Jacovich. I'm sorry."

I stood up, too. "That's all right, Ms. Strassky, I understand." I took the little brass holder from my pocket and gave her my business card. "If I can do anything, please feel free to call me."

"I guess no one can do anything for me right now. But I'm grateful for your kindness." She walked with me toward the door. "And I hope—if your client is really innocent—that everything works out."

The panorama of the lighted towers of downtown, which Duck Islanders call "the million-dollar view," glittered like the jewels in a pirate's treasure chest as I made my way toward the bridge and back to the east side. I thought Jane Strassky's final comment was an exceedingly generous one, under the circumstances. Of course, she had no way of knowing that McHargue was questioning Jason Crowell, and that he might indeed be the number one suspect in Dorothy Strassky's murder.

CHAPTER SEVEN

Jane Strassky's pain had been oppressive and stifling, like a layer of heavy air in the atmosphere. After I left her, I made my way out to the Crowell house where I'd arranged earlier to meet with Reggie Parker. It took me about half an hour to get there, long enough to get up a big head of worry over Jason's situation, which had gone from anonymously accused date rapist to murder suspect all in one fell swoop. I imagined the kid must be reeling.

I thought about Dorothy Strassky dying in an ugly, lonely way, beaten to death with a log in a dreary, muddy backyard. Robbery might have been a motive, and the killer could have been scared off before he—or she—was able to take the money from Strassky's purse. In years past, Duck Island was a wild and woolly neighborhood, and while it's settled into a kind of middle-aged, blue-collar gentility in recent years, it still isn't a place I'd want to walk around flashing a big bankroll.

But her purse had been left untouched, so if robbery, at least in the traditional sense, *hadn't* been the beginning of the end for Dorothy Strassky, and if it wasn't a sex-related crime—and there seemed to be no indication that it was—then someone had killed her for another reason. Perhaps for something, some incriminating document she'd been carrying in her briefcase.

Or for something she'd found out, what she'd invited me to her office to tell me about.

Secrets.

I didn't know anything about Strassky's life, so I couldn't say what other secrets she'd been harboring—whether she had a married lover, a coke habit, a gambling jones, or ten other sexual-harassment cases pending at Sherman. But failing any of those, I couldn't really blame McHargue for considering Jason Crowell the most likely suspect in her killing. Hell, I hadn't quite eliminated him in my mind myself.

It was dark by the time I got to Crowell's. As I parked my car it seemed as if every light in the house was on, looking warm and autumnal and inviting. When I stepped up onto the porch it was quite a different story. Through the closed door I could hear Mr. Crowell ranting and shouting, his voice higher in pitch than usual, and shrill. About as warm and inviting as a hockey arena.

I rang the bell with trepidation. The yelling stopped, and someone pounded down the stairs calling out, "I'll get it." Cherie, the older of Jason's two sisters, opened the door and gave me a curt nod of recognition as she stood aside for me to come in.

The Crowells and Reggie were all standing up in the living room like characters on a stage set in various stages of distress. Jason, who could have served as poster boy for the terminally hangdog, looked as if he had been crying. His mother was white-faced and mournful, Reggie looked irritated, and Jim Crowell was red-faced and sweatily apoplectic.

Before Cherie could close the door behind me, Crowell wheeled around at me like a six-incher on the deck of a battleship. "The bastards have suspended him!" he bellowed without so much as a hello, and punctuated his words by slamming his right fist into his left palm.

"Let's all sit down and relax," I said.

"Bullshit! Two weeks ago I'm living a normal life, then my son is accused of rape! Next thing you know, he's suspended from school and the police suspect him of murder!" Spittle flew from the man's mouth when he spoke. "How the hell am I supposed to relax?"

I decided I'd get a cooler reading from Jason himself. "They actually suspended you?"

The young man nodded. "The chief of the campus police came to my place first thing this morning, and he stood there resting his hand on his gun while I packed a bag. Then he made sure I got in my car and headed back toward Cleveland. He told me Dean Lilly said it was for the good of the whole school. I went to my freshman advisor, Trey Dotson, but he said he couldn't do anything about it. He was kind of my last hope."

I made a note of Trey Dotson. "What's this security chief's name?" I said to Jason.

"Dunwoodie."

I asked him to spell it but he wasn't sure how. I wrote it down in my notebook the way it sounded. Then I clapped Jason on the shoulder sympathetically and moved over to the sofa. "Well, I'm going to sit down if no one else will," I announced. As I figured, as soon as I was on the sofa, Nola Crowell sat down too, and then Jason. That left Reggie Parker and Jim Crowell still on their feet, with Cherie hovering unobtrusively in the vestibule.

"I've been telling the Crowells that at this point a lawyer isn't optional anymore," Reggie said.

"I agree. First of all," I said, ticking off items one by one on my finger, "Sherman College has no right to suspend Jason when no one has proved he's done anything wrong. Second, as soon as I find out who's behind Women Warriors, I think you have grounds for a suit against them. And most important, you don't want to be talking to the police about any murder without counsel present."

"I've already called an attorney for them," Reggie said. "Jeremiah Locke. He's an old friend."

"That's good," I said.

Jim Crowell shoved his hands into his pockets. "This is going to wipe me out financially, you know. These goddamn lawyers, some of them charge two hundred bucks an hour." He looked accusingly at his son.

"When this is all over, Mr. Crowell, you'll find it's money well-spent. You could even sue Sherman College if you want to for a wrongful suspension. Of course, that's only if Jason is cleared of the rape charge."

Jim Crowell shot a worried glance at his daughter, still standing tentatively by the entrance to the living room. "Get upstairs," he ordered.

"Yeah, right, like I don't know what's going on," Cherie said, rolling her eyes. Crowell took one step toward her in a manner that could only be described as menacing. She started up the stairs, but slowly, as if it was her own idea. "I'm so sure *Jason* is going to *rape* anybody," she mumbled as she disappeared onto the second floor. She pronounced the word "sherrr."

I waited until she was gone. "What kinds of questions did Lieutenant McHargue ask you today, Jason?"

"Mostly where I was yesterday afternoon and last night."

"And where was that?"

"At home." He flicked a glance at his father. "I mean at home in my apartment. I was studying."

"I don't suppose you can prove that."

"I was alone."

"You weren't studying with Marika?"

"No," he said. "We don't see each other every day. She said she was going to a movie last night."

"You told the police that?"

"No. And I wish you wouldn't, either, Mr. Jacovich. They

don't know anything about Marika. She's got nothing to do with any of this."

"Who's this Marika girl?" Jim Crowell demanded.

Jason didn't seem to want to tell him, but finally capitulated. "She's a friend. Marika Rollins."

"She's just Jason's friend," Nola said to her husband, almost too quickly. "They sometimes study together."

Crowell ignored her. "Is that right, Jason?"

Jason bobbed his head in assent.

"Is that *all* you do together?"

The boy flushed scarlet.

"She's not involved in this rape business, is she?"

"There *is* no rape business!" Jason said desperately. "Why can't I get through to you about that?"

"You just watch your tone of voice with me, young fella!" Crowell said, advancing on Jason with fists clenched.

I've never cared for bullies. "Knock it off, Mr. Crowell. This isn't getting us anywhere."

Reggie broke in. "It's not going to do any good to panic. I think everyone ought to just relax and not even talk about it for a while. Mr. Crowell, the best thing you can do is to call Jeremiah Locke the first thing in the morning. He can tell you how to handle all of this."

"What about you?" Crowell said to me, his anger spilling out over everyone, even the innocent bystanders. "Now that this murder thing is hanging over Jason's head, are you going to crap out on us?"

"I'm going to do just what you asked me to in the first place. If we clear Jason of the rape charge, chances are the police will lose interest in him about Ms. Strassky's death. So what I'll try is to find out who's behind Women Warriors and who accused Jason. And why."

"How?" Nola Crowell asked, twisting the fingers of one hand with the other.

"I'm working on that," I said.

• • •

After finishing up with the Crowells, Reggie Parker and I drove downtown in separate cars and met at the lively bar of the Velvet Tango Room on the other side of the Lorain-Carnegie Bridge, just a block from the West Side Market. From the Crowells' home it isn't that far to the neighborhood tavern of my youth, Vuk's, which would have been more convenient, but I didn't think Reggie would have been comfortable there. It isn't that Vuk, the tavernkeeper, has anything against African Americans; he and his regular customers just prefer they do their drinking somewhere else. Yeah, right.

Marybeth, the statuesque brunette who minds the stick at the Tango, makes everyone feel welcome—unless they have big hair (a brass plaque on the door warns you that's forbidden) or are wearing baseball caps, in which case they get a stern lecture on the proper attire for barhopping in Tremont and are shown the exit.

"This is getting to stink more with every passing day," Reggie said.

"Big time. They had no business suspending him. When this is over I think Crowell could sue the pants off Sherman College. If we can clear Jason of this bogus rape charge."

Marybeth knows what I like to drink without asking and brought me a Stroh's beer with no glass; it's what I've been drinking ever since I can remember. Reggie opted for a premium bourbon, and I knew that if Marybeth ever saw him in there again, she would remember what he drank, too.

"Will Jason be off the hook for the killing if you prove he didn't sexually assault anyone?"

"I'm just about sure of it," I said. "He didn't even know Strassky until those flyers started showing up, so the only motive he'd have for killing her is if she'd found out he was really a sexual predator and was ready to blow the whistle on him. And he's eighteen now and would be tried as an adult." I grimaced. "Going down for a sex crime, he'd do some hard time, a kid like that."

"Jason Crowell is no sexual predator."

"For what it's worth, I don't think so, either. And I'll do what I can to prove it."

"I hope you can," Reggie said, and with hope we tinked glasses.

"And if I do, along the way that might shed some light on the Strassky killing, and clearing that would put a much-needed star in my crown with Lieutenant McHargue."

"Florence McHargue," Reggie said. "I knew her when she was a vice cop. Two of my girls at the school got into trouble a couple of years ago for turning tricks in their spare time. McHargue is—direct, I guess you'd say."

"She's a hard-ass, I guess I'd say."

"I'm glad it's you dealing with her and not me."

There were no other vacant seats at the bar, and behind us, two men wearing expensive suits and talking about the tele-communications industry were violating the three-foot rule, almost touching my back. I turned around and glared them a few feet farther away.

Reggie chuckled. "Speaking of hard-assess . . ."

"I just looked. Reggie, how did you get involved with Jason Crowell's troubles in the first place?"

"Jason and I have always been close. When I had him in school he was a good student and a good kid. He still is, in my opinion. He called me in a panic the day those flyers first started turning up—even before he told his family. For advice."

"And I suppose as a buffer against his father. What an unpleasant man. He acts like he's mad at the world. And a little tin tyrant around the house, too."

Reggie nodded. "Jim Crowell is a piece of work, all right. He treats those kids like employees. You'd think he'd be backing his son a hundred percent, instead of blaming him."

"I still don't think he's really sure Jason isn't a rapist."

"Maybe, maybe not. But he's pissed off at him anyway—for causing trouble."

"And worrying about how much it's costing him."

Reggie tasted his Maker's Mark and smiled with pleasure. "That brings up kind of a delicate point, Milan."

"What's that?"

"This business has gotten more complicated than it started out, what with Dorothy Strassky getting killed and the Cleveland police in the mix now. I don't see why you should be working gratis."

"Hey," I said. "It's the least I can do. Right now if it wasn't for you, I'd be designing a security system for the pearly gates and making sure nobody ripped off a harp."

"Anybody would've done what I did," he said. "That was no big deal."

"Maybe not to you. It was the biggest of big deals for me. Risking your ass for a guy you hardly knew."

"What was I supposed to do, let you die?"

"I still can't take your money, Reg. And I'm sure as hell not going to get any from Crowell. Besides, I'm not allowed to go near the Strassky beef. Lieutenant McHargue made sure I understood that."

He ran a finger around the rim of his glass. "It's different without Marko Meglich sitting in that seat, isn't it?"

"It is—different," I agreed, the pain taking me by surprise as it always did, like an ingrown toenail in my heart.

"I know you must miss him."

"Every day. And that's another reason I'm in with Jason for the duration."

"How's that?"

"Marko put his ass on the line for me, just like you did— only it didn't turn out so well. He didn't have to, it wasn't even a Cleveland PD case. But he was my friend. And I'm your friend. So just shut up about the goddamn money. I don't want to hear about it again."

"But—"

"No! Treat me to a Cavs game if you feel funny about it." I shook a Winston out of the pack. "The two of us—courtside seats. That'll probably cost you more money than if you paid my going rate, anyway."

"You got it." We clinked glasses and drank to it. Then he looked pointedly at my cigarette. "That is, on the off-chance that you live that long, smoking those damn coffin nails."

"Shut up about my smoking, too," I said.

CHAPTER EIGHT

Mel Dunwoodie, the chief of campus police at Sherman College, must have been at least sixty years old, but his pinkish cheeks were completely unlined, although a network of broken veins beneath the skin gave him away as a man who liked strong drink. The owner of multiple chins, he was several klicks past chubby, blue-eyed, almost completely bald, and had the scarlet mouth of a Renaissance cherub. Except for the fleshy pouches beneath his eyes he looked like an eight-month-old baby.

He fingered the business card I'd given him, rubbing his thumb across its face. A tarnished gold wedding band encircled his pudgy finger. Then he examined me intently from across his steel desk in the tiny basement security office of the administration building at Sherman College. "You used to be on the job, didn't you?" he said knowingly.

"You're observant, Chief."

He nodded. "An ex-cop. I could tell right away. It takes one to know one." He tried to puff out his chest but succeeded only in inflating his tummy. "I put in my twenty-five and retired from the force in Dayton about eleven years ago."

I guess it did take one to know one, because I'd spotted him as an old-time, old-fashioned cop, too, the minute I had walked in the door. He had the mean, confident strut of a bully; in his heavily-starched black uniform with the dark gray epaulets and pocket flaps, and the black high-peaked hat with the polished brim on the desk next to him, he could have passed for an overweight stalwart in the Waffen SS.

The only thing that didn't fit was the jar of jelly beans on the desk. He was probably trying to emulate another, more famous jelly-bean aficionado, Ronald Reagan—only Dunwoodie was less the elder statesman than the movie cowboy, quick on the draw in the name of law and order.

"You don't look old enough for retirement," he observed.

"I left the Cleveland PD a long time ago."

His demeanor cooled perceptibly; most veteran cops and career military people can't understand why anyone wouldn't want to do what they do. "I'm not sure but this college beat is harder than the old job," he said, vigorously swiping a hand across his hairless dome. "Goddamn kids in this school, they teach 'em physics and art appreciation and all that crap, but they don't teach 'em respect anymore. 'Course, you wouldn't know anything about that since you turned in your badge and weapon and went private." He left no doubt as to his feelings about ex-cops who go into business for themselves.

"Didn't Jason Crowell have any respect, either?"

"Who?"

"The kid you rousted out of town yesterday."

"Who?" he said again. "Oh, yeah. The little rapist."

I let it go.

"What's the Crowell kid to you?" he wanted to know. "Are you family or something?"

"He's my client."

He screwed up his face. "You're working for a rapist? For a kid who took advantage and forced himself on a nice young girl and ruined her life forever? Shame on you, Jacovich. That's a disappointment to me."

"It was a disappointment to me when you ran him out of Dodge."

"It wasn't me that suspended him, it was the dean. Dean Lilly."

"That meant he couldn't attend classes, not that he had to leave his apartment."

"Listen," he said, "when I was on the job in Dayton, I saw it all. Rapes, murders, drug deals, drunk driving, domestic abuse, until just the thought of it used to get me sick every morning before roll call. So I finished up my twenty-five years and then took my pension and came here because I thought it would be quiet and peaceful. And my job is to keep it that way. I don't want his kind running around loose anywhere near campus raping women."

" 'His kind'?"

"Fucking little pervert."

"His apartment wasn't on campus."

"Close enough," Dunwoodie said.

"You had no jurisdiction."

He stuck his chin out from between the rolls of suet that surrounded it. "I make my own jurisdiction around here, mister."

"You questioned him last week, didn't you?"

He sat down behind his desk, and the chair cushion gave a tired little put-upon sigh. "A complaint was made and I followed up on it."

"An anonymous complaint."

"Makes no nevermind. That's my job."

"You talked to the kid. Do you really think he raped anybody?"

"That's what the flyer says."

"Anybody can print up a flyer."

"Are you really that naive? Nobody makes an accusation like that if it's false—you should know that, an ex-cop like you." He looked at me with what seemed like infinite sadness—but I know a good actor when I see one. "And what's really putrid here, what really frosts my knockers, is that now you're working for the bad guy."

"I don't see it that way."

"I imagine the shine from your thirty pieces of silver blinds you."

"And I imagine your selfless devotion to truth, justice, and the American way blinded you to the fact that you have no authority to run anyone out of town."

"I have all the authority I need!" he rumbled. "See this badge?" He thumped his chest. "That means I'm King Shit on this campus, and I don't care who knows it. If it wasn't for me, these goddamn kids would be humping in the bushes on the quad in broad daylight, smoking marijuana until their brains turn to Cream of Wheat, or getting all boozed up behind the gymnasium and driving their car into a tree, or even worse, into a family of five on their way downtown for a pizza! And heroin, too. Did you know that horse is back in a big way with the kids these days? So don't give me any crap about what my authority is." His baby-blue eyes turned mean and crafty. "I have the authority to shoo you off this campus if I want. You're not a student, you're not a parent, and you're sure as hell not official law enforcement. So I'll run you right back to Cleveland if you don't watch your ass."

I finally got mad. "No, you watch yours, Dunwoodie," I said. "You try pulling a Wyatt Earp and roust me off this campus for no good reason, and you and Sherman College will be looking at a lawsuit that'd curl your hair—if you had any." His pinkish cheeks flushed bright red and the dim candles of humanity behind his eyes guttered and went out. He started to say something, but I bulldogged on. "And afterwards you'll be lucky if you can get a job as a night watchman in a 7-Eleven! So don't flex your flabby muscles at me, because I don't intimidate easily."

His face got even more scarlet, and wet with perspiration,

and a purple vein in his forehead throbbed and swelled. He took a few deep breaths and settled back into his chair, visibly willing himself to relax. He took the lid off the jelly-bean jar and twiddled through them with his fingers until he found a green one, which he extracted and popped into his mouth. Tranquilizers with calories.

"You're a bad man, Jacovich," he said wetly, talking around the jelly bean. "You and me must've shared certain ideals at one time or you never woulda pinned on a badge. And now here you are going against your own kind and sticking up for a cheap, oversexed punk."

"That cheap, oversexed punk might just be an innocent kid who got caught in a rundown," I said. "There's no proof, no accuser, there might not even have been a rape at all. When you were on the job, didn't anyone ever tell you that in this country the courts maintain a presumption of innocence?" I drew myself up to my full height; six foot three isn't a giant, but it sometimes gets people's attention. Especially bullies. "Or were you that other kind of cop?"

He looked up at me, not intimidated at all. "I was the kind of cop that put away scum like your Jason Crowell," he said. "I haven't got enough on him yet; but punks like that always slip up, and I will, sooner or later. And then"—he jerked his thumb toward the floor—"he goes down. Count on it."

I was too angry to say anything, so I turned and started for the door.

"Jacovich," Dunwoodie said. "You walk real softly around this campus, you hear. Because I'll be watching you. You fuck up just one time—and you go down, too."

I made my way across the quad to the poly sci building, wondering why Mel Dunwoodie had been so hostile. Was he one of those scary cops with a messianic drive to rid the world of everyone he perceived as an evildoer? Or did he have another agenda that cut a little closer to Jason Crowell's bone?

Either way, I resisted smoking a cigarette as I walked. I might get careless and toss it on the sidewalk and Dunwoodie would have me hanged for littering.

A cold wind set the fallen leaves to dancing a spirited fandango. In a few days or weeks, winter would spread its shroud over the North Coast, and Ohioans would become clinically depressed from a four-month-long lack of sunshine.

It was time to talk to Jason's faculty advisor, Trey Dotson. On my way I tried to imagine what "Trey" was short for.

Inside the building I checked the directory and found Trey Dotson's name, and one mystery was solved. He was listed as Schuyler Dotson III. The "III" had evidently turned into "Trey" somewhere along the line, probably because you couldn't call a little kid Schuyler.

His office was on the third floor, and I made my way up the stairs past several groups of earnest-looking young men and women on their way to or from classes. Poli sci majors always look earnest.

Trey Dotson was in his early thirties, and even though he wore a cardigan sweater with leather patches at the elbows over a blue-striped white shirt and plain navy tie, he managed to seem almost jaunty—maybe because the sweater was powder-blue and the shoes peeking out from under the cuffs of his tan cords were immaculately clean Nike crosstrainers, and because he looked like the kind of one-hit rock star who used to make the cover of *Tiger Beat* in the seventies—the baby face not quite masking a cocky sensuality.

When I walked into his office, he was straightening up the surface of his desk. It didn't look as if it needed much straightening; he was a lot neater and more organized than most college teachers in my experience. I had called him before I left the house that morning and told him who I was and what I wanted, so he'd been expecting me.

"I've got a class in fifteen minutes," he said, "so I want to grab a coffee while I can. It's been pretty hectic around here—we've just lost one of our faculty people in a terrible way."

"I know," I said. "That was too bad."

"Walk with me, okay?"

It was okay with me. I was sick of cramped offices anyway. We went down to the second floor where we confronted a gleaming machine that dispensed coffee, tea, and soup.

"Want anything?" he asked, digging into the pocket of his cords for change.

I decided to pass. As much of a coffeeholic as I am, I hope I'll never be desperate enough to drink any out of one of those machines. Even the industrial-strength brews in police stations are better than that.

He put in his fifty cents and waited while the monster dispensed coffee with cream into a little cardboard container, one with the collapsible handle on the side that is never strong enough to hold a full cup.

"Jason came to see me yesterday after he'd been suspended," he said, leaning against the machine with a kind of tousled insouciance and blowing into his coffee. "Naturally. I'm his advisor."

"And what did you tell him?"

"That there was nothing I could do." He might have been dispassionately discussing a TV show he'd watched the night before.

"You think suspending him was justified?"

"They don't pay me to make judgments like that," he said, so pleasantly it was making my teeth ache. "Only to teach political science and hold the hands of the freshmen who are assigned to me."

"And what about campus security making him leave town?"

He shrugged to indicate his lack of power. "I had nothing to do with that."

"How well did you know Jason?"

"Not very. I'd met him the first week, like I did all my kids. He seemed like a pretty good guy. Then I had him come in when the flyers hit the streets, to find out what was going on."

"You think he's a rapist?"

"I don't know. You can't tell by looking."

A pretty young woman walked by, laden down with a purse, a book bag, and a canvas duffel. "Hi, Professor Dotson," she cooed, batting her eyes in a way that I'm sure she thought was flirtatious. It looked pretty ludicrous to me.

"Hi, Georgia," he said casually. Everything he did was casual—drinking coffee, straightening his desk, flirting with students, or watching Jason Crowell go down the tubes. "I'm not a full professor," he confided to me modestly, when she was out of hearing range, "just an associate. But they don't really comprehend the difference yet."

As if I cared. "When Jason Crowell came to you about those flyers, what was your gut feeling? You must have those," I said, although I was beginning to doubt whether Trey Dotson had many feelings at all.

"I suppose he could have done it," he said, either ignoring the gibe, or too blissfully unaware to notice it. "Not that it was premeditated or anything. You know, kids this age, they don't know what to do with their raging testosterone, and sometimes it runs away with them. My guess is, he was out on a date, they were doing a little harmless nicmo—"

" 'Nicmo'?"

"N-C-M-O. An acronym for non-committed making out. And maybe Jason just got carried away. Maybe he was even on something."

"On something?"

"Drugs." He took a slug of caffeine. The face he made led me to believe he felt the same way about machine coffee as I do. "Marijuana, of course, but crack cocaine or heroin, too.

Heroin is making a comeback, big time. It's not just an inner-city problem anymore. Drugs are rampant on every college campus in America—except maybe Oral Roberts University."

He smiled and ducked his head, embarrassed at his own little joke. "No matter how hard we try, no matter how much educating we do, kids still spend their money to abuse illegal substances, and then they do crazy things." He knit his brows together in a frown and wrinkled his smooth forehead so I'd believe he was thoughtful and serious. "That doesn't excuse it. Not for a minute. When you're an adult—and that's what they're supposed to be when they come to college, young adult—when you're an adult, you're supposed to be able to control yourself. I guess Jason hasn't figured that out yet." He grimaced. "Or maybe by now he has—but for him it's already too late."

"You're talking as though he's guilty."

Again the charming, tolerant smile. "Why would he be accused publicly if he wasn't?"

"I can think of several scenarios," I said. "Maybe he had sex with a woman and then didn't call her again and she felt used and rejected and wanted to get him in trouble. Maybe the victim had him mixed up with somebody else. Maybe someone just had it in for him, and there wasn't any rape at all."

"That's a little fanciful, isn't it?"

"So is your drug theory."

"Could be."

"The point is, there's not a shred of evidence against him except some anonymous piece of paper."

He tasted his coffee. "A pretty powerful piece of paper, I'd say. Have you read it?"

"Sure I have."

"What did you think?"

"I thought it was execrable, cowardly, and grossly unjust."

"Well, that's your opinion," he said. "Colored, of course, by the fact that Jason is your client. You want him to be innocent. I understand that. Frankly, I do, too. I don't like to think one of the kids I've been advising is capable of anything so terrible. But by the same token, I can't think why anyone would make an accusation like that if it weren't true."

"You're his faculty advisor. Couldn't you have gone to bat for him, pointed out to the dean that suspending him without proof is grossly unfair?"

He blew on his coffee again and took another sip. "I'm afraid I know Dean Lilly too well to do anything like that. He's a pretty stubborn fellow once he makes up his mind."

Another gutless wonder, whose species seems to breed so prolifically in academia, I thought. "Can I gather that you don't have tenure?"

He recoiled as if I'd slapped him, and some of the muddy coffee sloshed over the lip of the cup, narrowly missing his spotless Nikes. "That's pretty unkind, Mr. Jacovich. And not fair. I'm an advisor, not an advocate. Disciplinary actions aren't my area, and I learned a long time ago that it's unhealthy to stick my nose where it doesn't belong. Don't you agree?"

"If I did," I said, "I'd be in another business."

"Maybe that'd be a good idea," he said. "I understand the Cleveland police have been talking to him about what happened to Dorothy Strassky. That could really get messy—for you, too, I should think."

"Thanks for your concern."

The smile wavered for just a moment, and then came back, brighter than ever. "I'm afraid I have to get to my class now," he said, dumping the dregs of his coffee into a plastic-lined trash can and sending the cardboard cup in after it. "Look, I'm really sorry about the boy, but there isn't a doggone thing I can do about it."

"A doggone thing"? As I said good-bye and made my way downstairs, I found myself experiencing a sugar rush.

CHAPTER NINE

Saturday morning brought cold, pelting rain, still another harbinger of the dreary winter to come. But Ruthie and Moe's diner, on East Fortieth and Prospect, seemed cheery enough, even though its walls and leatherette booths and stools are black and its ceilings are aluminum. Built in 1926 and doubled in size a few years ago, it's a midtown corridor landmark, notable for the eclectic makeup of its clientele. Despite its very casual ambiance, enhanced by the charismatic Moe and his graying ponytail, on weekday mornings half the diners are lawyers, judges, and businessmen wearing expensive suits to their power breakfasts; the other half are denim-clad laborers sporting baseball caps. On the weekends things get more relaxed.

I sat in a booth next to Reggie Parker. Across from us was his lawyer pal, Jeremiah Locke, a tall, astonishingly handsome man a few years younger than me, with skin the color of latte, curly dark hair like an Italian lounge singer of the fifties, and light-green eyes that seemed to drill right through me. His Saturday getup was a dark red jogging suit that looked as if it had never accompanied him on anything more strenuous than walking up the stairs.

Locke was trying to talk around mouthfuls of bagel with cream cheese. "This situation is iffy, guys. Sherman had no justification for Jason's suspension only on the basis of that flyer, which amounts to nothing more than an unsubstantiated rumor. But"—and he held up a cautionary finger—"with him being a suspect in the Dorothy Strassky killing, they might be on a little more solid ground, legally."

"But Jason hasn't been officially charged," I pointed out, as I dug into my hash browns. "And there's still no proof of anything."

"No," Locke agreed. "But the college does have a point about the way they're perceived by the public, the alumni, and the parents. Would you want your kid going to school side by side with a suspected murderer—never mind a rapist?"

"Isn't there anything you can do?"

"I can lean pretty hard on Dean Lilly Monday morning," he said. "I don't know if it'll get Jason reinstated, but it'll give the good gray dean something to think about. A messy, high-profile lawsuit isn't going to do much for Sherman's public image, either, and they damn well know it."

"Where do I fit in?"

He smacked his lips, judging the bagel. "Reggie tells me you're working on this pro bono, right?"

I nodded.

"And that means that officially you don't have a client. And even if you did, as you know, in legal terms a private investigator is just an ordinary citizen with an interesting job. Nobody has to talk to you if they don't want to."

"Well . . ."

"Legally speaking, you're simply meddling in an affair that doesn't concern you. The school can get a restraining order on you if you start getting up their noses, and the Cleveland police can kick your ass from here to Ashtabula for messing around in what's become a capital case. Right?"

"I suppose so."

"And then," Locke went on, "Security Chief Dunwoodie could clap you in irons if you so much as set a toenail on his campus. We don't want to give him the satisfaction, do we?"

"Jim Crowell has retained Jerry as Jason's attorney," Reggie said as he poured a little too much maple syrup on his pancakes, spilling over onto his bacon. I had to grimace; I hate it when the syrup gets onto my bacon. "So if Jerry hires you as *his* investigator, you'd have the same client-confidentiality privileges as an attorney. And you wouldn't have to talk to the police if they bother you."

"Crowell will never go for that," I said. "I'm too expensive."

"Oh, we'll let you continue to work for nothing, Milan," Locke assured me, trying to hide his amusement. "I have no problem with that."

I bet not. "The thing is, Jerry, I always run my own investigations. It's the only way I can work."

"I promise I won't do any detecting if you don't do any lawyering. Okay? And if everything comes out in the wash, if Jason comes up squeaky-clean and we do sue Sherman and win, I'll make sure you're taken care of out of the settlement. How does that sound?"

"It sounds all right as far as it goes," I said. "But I'm not sure what it is you want me to do."

"What you've been doing," Reggie told me.

"Only more so." Locke looked up as thunder rumbled in the northern sky from over the lake. An electrical storm was coming, the kind that might knock out the power in the northeastern corner of the state. "We've got to know who's behind Women Warriors. Once we know that, we can get the name of the woman who says Jason took advantage of her. And then if we can prove he didn't . . ."

"He gets reinstated at school," Reggie said, almost happily, "and they make a public announcement that a mistake has been made. His reputation is saved and we can all put this behind us."

"Better than that, Sherman is going to have to pay for suspending him. I'll see to that. Jason might end up a very wealthy kid." Jeremiah Locke was warming to the subject now that there was talk of profit. He smeared cream cheese on the other half of his bagel, then gestured with the knife. "And most important, that'll mean Jason had no motive to kill Dorothy Strassky so he'll be off the hook with Flo McHargue."

"You call her Flo?"

He smiled that big, wide smile again. "We go back a ways." He patted his mouth with his napkin and then set it beside his plate, looking at his watch; it was a Movado, I noted. "Sorry, guys. I've got a racquetball game in twenty minutes."

He slid out of the booth, pulled a roll of bills out of the pocket of his jogging pants, and dropped a twenty onto the table. "This is for breakfast."

"I'll get it," Reggie started to protest, but Locke held up a hand.

"No sweat," he said. "It's on the client." He gave a jaunty wave and headed for the door.

"Wait until Jim Crowell hears he bought breakfast for three," I said.

"With Jerry Locke, Crowell's lucky it's Ruthie and Moe's and not brunch at the Ritz."

Reggie moved over to the vacant side of the booth, and he and I watched through the big window as Locke scurried across the parking lot to a new-looking Saab sedan that almost matched the color of his clothing. I think he must have run between the raindrops, because he didn't appear to be getting wet at all. Some people are just like that—they never sweat, they never crease, and they never wake up in the morning with bedhead.

"Racquetball," I said. "Funny, I figured him for a golfer."

Reggie gave an elaborate shrug. "How the hell are you supposed to play golf in this weather?" He tried to mop up more syrup with an already saturated pancake. "Don't sell Jerry

Locke short. He's got all the fancy downtown-lawyer moves that aggravate people, but he's smart as they come, and once he gets hold, he hangs on like a pit bull."

"I hope so. Jason's going to need him."

"You think if I went down and talked to this Flo McHargue it would do any good?"

I shook my head. "She'd probably tell you to save it for the trial. And she'd be right. She can't stop doing her job just because you walk in and tell her that her chief suspect is a good kid."

I finished the last of my coffee and took a quick glance at my watch. "Well, I'm out of here," I said.

"You have a racquetball date, too?"

"Slovenians don't play racquetball. We polka."

"So you're going to polka, then?"

"No," I said. "I'm going to a funeral. Dorothy Strassky."

He sobered. "Oh."

"Just to check out who shows up. You never know . . ."

Reggie shook his head and clenched his fist in frustration, the fist that wasn't holding the fork. "I just wish I could do something. Now that you and Jerry are both on board, I feel so useless."

"You're best at doing the Green Beret stuff, Reggie. And we don't need that here." I stood up. "At least I hope we don't."

"What do you mean, Milan?"

"I'm kind of afraid that if I ever do track down Women Warriors, they're going to punch the shit out of me."

I drove back up the hill, showered, and changed into a dark brown suit and muted tie, which better matched my mood and my destination. My son Milan was playing football for Kent State at Bowling Green that afternoon, and even though as a freshmen he was unlikely to see much playing time, I would have given anything to be there to cheer him on.

Besides, I hate funerals, and I didn't want to go to Dorothy Strassky's. I didn't really know her or her family, so nobody's feelings would be hurt if I didn't show up. But I thought I might learn something just by being there, and with the stone walls I'd been running into looking for Women Warriors, I needed every scrap of knowledge I could lay my hands on. Jason was sinking into a quicksand that seemed to get deeper with every passing day.

Funerals are, by nature, depressing. But we aren't really sad for the departed most of the time—we're sad for ourselves, because now they're gone and we'll never see them again. Funerals are also an uncomfortably startling reminder of our own mortality, that the next time around it could be us in that box. The bell tolls for thee, all right. For thee and for me.

It was a funereal day, anyway, matching the sad occasion, and the twin bullet-shaped towers of St. Colman's Catholic Church on West Sixty-fifth Street reared up against a wet gray sky that was intermittently brightened by forks of lightning. Originally this had been an Irish neighborhood—St. Colman is the name of a whole handful of early Irish saints—but in recent years it's become part Latino and part African American, with a smattering of Eastern Europeans, and the oldline Irish still hanging in there. A waist-high fence of black iron pickets separates the church grounds from the sidewalk, and several people were leaning against it despite the rain, smoking a final cigarette before the funeral mass began.

A small but steady stream of mourners was filing into the church when I parked around the corner, pulled up the collar of my raincoat, and started for the door. It wasn't a "big" funeral, the kind reserved for local politicians, high-profile industrialists, or former linebackers for the Cleveland Browns. Since the report of Dorothy Strassky's murder had been in the Metro section of the newspaper and on television, though far from the lead story, there were probably a handful of morbidly curious strangers on hand, as well as a sprinkling of representatives from the media. But most of those in attendance, I suspected, were from the ranks of Strassky's friends and colleagues.

As I entered the nave, I genuflected out of long habit—I was raised Catholic as a member of St. Vitus Parish on the east side, but I hadn't been to Mass in fifteen years. I slipped into a seat near the back, taking advantage of my position to study the crowd, which only filled up about a third of the seats. A haggard-looking Jane Strassky, in a black dress and dark gray coat, occupied the front pew, a black-and-white scarf around her head, along with a couple in late middle age. From the remarkable resemblance between Jane and the woman, I presumed they were an aunt and uncle.

Dean Lilly was there, a few rows back, wearing a dark three-piece suit and his officious air, along with several other middle-aged people, a few of them black, who I felt sure were administrators or faculty at Sherman. Otherwise, most of the attendees were women, a large number of them of college-age, who had probably searched their youthful wardrobes for something suitably somber.

The gleaming mahogany casket was at the front of the church before the altar, draped with a blanket of flowers that would have been more appropriate for a Kentucky Derby winner. The mourners would have to pay their respects to a closed lid; Strassky had been beaten about the head and face with a heavy wooden log, and delicacy precluded any public viewing.

Lieutenant Florence McHargue—I found it impossible to think of her as "Flo"—and Detective Bob Matusen walked in and took seats in the last row of pews. She was wearing a black Borsalino hat that made her look like a gangster in a European movie. I couldn't see her eyes, masked as they were by the blue lenses of her sunglasses, but she caught me looking at her, and I could tell she was surprised, because her back stiffened just a little. Her acknowledgment of my presence took the form of a brusque and disapproving nod.

Matusen nodded too, but the glint in his eyes gave me at least a hint that he was glad to see me. He was one of those people you could spot as a police officer anywhere, even if he'd been wrapped only in a towel in the famous old *schvitz*, the steambath on Kinsman Avenue. He'd been Marko's partner for a year, and I'd gotten to know him fairly well, especially after Marko was killed and he became temporary head of the homicide division. He was probably smarting that the department had bumped him back into the ranks and installed McHargue over him, but he was a realist and a loyal and tough cop and he knew McHargue had rank, and you could pull his fingernails out one by one before he'd ever admit his disappointment.

I suppose the police contingent was there for the same reason I was—to check out the attendees and perhaps learn something they hadn't known before.

Jane Strassky and her aunt and uncle were crying. So were several of the young women, although they were doing it louder. Almost everyone else was suitably subdued but not exactly grief-stricken. I figured the faculty crowd from Sherman had attended out of courtesy, to show the colors, and not because of any deeply felt remorse for the departed.

A couple of people caught my attention, though. One of them was a fiftyish woman in an inexpensive cloth coat and run-down-at-the-heels sensible shoes. She stood out because everyone else in the church had dressed in their Sunday best or in undergrad thrift-shop chic. She seemed extremely nervous, as if she didn't really belong at the funeral but was there to get in out of the rain. She kept darting covert glances around, as if at any moment she expected someone to come around and throw her out.

Sitting on the opposite side of the church from me were two young women, both dark-haired and sallow, one with startling blue eyes and the other with dark brown ones. They hadn't made any apparent effort to dress for the occasion; both wore chino slacks and loafers over sock-clad feet. One had on a Sherman College sweatshirt, hardly apropos for a funeral, and the other, a mud-brown sweater with a black scarf knotted at her throat. They weren't red-eyed or solemn like the family, nor did they seem as disengaged as some of the others, but were angry and almost defiant.

As though it had been orchestrated, a rumble of thunder announced the entrance of the officiating priest, who conducted the requiem with all its intended pomp and ritual. The things he said about Dorothy Strassky in his eulogy were pretty much boilerplate, but touching nonetheless, and then he did a commercial for stopping the senseless and random violence in our cities. The drone of his voice was punctuated by thunderclaps, by Jane Strassky's quiet sobbing, and by the occasional annoying and shockingly anachronistic chirping of some of the mourners' cell phones and beepers.

Finally it was over, and I made my way down to the front to pay my respects to the family. Jane squeezed my hand and thanked me for coming, as did her aunt and uncle, who hadn't the foggiest notion of who I was and what I was doing there.

On my way back up the aisle I nearly bumped into Dean Lilly.

"I'm sorry we have to meet again in such tragic circumstances," he said. "This is a terrible thing, Mr. Jacovich."

I mumbled something trite and innocuous.

He shook his leonine head sadly. "You see? This is what I was talking about when we spoke a few days ago. This is what happens. This is a terrible black mark for the college."

His concern for Strassky was touching. "Why? She wasn't killed on campus."

"Yes, but"—his hand fluttered to the knot in his tie—"with all this other business, though—this rape business . . . Well, I don't want it turning into a media circus." He took his hand from his throat and placed it on my arm, and I felt myself stiffening. I don't like being touched unless it's by someone I want to touch me. "I hope Sherman College can count on your discretion."

Without waiting for a reply he hurried up to the front of the church, gave the closed coffin a cursory glance, and bent over Jane Strassky almost unctuously, taking her hand and stroking it.

I continued up the aisle. In the narthex, just inside the door, I caught up with McHargue and Matusen.

"Whattaya say, Milan?" Matusen shot a quick look at his boss and decided not to shake hands.

"Hello, Bob. Lieutenant."

"Paying your respects, are you, Jacovich?" McHargue said.

"Something like that."

"I thought we agreed you were staying out of my case." Her eyes were unreadable behind the dark lenses.

"I am staying out of your case," I said. "But I'm staying in mine. I've been retained by Jason Crowell's lawyer."

"Who's that?" she demanded.

"Jeremiah Locke."

"Jerry Locke," she said dully, and her shoulders sagged beneath her dark suit. She took off her blue glasses, and her eyes looked angry and tired. "That's all I needed on a rainy Saturday."

"You know him?"

"I know him." She sounded grim.

"Then he can tell you that I'm looking into the alleged rape—not Dorothy Strassky's murder."

"But in your mind they're related."

"In yours, too, it would seem." I gave her what I thought was a disarming smile. "I try not to jump to conclusions before I have some facts," I said. "Don't you think that's a good idea?"

Bob Matusen covered his mouth and coughed so she couldn't see him smile.

"You'd better remember what I said to you, Jacovich," Florence McHargue said. "You and Jerry Locke both. About staying out of my way." Her lip almost curled when she spoke Locke's name.

"I'm having it stitched on a sampler for my office wall. Just so I don't forget."

I walked out the door and down the church steps onto the sidewalk, feeling her eyes burning through me. The rain had gotten heavier during the mass, drumming on the cars and creating mini-rivers in the gutters, and bolts of lightning split the sky. The temperature had dropped perhaps eight degrees, and I pulled the belt of my raincoat tight around my waist and ducked my chin. By the time I got around the corner to where I'd left my car, my hair was plastered to my head and water was trickling into my collar and down the middle of my back.

I was feeling extreme dislike for Dean Arthur Lilly, who was more concerned for the college's public relations than for Dorothy Strassky. And then I had to remind myself once more of Florence McHargue's warning—I wasn't working the Strassky case, I was trying to ferret out Women Warriors.

While I was unlocking my car, the two young women I had noticed, the ones who had seemed so angry, were across the street just getting into theirs, a little blue Geo with a Sherman College decal in the rear window. They didn't even look up at me, so I had a chance to study their faces more closely than I had inside. They looked belligerent enough to be warriors; one of the women, the one wearing the sweatshirt, almost ripped the door off the car when she opened it. She got inside, slammed the door, and put her head down on the steering wheel for a few moments while her companion climbed into the passenger seat.

They didn't move for almost a minute. Then the passenger

said something to the driver and put a soothing hand on her arm, and they talked animatedly for a while. They still looked angry.

Finally the driver cranked up the engine and slammed the transmission into gear. As they pulled out of the parking space, laying down some rubber, and did a half-stop at the corner before turning onto West Sixty-fifth, I memorized the license-plate number, which I transferred to my notebook when I got into my car out of the downpour. I also noted their license-plate frame: SHERMAN COLLEGE, it had said.

CHAPTER TEN

I went back to the Flats, climbed the stairs to my office, took off my coat and jacket, loosened my tie, and did some housekeeping. I ran the vacuum cleaner over the hardwood floors, rinsed out the coffeepot and dumped yesterday's grounds. After I straightened out some of the clutter on my desk, I went around the room with a feather duster. Then I gave the room a couple of sweeping sprays with a can of Lysol. The lingering smoke smell from the office fire that spring was almost gone, although I was pretty sure it would never completely dissipate.

I checked my watch; Strassky's funeral had ended an hour earlier, and while many of the mourners had probably gone to the cemetery for the interment, I didn't imagine McHargue and Matusen had bothered.

I got my notebook from my pocket, sat down at my desk, and dialed the number of the homicide bureau, and waited until Bob Matusen got on the line.

"Hello, Bob, it's Milan Jacovich."

"Yeah, Milan. How's it going?"

"It was good seeing you today, Bob. It's been awhile."

"Yeah," he said. "I guess you know I'm not running the division anymore. I'm just a grunt again."

"You get along okay with the new brass?"

He paused a tick too long. "She's all right." I heard him

slurping something—pop, maybe. "She's sure got a woody for you, though. What'd you do to her?"

"I think I called her ma'am."

"That's what I *have to* call her," he said.

"Bob, I need a little favor."

There was another silence, considerably longer than the first. "Don't ask me, Milan, all right?"

"I'd just like you to run a license plate for me."

"I can't."

"It has nothing to do with the Strassky murder," I told him.

"Yeah, but you're working for the Crowell kid. And if it has to do with him, it has to do with the Strassky murder. In this office, anyway. The lieutenant likes him for it. A lot."

"Have you met him, Bob?"

"Not yet."

"If you do, you'll stop suspecting him."

He exhaled noisily into the receiver. "I suspect who my boss tells me to."

"If he didn't do the rape, he'd have no motive for doing the killing."

"None that we know of," he agreed.

"Did you ever think that maybe I'll find out he *is* guilty?"

He considered it. "You might. And if you do, of course you'll tell me, right?"

Now it was my turn to pause. "I'm working for his lawyer now, Bob. Attorney-client privilege. I couldn't tell you if I wanted to."

"And you're not gonna tell me about this plate number you want me to run, either, are you?"

I didn't say anything.

"You got the guts of a guy wrestles alligators, asking me for that kind of a thing."

"You want to find out who did Dorothy Strassky, don't you?"

"I want to keep my badge even worse," he said.

"I don't believe you're that kind of a cop, Bob. Marko Meglich didn't train you like that."

"Believe it. Marko isn't here no more, Milan. Things are different." He swallowed something liquid again. "I can't run any plates for you, I can't let you look at files, I can't even tell you what's going on. I'm sorrier than hell because I know you and Marko were tight—but the LT would cut off my nuts and nail 'em to the front door if she knew I was even talking to you."

"All this couldn't be because I called her ma'am."

"She's pissed off that Marko let you get away with stuff all the time, that he—how the hell did she put it?—he violated the integrity of the department by telling you things you weren't supposed to know. She's strictly by-the-book, Milan."

"So was Marko."

"Marko did what it takes to get the job done, even if it meant cutting a corner here or there. But this McHargue, when she talks in her sleep, she recites the penal code."

"I think I know how to find that out for sure," I said, and said good-bye to Bob.

From my wallet I dug out the card Jeremiah Locke had given me that morning. He wouldn't be in his office late on a Saturday afternoon, but he'd scrawled his home phone on the back. I tapped out the seven numbers.

"How was racquetball?" I said, after we'd gotten the hellos out of the way.

"I was invincible," he said. "What's up?"

"I ran into your old friend Florence McHargue this afternoon. Flo."

"Oh?"

"At Dorothy Strassky's funeral. I don't think she likes me very much."

"I don't think she likes any private ticket very much. Especially one who left the department voluntarily. In her mind that's akin to desertion."

"I can understand that." Marko had felt the same way—it was only thirty years of friendship that had kept him from booting me out of Third District headquarters at least a dozen times.

"She's very focused," Locke went on. "She wouldn't give a damn about an alleged rape in Sherman, because that's not her job. And she probably doesn't want you fooling around with that and getting in the way of her murder case."

"I mentioned your name to her," I said. "She made a face."

"I imagine she did."

"You want to tell me about that?"

"No, I don't. But I suppose I should. Flo and I dated for a while. Three or four years ago. In her mind, I think we ended badly."

"And in your mind?"

"We just ended, that's all. I told her from the beginning I wasn't looking for 'off into the sunset' and 'happily ever after.' "

"So I don't suppose she'd take it well if you were to call her up and ask her to cut me a little slack."

"I shudder at the thought."

"What's she like, Jerry?"

He laughed. "In what spirit are you asking that, exactly?"

"Come on," I prompted.

"Okay. She's a very serious woman. She takes things hard. She has a very strong sense of what's right and what's not, which is what made her become a police officer in the first place. And I can imagine she saw some pretty sickly shit when she was working vice. There's no middle ground for her, no gray areas. To Flo, you're either part of the solution or part of the problem. And I guess you know what that makes you."

I did. "I guess we'll just have to live with that."

"You get anything at the funeral?"

"Nothing I can brag about," I said. "I'll let you know in a day or two."

"There isn't much I can do until Monday when I talk to the dean."

"I can't do much, either," I said. "Tomorrow is my day to spend with my sons."

"You married?" he said.

"Divorced. That's why it's so important that I don't miss a day with my kids. Nothing's going to happen to Jason tomorrow."

"With any luck," he said.

After I hung up, I finished my dusting chores and started for home. As I drove up Eagle Road out of the Flats and made a half-circle around Jacobs Field onto Carnegie Avenue, I thought hard about what Jerry Locke had told me of Florence McHargue and her rigid sense of right and wrong.

No wonder McHaruge and I got on one another's nerves. We were just alike.

Connie came over later that evening for our traditional Saturday date. She didn't ask me about the Jason Crowell business—in fact, she seemed determined to avoid mentioning it at all—and I didn't volunteer anything; it was a sensitive subject for us.

We finally got to that Italian flick at the Cedar Lee that evening—it wasn't worth the wait—and stopped for a late supper at a restaurant called Cena Copa almost right across from the theater, then drove back to my place, where we went to bed early and got to sleep late.

We had eight A.M. coffee sitting on the sofa in the morning because I was to pick up my younger son, Stephen, at ten.

"When am I going to meet these kids of yours, Milan?" she said, wiping crumbs from her English muffin from the corner of her mouth.

"One of these days, I guess."

"Are you keeping me a secret?"

"Hardly. They know we're seeing each other. Your picture is right there." I nodded at the framed snapshot on top of the bookcase, right next to the most recent school photos of both boys. It had been taken by Connie's brother Kevin one evening while we had dinner at her father's restaurant. I don't care for the way I photograph, and don't normally put pictures of myself on display in my apartment, but she'd looked so radiant in this one that I couldn't resist.

"And do they approve?"

"Of my dating? It's hardly an issue anymore, Connie. I've been divorced for a long time."

"So? When do I get to meet them?"

"Soon," I said, trying not to sound deliberately vague. "It's harder now, with Milan away at college."

"I'm going to hold you to that."

I didn't particularly want to tell her that because I saw my boys so infrequently, every moment I was with them was precious to me, and I didn't want the distraction of having someone else along, didn't want to worry if she was having a good time, didn't want Milan Junior and Stephen to think they were tagalongs, an afterthought to my social life. I couldn't very well say that to her, because I wasn't sure how well she'd take it.

It's not that I wasn't committed to Connie; I hadn't dated anyone else since I'd met her. But twice before since my divorce, I've been in relationships I thought were for the long haul and they hadn't worked out. From experience, I was taking this one slower and easier.

The rain had played itself out somewhere in the middle of the night, although the streets were still dark and damp. I got to Lila's house—I've finally gotten over thinking of it as *my* house—a few minutes before ten. I rang the doorbell and settled in for the usual long wait, enough time for Lila's live-in boyfriend Joe to scurry upstairs and hide in the bedroom the way he always does when I arrive on Sunday to pick up the boys. At first he had his reasons—he knew I would have just as soon laid him out as not—but the years have mellowed me, I guess, and now I consider Joe not much more than a wimpy pain in the ass.

I guess that's why Lila puts up with him. Because she can run him, which, given her fiery Serbian temperament, is important to her. Historically the Serbs and the Slovenes have never gotten along, so I suppose our union was doomed from the start. That's the way her parents always looked at it, anyway.

My son Stephen opened the door. "Hey," he said.

At twelve years old, Stephen is no longer the golden, tumbly doll he was at three and four, nor the sweet love he'd turned into at nine and ten. He was tottering on the edge of adolescence now, and had all sorts of preadolescent issues. One of them was that he no longer kissed or hugged his parents; indeed, when he was around his friends, he was loath to admit he even had any. The only time I ever got to touch him was when we were roughhousing.

Still, Stephen was a smiling child. The genes from my Slovenian side of the family had made him fair-haired and blue-eyed, and as easygoing as a twelve-year-old can be, and my heart bloomed in his warmth every time I saw him.

"Hey," I said. He flashed me a grin and then skipped nimbly out of reach of a potential hug or kiss, heading for the front closet where his jacket was.

Lila came down the stairs in a pink jogging outfit, her head held regally high. For a blue-collar Serbian kid from the old neighborhood, she could make a dramatic entrance that would put Tallulah Bankhead to shame, even when, as this morning, she was wearing polyester sweatpants. "Milan," she said.

"Hi, Lila. How are you?"

"All right." As she passed Stephen she put out a hand to

touch his hair, but he squirmed away from her. It didn't bother her any more than it did me. "What time will you be bringing Stephen home tonight?"

"About six o'clock," I said. "As I told you."

"Well, please don't be late, because we've made plans for dinner."

"I won't," I said, resenting it; I *never* brought the kids home late. It was just one of the many ways Lila made things difficult.

"You look tired, Milan," she said. "Are you all right?"

I couldn't help but be touched by her concern. We all have old tapes in our head that get activated when we least expect it. "I'm fine, Lila."

"Have you been getting enough sleep?"

I hadn't gotten enough sleep the night before, but I was damned if I was going to tell her why. "I've been working hard."

"That's good. It's good for you to keep busy. I know these past few months have been rough for you."

She was referring to the quiet morass of grief into which I'd slipped when Marko Meglich was killed. Marko and his former wife and Lila and I had been a steady foursome before our respective divorces, and his death had hit her pretty hard, too. But by nature, Lila is much more stoic than I.

Stephen had struggled into his jacket and was now bouncing around between us like a puppy. "Let's go, Dad."

"Stephen," Lila said in a severe tone, "I think you ought to tell your father about what happened at school Friday."

"Mom," he said, giving the word two syllables and an upward inflection.

"Do it, or I will," she warned.

"Stephen will tell me," I said.

"And then you can deal with it."

I sighed. I see my sons so infrequently that I dislike the role of disciplinarian. I want our times to be happy and warm. I suppose divorced fathers everywhere feel that way, which sends the mothers around the bend.

"Well, have fun, you two," Lila said, and watched as we made our way down the walk to the car.

Having fun with Stephen was never a problem. Full of life and bubbling with high spirits, he always managed to raise mine.

We started the morning with pancakes at a restaurant on East 185th Street. Stephen liked his with blueberries.

"So what's the problem at school?" I said.

"It's dumb," he said. "It's so dumb you won't believe it."

"I'll believe it."

"Okay," he said. "Okay, so we're studying the American Revolution in school. And Friday the teacher goes, 'We're going to put on a little play about the Founding Fathers,' and he goes, 'and each of you will play a different part.' "

"Is that how he went?" I said.

"Huh?"

"Skip it, go ahead." I figured an English lesson, no matter how badly needed, would interfere with the story Stephen was telling.

"Okay, so then he goes, 'And so you'll remember which of the Founding Fathers you're supposed to be, and who everyone else is supposed to be, we're going to pass out these little name badges with your character's name on them.' "

He stopped and looked across the table at me, grinning wickedly.

"So?" I said.

"So then I go"—and here he crinkled up his face in an outraged scowl like Alfonso Bedoya's in *Treasure of the Sierra Madre*—"then I go, 'We don' need no stinkin' badges!' "

I began laughing so hard I almost blew my coffee through my nose. I had rented the classic Bogart film about a year earlier and watched it with Milan Junior and Stephen, and we'd rewound the tape so we could watch the marvelous "stinkin' badges" sequence again. I guess Stephen took after me in more ways than his blue eyes and light hair and complexion—he was a vintage-movie buff, too.

"I guess your teacher never saw that movie," I said, when I finally stopped laughing.

"I got into a lot of trouble. I had to go to the office for disrupting the class. And then the principal called Mom."

"Did she yell at you?"

He lowered his chin and looked at me with the tops of his eyes. "Are you kidding?" he said.

"Well—it was really funny, Stephen, but sometimes you have to know when to be funny and when not to. I guess this was a 'not to' time."

He nodded. "I knew I was gonna get sent to the office before I said it." He shook his head and smiled, relishing the memory. "But I would've said it if I got sent to the guillotine."

I looked across the table at this fair, laughing child I'd sired, and love and pride swelled inside me. I would've given the whole enchilada to be able to reach over and hug and kiss him—but I just winked at him and gave him a thumbs-up instead.

I couldn't imagine how Jim Crowell could not get behind his son one hundred percent, with love and support and, most important, faith. It made me feel bad for Jason—and it made me want to help him even more keenly.

After breakfast we spent some time playing video games at the mall; I'm really bad at it. I think along about twenty years ago, kids began being born with an extra gene or so that made them understand the electronic age and gave them the hand-eye coordination to play those damn games. Stephen always got a kick out of cleaning my clock when we played, as had his older brother before him.

Then we went to one of the Metroparks and got ourselves

into a pickup touch-football game with what evidently was a group of other weekend fathers and their sons. The wet grass and mud played havoc with our clothes and shoes, and I imagined I was going to catch hell from Lila about it when I brought him home. My alternate Sundays with my boys were easier to fill up during baseball season, when, despite the inevitable sell-out at Jacobs Field, Ed Stahl was usually able to wangle some press tickets for us.

I watched Stephen play with a surge of parental pride. He didn't have the exceptional athletic ability of his older brother, but he was a scrapper, always in and around the play, and managed to catch a couple of passes for positive yardage.

Afterwards we went back to my place, I popped some Orville Redenbacher in the microwave, and we watched the NFL on television—the Packers were playing the Bears in the late game, and Green Bay quarterback Brett Favre was one of Stephen's favorites. Personally I don't much enjoy watching football when I don't have anyone to root for, but I got a kick out of Stephen's enjoyment. Playing, spectating, studying, or goofing off, he invested everything he did with an enthusiasm and intensity I found charming.

Then again, I find anything Stephen does charming; I adore him, adore both my boys, and for many years my heart has ached that they were growing up several miles away from me, my time with them scheduled by a divorce judge. And although I talk to them both on the telephone several times a week, Lila has rarely let me deviate from that court-mandated, every-other-Sunday pattern unless it was a special occasion, like the time I got World Series tickets to see the Indians play the Florida Marlins, or the summer I drove them to Myrtle Beach for a precious week of sun, sand and surf.

It was a tough way to go for a devoted family man like me. I missed my boys every day.

At five minutes to six, I dropped Stephen off at the curb in front of his house—I didn't feel like sending Joe Bradac scurrying up the stairs—and then set off toward Kent for the second half of my bimonthly father's day, to have dinner with Milan Junior.

It had been awhile since I'd had the pleasure of having both my kids together on a Sunday. Milan's football schedule and his classes kept him pretty busy, and he'd chosen to spend the day studying, opting for a late dinner instead.

It was just as well, I thought, that I'd spent the morning and afternoon with Stephen and now would have Milan alone. Apart from wanting to be with him because I love him, he was the same age as Jason Crowell, at the same place in his college life, and could perhaps give me some insight on the case I was working.

In short, I wanted to pick his brain.

CHAPTER ELEVEN

The drive to Kent took the better part of an hour, and darkness had fallen by the time I got there. The beautiful black squirrels famous for gamboling about all over the university grounds were nowhere in evidence; they had evidently turned in for the evening. I was sorry to have missed them.

My son Milan was staying in a residence hall on campus in a neat little two-bedroom suite he shared with a redheaded electrical-engineering major and fellow football hopeful, Bert Corcoran. Milan, like me, is a lifelong east-sider, and Bert was from the western suburb of Avon Lake; the two of them together in the same apartment was something of a culture shock.

The east and west sides of greater Cleveland are as different as Los Angeles and San Francisco—different lifestyles, different mindsets, and different ethnicities. On the east side is most of the African American community, the Slovenians and Croatians, the Poles of Slavic Village, the Russians, Jews, Asians, and the Italians of Little Italy. West-siders tend to be Irish, Polish, Puerto Rican, Serbian, Ukrainian, Lithuanian, and German, as well as Gen-Xers and late boomers. Not for nothing do many people refuse to cross the Cuyahoga from one side of town to the other; for most of them it's terra incognita.

Bert was the one who answered my knock, a pencil behind his ear. He was wearing blue running shorts and a T-shirt, showing off the solid physique that had made him second-string tight end on the varsity squad, with white rubber flip-flops on his sockless feet. Apparently the young don't ever get chilly.

"Hey, Mr. Jacovich," he said, and shook my hand; he was one of those young men who shakes hands at every opportunity. I imagined if he had to make a pizza run for a bunch of guys in the dorm, he'd press flesh with everyone both coming and going. "He's getting dressed," he said, with a nod toward the door of Milan's little cubicle.

There were two small bedrooms in the suite, and a central room with two computer desks and a small sofa. No ashtrays in sight—I was pleased my son had not picked up my cigarette habit. As athletes, he and Bert both had more respect for their bodies.

"I'll be right out, Dad," Milan hollered from the other side of the door.

"Good game yesterday, Bert?" I said.

"We lost by a field goal."

"Yeah, I know."

"I was only in for two plays—in the last quarter. I blocked."

"That's not too bad for a freshman. I think I only ran nine plays all season my first year. Be patient—you'll get your chance."

He shrugged and took the pencil from his ear. "It's not like I'm going into the NFL anyway."

"You never can tell," I said.

"Nah—I'll never be good enough. Football's a great game when you're in school. And it impresses the hell out of women." He grinned, his cheeks coloring. "But I'd rather be an engineer. I can't imagine getting hit by a 280-pound line-backer when I'm thirty years old."

"When I was your age, I couldn't imagine even *being* thirty years old."

I sat down at Milan's desk and chatted with Bert for a few

minutes. He was a nice kid, freckled and serious and respectful. Like Jason Crowell. I wondered how Bert would hold up under the kind of pressure Jason was enduring.

Milan came out of his room, his hair still damp from his shower, and smelling slightly of Brut, wearing the off-white sweater I'd given him for his birthday over a dark blue shirt and blue slacks. While Stephen was blond and fair, Milan Junior had inherited the Serbian dark hair and eyes of his mother, and her grave Serbian disposition, too. He'd never been as rowdy or effervescent as his brother, but was always reserved, almost dignified. From the time he was too little to raise his head, it has never occurred to anyone to call him just "Junior."

"Hey, Dad," he said, hugging me. He'd passed the stage Stephen was in now—it was okay to hug his old man again. Gratefully I hugged him back, noting he was just an inch shorter than I, and probably still growing. I wondered what it would be like, having to look up to my son.

I invited Bert to join us for dinner, even though I wanted some time alone with Milan; fortunately, he decided that he had to hit the books. Milan put on his team jacket, Bert shook hands with both of us, and we went out into the brisk autumn air.

We took my car and drove to a little eatery on one of Kent's main streets. It was, not surprisingly, a school hangout, and I found myself the oldest one in the place by a good twenty years. The decibel level of conversation was higher than I would have liked, but at least they weren't playing loud, clanking rap, so we found a small table against the wall and settled in. I ordered a seafood platter—shrimp, crab, and scallops— and a Pepsi. Milan got a bowl of clam chowder, a green salad, a grilled chicken sandwich on pita bread, and a glass of milk.

"Have you been studying all day?" I said.

He nodded. "My eyes are ready to fall out."

"It'll all be worth it."

"I hope so," he said. "College—I'll tell you, it's a whole lot different than high school."

"It's supposed to be. But it's supposed to be fun, too." I unfolded my napkin and put it in my lap. "Are you having any fun?"

"Sure," he said. "Playing ball—even though I don't get to play much."

I tried to make it casual. "Dating anybody?"

"Nobody special. I don't have the time to get into a totally heavy-duty dating thing right now."

"But you do date?"

"Sometimes."

"You know, now that you're in college, it's different than when you were a kid. These are grown, mature women. I mean, it's not like the backseat of a car anymore."

Milan gave me a skeptical look; he knew me too well. "Is this going to be the foreplay lecture?"

I laughed. "Never mind," I said.

"Thanks."

"How about friends? Are there any women you're just friends with? No romance, just like buddies?"

"A few. There's this girl Kristi—Kristi Miracle."

"Cute name."

"Cute girl."

"But you're just pals."

"Right. She's in my physical-geography class."

"I took physical geography, too. I barely scraped by."

"All you've got to do is read the book," he said. "That's what I've been doing all day long."

His chowder arrived. He shook a whole packet of oyster crackers onto the top of it, then loaded it with pepper.

"So you don't date her?"

"Who?"

"Kristi Miracle."

He paused with the soup spoon halfway to his mouth. "Depends on what you call a date."

"Come on, Milan, you know what a date is."

"You mean fooling around?" He shook his head. "That'd just louse up a perfectly good friendship."

"But the two of you are tight."

"Tight enough."

"You tell her things?"

Milan looked puzzled.

"I mean, like confide in her? Tell her your troubles? Talk about some of the women you do go out with?"

"Sometimes. It's easier talking to a woman about things like that than it is telling one of the guys." He wiped chowder from his mouth, sat back and crooked one arm over the back of his chair. "Okay, what's the deal here?"

"What deal?"

"Why are you suddenly so interested in my sex life?"

I winced. I had no illusions that my son was still a virgin—I sure hadn't been when I was eighteen—but nevertheless it gave me a twinge to even hear him use the words. "It's not exactly sudden," I told him. "I've always been interested in who you were dating."

"Yeah, but . . ." He ran a hand through his hair, which was almost completely dry by now. "Not like this. I know when you're being pointed."

"Pointed?"

"When you bring something up for a particular reason." His gaze was level. "Pointedly."

I sighed. "Sometimes I think you're so smart already, you don't need to go to college."

"Is it a case you're on?"

"Yeah. By the way, have you given up your lifelong affair with cheeseburgers or are you just trying to impress me?" I said.

"I've got to stay in shape or I'll never see any playing time. I'm a wide receiver, we've played seven games, and I've never even touched the ball yet." He smiled; Milan was not much of a smiler, so whenever he allowed himself the luxury it was like the sun breaking through a January cloud cover. "I still scarf down a lot of pizza, though."

"Bad."

"It's okay—I have mushrooms and peppers and onions on it. Veggies are good for you." The waitress brought our drinks and he gulped down half the milk the instant she put it down on the table. "Now, what's all this business about dating?"

"Back in high school, did you know a kid named Jason Crowell?"

He had to think about it for a while. "I know who he is," he said. "We graduated together in June. But there were five hundred and some kids in that class. I didn't know him very well."

"What did you think of him?"

"I didn't think anything of him," he said. "I can't remember if we ever had a conversation. He was just a guy around school." He leaned forward, his mouth tight and serious. "Does he have something to do with your case?"

I took a deep breath and proceeded to tell him all about the rape accusation. I omitted any mention of the Strassky killing because I didn't want to upset him. He'd seen me hurt before—knifed, shot, beaten up—and he'd spent a lot of his adolescence brooding about it.

"That sucks," he said when I'd finished the story. "The poor guy can't even defend himself."

"I know."

"Did he do it?"

"He says he didn't."

"What do you think?"

"I don't know him well enough to make that kind of judgment. I guess I'll believe him until I find out otherwise." I took a sip of my Pepsi. "Ever hear of anything like that happening here at school?"

"What?"

"Date rape."

"I haven't heard of it, but I imagine it happens."

"Why?"

"Some guys can be real assholes. They don't even like to think a girl doesn't want to, even if she says no. You know, it's a male-ego thing." He cracked his knuckles; it was like the sound of castanets. "Or sometimes they just get carried away."

"That makes it right?"

There was an edge to his tone I'd never heard before. "No! All I'm saying is, I can imagine it happening."

"But it's never happened to you, has it?"

His look was withering. "Get real, Dad," he said.

Milan wanted to go back to the books after dinner, so I was homeward-bound before ten o'clock. It was a long drive just to spend two hours with him, but worth it. The rain was starting up again, drumming on the roof of the car, and in the white glare of my headlights the drops looked a lot like snow. With November almost upon us, it wouldn't be long now before they were.

My son had given me a lot to think about. He didn't approve of date rape, which was no surprise, but he knew that it happened, more often than I realized. Maybe Jason *had* lost control, and in his mind he didn't think about it as rape at all. But then that would mean he was lying to me about never having a date. Even Milan didn't quite buy the idea of his innocence after I told him the story.

And if Jason was lying, if he *was* a rapist, then it was entirely possible that he was a murderer, too.

Jesus, it makes it tough when I begin having doubts about a client. This was getting messy, and I wasn't any closer to unraveling it than I had been when Reggie Parker had first sat down in my office and asked for my help.

As I squinted through the water on the windshield, I thought about Milan's friend Kristi, too. He admitted he told her things he wouldn't confide to any of his male friends, which made me wonder if Jason had done the same thing with Marika Rollins and she hadn't told me all that she knew.

I decided to go back out to Sherman College in the morning and see if I could turn over any fresh clods of dirt. I didn't know what else to do.

I walked into my living room at five past eleven, shucked off my jacket, and stretched away the many miles of driving I'd logged. It had been a long and ultimately tiring day, but I wouldn't have given up thirty seconds of it—seeing my boys always refreshed and restored me.

I headed into the kitchen and took my first beer of the day from the refrigerator. I tore off the top, then took it into the den and saw that my answering machine was blinking. Apparently I'd gotten three calls.

I pushed the machine's button before taking a long swig.

"Hi, Milan," Connie's voice said. *"I know you're with your kids today, and I just wanted to let you know I hope you had a great day. Call me tomorrow. 'Bye."*

That was good, I thought. It meant she wasn't really ticked off about not being introduced to Milan Junior and Stephen. I wasn't surprised; except for the Jason Crowell business, Connie had always been easygoing. Relationships are like minefields. You never know when you're going to step somewhere you shouldn't, and you're always relieved when you manage to get through one unscathed.

BEEP! went the machine.

"It's Ed, Milan. I looked up Sherman College in my files. There was a similar date-rape incident three or four years ago, just like I remembered. No flyer like this time, but it made a

pretty bad stench on campus and hit most of the newspapers, too. The difference is—and I'm sorry to be the bearer of shitty tidings, big guy—is that that time, the accused kid really was guilty. Call me when you get anything printable."

That didn't bode well for Jason's chances with the powers that be, I thought. They'd been burned once before, and probably were going to take it out on Jason just so they'd look good.

The machine beeped again.

"Milan, it's Reggie." His voice sounded ragged and tired. *"May Day! May Day! It's—uh—eight forty-five now. Call me at home as soon as you get in, no matter how late."*

The urgency of his message made the hair on my arms stand up. I lit a cigarette, settled into my leather recliner, and punched out Reggie's number.

"Hello," he said, quiet and low.

"It's Milan. What's the matter?"

"Plenty. I just got a hysterical call from Jim Crowell. Jason was arrested at about seven o'clock."

"Arrested? What in hell for?"

"Possession."

"Possession of what?"

"Heroin," he said.

CHAPTER TWELVE

Mel Dunwoodie seemed more pink and glowing than the first time I'd seen him. Even his extra chins looked healthily florid. Perhaps it was the heat in his small basement office that was causing the rosy flush, the pipes clanking noisily on a morning that had turned raw and cold. Or maybe it was just because he was happy.

"I don't know who called in the anonymous tip," he said, not quite able to suppress the glee that was turning up the corners of his mouth. "It was a male voice, that's all I know."

"And this Mr. Anonymous told you Jason was holding heroin in his apartment?" I said. "That was the basis for your busting in there to search?"

He nodded at me, beaming satisfaction. "Well, now, let's think this out, 'kay? Officially, that was a vacant apartment, so it's not like I 'busted in.' Besides, a guy involved with drugs is just as likely to do anything else—rape, steal, maybe even kill. You wore a badge long enough to know that a bad apple is a bad apple. Or don't you remember anymore, Jacovich?"

He certainly know how to activate my hot buttons. I put up a hand. "Chief—if you want to call me by my first name, that's fine—or you can call me Mr. Jacovich if you're more comfortable with that. But just plain 'Jacovich' is not acceptable. Do we understand each other?"

His eyes bugged out in surprise, and before he could answer,

I cut in. "Good. Now—has Jason been tested for drugs?"

It took him a moment to regain his composure; then he shook his head. "Not yet, no. He'll probably test clean, anyway. A smart pusher doesn't sample his own product."

"Pusher?"

Once again on solid ground, he leaned back in his chair and laced his fingers together at the back of his neck. There were wet, white smudges under the arms of his black shirt where he'd sweated off his stick deodorant. "There was nearly a quarter of a pound of smack taped inside his toilet tank in a plastic bag. That's a hell of a lot for purely personal use. I imagine the DA is going to charge him with intent to sell."

"It's a hell of a lot to leave behind when you move out, too."

He had an answer for that. "When Jason Crowell, ah, 'moved out,' I was standing right there watching him pack. He didn't have the opportunity to take the drugs with him."

"I assume you had a warrant?"

The happy smile diminished. "I'm no dumb briarhopper cop, Jacovich. Of course I got a warrant. What with the other charges against him, I didn't have any trouble getting a judge to sign one."

"What other charges? He's never been formally charged with rape."

"Nevertheless," Dunwoodie said. He took his hands from behind his head and reached for his jar of jelly beans, lifting off the glass lid. This time he selected a purple one. "I'll tell you," he chuckled, "that colored woman from Cleveland is fit to be tied that I'm beating her time."

"I assume you're talking about Lieutenant McHargue?"

He popped the candy into his mouth. "She wants a piece of the Crowell punk, too. Thinks he might have had something to do with killing that dyke from the college. But she's just going to have to get in line."

"Where is Jason now?" I said.

He made a face. "The sheriff's got him out to the county jail. Only place *to* put him. For the time being." He seemed almost disappointed that he and campus security didn't have their own lockup, but it didn't keep him from chuckling again. "I imagine those other inmates'll take real good care of him over there—a good-looking young boy like that."

I was fast losing patience. I've always found political correctness stiflingly insufferable, but "colored woman," "dyke," and the gleeful anticipation of someone suffering forcible sodomy all in one conversation, was making me sore. "This is personal with you, isn't it, Dunwoodie?"

The phony affability disappeared, replaced by messianic righteousness. "It's personal with me every time someone breaks the law, *Mr.* Jacovich. I've spent my whole life upholding that law, and whenever somebody shits all over it, you're damn right it's personal." This declaration would have been a lot more dramatic if Dunwoodie's tongue and lips hadn't turned purple from the jelly bean.

"What if you've got the wrong guy?"

He wagged his head from side to side like a bison; the smile had returned. "Oh, he's the right guy, all right. No question. It's his apartment. His toilet."

"He used to have a roommate. Isn't it possible—?"

"—that a kid moves out and just forgets to take five thousand dollars' worth of illegal drugs he hid in the tank of the john?"

"What if it was planted?"

"Now, who'd want to do that? The kid's only been on campus four weeks, and already he's accused of rape and we find a stash of horse in his place. And you actually believe he's innocent of both charges? You're either pretty naive, which I doubt because of all the years you spent with the police department, or else you're in denial. Isn't that the latest psychobabble? Denial?"

"I want to talk to him," I said.

"Don't see how you can do that."

"I've been engaged by his attorney. That's how I can do that."

Dunwoodie scowled. "Well, you'll have to take that up with the Sheriff's Department, then."

"I will."

"Although those county boys aren't going to like a fallen-away cop any more than I do."

"I'm not sure you really like anybody, Chief Dunwoodie," I said, getting up from my chair across the desk from him. "You seem to think you have the franchise on righteousness, and the rest of us—like the ones you call punks, dykes, colored people, and fallen-away cops—just don't come up to scratch. I don't think you're a police officer because you want to help people—think it's because you get off on busting everybody who doesn't fit your standards."

He smacked his purple lips. "You can't talk to me that way in my own office," he said, rising too—but the gesture wasn't threatening; he wasn't armed, and even in his blind zeal for truth, justice, and the American way, he surely couldn't have believed he could stand up to me in a physical confrontation.

"I'm doing it, though," I said. "You're a small-minded, vengeful man, Chief. You think you're a good cop, but you're really the worst kind, because you have no compassion or humanity."

The rosy glow on his face had turned an apoplectic crimson, and there was yellow wolf-heat in his eyes. "You just get your ass off this campus right now," he ordered in a voice sandpapered by rage, wagging a pudgy finger at me. "And stay off."

I walked slowly—infuriatingly so, for Dunwoodie—toward the door. "I'm sorry, Marshal Dillon," I said, "but you'll have a hell of a time making that one stick."

. . .

The Lorain County lockup was in Elyria. It took me fifteen minutes to get there, and another fifteen to talk the sergeant at the desk into letting me see Jason Crowell.

When she finally relented and they brought him into the visiting room, he was pale and drawn, looking as sorrowful and stricken as a mourner at the tomb of Jesus in some medieval Italian painting. He was wearing the TV-familiar short-sleeved orange jumpsuit that was standard issue for all prisoners; they strip you of your individuality in jail—they give you a number and make you look like everyone else. They take away that essential part of you, that spark, that makes you human. Jails are necessary, but they're not rehabilitating. It's punishment, pure and simple, and don't let anyone try to tell you otherwise.

Jason shuffled in, his feet dragging across the floor even though they weren't manacled. He slumped into the uncomfortable straight chair across the table from me, his pale bare arms hanging limp at his sides as if they'd both been broken.

"Are you all right?" I said. I knew that an eighteen-year-old middle-class kid who'd just spent his first night in jail was anything but all right; I felt obliged to ask anyway.

He shook his head slowly from side to side. "This is like a nightmare," he said without intonation, like a computer-generated information operator on the telephone. "And I can't wake up."

"Mr. Locke, your lawyer, is going to look after you now. And so will I."

"Are you going to look after me when they send me to state prison?"

"Innocent people don't go to prison," I told him. But I knew it was a lie as I said it. Lots of innocent people get locked up, and Jason Crowell—accused rapist, suspected drug dealer, and the most likely suspect in a brutal murder—was playing against house odds.

He took a deep breath, as if he was having trouble getting enough air into his lungs. "I don't know if I can stand it. The guy in my cell jerks off four or five times a day, and somebody two cells down has bad dreams and screams all night. How long are they going to keep me here, Mr. Jacovich?"

"Until the hearing tomorrow morning."

"God, another night in this place." He shuddered with his entire body.

"They'll probably set bail then, and you can go home."

Tears welled in his eyes. "More money my father has to pay out," he said.

"That's the last thing you should be worried about, Jason. Your father wants you out of jail, no matter how much it costs."

Looking as if he didn't believe me, he wiped his nose with the back of his hand, the gesture of a small, frightened child.

"Tell me the truth," I said. "Was the smack yours? The heroin they found in your toilet tank. Was it yours?"

He shook his head slowly from side to side. "I don't even know what heroin looks like."

Was this kid too ingenuous to be true? I wondered. Had he somehow grown up encased in a bubble that protected him from the three *B*'s, the plagues of his generation—*Beavis and Butt-Head, Baywatch*, and Buttafuoco—the abandonment of ethics, the designer drugs and body piercing and the disaffection that was the natural reaction to priapism in the Oval Office, enormous greed in professional sports, and cynicism in business and politics? Or was this dewy-eyed naiveté of Jason's a gigantic put-on? I've been lied to by a client before.

"Then how did it get there?"

His shrug was eloquent.

"When's the last time you cleaned your toilet?"

"I do it every couple of days," he said. "But I don't clean the inside of the water tank. I mean, who does?"

He had me there. "Who else had a key to your apartment?"

"My mother."

"I think we can safely rule her out," I said. "What about Marika? Did you give her a key?"

"Uh-uh."

"How about Terry Yagemann?"

"No, he left his key on the kitchen counter before he moved out."

"But he could have had another one made."

"I suppose. But why?" He shook his head as if clearing away the cobwebs. "I mean, why would Terry try to frame me? I never did anything to him."

I had a possible answer to that, but I didn't think it would do Jason any good to hear it. "Why would *anyone* try to frame you? Why would anyone circulate that flyer in the first place? You must have cheesed someone off royally."

"I can't imagine who. Or why." He sniffled, and his chin wobbled a little. "I'm so scared."

I took out my notebook and flipped it open to a fresh page. "I've got two jobs now, Jason," I said. "To find out who Women Warriors are, and to figure out how the smack got into your toilet tank. Can you give me any help?"

"I can't even help myself."

"All right, let's do it this way—do you know anybody on campus who uses drugs?"

"Half the school smokes grass," he said. "But I don't know anything about heroin. I swear to God."

"You're sure?"

He nodded miserably.

I closed my notebook and put it back in my pocket. Frustration boiled up inside me like bile in the back of my throat. "Okay," I said.

It took me ten minutes to drive from the Lorain County lockup to the Sherman campus, ten minutes to reflect on a client who, it figured from a lot of circumstantial evidence, was guilty of a hell of a lot of things, a client whose protestations of innocence were all I had to go on.

I felt like a guy who'd just invested his entire life savings into a new soft drink called 6-Up.

I parked in the visitor's lot closest to the poli sci building and went inside, climbing the two flights of stairs to Trey Dotson's office, taking the chance that he'd be in. He was, wearing a corduroy sports jacket with elbow patches—naturally—over a pinkish sweater, conferring with yet another attractive female student. The door had been carefully left open so there would be no talk, no gossip.

"Mr. Jacovich," he said. He looked surprised, but not pleasantly so. "What can I do for you?"

"You have a few minutes, Mr. Dotson?"

He consulted his watch before he answered. "We'll be through here in a little bit. If you want to wait."

"I do," I said.

I walked down the hall and sat on one of those same torture-rack benches that they had over in the administration building just outside Dorothy Strassky's office. The late Dorothy Strassky. By the time Dotson's student—heartbreakingly young and fresh and pretty—emerged from his office, it had been considerably longer than "a little bit" and my butt was hurting from the bench. I rose stiffly, feeling like an old man for a couple of different reasons.

"I'm afraid I don't know a damn thing more than I did the last time we talked," Dotson said, when I appeared in the doorway of his office.

Then why did you make me wait out there for twenty-five minutes, you inconsiderate prick, I thought. What I said was, "I just want to go over a couple more things with you."

"Have a seat, then."

I sat down in the chair the student had just vacated. It was still pleasantly warm.

He splayed both hands flat out on the top of the desk. "So. What 'things', Mr. Jacovich? I'm afraid I have a limited amount of time today. Two classes, student conferences, et cetera . . ."

"When students come in here for a conference, Mr. Dotson, what do they generally talk about?"

"When I'm wearing my political-science professor hat or my freshman-advisor hat?"

I am not by nature a violent man, but there are some people you just want to slap. However, I was loath to muss up his razor-cut hair. "Was Jason Crowell in one of your poli sci classes?"

"No."

"But you were his advisor?"

"Not all the students I advise are poli sci majors."

"Well, then, let's talk about your student-advisor duties."

"All right," he said. "What?"

I started to count to ten, but I got only as far as four. "Do you counsel your students about academics? What courses to take? Things like that?"

"Exactly. And I help them with their schedules, getting them into their required courses, at the beginning of the semester."

"And maybe about things in general on the campus? How to get around? Various student activities and organizations?"

"Uh-huh."

"So you know about the glee club or the French club or the Students for Jesus club, and you tell the kids who to talk to and where to find them?"

"There is no Students for Jesus club per se," he said. "Although there are several Christian—"

"Do you ever tell them about Women Warriors?"

"I never heard of Women Warriors until that circular about Jason Crowell showed up all over the place. They're not on the approved list."

"But there are similar organizations on campus that are? Gender-specific groups?"

He nodded. "There's a NOW chapter. There's a Women in Communications chapter—that's mostly speech and communications majors. And there is a small but active women's-studies program."

"And if a student came to you and asked you to suggest feminist groups, that's where you'd refer them."

"Probably."

"Okay," I said. "Now, do some of the kids assigned to you as their advisor ever come to you with personal problems?"

He squinted at me. "I'm not sure what you mean by 'personal problems.' "

"Things that are more—social, let's say, than academic."

"You mean romantic problems? Dating, things like that?" He opened the top drawer of his desk and rummaged around inside. "Not specifically. I'm not qualified to do that. I send them to the counseling center."

"But sometimes?"

He waved a hand in the air like the Queen of England greeting the multitudes from her carriage. "Sometimes the conversation just drifts in those directions, I suppose. It depends on the individual advisee."

Advisee, eh? I thought, and my gut twisted. "Do you ever advise your advisees about drugs?"

His eyes popped open like a baby doll's when it's held upright. "Drugs? Illegal drugs? You're asking if anyone comes to ask me where to score drugs? Are you insane, Mr. Jacovich?"

"Not where to get them. But what if a kid has an existing

drug problem? "Would he—or she—come to you for help?"

"Drugs are against the law. A student wouldn't normally come to a faculty advisor voluntarily and confess to a felony, no."

"You told me the first time we talked that there were drugs on campus. Heroin, specifically."

"That's fairly common at schools all over the country—unfortunately," he added.

"So nobody ever came to you and said they were hooked on crack or heroin and wanted help?"

"No, thank God. That'd be difficult for me to handle. I'm not trained—"

"Then you wouldn't have any idea where the ones with drug problems get their supply from?"

He slid the desk drawer shut—more loudly, I thought, than was strictly necessary. "Certainly not."

"Mr. Dotson, I've never used an illegal drug in my life. But if anyone asked me, I'd sure as hell know where to go to get some."

"If you're asking whether I knew Jason Crowell was dealing—"

"Who said he was dealing?"

"As I understood it, he had enough heroin in his apartment to open a store. Look, you'd better talk to Dean Lilly about this," he said. "He's the one who . . . Well, he's fairly convinced now of Jason's guilt, and he wants him prosecuted—for giving the school a black eye and for bringing heroin onto this campus. I mean, what else are we supposed to think?"

"So you think he was a dealer?"

"It's a damn shame, but it looks that way."

"And it looks like he's a rapist, too?"

"Somebody says he is."

"And you believe it?"

"I hope with all my heart that Jason is innocent, Mr. Jacovich. But someone is claiming she was raped by him, and the police found heroin in his apartment. How can any reasonable human being not believe it?" Trey Dotson said.

I was beginning to wonder myself.

CHAPTER THIRTEEN

$$T$$he trip back to Cleveland was pretty depressing. It wasn't just the gray skies and the chilly winds that were squashing my spirit, either.

I made a pot of coffee, French roast from the Arabica coffeehouse up near Coventry Road, and stared out the window at the river while I drank it. Things were looking pretty damn bleak for my client right now, and I'd flipped over all my available rocks to see if something crawled out from under them. I was at a dead end.

I took out my three-by-five cards again and started shuffling them around on the desk, trying to make some sense out of them, but nothing seemed to fall together. Everyone was connected to Jason in one way or another, but none of them seemed to be connected to another.

I sighed and put the cards back in the folder. I would have been better off playing solitaire with a real deck of cards, because I usually win. That's because I cheat.

But after I'd been in my office for fifteen minutes, things got worse.

The bad news came in the form of a thirtyish man who walked in carrying a London Fog raincoat, wearing a form-fitting gray suit, a too-short blond haircut, and one of those nasty, self-confident looks usually sported by people who know they have a lot of authority and just love to exercise it.

"Are you Milan Jacovich?" he said.

I couldn't help being impressed; he'd pronounced it correctly, first try. "That's right."

He flipped open a leather wallet and flashed me a buzzer with a government eagle engraved on it. It wasn't really necessary; I'd made him for federal heat the moment he'd breezed through the door. G-men carry an attitude around with them you can spot a mile away.

"Special Agent Richard McAleese," he announced, pronouncing it "MACK-a-leese." He didn't look as though he wanted to shake hands, which was fine with me, because neither did I. "DEA."

With my left foot I flipped the switch under the desk that activates a recorder built into the telephone console, which would tape anything said in the office. The federal government gets all excited about tape recordings, which you probably know if you've ever read a newspaper.

I should have guessed that the drug enforcement feds would show up sooner or later. He draped the raincoat over one of my client chairs and sat down in the other one, careful not to disturb the knife-crease of his trousers. I could have shaved in the reflection from his highly polished brown Florsheims.

"Have a seat, Agent McAleese," I said, repeating his name so it would be on the tape; besides, I was irritated that he'd already done so. The irony seemed lost on him. "Would it be considered attempting to bribe a federal officer if I offered you a cup of coffee?"

"No, and no," he said. "Thanks anyway. I imagine you know why I'm here."

"I imagine I do," I said, "but tell me anyway.

"I want to discuss the Jason Crowell matter with you."

"The Jason Crowell matter."

"That's right."

"I think you should be discussing the Jason Crowell matter with Jason Crowell's attorney."

He cleared his throat. "I've tried to get Mr. Locke on the phone twice already today. And I even visited his office. He seemed to be unavailable." He raised his perfect dark eyebrows. "I think he's avoiding me."

"Don't take it personally, Agent McAleese," I said. "I doubt Mr. Locke is deliberately avoiding you. He tends to approach things head-on. But he is my employer, and it would be inappropriate for me to—"

"Look, let's not play games," he said. "I'm not here for information. I've come to ask for your cooperation."

"Always happy to cooperate with my government."

"Good. That's good news." He cleared his throat again, and I realized it was a nervous habit. "Here's the thing."

I waited while he considered what the thing was and formed his sentences in his head. I knew that when they eventually came out, they would be concise, lucid, and would irritate the stuffing out of me.

"We've got a problem out at Sherman College," he said.

"We?"

"My agency. A heroin problem."

"Worse than at any other university?"

"We're not talking about any other university," he said impatiently.

"Oh."

"Now, we know that your client is a small-potatoes dealer . . ."

"We don't know he's a dealer at all."

"Come on, sir." He crinkled his nose at me, cute as a button. "He had a stash of heroin big enough to choke a hippo taped in the tank of his crapper."

"He says he doesn't know how it got there."

He checked his fingernails for alien material and found none.

It seemed to disappoint him. "And elephants have wings." He seemed to have a fondness for pachyderm metaphors. "We don't want to hurt this kid," he went on. "I know how it is— you go away to college for the first time, money's tight, there are all sorts of temptations, and then you have to face the consequences. But for Crowell, those consequences can be major or minor. Depending."

I waited. I was willing to wait all week; this was his meeting, after all.

He smiled. He had a nice smile—like a crocodile right after polishing off a wildebeest entrée. "You guess."

"Guess? And here I thought you said you didn't want to play games."

McAleese dropped the smile; I guess it was too much trouble for him. "We want his source," he said. "His supplier. He's just an eighteen-year-old snotnose, he's not bringing those quantities of shit into town himself. We'd like to know who is."

I still didn't say anything. I didn't know what I was supposed to say.

"You're close to him, I understand."

"Where do you understand that from?"

He held his hand up, palm out. "Unimportant to this discussion," he said. "Here's what I'd like you to do. Explain to the boy what's what. He can do this the easy way and do easy time, or he can do it the hard way and do hard time. Hard federal time." McAleese had an annoyingly precise way of talking, as if he were about to recite *Evangeline* for extra credit.

"Or," I said, "he's innocent and you can go fuck yourself."

He sat up a little straighter. "Let's not dick each other around, all right? You and I are on the same side."

"What side is that?"

He smoothed the knot in his tie. "We want what's best for the boy."

"Doing easy time is best for the boy?"

"Sure—maybe six to eighteen months in a county lockup somewhere. Have you ever been inside a federal correctional facility, Mr. Jacovich? I don't mean one of those white-collar country-club prisons they send Washington big shots to—but a hard-core pen. It's no place for a kid like that. He'll be a happier camper if he plays ball with us. Trust me."

"But if he doesn't play ball with you, you've got no problem with locking him up with pond scum."

"That's the way it lays out," he said.

"Uh-huh."

"Talk to him," he oozed. "Explain what's in his best interests. We don't really care about him. He's just a kid, not a hard-core pusher. We're not after the mules, we're after the mule-drivers." He stood up and took a business card from his side jacket pocket. I'm sure there was only one of them in there—any more would have ruined the drape of his suit.

"The federal government is very interested in breaking any drug rings operating at Sherman. Don't let them get interested in you, too." He held out his hand as though he were about to stroke a large, invisible dog on the head. "I know the state issues your license to operate, but you know as well as I do that a well-placed word from a federal judge is often listened to, one way or the other. It's in your best interests to help us out here." He put the business card on my desk and turned it around so I could read it. It was Special Agent Richard J. McAleese, I noted, and thought it would not profit me to speculate aloud on what the J stood for.

"Do what's right," Special Agent Richard J. McAleese said, and then drifted out of my office smoothly and quietly as if he were on casters.

That evening Jeremiah Locke joined Reggie and me in the living room of the Crowells' house, along with Jason's parents. Five people, four of them rather large men, made it a bit crowded in there. They'd sent Cherie and Yvonne upstairs to their room before we even arrived.

There was no cheery fire on the hearth tonight; we were just five very grim adults in a room that trouble had turned cold and dreary. And I was probably the grimmest of all—because I had a client who looked as guilty as hell, and everyone from his freshman advisor to the United States government thought so, too. Doubts were beginning to nag at me.

"The bail hearing is at nine o'clock tomorrow morning out in Lorain County," Locke was saying. "I'm sure the district attorney's office is going to suggest Jason be held without bail, but I'm not letting that happen without a fight. The judge'll probably set it high, but he'll let us have it."

"High?" Jim Crowell said worriedly.

"A hundred thousand would be my guess."

"Where am I going to come up with that kind of money?"

"Just ten percent of it," I said, not liking him very much at all right then. "You only have to pay the rest if Jason runs away. You borrow it, you mortgage your house to get it, you sell your car if you have to. But you don't leave a kid like that languishing behind bars."

"Does that mean Jason will come home?" Nola Crowell said, the mark of hope on her brow like a pilgrim to Lourdes.

"For the time being. Then it goes to the grand jury; they'll decide whether or not to try him."

"We'll just be there for him, then."

"No, Mrs. Crowell," Locke explained. "The grand-jury hearing is strictly the DA's show. No visitors. Not even me."

"Son of a bitch!" Jim Crowell slammed his fist into his palm again, which seemed to be his favorite way of expressing displeasure. "He's just a kid."

"He's eighteen," Locke reminded him. "They'll try him as an adult."

"I think you should understand," I said, "that this is only

about the heroin charge. The rape business is another thing altogether, and they still haven't got any proof except that flyer. But you'd better believe that the DA would love to go before the grand jury and tell them Jason is both a pusher *and* a rapist."

"There's been a federal drug enforcement officer hounding me all day, too," Locke said. "I managed to duck him."

"I wasn't so lucky," I told him.

Locke glanced sharply at me. "A guy named Mc-AL-leese?" he said, mispronouncing it.

"MACK-a-leese. Yeah."

"What'd you say to him?"

"It's what he said to me, Jerry. Which is that if Jason rolls over on his wholesaler, his drug supplier, the feds are willing to cut a deal."

"What kind of deal?" the father wanted to know.

"Minimum jail time in a county facility instead of ten to twenty-five in federal prison."

Mrs. Crowell started to cry again.

Crowell looked twenty years older than he really was. "Maybe that isn't a bad idea," he said hoarsely.

I couldn't believe it. "What?"

His deep breath rattled in the back of his throat. "Play ball with them."

"Wait a minute," I said. "Jason swears he doesn't *have* a supplier."

"Doesn't he?" Crowell whispered.

"Jim . . ." Mrs. Crowell entreated him, her eyes as big and round as twenty-dollar gold eagles.

Crowell ignored her and turned to Jeremiah Locke. "Can't he plead 'no contest' or something?" he said. "That's not like saying 'guilty,' is it?"

Locke shook his head. "You don't want to do that, Mr. Crowell. It'll be on Jason's permanent record. It'll hang around his neck for the rest of his life."

I leaned forward, my elbows on my knees. "You're forgetting something important here, Mr. Crowell."

He turned his body toward me, hostile again. "Oh?"

"The Cleveland police are trying very hard to hang a murder rap on your son. And there's not going to be any dealing there."

"Oh my God," Mrs. Crowell moaned.

"You're talking as if you think Jason's guilty of all this stuff."

"Well, what am I supposed to think?" he exploded at me. "I don't want to believe it, but there's all this evidence—the heroin in his apartment, those flyers . . ." He ran his hand roughly over his face. "Look, I don't think he's the kind of kid who'd hurt anybody—and he's never been involved with drugs that I know of. But God—he's always been kind of strange—different. How do I know what's going on in his head? Who the hell really knows their own kid, anyway?"

"Jim, whatever are we going to *say to him* when he comes home tomorrow?" Mrs. Crowell said.

I wondered that, too, or would have if I hadn't been so damn furious. I stood up. "I don't think there's much point in going on with this discussion."

Reggie took hold of the sleeve of my jacket. "Take it easy, Milan."

I glared down at him. "*You* talk to these people, then."

"Perhaps we should all call it a night," Jeremiah Locke said, rising from the sofa with no effort at all. "I'll take care of the bail hearing in the morning and then we'll see what happens. All right?"

He cast me a meaningful, "shut your mouth" look and began saying good night to the Crowells. I didn't bother; I just stomped out the door and waited for Locke and Reggie at the curb where I'd parked the car.

What was burning a hole in my belly is that I'd had doubts about Jason, too. But now that his family seemed to be sharing them, I wanted off the bus. *Somebody* had to be on the kid's side, to believe in him. And despite my misgivings, I had just elected myself.

"That son of a bitch thinks his own son is a murderer!" I fulminated when the two of them came down the walk toward me.

"Calm down, Milan, they'll hear you," Reggie said. The three of us stood there in the dark, hunching our shoulders against the wind.

"I hope they do!"

"Cut people some slack, Milan," Locke admonished. "This is a tough time for the Crowells. If they didn't care anything about Jason, they wouldn't have hired me, would they? But we're looking at evidence here that—"

"You think he's guilty too, don't you, Jerry?"

"It isn't my job to determine that," he said sternly. "It's to help him, and hopefully get him off. And I intend to do that with everything that's in me." He softened a little. "I practice criminal law, Milan. If I only defended people who were innocent, I'd be the lonesomest guy in town."

He clapped me on the shoulder. "Get some sleep. You've still got work to do. Finding who's responsible for those flyers is the key here. And, of course, proving that heroin was planted."

"That won't tell us who killed Dorothy Strassky."

"I don't really care who killed Dorothy Strassky," he said. "Our job is to get Jason Crowell out of jail and out of trouble. We solve the heroin mystery, he's off one hook. We find out who Women Warriors are, he's off the other. And then he has no motive for killing Strassky and Flo McHargue is out of our face." He walked down the sidewalk toward his car. "*Ciao,*" he threw over his shoulder.

" '*Ciao,*' my ass," I muttered. I don't think he heard me—at least, he didn't react. I wouldn't have cared if he did. I was mad enough to eat something.

Reggie waved at Locke's retreating figure and then turned back to me. "You get so excited, Milan. I know you. Don't get excited. Just keep the lid on."

I looked at my watch, then at Reggie Parker. "Racquetball game at nine-thirty in the evening?"

"He's a good lawyer," Reggie told me.

"It'd be nice if he believed in his client!"

"We all do."

"Locke doesn't. The school doesn't. Jason's own father doesn't." I shoved my hands into my pockets because they were getting cold and I didn't have my gloves with me. "And I was starting to have my doubts, too. I was ready to pull out, Reggie. I was almost as convinced that Jason was guilty as everyone else is."

"And what happened?"

I turned and watched the departing taillights of Locke's car. "When Jim Crowell started talking as if Jason was already convicted, I kind of lost it. Somebody's got to back him, and if it's not his own lawyer and his own family, who else is there?"

"You?" he suggested.

"And you."

Reggie stuck out his hand, and I pulled mine out of my pocket to clasp it. "Jason needs a good friend like you now, Milan."

"And what I need now," I said, "is a beer."

There's only one place I wanted to drink it. Reggie had a conference first thing in the morning, so he went straight home, and I stopped off at Vuk's Tavern, on St. Clair Avenue in the old neighborhood where I'd grown up. It was a typical local booze joint, ethnic down to its toes, its clientele mostly Slovenians and Croatians who lived within a ten-block radius. Sometimes they brought their friends, newcomers, but a stranger wandering in alone was usually given a welcome like the hospitality extended to a Hasidic rabbi on the streets of

Amman. Local ethnic taverns are usually suspicious of anyone they don't know.

Vuk, whose real name was Louis Vukovich but who has been called Vuk by everyone in living memory except his nonagenarian mother, was something of a philosopher, in the manner of neighborhood barkeeps everywhere. He opened the tavern at six A.M., stayed on duty until noon, went home and took a nap until eight, and then came back on duty until closing. He'd stand behind the bar with his Popeye forearms crossed in front of him, his trademark walrus mustache now streaked with gray, sending the message to one and all that he brooked no nonsense in his joint. That is, when he wasn't pouring shots or twisting the tops off beer bottles. Vuk's Tavern was the kind of place where anyone foolhardy enough to order something like a frozen daiquiri or a Fuzzy Navel was likely to wind up the worse for wear in the Dumpster out back.

Vuk moved the slightest bit when I walked in. "Whattaya say, Milan?" It was his standard greeting to me. If he even knew the word "hello," I hadn't heard it escape his lips in more than twenty-five years of drinking across the bar from him.

"Hey, Vuk," I said, and swung myself up onto a stool. He turned, reached into the cooler, and brought out a frosty Stroh's, which he set on the bar in front of me. No glass. Vuk knows his customers.

"How's it goin'?"

"All right."

"How are the kids?"

"They're fine."

"Are you mad at me?"

"I'm not mad at you."

"You look like you're mad. Trouble with the lady friend?" He always referred to the women I dated as "the lady friend," because he couldn't ever remember their names. Probably because most of them never stuck around long enough for him to learn them.

"No, she's fine, Vuk. It's just a case I'm working."

"And it makes you mad?"

I gave in and went with it. "It bothers me when a father doesn't back his own son," I said.

"That's bad."

"Yeah."

"Families, you know, that's a special thing."

"It's supposed to be."

"Young kid, is it?"

"Eighteen."

"Milan Junior's age, huh?"

"Yep."

"Sounds like he could use a friend," he said.

I just nodded.

"So be his friend, Milan."

I shrugged. "I'm not his father."

"I didn't say 'father,' " he reminded me.

"Uh-huh." I brought the bottle to my lips and tilted my head back, enjoying the icy rush as the beer hit the back of my throat.

"Somebody he can talk to. Sometimes a kid can talk to a friend better than he can to his old man, you know what I'm sayin'?"

"I know what you're saying, Vuk."

He stood there looking at me for a while until someone called for another beer. He started down toward the other end of the bar. "Just do it, Milan. What's it gonna cost you, right?"

CHAPTER FOURTEEN

Nola Crowell was the only family member to show up at the bail hearing with Jason the next morning. She seemed to be trying to hide, sitting in the back with her head down, not making eye contact with anyone; she'd probably never been in a courtroom before in her life. There was no sign of her husband—apparently he had more important business elsewhere.

I, however, did not. I was in the first row of spectator benches, where Jason could see me and take whatever comfort he might in my support. I was nursing a flowering hangover from the excesses of the night before and wishing I carried a purse so I could dive into it for some Aleve, when Jeremiah Locke walked in with his soft-sided ostrichskin briefcase under his arm, wearing a light beige suit and a yellow power tie that looked curiously out of place in rural Lorain County.

It might have looked just as out of place in the lobby of the Beverly Hills Hotel.

"Milan," he said when he saw me, looking surprised and not entirely pleased. "What are you doing here?"

"I figured Jason needed as many friends here as he could get," I said, and gave him a look that brooked no challenge.

"Well . . . Thanks for coming, then." He recovered nicely as he went to his position at the defense table. Lawyers are trained to recover nicely, and Locke must have aced his Recovering Nicely 101 final.

The hearing only took a few minutes, and as expected, Jason was bound over to the grand jury. Despite the district attorney's attempt to paint Jason as a menace to society and have him held without bail, Locke managed to get it set at twenty-five thousand dollars, lower than he'd predicted, although Nola didn't seem to appreciate the difference as she wrote out a check for $2,500 with a trembling hand. Afterward, Locke pleaded that he "had to run," shaking hands with me, Jason, Nola, the DA and the bailiff, and everyone else in sight before he did so.

When the technicalities were taken care of and Jason was at least temporarily free, I found myself out in front of the courthouse with Nola and her son.

"What about the grand jury?" she said. "When do we have to go through that, now?"

I tried to sound more reassuring than I felt. "In about two weeks. You just have to relax and leave everything to Mr. Locke. He's very good at what he does. This is going to be all right."

She rotated her head around as though she had a crick in her neck. Come to think of it, she probably did, from the tension. "I don't see how it can be. Jason's been kicked out of school . . ."

"Don't worry about that part of it." I smiled modestly. "I'm pretty good, too."

Jason, like a drowning man grappling for a hold on a hunk of driftwood, pumped my hand and thanked me profusely even though I hadn't done anything yet.

"Come on, Jason," his mother said, "let's go home."

A shadow came over the kid's face, as if a cloud had just scudded over the sun, and he dropped my hand and his chin at the same time, and he and his mother began walking toward their car.

I took a deep breath. "Mrs. Crowell."

She stopped and looked over her shoulder at me.

"I did some thinking last night and came up with an idea. You might not like it, but I think it's a good one."

"Well?"

I moved closer to them. "I think it might be better for everyone if Jason stayed somewhere neutral for a while—away from the family. It would ease tensions a lot, I think, and be easier on everybody—Jason especially."

She looked dumbfounded. "Neutral?"

"Well—I was thinking that maybe he could stay with me for a while."

Jason gazed up at me with admiring wonder, as if I'd just broken off a 99-yard punt return or won an Oscar or found a cure for herpes.

"With you?" Nola said.

"Just temporarily, until things smooth out a little. I've got a spare bedroom that my kids use when they visit me. He won't be any trouble."

"I don't see the necessity of it," she said stiffly.

"Necessity, no. But tensions are running pretty high in your house right now, and this might give everyone a chance to cool off and be objective. Your family needs a little peace, and so does Jason." I turned to the boy; he was, after all, eighteen and fully able to make his own decisions. "You think?"

"It's fine with me," he said, trying not to appear too anxious so as not to offend his mother. But he was so grateful, he was almost crying.

"Jason belongs at home with his family," his mother said, but it didn't exactly ring with conviction. After all, she knew her husband better than I did.

"He'll get there, Mrs. Crowell. But these are tough times.

Besides," I added, "I'll be needing to talk to him a lot over the course of my investigation, to consult with him." That sounded pompous and false even to me, but I was committed now, so I rushed on. "Having him right there with me will make it easier."

She wasn't convinced. Neither was I, to tell the truth. Jason was, however, so I told him where my apartment was and gave him an extra key. I walked them to their car, and I half expected his mother to talk him out of it on the way back to Cleveland. But it was an offer I had to make; the atmosphere of hostility and suspicion in his house wasn't healthy for anyone, especially for a kid going through the kind of walking nightmare that Jason Crowell was living.

I had made up my mind to believe him innocent of everything, across the board; it's the only way I could live with myself. And having arrived at that conclusion, I felt I had to get him away from his parents, specifically from his father. I couldn't imagine him living in that house, under the dark clouds of resentment and suspicion and recrimination that seemed to hover over the Crowell family. Offering him my spare room was the only solution I'd come up with during a long evening of drinking Stroh's at Vuk's Tavern.

I also realized that there were two ways I could prove his innocence. The first was to find Women Warriors and track down the accuser, which would clear him of the suspicion of rape, and probably send Lieutenant McHargue looking in another direction for Dorothy Strassky's killer. It was beginning to look like Jason Crowell was on the receiving end of a pretty elaborate frame-up, and that someone was, for whatever reason, using him to take the blame for all their sins. The second, and more immediate, was to find out how that heroin had found its way into his toilet tank, and to do that it seemed to me my only recourse was to nail the person or persons who had put it there.

Since I was in Lorain County anyway, I decided to go and talk once more to my most logical suspect.

But Terry Yagemann was not at home. It was still midmorning, and I supposed he had a class. Since I was not exactly Sherman College's Man of the Year, I didn't imagine the administration office would tell me where he was at any given moment, so I decided to wait for him. My car was parked half a block from his apartment; I got myself a container of very hot coffee from a nearby Mickey D's, unfolded the newspaper I'd picked up outside my door that morning but hadn't had time to read, and hunkered down behind the steering wheel for the most boring aspect of any private investigator's job: waiting.

They say (that ubiquitous, mysterious, never-identified "they") that time seems to pass more quickly as you get older, that the period between the beginning of school and Christmas vacation that seemed like an eternity at seven years old is the merest flicker of an eye at fifty.

Well, "they" never had to sit in a cramped car while the day crawls by and the light changes as they try to be unobtrusive so no well-meaning neighbor will call a policeman to bang on the window and find out why they're loitering. "They" never had to eat three candy bars for lunch or pee in a coffee can. "They" obviously never had been on a stakeout, or they'd know how slowly time can move.

The morning was still, with no wind to speak of. Ohio weather never bothers me, as long as the wind isn't blowing, and Sherman is far enough from the lake that it isn't often subject to the icy breezes that scream down from Canada. The sun was making a valiant effort to cut its way through the low cloud cover but wasn't doing a completely successful job of it. Still, for less than a week shy of November, it was a felicitous day.

But not if you were Jason Crowell, out on twenty-five-grand

bail, facing a drug-selling charge and suspected of murder and rape by everyone, even his attorney and his own father. Not if you were Dorothy Strassky, cruelly murdered, either at random or because she knew something she shouldn't. And not if you were Milan Jacovich, a man with a million questions and not a single answer, sitting in his car drinking coffee and willing the time to pass more quickly, waiting for someone who might or might not be a murderer, who might or might not be able to help him—who might or might not show up.

It made me think about all the other people who were having a lousy day, too—the ones with tension headaches or broken marriages or polyps in their colons or upcoming tests they hadn't studied for. I learned a long time ago that life is good, but where is the fine print in your contract that says it's supposed to be easy?

It took me about forty-five minutes to read everything I wanted to in the paper, and just as I had started on the comics—a sure sign of desperation—my beeper chirped and vibrated. Since it was in my pants pocket, it took an act of will on my part not to become emotionally involved. I fished it out and looked at the readout: Marika Rollins was calling me.

I activated my car phone and called her back. I think she was surprised to get such a quick response.

"Mr. Jacovich, I have to talk to you," she said, squeezing the words out in a strained little voice.

"You're in luck," I said. "I'm just off campus. Are you free now?"

"Until three o'clock, yes."

"The tearoom?"

"N-no. That's too public. Can you come to my place?"

"Sure," I said, wondering what she had to say to me that no one else should overhear. "I'll be right over."

She gave me directions to her apartment, which was only five minutes away—but then, everything in Sherman was five minutes away from everything else. I felt a little off-kilter about abandoning my wait for Terry Yagemann, but she'd sounded as if she had something important to say.

Like Jason's, Marika's student digs were in an old home artlessly converted to tiny private suites. Hers was not nearly as nice as the others I'd been in. In the single room was a sofa that was too short to stretch out on and so must have opened outward into a bed, a desk, and, in a five-foot-square alcove, a small refrigerator atop which sat a two-burner hotplate, and a sink. It was no bigger than the bathroom in my office, but the little place was as neat as a pin.

Marika, however, was not. She was clad in a gray T-shirt and red sweatpants that made her look dumpy, her usually-tight curls hung loose and messy, and her eyes and nose were reddened as if from crying.

"What's the matter, Marika?" I said.

She just shook her head wearily. "It's been a bad few weeks."

There were only two places to sit in the room—the floral-patterned sofabed and the straight-backed chair at her desk. That's the one she practically fell into, so I took what was left. The sofa cushion was unyielding; one of the biggest drawbacks of the Crowell case was turning out to be a distinct lack of comfortable furniture.

"I just came from the hearing," I said. "Jason's out on bail now. Which is the good news. And he's going to be staying at my place for a while, just to get him out of his parents' house, if you want to get in touch with him."

"That's great," she said, sounding as though she meant it.

"He's got a good lawyer now. We're going to get him out of this mess, Marika. Don't worry."

She ran both hands through her hair, pushing it back behind her ears. She looked so young and vulnerable—and sad—she broke my heart.

"Did you ever know Jason to have anything to do with drugs?" I said.

"God, no. He's such a straight arrow about things like that."

"I don't mean using them."

"*Selling* them?"

"That's what they're charging him with."

"That's ridiculous. He'd never . . . I'm sure of it." She dabbed at her nose with a wadded-up tissue that had been in her hand the whole time. "He doesn't drink much—maybe one or two beers a week. He doesn't even smoke."

"If it comes down to it, will you testify to that in court? Since you know him better than anyone else at Sherman, it might be helpful."

"Absolutely," she said with a fervor that burned from within. "I'd do anything to help him."

"In court, you take an oath to tell the truth," I reminded her. "That means the *whole* truth and . . . et cetera."

That seemed to trouble her. She looked away, falling silent.

"Is there some part of the whole truth you're not comfortable with?" I waited for a moment or two, but it didn't seem as if she was going to answer me anytime soon. "You called me, Marika," I reminded her.

She didn't move.

"You said you had something to tell me."

She tried to look as if she didn't understand the language, but it didn't work too well. So she combed her hair back from her face again, and wet her lips with her tongue. "I feel so stupid . . ."

"Why?"

"Because—I should have told you before. I should have told somebody. It might have helped."

"Maybe it'll help now."

"I promised I wouldn't tell. I feel funny about breaking a promise. Even if it's for a good cause."

She got up from the chair and paced the room as best she could; there wasn't much space in there for maneuvering. "I was never one of those popular girls, Mr. Jacovich," she said. "In grade school or in high school. I never had a lot of friends."

Obviously this was going to be the long form, complete with autobiography, but I had to let her tell it in her own way. "That's not a crime," I said. "Lots of people are loners."

She gave me a sad smile. "Don't be kind. I know people think I'm a geek." I started to reassure her that she wasn't, but she stopped me. "That's okay—I've learned to live with it."

I didn't answer her, but reflected on how very cruel the human animal can be, especially the young of the species.

"But Jason . . . Even though I've only known him a couple of weeks, he's the best friend I ever had."

I didn't dare speak. I sensed that she was about to confide something important to me, and I didn't want to say or do anything that would shatter the mood or break her rhythm.

"When your best friend tells you something—in confidence— it's hard to betray that confidence, you know?"

I nodded.

"Well, Jason told me something—he said he had to. He made me promise I'd never tell anyone. And I haven't, up until now. But I think I have to tell someone. I have to tell *you*."

My neck hairs bristled. Here it comes, I thought, the big revelation, the one that's going to put Jason Crowell behind bars for rape, even if he manages to beat the drug charge. My mother had always told me never to ask a question I didn't want to hear the answer to, in which case I was in the wrong business.

"All right, Marika," I said, and braced myself.

"I've never had a real boyfriend, Mr. Jacovich," she said. "I mean, I'm not a virgin, but"—she blushed and turned her face away—"I've never really, you know, *gone* with anybody. I guess you've already figured out that I'm crazy about Jason. He's kind and sensitive and funny, and really nice-looking . . ."

I smiled my most understanding smile.

"And I know he likes me. So we were hanging around together a lot, and when nothing, you know—happened—between us, I couldn't understand why. So I just asked him, right out."

She turned to face me squarely, wringing the fingers of one hand with the other one. "That's how I know he couldn't possibly have raped some woman. I don't know about the drug business, but he didn't commit rape."

"Why not?"

She took a deep breath, the way one does before plunging into icy water. "Jason is gay," she said.

It hit me with an almost physical impact, rocking me back against the back of the sofa; I sat there, my hands between my knees, stunned. Finally I said, "Are you sure?"

She nodded; her mouth was slack, almost as though her face were numb. The betrayal of Jason's confidence had cost her dearly. "He made me swear not to tell. Anyone."

I gave it some thought. Jason's being homosexual certainly made it less likely he'd raped anyone, but it wouldn't necessarily render him incapable of it. Rape was all about power and control, no matter what the rapist's sexual preference is. I didn't want to tell her that, though.

"But why the secrecy?" I said. "Being gay still isn't going to get you elected president of the Kiwanis Club, but there isn't the stigma attached to it that there used to be. And coming out *might* have gotten him out from under the sexual-assault business."

"If you had a father like Jason's, would you admit you were gay?"

To stay out of prison, I might. But she was missing something, probably because she'd never seen Jim Crowell interact with his son.

Because I think that in his heart, Jim Crowell knew about Jason. At least, he had sensed it. He'd told me Jason was "different." And it would certainly explain his anger, his seeming dislike of the boy.

And maybe that's why he was willing to believe Jason was guilty of rape. Maybe, somewhere down in the darkest recesses of his soul, he *wanted* him to be guilty, because that would, to him at least, mean his son was "normal."

My heart was heavy in my chest. If people aren't prepared to love their kids unconditionally, to stand by them no matter what, to accept them however they turn out, they shouldn't be allowed to have them.

It wouldn't do any good to tell Marika I thought that if she'd said something at the beginning, or that if Jason had, maybe none of the rest of it would have happened. Not the drug bust, not the flyers—perhaps not even Dorothy Strassky's murder. All of that was history. Now it was up to me, and to Jason, to do that which delineates a successful life—to play the cards we'd been dealt.

"The question is, then, why was he accused? And by whom?"

She shook her head.

I wondered if someone else had managed to discover or discern Jason's sexual preference, perhaps some homophobic moron who was on a mission to rid the campus of gay people and had mounted a personal vendetta against him. "If we're going to help him," I said, "we have to find out. I have a feeling that all his troubles go right back to that damned flyer."

She sat back down on the straight chair. Her hands were shaking and she clasped them together to still them. "What can I do?"

"Ask around. Contact people in some of the women's groups on campus—they're more likely to talk to you than me. If you find out anything—anything at all—let me know, and I'll take it from there."

"I'll try," she said.

"Good girl." I heaved myself up off the sofa, took a business card from my pocket, and scribbled my home phone number on the back. "Here," I said. "This is where Jason is, in case you want to talk to him. I kind of wish you would—he could use your support right now."

"I will." She looked as though she had something else to say, so I waited until she geared herself up to say it.

"Mr. Jacovich? If this Women Warriors business had anything to do with Ms. Strassky getting killed . . ."

"We don't know that for sure."

She hunched her shoulders nervously as if being buffeted by a cold wind. "I mean, that's really serious. Do you think my asking around could be dangerous?"

"Marika," I said, "sometimes just getting out of bed in the morning is dangerous."

I drove back to Terry Yagemann's place and tried his doorbell again, but he still wasn't home, or wasn't answering the ring. I spent another crushingly boring hour in my car waiting for him, and then the rumbling of my stomach reminded me that I hadn't eaten since breakfast. Screw it, I thought. Yagemann could wait until morning. At least Jason was out of jail.

And in my spare room.

CHAPTER FIFTEEN

I made my way up the two-lane and back onto I-90 but I didn't go all the way downtown. I got off in Lakewood, just west of the city limits, and headed for the restaurant Connie's family owns, the White Magnolia.

The White Mag wasn't open for lunch, but I figured that, being a friend of the family, so to speak, they could rustle something up for me. When I walked in, Kevin, Connie's brother, was taking his daily inventory behind the bar, wearing a bright green sweatshirt that read, *Kiss Me, I'm Irish*, which I knew would give way to a white shirt, black tie, and black vest in the evening before the customers started arriving.

"Hey, Milan," he said. He leaned over and shook my hand, then opened the refrigerator below the bar and brought out a bottle of Stroh's, snapped off the cap, and set it in front of me on a serviette. No glass. It occurred to me that entirely too many bartenders were conversant with my drinking habits.

Kevin glanced at the telephone on the back bar; one button was lit. "Connie's on the phone in the office I think."

"How do you know it's Connie and not your dad?"

"He *hates* talking on the phone."

"That's okay, I'll wait. Any chance of me getting something to eat?"

He looked at his watch. "Maybe I could have Sean rustle you up a cold roast-beef sandwich."

"That'd be terrific. With cheddar."

"We can do that." He came out from behind the bar and went back into the kitchen.

I drank my beer while I looked around the empty restaurant. By nightfall they'd turn on the flattering recessed lighting and it would be pleasantly crowded with the semi-young and semi-rich boomers of Lakewood and Rocky River, desperate to spend their discretionary income. Since it had opened the year before, the affluent west-siders had discovered it and anointed it an "in"-spot.

In a way, it was too bad. In Cleveland, restaurants that are trendy usually remain so for about two years and then die a slow, lingering death, like the fondly remembered and recently departed Caxton Cafe, Piperade, and 600 St. Clair. I hoped for better for the White Magnolia.

After a few minutes Leo Haley, Connie's father, came out of the office to say hello. Even with his ramrod-straight back, his compact, muscular body, and his graying brush cut, you couldn't really spot Leo right off for a retired Marine Corps officer. Instead, you might think he was a retired cop, a retired Secret Service man, or maybe a retired leg-breaker for the Irish mafia.

"You're late for lunch and early for dinner," he said. I'd already prepared myself for his crushing handshake; I'd made its acquaintance before.

"I didn't eat lunch," I told him, "and I have nothing going on for dinner, so I stopped in for one of Sean's famous throw-it-together-while-the-store-is-closed sandwiches."

"Good, good," he said. "The boys're taking care of you, then?" He went behind the bar and got himself a Perrier; Leo had a strict rule—he never drank the hard stuff until the last customer had left for the evening. After that, it was usually an Irish like Bushmill's; the Haleys take their ethnicity seriously.

He uncapped the bottle, took a gulp or two, and leaned over the bar. "How's it going?"

"Working hard, Leo."

"Me too. See what happens when you're not born rich?"

"Or lucky," I said.

Sean, Connie's other brother, came out of the kitchen bearing a plate. The whole family had faces right out of the Book of Kells. "Hiya, Milan," he said, putting it down in front of me. On it rested a sandwich big enough for three, roast beef and cheddar on warm French bread sliced lengthwise, with a handful of crisp potato chips that hadn't come out of a bag. He placed a white napkin wrapped around some silverware next to the plate and adjusted his starched chef's coat. "I put the horseradish on the side. That stuff can really clear out your sinuses."

"Connie tells me you're working on a rape case," Leo said.

"That's right."

"That's some ugly stuff."

"They don't pay me for the pretty ones," I said, uncomfortably aware that they weren't paying me for this particular ugly one, either.

"Why would you want to fuck around with a guy like that?" Sean asked, as if he really wanted to know.

I slathered the horseradish onto the bread, closed up the sandwich, and took a bite. Sean was right about the horseradish; it made my eyes tear up. "Because I think he's innocent."

Leo made a skeptical face. "They're all innocent, aren't they?"

"I think this one probably is."

He shrugged, his expression turning blank. "Whatever pushes your buttons," he said.

Connie came out of the office, wearing an above-the-knee khaki skirt and a blue blouse, with a white sweater across her shoulders, the arms loosely knotted over her breasts. She was somewhere in her middle thirties but looked young enough to blend right in with the student body at Sherman. "Hello, stranger," she said cheerily, and jumped up onto the bar stool next to me.

Leo and Sean exchanged meaningful looks and disappeared, as if by some tacit agreement, Sean into the kitchen and Leo back into the office.

"I thought you'd died and gone to heaven," Connie scolded. "You haven't called me for days."

"Two days. I've been kind of tied up."

She cocked her head to one side. "With that rape business?"

"Uh-huh."

"Still, you could have made time for one little phone call."

I'm not one for calling up just to say hello or to chat, even with people I care about as much as I do for Connie. I'd had this same conversation before, in other places and with other women, and I hadn't liked it much better those times. The roast-beef sandwich suddenly became hard to chew. "The phone works both ways," I said.

"Hey, I'm just a little Irish Catholic kid. I was taught that the men are supposed to do the calling."

"What do nuns know about who's supposed to call who?"

"Nuns know everything," she said. "How's your sandwich?"

"Excellent." I took one more bite, put it down and swallowed some more beer.

"So what's been happening, Milan?"

"Not much."

"With your rape case."

I wasn't sure I wanted to discuss it. "You really want to hear?"

She nodded. I saw no way out of it, so I told her about the drug charge. She didn't say anything until I was finished.

"Heroin," she said, shaking her head in dismay. "Along with

the rape, and maybe even murder. He's something, Jason. A real lulu."

"He says he doesn't know how the smack got into his apartment."

"Just like he says he didn't rape anybody."

As hungry as I'd been, my appetite was fading rapidly, so I pushed the plate away with about a quarter of the sandwich uneaten. And I'd barely touched the chips. "Let's not get into this again, all right?"

"You don't have to get touchy about it," she said, leaning her upper body slightly away from me.

"I don't want this coming between us, Connie."

"I didn't know it was." She drummed her painted fingernails on the top of the bar. "Is this our first fight? I should put up a plaque or something . . ."

"I don't want it to be."

"You could've fooled me."

"I'm not fighting, I'm just doing a job."

I could see the wheels and gears working behind her eyes as she decided whether or not she wanted to continue. I guess she chose not to, because her eyes changed, got warmer. "Will you be on the job tomorrow night, Milan? I was thinking about coming over." She smiled, making her dimples as deep as a well. "You should be flattered. A west-sider crossing the river to the east side is a real act of faith."

"Uh . . ." I said.

She frowned. "What?"

I fumbled in my pocket for a cigarette. "I'd love to have dinner, maybe go to a movie if you want. But—I have a houseguest."

She raised one eyebrow. "What's her name?" she said mildly.

"It's Jason Crowell."

The dimple all but vanished, and her face lost its light, as if someone had turned off a switch. "You're kidding!"

"He got out on bail this morning, and I thought he'd be better off away from his family for a while. They're giving him a pretty rough time of it."

"But to take him into your own home . . . ?" She pushed herself away from the bar and stood up. "Who do you think you are, Father Flanagan of Boys Town? That's not part of your job."

"No," I admitted. "It's not."

"Well, then?"

"The kid needed a friend, that's all."

"So do I."

I looked around like a trapped animal, but there are no clearly marked Exit signs in arguments. Finally I said, "It just seemed like the right thing to do."

She regarded me narrowly. "That's a big thing with you, isn't it, Milan? Doing the right thing."

"I hope so."

"And what about us?"

"This has nothing to do with us."

"It has everything to do with us," she said, and then lowered her voice, but her whisper was as intense as the hiss of a cat. "I told you what happened to me in college. How can you damn near adopt this kid after that? How can you even be in the same room with him, much less make him your room-mate?" Her voice got a little bit louder. "How can you possibly think this isn't about us?"

I felt my insides turning hard and cold as if my vital signs had all shut down and I was flatlining. I could sense my heels digging in for a stand, and I could not help myself, any more than I could fly. "This is business, Connie." My tone was colder than I'd intended.

"Protecting a rapist?"

"Jason isn't a rapist."

"*He* says."

"No, *I* say." I lit my cigarette. I inhaled and then turned my head to blow the smoke away from her. "He didn't rape anybody, Connie. He's gay." Marika had told me a confidence, but Connie didn't know any of the parties concerned, so I didn't think it would make any difference to betray it.

The angry spots on her cheeks faded, and she blinked her eyes as if she'd been struck. "Why didn't you tell me?" she said softly.

"I didn't know until today."

She chewed off some of her pink lipstick. "Oh."

"Yeah."

Taking a deep breath to compose herself, she got back onto the stool and forced a smile. "Well," she said, resting her fingertips on the sleeve of my jacket. "That's different, then."

"Is it?" I said.

I got back to the office about three forty-five. I hadn't been there very much in the last week or so, and I'd missed it— missed the feeling of ownership it gave me, the familiarity, missed the view, missed having my "stuff" all around me, and it took me a moment to enjoy it now, even though the clouds had come in low and dark and Terminal Tower stood stark against the gray sky.

I was pretty upset about Connie. I don't have the easiest job in the world, certainly not the nicest, and she had known it before we ever got involved. I didn't see why I couldn't have her understanding now. It wasn't enough that she changed her tune after she found out Jason Crowell was probably not a rapist. She should have trusted my judgment enough to back me up in the first place.

I guess that's what defines friendship for me. Being there. Standing firm. Taking the good with the bad. I'd had that with Marko Meglich, I'd had it with Reggie even when I barely knew him, and for that matter, I'd had it with Lila during most of our marriage, before it had turned sour and before Joe Bradac had come into the picture. I needed that from any woman I was going to be involved with—needed it desperately. For me it was *the* minimum requirement.

I tried calling Reggie Parker at the school, but his assistant said he'd gone to a meeting. I didn't leave a message, figuring to catch him at home that evening. I wasn't in the mood to talk to him anyway.

I wasn't in the mood to talk to anybody. The grayish cloud cover which was socking in downtown Cleveland was dogging me as well.

I riffled through my mail. The most interesting thing was a catalog from an electronic surveillance company, and as I thumbed it, I was struck by the variety of devices virtually any-one off the street can purchase that are invasive of privacy. Wiretaps are illegal, but there's nothing that says you can't point a highly sensitive microphone at someone's window and pick up and record the gurgles of their gastric juices from three blocks away, or take a close-up photograph of their left nostril from across the street with a pinpoint camera mounted in your eyeglasses.

If the general public realized how easy it was to find out virtually anything about anyone, there would be no need for private investigators and I'd have to get a real job.

The rest of the mail was bills or junk or duplicates of the catalogs I was getting at the apartment, except for a check from a client who'd been paying off my fee in monthly installments since early spring. I endorsed it, made out a deposit slip, and slipped them into an envelope to put into the ATM on my way home.

I pulled into a parking space around the corner from police headquarters on Payne Avenue just before five o'clock. Inside, the desk sergeant looked up, recognized me from my former tour of duty there, and waved me up the stairs.

Florence McHargue wasn't in her office. I walked farther on, to the bullpen where the homicide detectives hung out, and was grateful to find Bob Matusen hard at work.

He looked up and saw me, put down his pencil, and closed the file he'd been working on, shoving it into the top drawer of his desk. "Milan," he said.

"Hello, Bob. Where's the lieutenant?"

"The lieutenant is in the ladies' room," he said, and then laughed sourly. "I didn't think I'd ever hear that sentence coming out of my mouth."

"I've got something for her."

"I hope it's warm and fuzzy and wags its tail, to put her in a more kindly mood . . . Sheesh! And I thought Meglich was a hard case."

"Anything new on Dorothy Strassky?"

He looked away. "Nothing I can talk to you about."

"Figured."

He glanced discreetly toward the hallway before he said anything else. "Hey, do yourself a favor, Milan. Cut yourself loose from the Crowell kid. We're gonna make him for this sooner or later, and I'd hate like hell for you to go over the side with him."

"We'll see," I said.

"What the hell is that—'We'll see'?" He rummaged through the papers on his desk and found a soft pack of Camels. "That's what my mother used to say when I'd ask her if we could go to Cedar Point and ride the coasters when I was a kid. And it usually meant no. Fuck 'We'll see,' Milan."

He stuck a slightly bent cigarette into his mouth, and I leaned over and flicked my lighter so he could ignite it. "Did your mother also used to warn you about not counting your chickens?"

"She told me a lot of things," he said, sucking in the smoke. "And when I became a cop I forgot almost all of them."

His eyes focused somewhere behind me, and I turned to see Florence McHargue heading down the hall toward her office.

"If you'll excuse me," I said.

He shrugged expressively. "*I* will," he said. "I can't vouch for anybody else around here."

I went down the hall to McHargue's office. She was squatting down in front of her file cabinet, taking a folder out of the bottom drawer. "Got a minute, Lieutenant McHargue?"

She looked up at me over the rims of her glasses and frowned. "Do I have a choice?"

"Sure you do. You can tell me to pound sand. But I wish you wouldn't. I have something you might be interested in."

She straightened up, nudging the file drawer with her foot. It clanged shut like the closing of a prison-cell door. She put the folder on her desk. "How are you at getting to the point quickly?"

"That was my major in college," I said.

"Good." She perched on the edge of her chair. "I hope you paid attention in class."

"May I sit down?"

"Suit yourself, but you're not going to be staying that long."

"Even two minutes will do wonders for my aching feet," I said, and sat, reflecting on how many times I'd been in that chair when Marko was on the other side of the desk. "I think there's a very good probability Jason Crowell is not the phantom rapist."

"Probability doesn't pay the rent around here." She clasped her hands atop the file like a second-grader wanting to impress the teacher. "What've you got?"

"Jason Crowell is gay."

She looked at me levelly. "So?"

"So there's a good chance he didn't commit date rape."

"Rape has nothing to do with sex, you know that. Besides, he hasn't been charged with rape."

"Not officially."

"That's how I talk, Mr. Jacovich. Officially. And speaking officially, I don't care if he had a sex orgy with the Ohio State football team. This is the homicide division, remember? We solve murders here. Murders committed in Cleveland. Like in Duck Island. Get the picture?"

"But if he didn't do the rape, he'd have no reason to kill Dorothy Strassky to shut her up."

"What about the heroin in his toilet?" She took her glasses off, plucked a tissue from a box at her elbow, and began polishing the lenses, blowing on them first. "That's turning into a major pain in the ass. If there's one thing I hate—besides murderers, rapists, and drug dealers, that is—it's some federal dickbrain waltzing in here in a tight suit and telling me his case is more important than my case and if I know what's good for me, I'd better help him make his."

"McAleese?"

"You've made the gentleman's acquaintance?"

I nodded. "He told me it was my job to get the Crowell kid to roll over on his supplier."

She was fighting to suppress a smile. "Or else?"

"He made noises about siccing some federal judge on my license."

"That scare you?" McHargue asked.

"Can't you hear my knees knocking?"

Now the smile came out; grudgingly, I admit, but a genuine smile nonetheless. "Deliver me from the G," she said. "If a local cop pulled shit like that, he'd wind up rattling doors in Hough and taking open bottles of Thunderbird away from old men on park benches."

"Forget McAleese. And forget the heroin beef. I'm working on that. What I want to know is, now that Jason's motive seems to have gone up in smoke, will you lean in another direction for a while?"

"Can't be done," she said.

"Why not?"

"I don't have any other direction. We've poked around and Jason Crowell still comes up heads, no matter how many times we toss the coin. Strassky wasn't romantically involved with anyone, she had no enemies that I can find, and the motive wasn't robbery because nothing was taken."

"No money was taken. But her briefcase was open, remember? We don't know what was in it."

"I still don't have anywhere else to look," she said. "We're going through her office files, but as yet we haven't found any reason for someone to be really mad at her. The Crowell kid is all I've got right now, his sexual preference notwithstanding." She examined her glasses, put them back on, and began to think aloud. "He's young, he's away from home for the first time, maybe he's a little confused about the whole sex thing. He doesn't want to admit that he's gay, or maybe even bisexual, even to himself. So maybe he asks a woman to go out with him, for the end purpose of having sex with her, just to prove he's a 'real man,' and he strikes out. So he forces the issue. In the most violent way he can." She made two sets of quotation marks in the air with her fingers. "Macho man." She leaned back in her chair, pleased with her analysis. "Makes sense to me. Does it to you?"

"Not a lot, no."

"Then you prove to me I'm wrong," she said.

CHAPTER SIXTEEN

So now, not only was I striving mightily to clear my client of a rape accusation, I was trying to solve a murder for the Cleveland PD and doing the DEA's job for them. All for the princely sum of zero. I didn't have to hearken back to all the economics courses I'd suffered through at Kent State to realize that this was no way to run a business.

I headed east on Chester Avenue, then negotiated the weird traffic pattern at University Circle which I've never gotten used to, even though I've spent my whole life in Cleveland, and drove up Cedar Hill to my apartment. In the vestibule I grabbed my mail and perused it as I walked up the stairs to the second floor. It didn't take long; the delivery here at home was no more interesting than the one at my office had been.

Jason Crowell was sitting in the living room when I walked in, a small suitcase on the floor beside his chair. In court, he'd looked uncomfortable in a blue suit; now he'd changed to khakis and a ski sweater, but he still appeared ill-at-ease, tentative—as if on a moment's notice he was ready to fly from the wire on which he seemed perched. He was reading an old, dog-eared copy of John Steinbeck's *The Pearl*, which I'd picked up at a Friends of Cleveland Heights Library book sale.

"Hi, Mr. Jacovich," he said, putting the slim volume down on the coffee table and getting to his feet.

"Hi, Jason. You got in all right, I see."

"I wasn't sure where you wanted me to sleep so I've just been sitting out here reading one of your books. I hope it's okay."

"Sure it's okay. That's what they're for." I went into the kitchen with the stack of mail and tossed the whole thing into the trash, then came back out, pulling my tie down from my throat and opening my top shirt button. "I want you to make yourself at home here. And feel free to smoke—I do."

"I don't," he said.

"Good for you, it's a lousy habit. Well, you can eat, drink, use, or otherwise consume whatever you want. Except my toothbrush."

"Thanks, but I brought my own." He looked over at the bookcase. "You've got some neat books."

"I read a lot. Always have, ever since I was old enough to. Have you ever read Steinbeck before?"

"No. I don't read a lot of fiction."

"You should," I told him. "Most of what I've learned about life has come from good books." I took off my jacket and hung it in the front closet. "Come on, I'll show you where you're bunking."

He hefted his suitcase and I took him into the spare room where the twin beds my boys use, when I'm lucky enough to snare them for a weekend, were neatly made. On the wall, mostly collected by Milan Junior, were a couple of inexpensive Leroy Neiman sports posters and a signed photograph of Bernie Kosar, former star quarterback of the once-and-future Cleveland Browns.

"Take whichever bed you want," I said. "There are towels and washcloths on the top shelf of the closet. And I think the bottom drawer of the dresser is empty."

"This is really nice of you, Mr. Jacovich. Once I thought about it, I . . . I guess I really did need to get away by myself."

"Did your parents give you much poop about staying over here?"

He tested the mattress on the nearest bed with the flat of his hand. "My mom a little bit, but not much."

"And your father?"

He colored slightly. "He doesn't know yet. Well, I guess he does now, because Mom was going to call him to tell him about the bail." He straightened up from his examination of the bed and shoved his hands into his pockets. "He'll probably have some kind of fit."

"He'll get over it. Everything's going to be fine, Jason. You just relax and get your head on straight. And don't worry."

We went back out into the living room. "Hungry?" I said.

"Yeah, come to think of it. I didn't have much lunch."

I thought of the half-eaten sandwich I'd abandoned at the White Magnolia. Then I thought of why, and tried not to. "Me neither. I'm not much of a cook, but I'll do my best. You like klobasa?"

"I don't know," he said. "What is it?"

"Slovenians call it klobasa, but everyone else says 'kielbasa' or 'kielbase.' "

"I never tried it."

I was amazed. "You mean to tell me you've lived in Cleveland all your life and you've never had klobasa?"

"I don't think so."

"Well, your *real* education starts tonight."

Turning him back over to John Steinbeck, I went into the kitchen. When I'd left the house that morning, I hadn't known I'd be entertaining a houseguest, so I had to make do with what I had. I removed four large links of klobasa from the freezer and defrosted them in the microwave while I peeled and cut up three potatoes and two medium onions and set them to frying in my biggest pan. I boiled the sausage for a while, then drained it and put it into another frying pan. I took a loaf of *quattro formaggio* bread—four cheeses, baked right here in Cleveland at the Orlando Baking Company—and sliced it lengthwise, then stuck it in the oven to brown.

Not the healthiest meal in the world for a growing boy, I thought, and to remedy it, took a package of frozen broccoli from the freezer. The only time I'd ever agreed with George Bush was when he had made known his feeling about broccoli, but I eat it once in a while when I start feeling guilty about my usual diet. Just so dinner wouldn't be *too* healthy, I cut up part of a wedge of sharp cheddar, sprinkled the pieces over the vegetables in a large glass bowl, and nuked the whole thing while the klobasa, potatoes, and onions simmered.

I brought plates, silverware, and napkins into the living room and set two places on the coffee table in front of the sofa.

"You want a beer with dinner, Jason?"

He looked uncertain.

"It's okay, I won't tell the cops I'm serving alcohol to minors if you don't."

"It's not that. Uh . . . I think I'd rather have a Coke, if that's okay."

"No Coke, Pepsi," I said, belatedly realizing Jason was too young to remember the classic John Belushi *Saturday Night Live* routine, and went back into the kitchen, my comedy career stillborn.

We didn't talk about anything significant while we ate. In fact, we hardly talked at all. Jason was a quiet kid at the best of times, and I think he was still a bit hinky about living in my apartment.

I'm not much of a sweets eater so there was nothing for dessert, and though I offered to take him across the street to Baskin-Robbins, he declined. Instead he cleared away the detritus of the meal, put the dishes in the dishwasher, and cleaned off the kitchen counter. I decided to let him do it, trying in vain to recall the last time either of my sons had made a similar gesture.

I drank a second beer and smoked a cigarette as I listened to him moving around in the kitchen. When he came out, I said, "I've got some paperwork to do, Jason. You can watch TV in the den if you want to. Or do you want to read?"

"I'd like to finish the book," he said.

"Good. Every time you read—anything—you learn something." I went over to the bookshelf and took down another book. "When you finish *The Pearl*, this one might interest you," I said, handing it to him.

"*Giovanni's Room*," he read from the jacket.

"James Baldwin. He was an African American writer, very big in the sixties at the beginning of the civil-rights movement. His stuff is great."

"I've heard the name," he said.

"He was also one of the first openly homosexual authors in this country to become popular."

He stood there with a book in each hand, as if trying to decide which one weighed more, the color draining from his face, leaving his lips white and thin. He looked at me in shock and surprise.

"You really should have said something earlier," I went on, "when those flyers first started appearing. It might have made life a lot easier."

He swallowed, his Adam's apple working hard. "How did you find out?" Then he shook his head bitterly. "Never mind, there's only one person who could have told you."

"Don't be angry with Marika. She was worried and scared—she was just trying to help you."

He practically staggered over to the sofa and lowered himself onto it, half sitting and half lying, like a Victorian lady on a fainting couch. "Some help," he muttered.

"It's not a bad thing, you know," I said.

"It is if you've got a father like mine."

"Is that why you didn't say anything? Because your father would be mad?"

He shook his head. "Don't you understand, Mr. Jacovich? If my father knew I was gay, it'd kill him. My whole life I was never enough of a . . . a regular guy, I guess . . . to suit him. I didn't like to play with toy soldiers, I wouldn't go out for football—I was never the kind of son he always wanted." His eyes filled up and a single tear began running down his face; either he didn't notice it or he didn't care, because he made no effort to wipe it away. "Jesus, I couldn't tell him. Even now I can't tell him. That's why I made Marika promise to keep her mouth shut about it."

"You'd rather the rest of the world thinks you're a rapist than for your father to know you're gay?"

He filled his lungs with air and let it out slowly, like a tire that had sprung a slow leak. "I guess so."

"How long do you think you can keep it from him?"

"I don't know," he said miserably, his voice breaking and his breath coming in little, hiccupy gasps. "Until I finish school, I guess. He'd never spend another nickel on my college if he knew."

He stuffed both books under one arm and studied his shoes. "Does this mean you won't let me stay here?" he said, not looking at me.

"Of course not. Nothing's changed."

He shot me another of his grateful looks.

"You know," I said, "you might be underestimating your father."

"Not him. When I finally realized I was attracted to men, when I was about fourteen, I thought about killing myself rather than have him find out."

"You think he'd hurt you?"

"I think he'd never speak to me again. *Literally* never speak to me again." His eyes turned dark and haunted. "That'd be worse than hurting."

"He'd eventually come around to it, Jason. It's just who you are."

"He wouldn't see it like that. Especially when he's drinking."

"Your father drinks a lot?"

"Not all the time. Just when he's pissed off."

"Does that happen often?"

"I don't know," he said. "I don't have another father to compare him with. And then when he drinks, it makes him even madder." With thumb and middle finger, he twisted the short hairs at the back of his neck. "Meaner." He looked up at me almost resentfully. "I can't really blame him. How would you feel, if it was your son?"

"I'd like to think more than anything that it wouldn't make any difference," I said, standing up.

I went into the kitchen, got my special-occasion stash of Stoli from the freezer, and poured two fingers of vodka into a glass. I took it back into the living room and handed it to him. "Here, you'll feel better."

"No," he said, recoiling from it.

"It's for medicinal purposes. Drink it. Ease yourself."

His hand was shaking almost too badly to take the glass. When he finally got control of it, he shot the vodka down in one gulp. It made his eyes tear even more; he wasn't used to it.

"Take it easy," I said, and took the Baldwin book from him.

His face, flushed from the alcohol, blanched again. He couldn't seem to decide whether he was tough and together and wise beyond his years, or a frightened little boy anticipating a strapping when his father got home. "You're not going to say anything, are you?"

"I've already told Lieutenant McHargue," I said.

He scowled. "Great."

"I had to, to save your bacon. If you didn't rape anybody, you had no motive for Dorothy Strassky. At least that's what I figure."

"Is that what Lieutenant McHargue figured?"

I couldn't look at him and lie to his face, so I stood up and walked over to the bookcase to replace *Giovanni's Room*. "I'm not sure how she feels about it."

He swung his feet off the couch and onto the floor, set the glass down on the coffee table and put his head in his hands. "The damn flyer doesn't matter anymore. I'm going to jail for selling drugs anyway. Or maybe even for murder."

"You're not going anywhere just yet," I said. "Don't lose hope."

"Easy for you to say, Mr. Jacovich. You haven't lost almost every friend in the world. And when people find out that I'm gay, I'll probably lose the rest of them."

"You haven't lost me," I said. "Or Dr. Parker or your mother and your sisters. And you haven't lost Marika, either."

His look remained unconvinced. He went into the bathroom to splash cold water on his face and I got myself another beer.

That was a pretty big secret Jason had been lugging around, a hard secret to keep. Most of the time secrets have a way of catching up with you anyway. I knew he'd be a hell of a lot better off if he just came out and told his father and everyone else, but I wasn't sure I'd ever be able to convince him of that.

I thought about the question he'd asked me: What if it was Milan Junior? Honestly, I have to admit that it would trouble me, sadden me—because of the grandchildren that would never be, and because I'd know that he'd be in for a tough time—being different in this country has never been easy.

I also knew that it wouldn't make me love him the slightest bit less, that I'd be proud of the young man he is, and would support him and be there for him, no matter what.

He's my son.

The doorbell intruded on my reverie. I wasn't expecting company, and as far as I knew, neither was Jason. I went to the callbox on the wall near the door and depressed the red button.

"Yes?"

"It's Trey Dotson, Mr. Jacovich. From Sherman College. I'm looking for Jason Crowell."

Jason came out of the rear of the apartment, his face splotched with red. I released the talk button.

"You want to see him?"

He shrugged and then nodded.

"Come on up," I said into the speaker, and then buzzed Trey Dotson in.

Jason shoved his hands into his pockets. "I wonder what he wants," he said nervously.

"We'll soon find out. Look, are you okay with this? Because I'll get rid of him if you're not."

"No, I'll talk to him." He went and sat down again, and together we waited for a knock.

Schuyler Dotson III was in the hallway when I opened the door, wearing a mauve Polo pullover, smiling as if he'd just dropped by with a gift of Tollhouse cookies. "Mr. Jacovich," he said. "It's nice to see you again."

I stood aside and let him come in. He immediately moved to Jason and pumped his hand warmly. It was a two-handed shake, the kind that says you're sincere. "How are you doing, Jason? I was worried about you."

"So you drove all the way in from Sherman to see how he was doing?" I said. "That was nice of you."

He beamed. The *"Yes, wasn't it?"* was tacit.

I pondered whether my duties as a host included offering him a beer, but I decided against it. I hadn't invited him and I didn't like him. Just letting him through the door had been a sacrifice.

I did suggest he sit down, though. He chose the big leather chair facing the sofa, where Jason had settled to resume his victimized slump. I just leaned against the wall and tried to pretend that years ago in the Orient I had learned the strange and mysterious power to cloud men's minds so they cannot see me.

Dotson was looking up at me expectantly, waiting for me to disappear. This wasn't my party, but it was my home and Jason was my guest and my client, and I'd be damned if I'd go hide in my bedroom like Lila's consort, Joe.

When it became evident I was there for the duration, he turned his attention to Jason, putting both hands on his thighs and leaning forward earnestly. "Well, now, it seems as if we have some problems, hmm?"

Jason didn't answer. I'm not sure Dotson expected him to.

"You're in some pretty serious trouble, Jason, aren't you? First that flyer comes out and accuses you of sexual misconduct, then poor Ms. Strassky gets killed, and now this drug business."

"I didn't do any of it," Jason protested.

"I'm not here to judge that," Dotson said, although it was clear he was. "I just want to help you. Even though you're officially not a student at Sherman anymore, I was your advisor, and I feel a responsibility."

Jason gave a mute nod.

"It's looking pretty bleak right now, but you need to know that there are a lot of people who care about you, whether you know it or not. Your family, your attorney, me, Mr. Jacovich here . . . He glanced up at me. "It's really kind of you to let Jason stay here, Mr. Jacovich. I know it must be an inconvenience."

This caring-nurturer posture was a turnaround from the last time I'd spoken to Trey Dotson. Maybe he'd had a change of heart. Maybe he knew something the rest of us didn't. Or maybe he'd come to Jesus.

"It isn't inconvenient at all," I assured him.

"Well, it's kind anyway," he said, and turned his attention back to Jason. "So, we all want the best for you, Jason—under the circumstances." He leaned farther forward, his head and shoulders jutting over the coffee table. "I've given it a lot of thought the last couple of days. I've talked to some friends, including a lawyer, and asked them what I should tell you to do."

He breathed in deeply, his chest and shoulders expanding under the sweater. "I think you should make a clean breast of it."

Jason blinked.

"Admit your mistakes. You're young—barely an adult. The courts tend toward leniency with someone your age. . . ."

"Wait a minute," Jason said.

"I know it sounds harsh to you right now. But they look a lot more kindly on a guilty plea. Your lawyer can probably make a very good deal for you with the prosecutor—"

"Wait a minute," Jason said again. "I haven't done anything, Mr. Dotson. I didn't rape anybody, I didn't kill anybody, and those drugs—I don't know how they got into my apartment." He threw his shoulders back unconsciously. "I'm not going to confess and go to jail for something I didn't do."

" 'You're just making it harder on yourself. If you try to stonewall them, they're going to come after you with all the artillery they have, and when it comes time for sentencing, you won't get any consideration at all." He sat back in his chair. "You have any idea what prison is like? You have any idea what those cons will do with a kid like you? I don't want to see that happen to you, Jason. Use your head, okay? Cooperate with them, give them what they want, and it'll lighten your sentence—just about guaranteed."

The boy didn't say anything. Ashen and practically immobile, he looked like he was about to faint. And I was tired of being silent.

"Mr. Dotson?" I said. He looked over at me pleasantly. "As an advisor I think you suck!"

If that offended him, he didn't let on. "You've been around, Mr. Jacovich," he said. "You know how the system works as well as I do. Tell him. Tell him it'll go easier with him if he comes clean."

"It'll go easier with you if you leave my home," I said, pushing myself away from the wall. "Because in about sixty seconds you're going to get very badly hurt. Do you know how hard it is getting blood out of a mauve sweater?"

I stood over his chair, and I'm sure that to him I looked even bigger than I am, because he seemed to get smaller, like Alice when she sipped from the "Drink Me" bottle.

"Don't do anything foolish, Mr. Jacovich," he said, the quaver in his voice belying the bravado. "You'd be looking at a lawsuit."

"And you'd be looking at stars," I said. I backed up a few steps so he could get up. "And the ceiling of a hospital room. Or you can look at the stairs going down—right now. If it were me, I know which one I'd pick."

He pushed himself to his feet. "You're not helping the boy any by being dishonest with him," he said. "Think it over. Think about the experiences you've had in the past. You'll know I'm right."

He moved past me to the door, and it was all I could do to keep from reaching out and tearing his head off his neck. His hand on the knob, he turned to give Jason one last volley. "Don't make it tough on yourself, Jason. You're young, you've got your whole life ahead of you."

Which is more than Schuyler Dotson III was going to have if he said one more word. As he opened the door, I moved toward him.

"There's something you need to be aware of, Dotson."

Jason jumped to his feet, afraid I was going to reveal his best-kept secret, but I put a hand up to reassure him. Trey Dotson was all the way out in the hall now, his mouth tight with fear, trying to decide whether to wait and hear what he should be aware of, or run like hell.

"I just want you to know," I said, "that if I ever see you again, anywhere—you'll be in play."

That froze him in his tracks for a second or two. Then, trying to salvage some dignity out of the situation, he drew himself up to his full height and went down the hall toward the stairway. I stood there until he was out of sight, then went back in and closed the door. I was mad enough to slam it after him, but I didn't see what good that would do anybody, and it would certainly annoy Mr. Maltz, my ninety-two-year-old neighbor across the hall.

Jason was still standing between the sofa and the coffee table, as if his shoes had been nailed to the floor. His mouth trembled involuntarily and his shoulders were shaking. I've never seen anyone with such a ghastly white pallor who wasn't dying from a gunshot wound.

"Your faculty advisor is a prime asshole," I told him. "Don't even think about what he said."

He struggled to swallow, his chest spasming, beads of sweat breaking out on his forehead, and for a moment I was afraid he was going to throw up. Then he said, "Maybe he's right."

"He's only right if you're guilty."

He shook his head violently from side to side.

"Then you don't confess to anything when you're innocent." I moved back into the room to face him across the table. "And you are, aren't you?"

"Yes," he said in a tiny voice.

"Of everything?"

Tears sprang to his eyes again, and he sat down hard on the

sofa. "Yes," he said again, and then let a bitter edge coarsen his voice. "Except of being queer."

Coming from Jason, the word seared like a branding iron. "That's nothing to feel guilty about," I said, and shook my head at him, but he wasn't looking at me. I wandered over to the window and looked out. Trey Dotson was doing some broken-field running through the traffic on Fairmount Boulevard, finally arriving safely at the side of a bright yellow Corvette. He rearranged his clothes and his dignity, wiped an imaginary fleck of dust from one of the fenders, and unlocked the door and slid inside.

The roar of the engine as he revved it carried all the way up through my closed window from the street.

Jason retired to his room shortly afterward, and I went into my den and put some Robert Lockwood Jr. blues on the CD player, and smoked half a pack of cigarettes before I decided it was my bedtime, too.

Just before I fell asleep, I heard him crying on the other side of the wall that separated our rooms. He wasn't crying like a woman cries. Or like a man, either. He was crying like a terrified little boy.

CHAPTER SEVENTEEN

"You're not a prisoner, Jason," I said.

It was eight o'clock the next morning. I had gotten ready for work—clean shirt, tie, jacket, polished shoes. He was still in his blue-and-white-striped pajamas and had yet to run a comb through his hair. Drinking coffee across the kitchen table from each other, we were a study in contrasts.

"You've got a key, your own car, you can go anywhere you want to. You don't have to stay in the apartment."

"I've got nowhere to go and nothing to do," he said. "Did you forget, I don't have to study, because I'm not going to school right now. I don't want to see a movie—and just about the only friend I have in the world—besides you, I mean—is Marika, and she's going to be in class most of the day. And I sure as hell don't want to go home. So"—he rested his chin in his hand—"I guess I'll just stay here and read. Finish the Steinbeck, start on the Baldwin . . ."

"Suit yourself. We can grab dinner out someplace. I'll be home around six, with any luck. If I'm going to be later than that, I'll call."

"You don't have to call and check in. I'm not your girlfriend."

I finished my coffee and stood up. "If you were," I said, "you'd figure out some way to break up with me, too."

I thought about that as I headed down Cedar Hill. Connie

had really thrown me a curve the day before. She'd been very stubborn and single-minded—a label that has often been hung on me. She hadn't been able to accept my working on Jason's behalf until she found out to her own satisfaction that he wasn't a rapist; she hadn't been willing to accept my judgment. I was wishing she could have trusted me, believed in me a little more. I didn't want a relationship in which I had to defend my every action.

I guess when you've been single as long as I have, you tend to adjust to the aloneness and use it to your advantage: I go to bed when I'm tired, and not before; I eat what I want; I watch television or not, as the moment suits me. When the baseball bug bites me and I can't get tickets to sold-out Jacobs Field and I take few days to go to Detroit to see the Tigers play, I don't discuss it with anyone; I just go. When I want to drive down into Amish country in Holmes County for a lunch at the Homestead Restaurant in the aptly named little village of Charm, or go for a spin in the country to look at the splendor of fall leaves, there's no need to take anyone else's feelings into consideration—I just do it. And when I crave a weekend around the house in my sweats, not shaving, watching football and reading and listening to jazz, I don't need to consider any-one else's feelings. I don't have to ask permission,

Of course, I'd exchange all of that in a New York minute, as well as some pretty lonely nights, for someone to love, and to love me back.

What I couldn't come around to, I didn't think, is justifying what I do. I haven't enjoyed being on the defensive since I quit playing football.

Given Connie's tragic experience in college, I could under-stand why she'd reacted the way she did. What I wasn't sure of is whether I could live with it, whether there would be other occasions where her personal feelings would ram head-on into my work or what I wanted to do.

I was going to have to give it some serious thought, and today I didn't have time to do that. Keeping Jason Crowell out of jail was my priority.

So I stopped being confused about Connie and went back to being angry with Trey Dotson—held over from the previous evening by popular demand.

Sherman College and its administration had not impressed me; they had been pretty quick to condemn Jason on the basis of an anonymous accusation of rape right from the beginning. And now with the heroin charge and the suspicion of murder, they wanted him to go away, leaving them to the important business of turning out good, responsible citizens. So they had sent Trey Dotson to convince him that he should fess up and take his medicine so the whole thing would blow over.

It hadn't occurred to them that someone, for whatever reason, might be doing an expert frame job on Jason. It hadn't occurred to me right away, either, but now I was sure of it.

Because of the overkill. First he was accused of rape, then suspected of killing a college official, and now, framed on a drug charge. Next they'd have him nailed for the JFK assassination, too. It was too much, and those clowns from Sherman were all too ready to buy it, all too ready to condemn without trial.

Well, I was going to make them eat it.

When I got to my office, Tony Radek, the owner of the shop that occupies the first floor of my building, was out in the parking lot smoking his ever-present cigar, a habit he'd cultivated long before it became trendy (I, don't think Tony Radek even knows the meaning of the word). One of his workers had complained about too much tobacco smoke in the workplace, and Tony—rather than face the towering righteousness of the new anti-smoking brigade—was reduced to coming outside to smoke, even in the dead of winter. I'm a smoker, but Tony's three-for-a-buck stogies must have been pretty hard to take indoors.

The thing about Tony that puzzled me was that he was always smoking a stub no more than three inches long. I'd never seen him with a new cigar; maybe he bought them that way.

"Hey, Milan," he said.

"Tony."

He shifted the cigar from one corner of his mouth to the other. Maybe he thought he could speak more clearly that way. He was wrong. "Listen, it's getting cold, so I turned the heat on this morning, and that radiator is clanking like a son of a bitch. I can't hear myself think."

This from a guy who makes wrought-iron gates and railings and disturbs me all day long with the metallic banging coming up through the floor. It's a good thing I'm not a psychiatrist.

"The building is ninety-two years old, Tony. What do you expect?"

"I think you need a new furnace."

"Or a new tenant," I said, and went past him into the building and climbed the old wooden stairs to the second floor. He finds something to bitch about at least once a week, and I usually get right back in his face, but by the end of the day he forgets about it and life goes merrily on. He's a pretty good guy under the Neanderthal façade, although I don't think his workers, whom I've heard him driving like Roman galley slaves, would agree.

I set a pot of coffee to brewing, sat down at the computer, and opened the Crowell file to review my notes. I was finally starting to get used to the damn computer; it was a lot easier to read than my handwriting.

Nothing was jumping out at me, though, as I scrolled through the file. I'd started out with a rape accusation, and wasn't any farther along than I'd been at the beginning. But in the meantime Dorothy Strassky was dead, there was a rapist running around loose, the federal government was up my nose, the Cleveland Police Department was mad at me, I had an unexpected houseguest, and I was in danger of losing the best relationship I'd had in years.

I'll bet Sam Spade never had days like this.

Two phone calls interrupted me before ten o'clock in the morning. The first was from DEA Agent McAleese, wanting to know whether I'd managed to convince my client to roll over on his drug supplier.

"He can't, because there is none," I told him. "That smack was planted and you know it."

"I don't know it," McAleese said. "And if you don't convince him to play ball with us, I'm going to have to try. And I know just where to find him. I know he's staying at your place."

"Call before you come," I said, "and make sure you bring a federal warrant with you."

I hung up on him none too gently, which didn't make me feel any better, and chain-smoked two Winstons. Somebody else for me to be mad at. Pretty soon I'd have to hire a secretary to schedule my angers.

The second call was decidedly more interesting. It was from Marika Rollins, and she sounded agitated.

"Mr. Jacovich, I think I have a name for you to talk to."

"What kind of name?"

"You told me to ask around on campus about militant feminist groups?" She said it as if it were a question.

"Yes," I said, picking up a pencil. The blood was pounding in my ears.

"Well, this isn't a group, exactly, but . . ."

I waited, doodling empty gallows on the pad.

"There's this woman. Diana Flaster is her name."

I wrote it down.

"She's a grad student and teaching assistant."

I waited some more, but nothing seemed to be forthcoming. "What about Diana Flaster?" I prompted.

"Well . . ." I could hear her breathing heavily through the receiver. "She doesn't belong to any of the groups or clubs on campus, but she's very outspoken about women's issues. Very militant, is what I heard."

"How did you get a line on her, Marika?"

I heard the soft sound of her breathing for a moment. Then she said, "I told a little white lie."

I didn't say anything.

"I told one of my art teachers that . . ."

More breathing.

". . . that some man grabbed me. And tried to . . ." She stopped.

"Marika . . ." I said.

"I couldn't just go around asking questions, could I? You said it might be dangerous."

"It could have been. That took some guts, putting yourself in that kind of position."

"It's the only thing I could think of."

"Jason is very lucky to have a friend like you."

"I guess that's all I can be. A friend."

"Lovers come and go, Marika." At least they did in my life. "But a good, loyal friend is forever." I was thinking of Marko Meglich, of course, and lobster claws of sadness nipped at my heart before I made a willful effort to send them scurrying back into the shadows.

"I guess." She sounded dubious. I didn't blame her.

"So what did your art teacher say?"

"Well, she said that ordinarily I should go to Ms. Strassky and file a formal complaint, but since . . . Well, anyway, she suggested I contact Diana Flaster."

"Is Flaster the one behind Women Warriors?"

"I don't know," Marika said. "But if there is such an organization, chances are she'd know about it. At least that's what my art teacher said."

"Where can I find her?"

"I don't know. I don't think she lives on campus. But this teacher told me she's majoring in women's studies."

"F-L-A-S-T-E-R? Just like it sounds?"

"I don't know," she said again. "Mr. Jacovich? Isn't all this beside the point now for Jason? I mean, with the heroin thing and all?"

I jumped as the office radiator made a sound like a pile driver; maybe grumpy Tony Radek was right. "The two might be connected, Marika. We won't know until I run it down. But you've been more help than you realize."

She didn't answer, but I heard a small sniffle.

"Let me get on this right away," I said. "I'll call you tonight and let you know what I come up with."

It was something, I thought, as I closed up the office and went back downstairs to my car. Not much, but certainly more than I'd been able to unearth since I'd gotten involved in this ugly and unpleasant business. Maybe it would break the log jam.

At the very least, as long as I was going to be on the Sherman campus anyway, I could try and catch up with Terry Yagemann again.

I realized I hadn't had any breakfast. I headed west and stopped at a little place on Detroit called The Big Egg. Just a few blocks off the west Shoreway, it's kind of a Cleveland in- stitution, featuring more varieties of breakfast than anyone could reasonably imagine, and it's open twenty-four and seven, which means that at any given moment you can find west-side boomers, downtown attorneys, salesmen on the run, school-age kids, and, especially at night, the dwellers of the darker side— pimps and hookers and gangstas—sitting at the counter or in one of the booths that look out at the traffic. Eggs on the griddle with fried potatoes is a common denominator.

Thinking that one of these days I was going to have to eat something that was relatively good for me, I ordered a cheese omelet with andouille sausage, which I washed down with three cups of strong black coffee.

After I'd found my way to I-90, the rain started, at first not much more than a mist peppering my windshield; after a few minutes, it grew heavier. By the time I crossed the Lorain county line, it was a bona fide gully-washer. I threw a quick glance over my shoulder to make sure my raincoat was in the backseat. I did not, however, have an umbrella. I never carried one, didn't even own one—perhaps out of some last vestige of leftover machismo, but more probably because when the wind comes in off the lake blowing a rainstorm ahead of it, it usually turns any umbrella inside out.

I still had my campus map, but it didn't show a women's-studies building, so I stopped at the information kiosk and asked the guard for directions.

He poked his head out of the kiosk; he was in his seventies, probably a retired deputy sheriff. The plastic rain bonnet protecting his hat made him look like my grandmother in her shower cap. "You here again?" he said. I was afraid he was getting used to me, and was a bit leery of me, too. Maybe I just look like the kind of pervert who skulks around college campuses.

He probably didn't get too many requests for women's studies, because he had to consult a mysterious list he kept in a drawer inside the kiosk to find out where it was; then he told me the program was run out of the social-sciences building, and gave me the directions.

He didn't tell me, "You can't miss it," because missing it would have been easy. There was such architectural uniformity on the Sherman campus that it was impossible to direct someone to watch for the white building with the green awnings or the one with the all-glass facade. The social-sciences building looked like nearly every other building in sight; I was able to identify it only by the free-standing sign on its front grass. I parked as near to it as I could, which was not very near at all, struggled into my raincoat, and headed for the front door. By the time I got inside my hair was flat against my head and cold water was trickling down the back of my neck.

The women's-studies office was listed on the directory board as being on the second floor. In the office was a middle-aged woman whose name, her desk plaque told me, was Audrey Helsing, departmental secretary. She had iron-gray hair, rimless glasses, and the chilly efficiency of a dominatrix, and she was clearly surprised to see me across the desk from her. And not very happy, either, when I told her I was trying to locate Diana Flaster.

"What for?" she demanded.

"It's a personal matter."

"We can't give out her home address to just anybody," she said.

"Of course not. But if I had some idea of where to look for her . . ."

She regarded me over the tops of her glasses with ill-disguised suspicion. "What is this in regard to?"

I produced one of my business cards, but it didn't satisfy her. "That doesn't answer my question," she said.

"It has to do with Dorothy Strassky."

Her lip quivered and her back stiffened. "Oh, Dorothy . . ." she whispered, momentarily shaken. She only allowed herself a second or two of real emotion, then quickly snapped back into her no-nonsense mode. "Surely Diana is under no suspicion . . ."

"No, not at all. If I could just talk to her—"

"I can't help you," she said. "For obvious reasons."

"They aren't obvious to me, Ms. Helsing."

"Then you mustn't be very perceptive."

It was one of those unanswerable insults. If I agreed with her, I'd be admitting stupidity; if I protested that yes I was too perceptive, I'd sound like a crybaby. She was good, Audrey Helsing.

"How about if you just give me a hint?"

"Dorothy Strassky is a murder victim. I can't discuss her with a perfect stranger just because he hands me a business card," she said. "And I'm very busy right now."

"So am I, Ms. Helsing, and this is important or I wouldn't be bothering you."

"But you are bothering me, Mr . . ." She looked at my card. "Mr. Jacovich." She pronounced it with the *J*, and the emphasis on the wrong syllable: Ja-CO-vich. This just wasn't my day. "I've told you I can't give you the information you want."

"I know," I said, "but I was hoping you'd have a change of heart."

All pretense of affability—and there hadn't been much to begin with—evaporated. "Well, I won't. Now I have to ask you to excuse me."

"I'm not sure I can," I said.

"Don't make me call campus security, sir."

"For asking a question?"

She stared at me intently, trying to intimidate me. It wasn't as good as Marko Meglich's hard look, which used to turn the knees of bad guys to water, but it was effective. Finally she said, "Good afternoon," and bent over her work.

My choices were to stare at the top of her head, or leave. I opted for the easy way.

I went downstairs again and stood at the front door, looking out at the rain, which had gotten heavier and nastier. I didn't relish the walk to my car, so I decided to stand in the vestibule for a while and hope it would abate sometime soon. It was the kind of situation that cried out for a cigarette, but the secondhand-smoke nazis have taken over Sherman College as well as the world. And there was no smoking allowed in the building.

It was ten minutes to twelve. I figured as soon as the rain quit, I'd grab some lunch and then try to run Terry Yagemann to ground.

I hoped I could find someplace to eat other than the tea shop, a pizza restaurant, or McDonald's. I missed my usual lunch haunts downtown.

I didn't like working so far from home. Lorain County wasn't exactly an overnight trip, but I was logging too many miles on the freeway, neglecting my other work, and spending a lot of time away from the familiar places where I was comfortable.

A bell rang, echoing loudly in the vestibule, signaling the end of eleven-o'clock classes. Doors began opening up and down the hallway as students emerged with their books, some singly and some in groups. Many of them were getting into their rain gear, preparatory to going outside to their next class or home. Almost everyone slowed their step when they approached the door, girding their loins before plunging out into the downpour. A few of the women refused to go out in it at all.

And then I noticed one of the young women I'd seen at St. Colman's at Dorothy Strassky's funeral—the one with the startling blue eyes who had been driving the Geo. Today she was wearing a similar Sherman College sweatshirt, only this one had a hood. She had a hard time getting into a yellow rain jacket while holding an armload of books—but this was the women's-studies building and, sadly, I was afraid of offending her with an offer to help. She finally got the jacket on and pulled the hood of the shirt out and up over her head to protect her hair.

Shifting her books to the crook of her other arm, she started through the door.

"Excuse me," I said, playing a big hunch, "are you Diana Flaster?"

She turned her head in my direction; her bangs were sticking out of the front of her hood, making her look younger than she was. Her dark, sallow skin was unadorned by makeup. She didn't seem to recognize me from the funeral; maybe I'm just not that memorable. In any event, she answered my question with one of her own. "Who are you?" she said almost defensively, suspicion drawing back the corners of her eyes.

I took that as an affirmative. "My name is Milan Jacovich. I'm a private investigator."

"So?"

"I'd like a few minutes of your time, if you can spare it."

Wary, she shifted her books to her other arm again. "I can't spare it."

"It's important."

"What about?"

"Women Warriors."

She took a second to catch her breath, and another one to formulate her response. "I don't know what you're talking about," she said, but the way her eyes changed shape from round to almond, and the rigid way her mouth set into a grimace told me she did.

"Sure you do. And we need to talk about it."

"Why should I talk to you?"

"Because Jason Crowell is my client and you've gotten him into a hell of a lot of trouble."

Her eyes got flinty and nasty, and her naturally thin lips turned into a line resembling a scar from a long-ago surgery. "Jason Crowell, huh? Well, I have nothing to say."

"I think you had plenty to say when you didn't have to sign

your name to it, Ms. Flaster. I'd like to see how well you do when you're speaking for attribution."

Her head shook as if wracked by a sudden pain. "Go fuck yourself," she said, and started out the door. The hissing sound of the rain filled the vestibule.

"A woman has been killed, Ms. Flaster," I said, shouting over the rain, "and a kid is looking at life in prison, and it's all on account of Women Warriors. All on account of you, I think."

She stood there with the door half open, staring at me.

"You can tell me I'm wrong," I said. "But you can't just walk away."

"Watch me."

"You can't walk away from the lawsuit Jason's parents are going to hit you with, though, and you sure as hell can't walk away from the police. And if you don't talk to me I'm going to be on the phone with them in five minutes and they're going to come to see you and ask some hard questions. And you can't tell *them* to go fuck themselves."

She slowly moved back into the vestibule and let the door swing shut. "What is it you want?"

"Some clarification. And some names."

"Fat chance."

"Me or the police, it's your choice. What you've done is illegal—it's called *libel*. And on the off chance you aren't prosecuted for it in a criminal court, you can take it to the bank that you're going to have your socks sued off by in civil court. So you'd be doing yourself a favor by cooperating."

I watched the color slowly drain from her face as I spoke. She seemed to be frightened by what I said, or at least it gave her something to think about. But Diana Flaster was a tough cookie, or enjoyed believing she was, and she wasn't ready to cave just yet.

"Why should I talk to you?" she said, not quite as surly as she'd been before. "What's in it for me?"

"Maybe I can help you—but only if you help me."

She was spared making a decision because Chief Mel Dunwoodie came blasting through the vestibule door like Wyatt Earp walking into the dance hall in Tombstone looking for the Clanton boys. He wore a plastic rain protector over his hat, as had the guard in the information kiosk, and the beaded raindrops were sliding around on its surface like Pachinko balls.

I'll bet Wyatt Earp never wore a plastic bonnet over his Stetson, I thought, trying to imagine Henry Fonda or Burt Lancaster or James Garner in one. They would have looked as ridiculous as Dunwoodie, except that he actually had his hand on the butt of his revolver. Guys with their hands on their weapons always make me a little nervous, ridiculous or not.

"Damn your ass, Jacovich, you don't listen!" he said, his head jutting forward eagerly, accentuating the multiple chins. "Didn't I warn you not to cause any trouble on this campus?"

"Trouble?" I wondered for half a second if he would really draw that police special and, once having done so, use it. I decided he would not.

"I get a call from Miz Helsing just now that you're nosing around in her office asking about young women."

I tried not to laugh.

"And now here you are, harassing one of our young girls right here in the public corridor." He puffed out his pouter-pigeon chest. "Well, you're coming along with me, mister."

"Fine, if you want to be sued for false arrest."

"There won't be nothing false about it," he growled.

"Just a minute," Diana Flaster said. She turned and stared directly into my eyes, and her gaze was level. "Nobody's harassing me. Mr. Jacovich and I are just having a conversation."

Dunwoodie took a step backward, clearly displeased with the way things were working out. "I can get this man to leave you alone, miss."

Flaster couldn't help flinching at the "miss." "We're just talking."

"Nice try, though, Chief," I said. I moved to take Diana Flaster's arm and together we walked outside into the rain, leaving Dunwoodie glaring and flummoxed in the vestibule.

"Thanks." I lowered my head in a vain effort to keep it dry. "He couldn't have arrested me legally, but it would have gotten messy."

" 'One of our young girls,' " She mimicked Dunwoodie cruelly. "I hate that fat son of a bitch. Don't flatter yourself, I didn't do it for you." But the angry edge to her voice and manner was gone.

"Does this mean you're willing to talk to me?"

She pursed her lips, considering it. "It means I'm willing to listen."

"That's a start. Are you driving?"

"No."

"Then can we go someplace in my car? Where we can talk? Or where you can listen?"

"I don't want to talk politics with you. I can't change your mind, and you won't change mine."

"This isn't about sexual politics anymore. It's much more serious than that."

"Nothing is more serious than that," she said, meaning it.

We ran through the rain to my car, and she directed me to her apartment several blocks off campus. It wasn't the standard, starving-student housing that Jason and Marika had lived in. It was in a fairly nice—though I'm sure inexpensive—brick apartment complex. She led me up the outside stairway to a second-floor unit. The hand-printed card in the slot in the door read, *Flaster-Naft*

"Wait here," she said, and let herself in with a key, closing the door behind her. I waited in the rain for more than a minute before it reopened. She'd taken off the yellow rain jacket and put the hood of her sweatshirt down. It had mussed her hair, but she didn't seem to care.

"I had to let my roommate know we had company," she said, and stood aside so I could go in.

The apartment was unremarkable—utilitarian furniture, the ubiquitous computer setup, a small TV set in the living room. Just off it was a kitchen larger than any I'd seen in Sherman, big enough for a metal-legged Formica-top table and two kitchen chairs along with the usual appliances.

Another woman came out from what was obviously a hallway to the bedrooms. She was the same one I'd seen with Diana Flaster at the Strassky service.

"This is my roommate, Judi Naft," Flaster said. Judi nodded glumly at me. Obviously she'd been told who I was and for whom I was working, and she wasn't any happier to see me than Diana Flaster was.

"You can take your coat off if you want," Flaster said, not the most gracious of hostesses. I followed her suggestion—my coat was soaked. She took it into the kitchen and draped it over one of the chairs, then came back out.

"Okay, so you're here," she said, hands on her hips. "And I'm listening. Go ahead and talk."

I looked at Judi Naft.

"Judi can hear anything you have to say to me. She's in this as much as I am."

"All right," I said. We were all standing, and the living room wasn't quite spacious enough for that, but neither of them seemed inclined to sit down, so I didn't, either.

"Are the two of you all there is of Women Warriors, or are there more?"

Shocked, Judi looked nervously at her roommate and crossed her arms defensively over her chest.

"It's all right, Judi, he's figured it out," Flaster said. There seemed to be no doubt which one of the two was the alpha animal. "Yes, Mr. Jacovich, there's just the two of us. So what?"

"So you've falsely accused someone of rape."

"Falsely?"

"Jason Crowell didn't rape anyone."

Judi Naft rolled her eyes. "Of course he'd say that."

"I know he didn't."

"How do you know?"

"Were you the victim, Ms. Flaster?"

Flaster looked astonished. "No."

"How about you, Ms. Naft?"

"No," Judi said.

"Then how do you know he did?"

That seemed to be a philosophical concept that was completely foreign to both of them. They looked uncertainly at one another. Then Judi Naft said, "Someone told us he did."

"Who?"

Flaster wheeled around to confront me directly. "Look. Women are raped by their dates all the time, and they're too frightened or ashamed to come forward about it—because chances are nobody will do a damn thing about it and then the whole world knows. This young woman came to us because she was afraid to go to the authorities and she had nowhere else to turn. She knew that with us she'd get a sympathetic hearing. More than that, that she'd get action. Satisfaction. Putting out that flyer was the only way we knew to punish Jason Crowell without punishing his victim, too." She took her hands off her hips and crossed her arms defensively in front of her. "Now why would this woman say something like that if it weren't true? Why would she lie for no good reason?"

"Let's put the best face possible on it," I said. "Maybe she made a mistake."

Judi came to stand next to her roommate, her eyes blazing. They were a formidable pair to confront. "You think a woman doesn't know the difference between making love and rape?"

"Let's dispense with all this bullshit!" Flaster said. "Crowell wanted to fuck her and when she said no, he forced her. It's as simple as that."

"Maybe the mistake was that it wasn't Jason Crowell."

There was a round white clock on the wall of the kitchen; in the ensuing silence I heard it ticking.

"I'm so sure this woman would go out with a man and not even know his name!" Naft said.

"Maybe he used Jason's name instead of his own."

"Yeah, right!"

"It could happen. Sometimes people use false names." I pulled a copy of the flyer the two women had written from my pocket. "And sometimes they don't use their names at all."

Diana Flaster stuck out her chin as if she was daring me to sock it. "Bite me," she said.

"But to take a woman on a date and not use your real name . . . ?" Judi shook her head. "How can that be?"

"It can't, Judi," Flaster assured her, but there was a slight tremor in her voice, a little uncertainty. I was leagues away from victory, but I'd done one of the things I'd come for—planted a little seed of doubt.

"You talked to this woman," I said. "How well did she know him before he asked her out?"

Diana Flaster swallowed hard. There was a little white fleck of spittle on her lower lip, and she wiped it away with the back of her hand. She looked at her roommate, at her fellow Woman Warrior, and then back at me. Her eyes were wide and round and troubled. This wasn't playing out like the tape she had running in her head.

She filled her lungs and then measured her words out carefully, giving equal weight to each. "I—don't—know," she said.

CHAPTER EIGHTEEN

I went to a Convenient Mart and bought a couple of magazines, then found a little diner just off Sherman's main thoroughfare and had an open-faced, hot roast-beef sandwich, the kind where they make a depression in the mashed potatoes and fill it with heavy brown gravy. After an hour had elapsed, as planned, I went back to Diana Flaster's apartment. Their other invited guest had not yet arrived.

Judi Naft had changed into the kind of white flannel leggings that look like men's old-fashioned long underwear, and a billowy maroon top. Flaster still wore her sweatshirt, but had combed her bangs back over her forehead and covered them with a wide black headband. Two large salad bowls, nearly empty, were on the table in the kitchen, along with half a loaf of Bread and a tub of I-Can't-Believe-It's-Not-Butter Light; evidently the women had taken time for dinner, too.

Judi Naft looked apprehensive. "I'm still not sure we're doing the right thing," she worried.

"You are," I assured her. "It's always better to get things out in the open."

"You aren't the one people are going to point their fingers at. You aren't the one who the whole world will know has been fucked." Flaster's fingers strayed to the edge of the headband to make sure there were no errant bangs peeping out. "What if it turns out your so-called client really is a rapist?"

"If he is, and that's still a big *if* as far as I'm concerned, then you'll have been justified, I'll apologize, and I'll blow him out of the water."

"Yeah, right."

"Really," I said.

She shook her head skeptically. "I hope you do. I don't think you will, but I hope you do."

"You know, Ms. Flaster, life would be a lot easier for everybody if you didn't automatically assume the worst about half of the entire human race."

"Not quite half," she said. "Women outnumber men." She seemed to take pride in it.

"When the shooting war starts, I'll have to remember that."

Judi began clearing the table, ducking into the kitchen with an armload of dishes and putting them in the small sink. Diana Flaster and I sat in mute and mutual dislike and discomfort, watching her through the doorway. When she finished, she joined us in the living room and all three of us were silently awkward together.

Finally, Flaster said, "When Joyce gets here, you have to go easy with her, or I'll blow the whistle and it'll be all over. Understand?"

"She's had a rough time," Naft put in. "Be gentle."

"I'm probably not as sensitive as I'd like to be," I said, "but I'm not nearly the slug you think I am."

"We'll see."

And we saw, when the Joyce in question turned out to be Joyce Hallen, who arrived about five minutes later, bringing a merciful end to the heavy silence. She was an eighteen-year-old freshman and the kind of pretty that would undoubtedly turn to beautiful as she matured. She was finely, if slightly built, with exquisite, almost translucent white skin, long blond hair, and enormous brown fawn's-eyes that showed fright and confusion. She took off her rain jacket to reveal a plain, full black skirt worn over pink opaque tights and clunky black shoes, and a pink jersey top with a tiny rose appliquéd at the neckline.

Maybe it was the rose that got to me, but she looked heart-breakingly vulnerable. The nervous eye contact she made with me when we were introduced was no more than fleeting.

Judi fluttered around her, taking her coat and helping her to get settled. Diana just watched with her arms folded, watching me more than the newest arrival, her eyes narrowed in suspicion.

When Joyce finally found a place to sit, she clasped her hands between her knees and hunched forward as if expecting a blow.

"As I told you on the phone," Diana said to Joyce, "Mr. Jacovich here is a private investigator, and Crowell is his client. He seems to be having trouble believing what happened. He's threatened Judi and me with lawsuits and the police."

"Threats don't scare us," Judi Naft added.

"But it'll probably mean this is all going to come out anyway. So I think it would be a good idea to talk to him now. He's *promised*"—and Flaster looked at me and leaned into the word like a blocking back opening up a hole in the defensive line—"to keep an open mind."

"I really appreciate your coming over here tonight, Ms. Hallen," I said. "I know how difficult this is—"

"No you don't," Judi said. "You have no idea."

I ignored her. "But there's been enough secrecy and whispering. It's always better to get things out in the open."

Flaster's laugh was derisive.

"What is it you want to know?" Joyce Hallen whispered.

"I just want to hear your side of it."

She mumbled something I couldn't quite make out.

"Pardon?"

She raised her voice a little along with her head. "I was raped," she croaked. "That's my side of it."

"I'm sorry," I said. "I truly am." I waited a decent interval, then asked, "How did you meet Jason Crowell?"

"At the Purple Raven."

"What's the Purple Raven?"

"A little bookstore over on Lowell Avenue," Judi said helpfully.

Joyce Hallen hung her head. "I guess you could say it was my fault, because he picked me up."

Flaster was out of her chair, shrill and angry. "Don't even talk like that! Don't start thinking it was your fault." She glared at me. "You see? You see why we distributed that flyer?"

Joyce Hallen seemed to shrink a little in her chair.

"Diana's right," I said. "It wasn't your fault at all. Nobody's blaming you and nobody's going to. Look, I believe you. What I'm trying to find out is whether it was Jason Crowell who did this to you. I don't think it was—at least I'm hoping that. You don't want the wrong person blamed, do you?"

Joyce shook her head almost imperceptibly.

"And you want to make sure who it really was so it won't happen again to some other woman, don't you?"

"Y-yes."

"Good. Then we're really on the same side."

"If you say so," she murmured.

"So—what happened?"

Joyce worried her bottom lip with her teeth. "We got to talking—you know, how people do in bookstores. We were both in the art-books section."

"And that's when he told you his name?"

She nodded. "He said he was an art major and I'm an art minor, so it seemed like we had a lot in common. I mean, I wasn't attracted to him or anything, but . . . Well, I don't know many people here yet. So when he asked me if I wanted to go for coffee, I said yes."

"Where? On campus?"

"He didn't tell me where he wanted to go. We got in his car and the next thing I knew, we were on our way out of town."

"Did you question that?"

"I asked him where we were going and he said he knew a nice place . . ."

A sudden thought struck me. "What kind of car was it?" I said, leaning forward so eagerly that it startled her.

"I didn't notice," she said.

"Two-door, four-door, American, import, red, blue? What?"

"I just didn't pay any attention. It wasn't a van or a sports car. Just a regular car. I'm not really into cars that much."

I sank back into my chair, disappointed. If she could identify the car, it might clear Jason and point a finger elsewhere.

Or if he really was her violator, it could nail him to the wall. "So then what?"

"Finally he told me he was taking me to the Lariat."

"The Lariat, what's that?"

"A country-western bar out on the highway," Judi said.

"Lowlifes and bottom-feeders who all wear tattoos and keep their cowboy hats on," Diana Flaster added. "Hardly anybody on campus goes there. It's more of a townie hangout."

"Did you know that, Joyce?" I said.

"Just what I've heard about the place. So I told him I didn't drink, that I wasn't twenty-one, and I didn't want to go there. And then I asked him to take me back to campus."

"And?"

"Well, he seemed kind of mad about it," Joyce said, "but he pulled into the parking lot and turned around."

"The Lariat parking lot?"

"Uh-huh."

"So he turned the car around and you were heading back to campus."

She nodded. "Except that he veered off on this little side road. Just a dirt road, really. And he stopped the car by this little grove of trees. I can show you where it is if you want."

I shook my head. "It doesn't matter. What happened then?"

She flickered a look at me, then away. "He told me he wanted to smoke some weed." Her breath caught, and her hands flopped around in her lap like two fish out of water. "I said I didn't do that either. Then he asked me, since I didn't drink or smoke dope, did I . . . fool around."

"That's what he said? 'Do you fool around?' "

She shook her head and looked away from me. "What he said was, 'Do you fuck?' "

Flaster sat down on the arm of Judi's chair. The glare she shot me was venomous. "I suppose now you're going to say that it was Joyce's fault for getting in the car with him in the first place."

"I wish you'd stop telling me what I'm going to say," I said. "I wasn't thinking anything like that." I turned my attention back to Joyce Hallen.

"I said no," she told me, without being prompted. "And I asked him to take me back to campus right now. Um—right *then*, I mean."

I waited.

"And then he grabbed me around the neck"—and she cupped her hand at the back of her neck by way of illustration"—and kind of pulled my head to him and kissed me. Well, it wasn't exactly a kiss. . . . I mean, I didn't want to kiss him, but he forced his tongue into my mouth."

She shuddered. "He had bad breath, too. Cigarette breath. It was like kissing an ashtray." That got me to thinking, all right. "I tried to fight him off, but he was a lot stronger than me. And then he started—you know, touching me."

Joyce Hallen went on to say how Jason Crowell had then pushed her down on the seat against the passenger door, reached up her skirt and torn off her panties, all the while with his other hand around her throat. How he'd slapped her hard across the mouth when she'd resisted, and how afterward he'd driven her back to campus without saying another word except when he left her off in front of her dorm.

She trembled while she was telling me, her eyes fixed on a spot on the opposite wall, and her voice broke a few times during the story, but she didn't start to cry until she'd recounted his last words to her.

"See ya," was all he'd said.

After she told us that, the floodgates opened, and she wept openly, her hands clutching the chair arms and the tears cascading down her soft cheeks. I wanted to do something to help, but of course there was nothing for me to do.

Nobody said anything or even moved until she stopped crying, except for Judi Naft, who sniffled a few times and wiped her own tears away.

When Joyce had finally sobbed herself dry and sat back in the chair, I said, "Telling me that took a lot of guts, Joyce. I know it wasn't easy. Thank you."

"Joyce has guts to spare," Diana Flaster said. "When we put those flyers out, it didn't take Dorothy Strassky long to figure out who was behind it. So she contacted me and really put the pressure on for me to tell her who the victim was. Joyce and I talked about it, and she agreed to let me tell Dorothy her name."

"When was that?" I said.

Flaster scowled. "The day she died."

"You'd given Dorothy Strassky Joyce's name on the day she was killed?"

Flaster nodded, and my pulse was racing double-time. That must have been what Strassky had wanted to talk to me about.

"I appreciate this," I said. "From all three of you. And I promise I'll see to it that the person who did this answers for it."

Diana Flaster stood up, her mouth a hard slash. "So you finally believe Joyce was raped, huh?"

"Yes, I do," I said. "But I'm more convinced than ever that Jason Crowell is innocent."

I got home more than an hour later. I'd missed the rush hour, but driving had been slow because of the weather, and squinting out the windshield through the raindrops had given me the beginnings of a headache.

But I felt good, too—relieved. Because I knew Jason Crowell had not raped Joyce Hallen. It wasn't because of his sexual orientation, it wasn't because he seemed like such a decent young man, it wasn't because I wanted to believe him, to believe Reggie Parker.

Joyce had mentioned her assailant's tobacco breath—and Jason doesn't smoke.

He was in the den watching television and eating from a large bag of barbecue-flavored potato chips, so I know he'd at least left the apartment to go to the store—the only potato chips I ever bought were the salt-and-vinegar kind. I stuck my head in to say hello, then went into the bathroom and popped a couple of Aleves, stripped off my wet clothes and changed into a dark blue sweatshirt and jeans, and got myself a cold beer. I needed one, if only in a celebratory sense: I thought I had the rape of Joyce Hallen, the murder of Dorothy Strassky, and the heroin in Jason Crowell's toilet tank all figured out.

Now the job was to prove all of it.

Because Florence McHargue wasn't going to listen to my theory about smoker's breath and back off. I needed more.

There seemed to be no way of getting Joyce Hallen to come down to the police station and look at mug shots. Just coming to Flaster and Naft's apartment to talk to me had probably stretched her limits.

And there was still that damned toilet full of heroin.

I checked my answering machine in the kitchen. There had been four calls all day, but they'd all been hang-ups, and since my home machine was much less sophisticated than my voice mail at the office, or my electronic beeper with caller ID that was connected to it, I had no idea who had tried to reach me.

I took my beer back into the den. Jason looked up, saw that I wanted to talk, and clicked the Mute button on the remote.

"How are you doing?" I said.

"I'm good, Mr. Jacovich."

"I don't want to sound like a parent, but have you eaten anything today besides potato chips?"

"I ran over to Aladdin's and had a pita sandwich," he said.

I sat down across from him in a chrome-and-leather director's chair that an ex-lover, Nicole Archer, had given me for my birthday. It had been meant for my office, but I thought it fit the decor of my den better. I set my beer bottle on the tall table at my elbow. "Talk to your folks today?"

"To my mom, yeah. And my sister, for just a second—she was the one who answered the phone."

"Everything all right at home?"

He bobbed his head. "My father threw a conniption about my being over here, but I don't even care anymore. I'm glad I came. I needed the time away from them. I don't think I could take living at that house right now. It's a bad fit." He swallowed hard as if his throat was sore. "They've got attitude and I've got secrets."

"You're going to have to tell them those secrets eventually, you know. And sooner rather than later. You can't live a lie for the rest of your life."

He rubbed at the corner of his eye with a finger. "I guess."

"It's always better to just be honest, Jason; I found that out tonight." That got his immediate attention. He looked at me with expectation, and I said, "Do you know a young woman named Joyce Hallen, a freshman at Sherman?"

He betrayed no nervousness, or even recognition, as he concentrated on the name for a second. Then: "I don't think so."

"Very pretty, slim, long blond hair, big brown eyes . . ."

"That could be about fifty different people on campus. Why? Am I supposed to know her?"

"She's the one who was raped. At least that's what she says."

"The one who claims it was me?"

"Yeah."

"I never even heard of her, I swear to—

"I know," I said. "Don't worry about it. You're off the hook. For the rape part of it, anyway."

"How?"

"Because once she sees you, she'll know it was somebody else." I looked at him hard. "Won't she?"

"Sure she will." He rolled the top of the chip bag closed. "Where'd she come up with my name?"

"The rapist told her he was Jason Crowell."

His body jerked as if someone had rammed into him with a hard shoulder. "Why?" he said, bewildered.

I shrugged. "That's what I'm going to find out," I said. "I think I've got it figured."

"Tell me," he urged.

"Not until I get it all sorted out."

"I've got a right to know."

"Yes, you do. But I'm not going to accuse anyone without proof. You of all people should know what that's like."

His chin dropped to his chest.

"Help me out here, Jason. You told me that Marika is the only one who knows that you're gay. Are you sure about that?"

He looked puzzled.

"What about Terry Yagemann? You shared an apartment for three weeks."

"I never told him."

"Did he even suspect?"

"I don't think so."

"You didn't come on to him in any way, did you?"

He snapped his head up angrily. "Of course I didn't!"

"Not even inadvertently? I mean, maybe look too long when he came out of the shower?"

"You're straight," he said angrily. "Are you sexually attracted to every woman you see?"

"No," I admitted. "But if one of them was in my apartment and naked, I think I'd probably sneak a look."

"Well, I don't get turned on by every man I see. That's a common misconception about gay people," he said, turning serious. "We're as selective as anybody else is. And I just wasn't interested in Terry that way. Even if I had been, I knew he wouldn't be—receptive."

"Okay."

The set of his jaw was stubborn, rigid. "I'm not attracted to you, either, in case you're worried about it and locking your bedroom door at night."

I felt my face growing warm. "Goddamn it, everybody seems to think they know what's in my head, and they're invariably wrong!"

He deflated a little. "I'm sorry, Mr. Jacovich, you didn't deserve that."

"That's okay," I said. "We're all stretched a little thin in the nerves department right now."

It was one of those awkward moments where someone should say something and no one does. Finally I got up and took my beer out into the living room to leave him with his thoughts and to marshal mine, and he unmuted the TV and settled back to watch it some more.

When the phone rang I was out in the kitchen recycling my empty beer bottles into a blue plastic bag.

"Milan, it's Connie." There was ambient noise in the background on her end, and music. I figured she was calling me from the White Magnolia

"Hi," I said, my stomach doing a small flip when I heard her voice. "This is a nice surprise."

"I called a couple of times earlier, but I guess you weren't home."

"Was that you? Why didn't you leave a message? I would have called you back."

"I'm not at the restaurant. Listen, can we talk?"

"You mean face-to-face? Sure. You want me to come out your way?"

"I'm just down the street from you. At Nighttown."

That was a surprise. It wasn't like Connie to drive all the way over to Cleveland Heights from the west side when I wasn't expecting her. "What are you doing at Nighttown?"

"Drinking a glass of wine, listening to the piano player, and getting hit on by a fat guy in a designer sweater who wants me to come up and see the view from his bedroom on Overlook Avenue. Are you going to rescue me?"

"I don't have anything more interesting to offer. I still have a houseguest."

"I know." There was the briefest of hesitations; I could visualize her on the pay phone at Nighttown, back by the rest rooms. "Why don't you come down for a while? I want to see you."

"I want to see you, too," I said.

I went back into the den and told Jason I was meeting my girlfriend downstairs for a drink.

A worried frown creased his forehead. "Listen, I can get out of here for a while so you can have some privacy. . . ."

"Don't worry about it," I said. "I'll see you later."

I had a scintilla of concern about my wardrobe and decided that the Kent State sweatshirt, although no match for a designer sweater on a fat guy, would simply have to do, because

I was getting tired of changing clothes all the time. Looking out the window, I could see it had stopped raining, so I just threw on a suede bomber jacket, gathered up my indispensible cigarettes and matches, went downstairs, and walked the block and a half to Nighttown.

The sound of piano music from the next room engulfed me when I walked in. Dennis Lewin, one of Cleveland's most popular entertainers, eschewed the usual "I Left My Heart in San Francisco" of most bar pianists and was playing something by Erik Satie. As I glanced in I could see he was surrounded by adoring fans, mostly women, and once more I reflected that I might have chosen the wrong career path.

Connie, wearing a short maroon skirt with knee-length socks that matched it, a black silky blouse, and her usual pigtail, nursed a glass of wine down at the end of the bar near the TV set, and a hummingbird fluttered inside my rib cage when I saw her. I walked the length of the room, and when I got to where she was sitting, she swiveled around and gave me a kiss on the mouth. Next to her, the attentive fat guy in the designer sweater, in a well-calculated display of body language, turned away from us, looking wounded and betrayed.

He showed no inclination to leave, however, so I just hovered behind Connie's stool, enjoying the way she leaned back against me. I signaled for the bartender. Nodding in recognition, she popped the top from an icy Stroh's and set it on a coaster on the bar without being asked. No glass.

Jeez.

"I wasn't sure you'd come," Connie said.

"Why?"

"I had the idea you were mad at me."

I took a pull from the Stroh's—it always tasted better out at a warm, welcoming bar than it did at home. "I wasn't mad."

"Not exactly."

"Well, no. . . ."

"Mildly pissed, then? Put off? Irritated?" She forced a smile. "Help me find the right word, Milan."

"I'm not sure I can find my own words," I said.

"I know that you were upset with me when I wanted you to back off from your case."

I nodded.

"But then you told me the kid is gay, and all my objections evaporated."

"I guess that's what made me—put off."

She crossed her legs, treating me to a flash of knee and thigh above the maroon socks. "Why is that?"

"It's not important," I said.

"Yes it is. It'll help me understand my honey."

"Is that what I am? Your honey?"

She shrugged. "For want of a better word."

"We seem to be having word problems tonight."

"Those are the only kind of problems I want with you. That's why you need to talk to me."

I fumbled for a cigarette in my jacket pocket. "It's kind of hard to explain. . . ."

She lifted one eyebrow. Apparently she was willing to wait— maybe a little trick she'd picked up from me.

"When I gave you what you thought was conclusive proof that Jason didn't rape anybody, that changed your mind, didn't it?"

She nodded.

"But before that—you were ready to hang him."

"I told you why."

"Yes, you did, and in a way I could understand that. But this is about you and me, Connie. It didn't seem to matter to you what I thought. Even though you'd never met Jason, hadn't talked to him, really didn't know anything about it other than what I told you, you just made up your mind that he was guilty and that I was wrong. I didn't expect you to give him the benefit of the doubt, but I expected you to give it to me. When you didn't, it bothered me."

The man in the sweater turned and looked at us with interest. The glare I shot back at him sent him spinning away on his bar stool, studying the other side of the room.

"Is that such a big thing?" she said. "Do I always have to agree with you?"

"Of course you don't. But . . ."

"Ah." She nodded knowingly. "The big 'but.'"

"But—you're supposed to give me credit for a little judgment."

She cocked her head to one side. "Why is that?"

"Because I care very much about you, Connie, and I think you care about me. So if you told me that so-and-so was an asshole, that he was giving you trouble, that he was a bad person—I wouldn't question it. I'd believe you and I'd back you. All the way. And if you said that someone else was a good guy, I'd believe you, too, and act accordingly."

"What if I was wrong?"

"I'd assume you were right until proved otherwise," I said. "That's just how I am."

I turned my body so I could slide in between her and her neighbor next to her, and put the beer bottle down, then leaned an elbow on the bar. Connie looked up at me, her blue eyes big and liquid, and put a hand against my chest so that I was painfully aware of my heart beating against her palm.

"What do you want from me, Milan?"

"Be on my side," I said.

She blinked.

"If I'm your honey, as you put it, you're supposed to always be on my side. You're supposed to trust my judgment, especially when it doesn't have anything directly to do with you and me."

She picked up her wineglass by the stem. "I'm going to have to think about that one for a while."

"I'm not always right," I said. "Often I'm not. But I always try to be." I lit the cigarette and turned my head to blow the smoke away from her. "When Reggie Parker asked for my help, I didn't want the best part of this case, because I don't like rapists any more than you do. But Reggie vouched for him. And Reggie's my friend. There's no questions asked—he's my friend and I believe in him. So I took the job, and as it turned out, Reggie was right." I took another puff. "And so was I."

"What if Reggie hadn't been right?" she said. "What if Jason *had* done the rape? Would you have just dropped the case?"

"Not only dropped it, but bent over backwards to put him behind bars."

The sweater guy was looking over his shoulder at us in open curiosity now. Irritated, I leaned toward him. "What're you, writing a book?"

He drew himself up stiffly. "As a matter of fact, I am," he said.

I turned back to Connie and grinned. "Cleveland Heights," I explained; a large part of the creative community of greater Cleveland—writers, actors, artists, and musicians—live in the Heights. Most of them eventually find their way to Nighttown.

"Why don't we get out of here?" Connie said. She started fumbling in her purse for money.

"On me," I said.

"Why? I invited you."

"We're on the east side. My side of town. When we're on the west side, you can buy the drinks." I put a twenty on the bar, took her arm, and started guiding her toward the Cedar Road exit.

"I'm parked in the back," she said.

We made a U-turn and headed for the rear door of the restaurant. She looked over her shoulder at the sweater guy.

"It was nice meeting you," she said, waving gaily.

He must have been angry about striking out, because he didn't answer her.

We got to her car in the big, sprawling, metered lot in back of Nighttown. The roof and hood were beaded with drops of the rain that had now subsided. She unlocked it and slid behind the steering wheel.

"Where do you want to go?" I said.

"Not another bar. Let's just sit in the car and talk for a while."

"Like our first date."

"Uh-huh. Get in."

I walked around to the other side, climbed in, and closed the door. She turned in the seat to face me.

"You know that this wasn't just another one of your cases to me," she said. "I had issues."

I took her hand. "I know. And it's been bothering me."

"How?"

I shrugged. "I feel terrible for you. It was an awful thing to happen, and even though it was a long time ago, I know it's something you don't ever really get over."

"Then you can understand how I was feeling about it?"

"I can understand it. But you're too intelligent to buy into that crap that all men are dogs and rapists. Some of us are okay when you get to know us."

"I know that," she said. "Or else I wouldn't be here. But you can't blame me for being judgmental, Milan. You, of all people."

"I'm very judgmental, I know that."

"You said you didn't want this to be a 'thing' between us."

I nodded. "All right, it's not," I said.

She raised both eyebrows. "It's not?"

"No. Now that we talked it out."

"Just like that?"

"Just like that."

She sat back against the door. "You're a dangerous man," she said.

"Why? Because I'm big and mean?"

"You're big—not mean. But you're dangerous because sometimes I can't figure you out."

"You always figure out your men?"

"I try to."

"Well, that makes me different, then. I like that."

"Being different?"

"Sure," I said, moving my hand from hers to slip it under the base of her braid, feeling the wondrously soft little hairs at the nape of her neck. "It keeps people on their toes."

She touched my leg. "It's a good thing I'm not on my toes right now, Milan."

"Why?"

She moved toward me across the seat. "Because they're curling."

Our faces met somewhere over the console and stayed there for a while. Then she broke away, adjusted the steering wheel to its highest position to give herself room to maneuver, climbed over the gear box, and straddled my lap, her wine-flavored tongue probing my mouth.

"Right here in the parking lot?" I said.

"Right here in the parking lot," she whispered. "Nobody'll see us, because in about two minutes the windows are going to steam up."

"This is illegal," I said, pulling her skirt up around her hips.

"They won't arrest you." She fumbled with my zipper. "You're an ex-cop."

"I know. But they'll arrest *you*. That'll make me real sad."

"Bastard," she said, and grabbed a handful of my hair.

• • •

An hour later I let myself back into my apartment. Jason was in his pajamas, getting a glass of milk from the refrigerator.

"Everything okay?" I said, aware that I was grinning idiotically.

"Sure. Listen, Mr. Jacovich, it might be better if I moved back home tomorrow, you know? I mean, this is too much trouble for you."

"Don't be silly, you're no trouble at all."

He blushed. "Yeah, but—my being here and all, it's kind of putting a crimp in your sex life."

"Thanks, Jason, but my sex life is just dandy," I told him, and went into my bedroom, still smiling.

❖   ❖   ❖   ❖   ❖   ❖   ❖

CHAPTER NINETEEN

❖   ❖   ❖   ❖   ❖   ❖   ❖

It had started raining again at about five in the morning, and hadn't let up. I'd squinted through the downpour all the way out to Sherman, where I'd taken up my vigil outside Terry Yagemann's apartment, glad for the protection of my car.

Huddling low in the seat while the rain tattooed the roof, I thought there was going to be flooding in Valley View and Independence. There always is in the low-lying areas around Cleveland when it rains for five or six hours solid like this. Roads would be closed under a foot of water and residents would be bailing out their basements with buckets by evening. The general capriciousness of the weather is something we accept in northeast Ohio, the way we do our height and eye color. It's just what we have to live with.

My fingers were wrapped around a rapidly cooling cup of coffee. I'd filled a thermos at Starbuck's on Cedar Road before undertaking the drive; by now it was almost empty.

I checked my watch in the gray light. It was quarter past eleven, winding down a very long and tedious morning, and I hoped I'd reap the reward of a result.

But Terry Yagemann's parking space behind the building where he lived had remained empty for three hours now, and I'd read through the morning paper and the three magazines and eaten the Clark Bar I'd picked up at the 7-Eleven just off the Sherman campus. I was cold, my socks were wet, and even though I'd made some small progress with Women Warriors and Joyce Hallen, I had nothing concrete enough on Dorothy Strassky's death to take to Florence McHargue, and Jason Crowell was still impaled on all three hooks—drug-dealing, rape, and murder.

My eyeballs were stinging from reading small print and from boredom. I'd cracked the driver's-side window for air, and errant drops of rain were pittering onto my left sleeve. I used a paper towel to wipe off the condensation from my breath on the inside of my windshield so I could see out. The car was like a stuffy and uncomfortable cocoon, and I felt trapped in it.

Finally, at about twenty minutes to twelve, a Chevy Cavalier in a bilious shade of turquoise pulled into the parking space and Terry Yagemann climbed out, carrying a stack of books and a gym bag. He made a beeline for the apartment building, charging head-down against the rain.

I checked my watch again, gave him seven minutes, and got out of the car.

Climbing up to the third floor was rough going—I was stiff from sitting behind the wheel all morning, and before I knocked on his door I stopped and stretched, hearing several joints pop in various locations on my body.

Terry Yagemann had apparently gotten right out of his wet things, because when he opened the door, he was bare-legged and wearing a bathrobe—blue with a red plaid collar and belt. Around his neck was a towel; he'd been drying his hair, and it stood up on all sides of his head like the spiked hairdos one often sees on Coventry Road in Cleveland Heights, one of the centers of our city's counterculture.

"Mr. Jacovich," he said, clearly not expecting me.

"You've been a busy boy, Terry. I've been looking for you for a couple of days now."

"Well—yeah." He fingered the towel. "Yeah, it's been kind of a hectic week."

"Mind if I come in?"

From the expression on his face, I could tell he minded. Instead he said, "Okay," and I followed him back into the little apartment. The shoes, socks, and outerwear he'd just taken off were in a pile against the living-room wall.

"I heard about all the shit Jason's gotten himself into," he said.

"Where'd you hear?"

"What are you, fuckin' kidding me?" He ran his fingers through his hair to tame the runaway cowlicks. "It's all over campus. All over town, even."

I nodded and sat down on the sofa without being asked.

Terry stood halfway across the small room, untying and then retying the belt on his robe. "That's a tough deal."

"Real tough. Did you have any idea he was selling drugs?"

"I never saw him."

"You didn't know the heroin was in the apartment?"

He shook his head. "I didn't look in the toilet tank very often."

"And you don't know if he was using it himself."

"He never did when I was around. I'd guess no."

"Why's that?"

His grin was crooked. "He's not the type."

"What is the type, Terry?"

"Ah, you know. He was a geek. A grind."

"And you don't know any geek hopheads?"

He took the towel from around his neck, draped it over his head, and began rubbing vigorously again. "I don't know any hopheads at all."

"I thought you were the big party animal."

"Keg parties," he said, his voice muffled through the towel. "Strictly beer. Guys get hammered and then throw up. Maybe somebody tokes once in a while, or pops an upper when there's a big exam scheduled."

"Where do you get your uppers?"

His face lost a little of its color. "I didn't say that I did speed, I said I knew guys who do."

"Okay, then where would they go to buy them?"

"Just around. This is a college campus, you know? There's drugs all over the place."

"Did Jason do uppers?"

"Jason didn't even do Tylenol." He sat down across from me on a straight chair, his hairy legs and large, very white feet extending from beneath the robe.

"Do you still have a key to that apartment?"

He appeared surprised. "No. I gave it back to him when I moved out."

"You didn't make a copy before you returned it?"

"Why would I? So I could sneak back in there and rip off some of his pastel pencils?" He made a face, as if the very idea was absurd.

"Well, someone had a key. That's how they went up there and planted the smack."

"The word I hear is that he was dealing it. That the stuff belonged to him."

"He was too much of a geek to deal it. You said so yourself."

"Anyone can deal," he said. "Because of the money. Big money, if you do it right. And even geeks like money."

"Did he ever offer you any drugs?"

"I was his roommate," he said dismissively. "You don't shit where you eat."

"But you go to all those parties, you know a lot of guys who might be interested. If Jason was dealing, it seems pretty funny he never asked you about it. Or asked you to take him to a beer blast so he could make those contacts for himself."

He appeared clearly uncomfortable. "Like I told you before,

we didn't hang out together. We just shared the rent on an apartment."

"You don't like him much, do you, Terry?"

"I don't not like him. He just isn't my kind of guy, that's all. You can't be friends with everybody."

He shifted his feet nervously, making me glance down. And what I saw made the skin on my back crawl.

"W-what?" he said, noticing where I was staring, and girlishly tucked his feet under his chair.

"You have big feet, Terry."

He tucked them even farther under, wrapping one leg around the other. "Yeah, so what?"

"Let me see your foot."

"Huh? What're you, nuts?"

"Let me see your foot," I repeated, and stood up, leaned over, and grabbed his left leg, pulling it up so that he almost tipped over backward on the chair.

"Hey, goddamnit!" he protested, and I struggled to control his wildly flailing foot.

I grasped his ankle in both hands and examined his foot while he struggled. Between the first two toes, and between the second and third ones, were the unmistakable marks of a needle.

I let go, and his foot clunked to the floor, his heel banging loudly. I stepped back and looked at him. "You're a junkie, aren't you, Terry?"

The silence was like wet cotton hanging in the air of the room. He sat there immobile for a minute, then rearranged his robe, which had fallen open to reveal white boxer shorts with red valentine hearts all over them.

"You're a heroin addict and you shoot up between your toes because that way no needle tracks show on your arms."

"Fuck you, man," he said. "Who the fuck you think you are?"

The young are often vocabulary-challenged, I thought. I said, "You're the one who planted that heroin in Jason's apartment."

He became agitated, rocking from one side to the other in the chair like Ray Charles in the middle of a blues riff. "The hell I did! Why would I?"

"To throw more suspicion on him because you were the one who committed that rape he was getting blamed for. You told the woman your name was Jason Crowell because you knew you were going to rape her."

"You're nuts," he said.

"It all fits."

"I didn't rape anybody," he blustered, "because I don't need to. I can get all the pussy I want, anytime I want. And I don't know anything about heroin in the toilet tank, either. You can't hang this on me."

"I won't have to. The police will. And maybe killing Dorothy Strassky, too."

At the mention of the police, his manner changed. His lower lip wobbled, and tears sprang to his eyes as he cringed in the chair, wishing he could disappear. His voice rose in terror. "I didn't kill anybody."

"It's not up to me to determine that, Terry. But I'd say you were in a world of hurt."

He jumped up suddenly, as if the chair had become electrified, and headed for the telephone on his desk. "I'm calling my father," he blubbered.

"Go ahead," I said. "But you'd be better off calling a lawyer."

If I still carried a badge I would have arrested him right there. But I don't have those powers, and I had to be content with leaving him quivering in a corner, trying to dial his father long-distance in Cincinnati. His hands had been shaking so badly it had taken him three tries to get the number right.

I drove straight back to Cleveland and to Third District Police Headquarters on Payne Avenue. Whatever pleasure I'd taken in visiting the Roaring Third when Marko was alive had evaporated; Lieutenant McHargue definitely didn't number me among her favorite people. I figured she'd start to give me a bad time the way she usually did, but maybe she'd be happy at my news.

I found her behind her desk, a cup of tea at her right hand, and sure enough, when she looked up to see me framed in her doorway, there was no twinkling welcome in her eyes.

"What?" she said.

"Be nice to me, Lieutenant. I've got something for you."

"Presents already? I hardly know you."

"It's a present you'll like."

"I don't wear perfume and I don't eat candy."

"How about a perp for the Strassky killing?"

She lowered her head and looked at me over her glasses. It was one of those skeptical, *"Yeah, right"* looks.

"Motive, means, and opportunity," I said. "Right out of the *Crimestoppers Textbook.*"

She exhaled through pursed lips like she was blowing out a candle. "The *Crimestoppers Textbook* was in the *Dick Tracy* comic strip, Mr. Jacovich. And it's sixty years old. Please don't be cute, because I have zero tolerance for cute even on my best days, and this isn't one of them."

"May I sit down?"

She looked up at the fluorescent-light fixture in the ceiling as if that's where divine guidance comes from. "Taxpayers bought that chair and you're a taxpayer, so I don't suppose I can stop you."

"I'll have to remember that the next time I want to spend a weekend in the Lincoln Bedroom." I took one of the chairs.

"Wait a minute, Matusen ought to hear this." She picked up her phone, punched three buttons, and listened long enough for one ring. Then: "Matusen. My office." She put the receiver down and glowered at me.

"You want a cup of tea?"

"No thanks, I'm trying to quit," I said.

Bob Matusen appeared in the doorway behind me. He was in his shirtsleeves, a cinnamon-colored shirt with a yellow-and-red tie pulled away from the undone top button. His .9-mm rested in a holster on his hip; he wore it way around toward the back, like Mike Connors used to do on the old TV show *Tightrope*, before he was *Mannix*. I never figured out how he perfected his fast draw from that position without shooting himself in the ass.

"Mr. Jacovich has solved the Strassky case for us," Mc-Hargue informed him, in a voice like crumpling parchment. "Isn't that swell?"

"Aw, jeez, Milan . . ." he said, not unkindly. He sat down in the chair next to mine, lifted one hand to his shirt pocket where he carried his cigarettes, and then remembered his superior officer didn't smoke and let the hand drop to his lap. That made two of us who wanted a smoke.

McHargue picked up a ballpoint pen and pulled a yellow pad toward her. "We're listening," she said. "In fact, we can hardly wait."

I gave it all to her—the rape of Joyce Hallen by a man with smoker's breath, the possibility of an extra key, Jason Crowell's sexual orientation, the tracks between Terry Yagemann's toes. By the time I'd finished, she'd filled up one page of the yellow foolscap with scribbled notes.

Then she put down the pen, scanned the paper, took off her glasses, and rubbed the bridge of her nose. "This is crap."

"Why?"

"You don't have a shred of proof, that's why."

"I don't mean to sound argumentative, Lieutenant, but proving it isn't my job—it's yours."

"There's not enough here for an arrest, Milan," Bob said.

"No," McHargue agreed, studying her notes. "There isn't.

But I think there might be enough to invite young Mr. Yage-mann down here for a little talk."

I took in a deep breath, then let it out. "That's what I figured," I said on the end of my exhale.

"Detective, why don't you take a run out to Sherman and bring the kid in?" she said to Matusen. "Take somebody with you."

"Right," Bob said, standing up.

"This isn't an arrest," she reminded him. "No storm-trooper stuff, no kicking down doors, all right?"

"What if he doesn't want to come?"

McHargue put her glasses back on, and a smile played at one corner of her mouth. "Oh, I'm sure he will," she said. "If you ask him nicely."

Matrusen nodded and walked out of the office. McHargue sipped at her tea.

I stood up too. "That's it, I guess. No thanks are necessary, Lieutenant."

She flickered an annoyed glance at me. "None are due yet. Not until we get something solid. Then I'll thank you."

I shrugged.

"Now I'll thank you to get the hell out of here. This isn't a social club, and I've got work to do."

I started to say, "Yes, ma'am," but rethought it very quickly. Instead I substituted a "See you around."

I was heading for my office, but on the way I decided to make a stop. I didn't like Agent Richard McAleese a dime's worth, but every once in a while I remember the good-citizenship lectures from my high-school civics class.

The Drug Enforcement Agency headquarters is in Court-house Square on Lakeside Avenue in a building that also houses radio station WMJI, where Lanigan and Malone hold forth each weekday morning. From their studios there's a smashing view of the lake and the new Browns Stadium, but I wasn't expecting any scenic wonders from a federal office.

The more-than-middle-aged woman on guard at the desk seemed irritated that I was interrupting whatever vital government work she was doing. When I told her who I was and asked to see Agent McAleese, her annoyance seemed to double.

"Did you have an appointment?" she wanted to know.

I admitted that I didn't.

"Well, you'll have to make an appointment. You just can't walk in here off the street—"

"Is he in?"

She sniffed. "He's in. But he might be busy."

"Why don't we ask him?" I suggested.

The receptionist withered me with a look better suited for Peeping Toms and pedophiles, got up from her desk, and marched stiffly across the reception room and into an inner office as if "The Stars and Stripes Forever" was playing inside her head, while I wondered why they are called civil servants when they so rarely are.

After about two minutes she reemerged, this time with McAleese in tow. His white shirt was so meticulously starched, he might have taken it from its original wrappings just moments before.

"Well, Mr. Jacovich," he said, but it wasn't what anyone would call a hearty greeting. "I was kind of hoping you'd brought your client in, ready to name some names."

"I have a name for you," I said.

He looked at his watch; it was one of those indestructible jobs you could wear skin-diving or mountain-climbing or jumping out of airplanes. "I can give you a few minutes, that's all."

"Wonderful," I enthused, and followed him into his office. The gatekeeper fluffed at her helmet of sprayed gray hair and actually turned her nose up as I went by.

McAleese worked out of a small cubicle near the rear of the

wren of offices. There was a window, but it didn't have a view of the lake; it looked across Lakeside Avenue at the wall of another building. I gathered he wasn't exactly a senior agent.

"So," he said when we'd both been seated, "you have a name for me."

I repeated what I'd told McHargue and Matusen. When I finished, he remained perfectly still, the way you do when you get to the end of a novel and all the loose ends haven't been raveled up or snipped off.

Then: "That's it?"

"That's it."

"So why are you bringing this to me?"

"Because it all comes together like a jigsaw puzzle. The Yagemann kid is an addict, which means he has access to heroin. And he could have a key to Jason Crowell's apartment. And that could explain the smack in the tank of the john, as well as the phony rape accusation and the suspicion of murder."

"It could also be a cure for cancer, but I doubt it," he said.

"You doubt it?"

"Look, Jacovich, your little theory is just fascinating, but this office doesn't solve murders or rapes."

"My fascinating little theory, it seems to me, is giving you the information you wanted about drugs on the Sherman campus."

He smirked. "We're not interested in busting some junkie," he said. "You think this agency is interested in busting junkies?"

I didn't answer.

"What *do* you think this agency is interested in doing?" he said. He must have been a third-grade teacher in another life.

"Busting balls, apparently."

He crossed his arms across his chest without wrinkling his pristine shirt. "Given your client is a drug dealer, I can see how you'd feel that way."

"It isn't a given at all. I've handed you a lead, Mr. McAleese."

"*Agent* McAleese," he reminded me severely.

"If you don't want to follow it up, that's your business. But I think you've got enough to ease up the pressure on Jason Crowell. Everything points to him being an innocent victim here."

"Federal penitentiaries are full of innocent victims," he said. "Just ask them, Jacovich."

"*Mister* Jacovich," I said. "And you know damn well Jason doesn't belong in a federal penitentiary."

"That's to be determined. All right, then—I'm giving you until nine A.M. the day after tomorrow to have that boy in this office, ready to talk. If I don't see him, I'm coming to get him." He uncrossed his arms and leaned back comfortably in his chair. "If I have to come get him, I'm going to be annoyed." He shook his head with a sad little smile. "You won't like me when I'm annoyed."

I stood up and moved toward the door. "I don't like you *now*," I said.

The gray-haired Cerberus gave me a nasty, triumphant smile as I walked past her on my way out. I was willing to bet she'd go home that evening and lace her cat's Tender Vittles with Tabasco sauce.

I went back to the office and called Reggie Parker at the school; he was out patrolling the halls, apparently, because it took the woman who answered the phone several minutes to find him. I didn't mind being on hold because it was quiet—the school didn't pipe in bad string arrangements of the music from *Cats* for me to listen to while I waited. Be thankful for small favors, I thought.

When Reggie finally came to the phone I told him what I'd found out about Terry Yagemann.

"Terrific news, Milan," he said. "That's a major break-through."

"I thought so, too. But it didn't seem to excite the DEA that much. They've given me thirty-six hours to deliver Jason to them, and they made it pretty clear that he'd better be in a talkative mood."

"Goddamn it!" he said. I heard him breathing heavily for a few seconds. "What about the Cleveland PD?"

"They're not completely convinced, but they sent somebody out to pick up the Yagemann kid for questioning."

"Maybe that'll do it," he said. "Have you told Jerry Locke?"

"Not yet."

"That's okay, I'll call him. Well, is this reason for celebration?"

"Cautious celebration," I said.

"Good. Shall we have dinner? Nighttown, maybe?"

"All right. Or I can come your way," I said. Reggie lived out in Euclid.

"That's okay—I spend all day in this neighborhood. Besides, you've done a lot of driving today—won't it be nice just to walk down the block to dinner?"

"You're right as usual, Reggie. About seven-thirty, okay?"

"I'll meet you at the bar. And we'll charge the dinner off to Jerry Locke."

"Deal," I told him.

CHAPTER TWENTY

I drove back up Cedar Hill to Cleveland Heights with my radio turned to the late-afternoon news on WCPN, mostly because I like to hear the way National Public Radio reporter Sylvia Poggioli says her own name, rolling it around on her tongue like fine Tuscan olive oil.

When I got into my apartment I found the note propped up on the counter in the kitchen where he knew I'd see it.

Mr. Jacovich—I'm meeting Marika for dinner.
I'll be back late. Jason.

Good, I thought, the kid isn't sitting around feeling sorry for himself. He was getting out of the house, out from under the oppressiveness that hovered over him, and trying to do something more or less normal. It had to be tough, under the circumstances, and on my personal score sheet I awarded him ten points for guts.

I hoped he wouldn't blame Marika too much for letting me in on his secret.

He wasn't the only one with a secret, though. Other people had them, too—like a rapist and a heroin dealer and a killer. Maybe they were all the same person.

Truth to tell, it was nice to have the apartment to myself again for a change. I've lived alone a long time, now. My sons—

or more recently, just Stephen—stay with me on alternate Sunday nights, and Connie's sleepovers are, of course, delightful. But they all go home in the morning, leaving me to my own personal space. Now Jason was actually living there, and it felt alien and a little claustrophobic to have another human being actually sharing my home.

Maybe I was turning into the old hermit of the hills, who's happy living in a cave in solitary comfort—but with Jason gone for the evening, I found myself luxuriating in the privacy, humming aloud some retro rock tune in an off-key baritone I'd never allow another soul to hear, secure in the certainty that no one was going to walk in and catch me at it.

I was also glad I didn't have to discuss my meetings with Lieutenant McHargue and Agent McAleese with anyone; they hadn't been tremendously heartening, especially the one at the DEA, and in Jason's current state of mind, only complete exoneration would give him any peace.

Not that the apartment was any messier than usual, but I decided to straighten up a little bit anyway, since I had a few hours to fill.

I try never to refer to it as "killing time," because the literalness of it cuts too close to the bone. Since I hit forty a few years ago, I've begun to realize that once we waste a day or an hour or a moment, we have indeed "killed" it; it's truly gone and won't ever come back. You learn that lesson when you get older, usually to your sorrow.

Jason was neater than most young men his age, I had to give him that. I supposed he was being particularly careful not to be intrusive or cause me extra work, the way people are when they're staying in someone else's home, making sure the bathroom counter was wiped down, the towels folded, and an adequate supply of bathroom tissue was on the roll.

Still, there was plenty to do. I stuffed the morning newspaper into a grocery sack for recycling, transferred the breakfast coffee cups from the sink to the dishwasher, cleaned off the counter, and then went out into the living room to fluff sofa cushions and vacuum a couple of dust bunnies from the corners. My apartment, in a building more than seventy years old, has polished hardwood floors, covered in places with sisal area rugs, and the dust really shows if I don't keep after it.

Maybe I was becoming a little compulsive about housecleaning; I'd been doing a lot of it of late, both at home and at the office—I didn't want to turn into the stereotypical rumpled bachelor slob.

When I was married, Lila had always taken care of those chores since she hadn't worked outside our home. After my divorce, when I set up an office in the front room of this apartment, I kept what I thought of as the "public areas" neat because clients frequently dropped in. Otherwise, though, the place was never really dirty, just—casual. It didn't bother me if a week's worth of newspapers had accumulated in the corner of the den, or a varied collection of sneakers and slippers in front of my chair, because nobody ever saw them anyway.

Now I cared.

They say (that "they" again) that the human body changes all of its cells every seven years. That includes brain cells. I wonder if these changes mean that we change as people, too.

Certainly there are visible differences between an infant and a ten-year-old, between a teenager and a forty-something, and differences in the way they act, the things they do, the activities they enjoy, and the way they think. Do we really ever stop growing, then, or is life a constantly evolving process?

I think it is. That's why I worried about Jason, about what this awful business was going to do to him. Life isn't supposed to be fair, necessarily, but it seemed to me that the gross injustice Jason was going through was going to imprint him considerably, no matter how it turned out.

I hoped it wouldn't make him bitter and cynical. Sour people—people like his father—never seem to have the potential to be very happy.

Finished with my cleaning duties, I got myself a beer and went into the den to check out the Channel 12 News with Vivian Truscott. It was only a week before election day, and as she reported on the last-minute gyrations of our local political candidates I was struck, as I often am, at how very beautiful she is and how much real credibility she brings to her newscasts. Someone else, I thought, who has made a 180-degree change.

During a story about a warehouse fire, the telephone chirred.

"This is McHargue," the abrupt female voice said when I answered.

"Good evening, Lieutenant."

"I'm calling from my car. I'm on my way up Cedar Hill, and I want to stop by and see you."

That couldn't bode well, but for a moment I was simply nonplussed that she'd bothered to ask permission. "Uh . . . sure. I'm at—"

"I know where you live."

"Second floor."

"I know that, too," she said impatiently. "I'll be there in three minutes."

Actually it took her six, but she probably had trouble finding a parking place. The always-busy Russo's Giant Eagle and Baskin-Robbins, as well as two bar/restaurants and a baby-boomer pool hall called Jillian's within a five-iron's reach, pretty well parked the block solid. This was, after all, attitude-adjustment hour, that period between the end of the workday and returning to home and hearth that, in less socially aware and more simple times, used to be known as the cocktail hour.

I was glad I'd given the living room a lick-and-a-promise cleaning. Since Marko Meglich had died, it wasn't often the

Cleveland PD paid me a home visit. And this was Florence McHargue's first.

When I opened the door, she took one step inside and made a fast but thorough inspection through her blue-tinted glasses. A woman always takes in a bachelor's pad with a critical eye: Does he keep the place clean, did he shove his smelly running shoes under the sofa, are there cobwebs in the ceiling corners, are dishes and pots and pans from several ancient dinners making mold cultures in the kitchen sink, and does he have better-than-hopeless taste in furniture, or is it all from discount stores and the Sally Ann?

I think the apartment passed muster. At least she didn't gingerly raise the hem of her skirt as she came in.

"I hope this isn't inconvenient," she said.

"Not at all." I guided her into the living room. I had seen her standing up before, but until now I hadn't realized she was about five foot ten, maybe more, atop her stacked heels. "Make yourself comfortable, Lieutenant. Can I get you something to drink?"

"This isn't exactly a social call."

"Are you going to arrest me, then?"

She chuckled. "When I'm going to make a collar, I don't usually ask whether it's convenient."

"Are you still on duty?"

"No, I'm off the clock. Even cops have to rest sometime. I'm on my way home—I live just up the street, on Meadowbrook."

"We're neighbors, then."

"Kind of."

"Then let me be neighborly and get you something."

She considered carefully. Florence McHargue was a woman who considered *everything* carefully. "What are you having?"

"I'm a beer drinker."

"That'll be fine, then. Don't bother with a glass."

Beer, no glass. Maybe she wasn't such a bad sort after all. I got two more Stroh's from the refrigerator and set one in front of her on the coffee table, then sat down on a chair facing the sofa.

"Since you're not going to read me my rights, I assume you have something to tell me."

"To tell you and ask you. We'll start with the asking, okay?"

Not exactly a surprise. She was, after all, a cop.

"What transpired between you and Terry Yagemann this afternoon? Give it to me as verbatim as possible."

"As I told you earlier, it had been raining pretty hard, and he'd just peeled himself out of soaking-wet clothes, so he was barefoot and wearing a bathrobe. I noticed there were needle tracks between his toes. I couldn't arrest him right there—as you've reminded me in the past, I don't carry a badge anymore. But I told him I'd contact you and that your department would probably be getting in touch with him regarding the Strassky business. The last thing I know, he was in a panic and pushing buttons on the phone, calling Daddy."

She heaved a weary and irritated sigh. "Since I'm in your home and drinking your beer, Mr. Jacovich, I hesitate to point out that was as dumb as a box of rocks on your part."

"Why?"

"Because you spooked him good. Young Master Yagemann has disappeared. Flown the coop."

"Just because he's not at his apartment? That's not unusual, he's out a lot. I've been surveilling him for the last few days and it was a long time before he showed up. He'll be around."

"No he won't. He's run out. Gone bye-bye. How can I make it clear to you? His apartment has been cleared out—no computer, no TV, no clothes. And no drugs," she said pointedly, taking a long swallow of her Stroh's. She drank beer like it was her second career.

"His car?"

"Not in his assigned slot."

"Did anyone see him leave?"

She shook her head. "The building manager works off-site at a regular job, Matusen said. He asked the other people in the building, but they're all students and were in class all day. So Yagemann got away clean."

"He's only nineteen years old, Lieutenant. Where's he going to run to? His parents live in Cincinnati—on Mt. Adams, which probably means they have some money. His father works at one of the TV stations there and his mother is with P and G, if that's any help."

"If you were running away, would you go to the first place anyone would look for you?"

"If I were a kid like that, I'd head for some sort of safe harbor. Like home."

"It'll be checked, don't worry. But my gut tells me Yagemann is just a poor, innocent little junkie. Probably it was Crowell who got him hooked in the first place."

"Jason Crowell is innocent," I assured her. "He's just a nice kid who for some reason has gotten himself in the middle of a frame."

"The pen down at Mahsfield is just full of nice innocent kids," she observed dryly. "Just ask them."

"Maybe. But I've gotten to know Jason pretty well, and I doubt if he's capable of anything like rape or murder or dealing drugs." I debated whether or not to give her the next piece of information. "He's staying here with me for a while."

"You think I didn't know he's been living here?" She lowered her head at me like a bull preparing a charge. "Don't underestimate me."

"I don't think I'd ever do that."

"Best not." She shifted her weight around, leaning forward, elbows on her thighs. "Don't get it into your head that this is any kind of a vendetta. I don't have a woody for the Crowell kid, not personally. I don't even have one for you. I've just got my job to do and you've got yours. They just happen to put us on different sides."

She put the nearly empty beer bottle down on the table. "Just make sure yours doesn't get in the way of mine, because I'm the one with the gold tin."

Inside her purse her cell phone twittered. She pulled it out, frowning, and looked at the readout. "A Lorain County number. Probably Matusen." She lifted an expectant eyebrow.

"Want some privacy? You can use the den. Or I can go in there."

She considered it for a moment. "No, I'll go. Why should you have to. It's your apartment."

She pushed herself up off the sofa and I showed her into the den, uncomfortably aware that I hadn't cleaned in there as well as I had in the living room. I was hungry, so I repaired to the kitchen and wolfed down a handful of Ritz crackers to hold me over until it was time to meet Reggie for dinner. Then I went back out to wait for McHargue. Through the closed door to the den I could hear her voice, low and urgent.

Terry Yagemann's disappearance troubled me. I could understand a kid getting scared and having the impulse to book, but surely if he'd talked to his father he'd have gotten better advice than that. And although I didn't like him much to begin with, and even less so now that I thought he was a rapist and possibly a killer, I couldn't help feeling a little worried for him.

He was only nineteen.

Not that his age took him off the hook for anything. I firmly believe that by the time kids are in preschool they have a pretty good idea of right and wrong, and a fairly informed sense of responsibility. Stealing from your mom's purse is wrong, shooting heroin is wrong, rape is wrong, and murder is most definitely wrong—and if Terry was guilty of any of them, it was his responsibility and his alone, and not the fault of his parents, teachers, or even his environment.

I'm sorry if somebody put him on the potty wrong when he was two, but it doesn't excuse antisocial or criminal behavior.

We're all capable of making choices.

I guess that's what troubles me about the way the world is going. Everyone has descended into a state of victimhood, where everything wrong is someone else's fault and no one has to accept responsibility. And I don't think it works that way. Call me intolerant, old-fashioned, and politically incorrect.

Go ahead, a lot of people do.

Still, only nineteen . . .

I heard Florence McHargue in the den, her voice rising higher in pitch and volume. After a moment she came back out, folding up her cell phone, frowning deeply. Her glasses were off, and she rubbed the bridge of her nose, as seemed to be one of her habits. Her jaw was set at a grim angle, and something in the rigid way she held her head told me she was very angry.

I hoped the anger wasn't directed at me.

She stopped in the middle of the room and looked at me.

"Well, shit!" she said.

I didn't say anything, pretty sure I wasn't going to like the next part.

I didn't.

"That was Matusen. The Sheriff's Department found the Yagemann kid. In a culvert about five miles outside of Sherman. With the back of his head shot off." She put the phone back in her purse. "Execution style."

I just nodded dumbly. She kept looking at me for a long time, and then finally turned away. I was grateful she wasn't going to push it. I felt terrible enough already.

Execution style. He must have been so scared. . . .

"Well," she said, "that pretty much knocks him out of the

sweepstakes for killer and rapist, wouldn't you agree?"

"Not necessarily," I said lamely.

"Oh, come on, use your head! Chances are, whoever did the rape and did Dorothy Strassky took out Yagemann, too." She looked around the room, a brownish red fingernail thoughtfully between her teeth. "Where *is* your roomie tonight, anyway?"

"He's having dinner with a friend. There was a note." I went into the kitchen and got it, brought it back, and gave it to her.

"What time did he leave?"

"I don't know, I wasn't here—that's why he left the note. I've been here about an hour, though." I suddenly felt large and ungainly standing in the middle of my own living room. "You're not thinking Jason killed Yagemann, too?"

"I'm not, huh?"

"Where did he get the gun?"

"Don't be a child, Mr. Jacovich. I'll bet I could purchase any kind of weapon I wanted, unregistered and untraceable, within six blocks of here." Her mouth twisted into a bitter grimace. "Within six blocks of anywhere."

I got myself a cigarette. She frowned and crinkled up her nose when I lit it; I knew she didn't approve of smoking.

The hell with her. It was my house. And I needed a cigarette very badly right then, almost as much as I needed another drink.

"It's not rocket science," she said. "Figure it out. Jason Crowell rapes a woman—for whatever reason, given his sexual preference, and I can think of a few. And when he finds out Dorothy Strassky has got wind of it and might be on to him, he follows her home and takes her out with a log."

"Rape is difficult to prove," I said, "more difficult to convict, because it's all 'he said,' 'she said' anyway. Pretty drastic to kill someone over, don't you think?"

"Not so much because of the rape. He's dealing heroin."

I started to say something, but she held up a warning hand.

"He doesn't want anyone poking around in his private life over the rape thing and discovering the horse, too. He's supplying his roommate, or ex-roommate, which would be natural. And then you come along and make Yagemann as a junkie. Yagemann calls Jason in a panic, and Jason tells him to clear out of his apartment before we can get to him, and maybe goes to help him move, leaving you a bullshit note that he's gone out to dinner.

"Now, he sure as hell doesn't want Yagemann talking to us or the DEA, does he? So instead of helping him move, he goes for another one of his little drives in the country and blows off the back of his head and drops him in a culvert out in Lorain County."

I shook my head. "That didn't happen. You don't know Jason Crowell like I do, Lieutenant. He's a sweet, sensitive kid who's scared to death at what he's suddenly found himself caught up in."

"That sweet, sensitive kid doesn't want to go down for dealing. That's a federal rap. Besides," she mused, "he must be making some pretty good bucks. Sure as hell enough money to kill for."

"Jason didn't have any money," I explained. "He was trying to get a part-time job to make up for Terry's half of the rent."

McHargue put a fist on her hip. "Trying?"

"It was pretty unlikely anyone in Sherman was going to hire him after those flyers hit the streets. It was worrying him plenty, he told me."

"And you believed him flat-out?"

"I had to," I said. "He's my client."

"You're a trusting soul, Mr. Jacovich." She shook her head with what might have been pity. "You've been around long enough to know that sometimes the worst killers have baby-faces and nice table manners. They don't all look pyschotic like Charles Manson. The way it seems to me, Jason Crowell has already killed two people, and one of them was in my patch. The Lorain County guys are looking for him right now, and I've got an APB out on him already." She waved the cell phone at me; then she sighed. "I told the dispatcher he's to be considered armed and dangerous."

The skin on my back crawled. "That means they might shoot him on sight."

"They'll make every effort not to," she said, but it didn't sound very reassuring.

"Lieutenant, you're making a big mistake here."

"You were the one who made the mistake, a big one, when you spooked Terry Yagemann into running—and he's probably dead now because of it. And you made another mistake when you stuck your nose into an open murder case when I specifically warned you not to."

I started to speak but she shut me up in a hurry. "Don't tell me about your responsibility to your client, because it doesn't mean jack. Police business comes first, and you were just too stubborn—or stupid—to let go of it." She poured the remainder of her beer down her throat almost angrily, then gasped. "The DEA isn't the only one gonna be taking a long, hard look at your license."

My license was the least of my concerns right then. Instead I was obsessing over Terry Yagemann, dead in a dark and lonely place. I was thinking about Jason, a heartbeat away from being shot dead in the street. I was considering my own culpability, and that gnawed at my vitals like a hungry and persistent rat.

"I'm putting a stakeout in front of the Crowell home in case Jason decides to go there," McHargue said. "And there'll be a shadow outside here, too, as soon as I can get one."

I shrugged, and she put the beer bottle down on the table, her cell phone back in her purse, and kind of hiked her skirt up at the waist. "And one other thing," she said.

"That would be what?"

"Keep Jerry Locke away from me. He's not only a smart-ass lawyer with a bag of tricks like the Great Houdini, but he's a weasel, too. I don't like weasels."

She started for the door.

"If I hear from Jason, I'll contact you right away," I assured her.

"That would be a *very* good way to stay in business," she said.

"Just being a good citizen."

"Yeah, right. They're gearing up down at city hall to present you with a plaque." She stepped out into the hallway. "Thanks for the beer," she said, and then the door snicked shut behind her.

Agendas again, I thought. Her agenda was Dorothy Strassky's murder, the DEA's was heroin suppliers, Women Warriors' was date rape, and for the honchos at Sherman College it was keeping their skirts pristine for the endowments.

Nobody ever looks at the big picture.

I took the two empties out into the kitchen and put them into the blue plastic recycling bag. Florence McHargue was a tough one to figure out. Conciliatory one moment, combative the next, so I couldn't be sure whether it was my ally or my enemy occupying the homicide throne on Payne Avenue. I wanted her to be on my side, but the deck was stacked against it.

Friend or foe, she was in a righteous rage at me. And with good reason.

I gave a brief thought to what she'd said about Jeremiah Locke. He must have given her a hell of a time. I could believe it; there was something irritating about him, with his impeccable clothes and his racquetball appointments. But I had the idea he was a pretty good lawyer, and that's what Jason needed right now, more than ever.

From the freezer I took the vodka bottle Connie had so

recently depleted, poured myself a straight shot, and belted it down. The cold was a shock to my stomach and gave me an agonizing pain behind the right eye. I pressed my tongue to the roof of my mouth to warm it—an old remedy of my mother's—and shook my head, trying to shake away the sorrow and guilt.

It didn't work.

I considered drinking another shot, but I needed a clear head, and finally put the bottle back.

With more than a little regret.

Jason Crowell, wanted fugitive. Armed and dangerous. Likely to be shot on sight. Because of me.

Indirectly—but because of me.

Like Terry Yagemann being dead because of me.

I'd had it all figured out. Terry was the phantom rapist and had used Jason's name for some reason, and I went after him like a hound from hell to prove it. If I hadn't, I never would have seen those needle tracks between his toes. If I hadn't braced him about them, chances were pretty good that he'd still be in his little apartment in Sherman, partying and drinking beer and shooting up and trying not to flunk out of another college.

What gave me I wondered, the right to interfere in other people's lives?

My chosen profession, I supposed. Granted, it wasn't my fault Terry had gotten himself a heroin jones, but if I'd been a dentist or a chef or a landscape gardener, he might not have died.

It was because of me that Marko Meglich was dead, too, and I lived with that agony every waking moment. Sometimes when I was reading a book or watching a ball game, his rugged Slavic features—with the Tom Selleck–type mustache he'd affected for the past ten years in the mistaken belief that it made him more attractive to women—would appear in my consciousness unbidden to smile at me or chide me.

In the bad times, like the one I was experiencing now, I saw him as he died in my arms.

I suppose we all affect each other's lives just by the simple process of living, and in ways we don't even realize. I've hurt some people, I know, and I've made some happier or better off, and in a few instances, I caused their deaths. Mostly the dead ones were bad people, but not all of them.

Not Marko.

And it ate away at me like a cancer.

Then again, I've saved a couple of lives in my day, and put a few more to rights, and this time, if I played it smart, Jason Crowell might not spend the next seventy years in the penitentiary for things he didn't do.

I hoped he hadn't done them. Hoped to God.

Florence McHargue had been spot-on; I had screwed up with Terry Yagemann, and royally. Now it was my job—my responsibility—to make things as right as I could. And I needed to do it fast.

I had to get to Jason before the police did.

I thought for a while about where I might find him, and then all of a sudden it hit me. Maybe it was the unaccustomed vodka that had blessed me with a brief moment of perfect clarity, but I knew—all of it, or most of it, anyway. With Terry Yagemann dead, I knew who had raped Joyce Hallen, and I knew who had planted the smack in Jason's toilet tank and why.

And though it gave me a sick, sad feeling, deep down inside my viscera where my often-exaggerated sense of the moral rightness and wrongness of things always lives just one klick from the surface, I knew who had killed Dorothy Strassky and Terry Yagemann.

I figured that two of us looking for Jason could cover more ground than one, so I went into the den and dialed Reggie

Parker's home number. All I got was his voice mail. He'd probably left the house already and was on his way to meet me at Nighttown, and I didn't have the number of his car phone—if indeed he had one.

I put down the receiver and headed for the guest closet just inside the front door.

I own two registered handguns. One I always keep in the top right-hand drawer of my desk in the office. It's a .357 Magnum, the so-called "Dirty Harry" weapon. I call it my "Justin"—"just in case."

The other was on the top shelf of the guest closet. It's a .38 police special, nestled in a custom-made shoulder harness. It doesn't have the Magnum's stopping power, but it's easier to carry around. I hauled it down, then went to the bedroom and took a box of ammo from the bottom drawer. I keep weapon and cartidges separate because my sons visit frequently, and even though I've trained them both in the proper handling of firearms, Stephen is at a curious age.

I loaded up in the living room and strapped the harness around my torso, aware of the revolver's heft and of the butt digging uncomfortably into my rib cage. With Florence McHargue after my scalp, I wasn't sure if this was the right time to be carrying concealed. But the feel of it gave me a certain sense of security.

Then I threw on a jacket and went downstairs. It was still raining, but not as hard as earlier in the day. Now it was more like a tease of rain, a heavy mist, cold and miserable, that peppered my face.

I headed toward my assigned parking space. Normally I'd walk the block and a half to Nighttown, but I wasn't planning on staying for dinner and didn't want to have to come back for my car.

As I bent down to put the key in the lock, something hard and cold poked into the back of my neck.

I didn't have to be a firearms expert to figure out what it was; the business end of a pistol has its own special, private feel.

The skin along my spine rippled. I straightened up very slowly so as not to make the trigger finger attached to that gun nervous. Then I stayed very still.

"Be easy," someone breathed in my ear. A hand patted me down, extracting the .38 from its nesting place. "Hey, now—you could hurt somebody with this. . . ."

"That's the idea," I said.

"Jus' open the door."

It was an unfamiliar voice, male, and seemed to have an African American lilt to it. An unfair stereotype, perhaps, because neither Reggie Parker nor Jeremiah Locke sounded that way, but that's how I perceived it. The metallic pressure at the base of my skull made it unwise for me to turn around and find out for sure.

I twisted the key in the lock and swung the door open slowly. No quick moves; a bullet from that angle would have taken off the top of my head.

"Unlock the back."

I pushed the button on the inside handle and heard the click as the three other doors unlocked. Then he took the gun from my neck and I sensed him moving a few feet away from me. "Get in," he ordered. "Slow. Easy."

I did. Slow. Easy. He got into the back seat right behind me and put the gun muzzle back under my ear. "Well, start the car, foo'."

I fired up the engine. A glance in the rearview mirror was only partly revealing; his face was directly behind my head so I couldn't see much of him in the dark. I saw enough to tell that he was dark-skinned and wearing a Cleveland Indians baseball cap with the bill pulled low over his eyes. I didn't recognize him, but I had the feeling this wasn't the first time I'd seen him.

"Get moving," he said.

I pulled out onto Fairmount Boulevard, and he directed me to the sprawling public parking lot right behind Nighttown. Orange-hued arc lights had been installed back there some years ago, but it was still pretty dark.

"Park it," he said.

I kept the car rolling slowly, looking around for some sort of assistance, but there was none forthcoming.

"Park it, I tol' you!"

"I'm looking for a meter with time left on it," I said.

The gun muzzle poked, hard. "Motherfucker, you wan' me to cap you right here?"

Some people can't take a joke.

I pulled into a vacant space, leaving the motor running.

"Cut the lights," he said.

I did, becoming aware that another set of headlights was following close behind us, eventually pulling into the space next to us. A savior? I wondered. Or my assailant's backup?

"Now what?" I said.

By way of answer, something very hard hit me behind the right ear, and my body slmamed forward, my face striking the steering wheel.

I didn't see stars.

I didn't see anything.

CHAPTER TWENTY-ONE

I was back in the womb again, floating snugly in forgiving darkness and a warm sea of amniotic fluid, rocking gentle and free with the steady motion of my mother's body as she went about her daily chores. No moment existed other than this one, because there hadn't been any other moments, and nothing was expected or required of me but to ride along, to wait patiently, just to *be*.

And then the birth trauma began with a heave and a sigh, and the sheer bulk of the pain in my head was being forced into a space far too small for it. I took the first desperate, gasping breath, and opened my eyes to blurred and indistinct light.

I was bitterly disappointed to discover that the swaying movement was not that of my mother as she strolled the Slovenian shops and bakeries on St. Clair Avenue, but of a car being driven at high speed on a smooth road. I was lying face-down on the floor between the front and back seats; the car might have been my own, but I couldn't tell. I've never been in the backseat of my car on the floor before, and so had no basis for comparison.

I did know that my hands were securely fastened behind my back with what felt like duct tape, and that my ankles were taped together, too, cutting off the circulation in my feet. When I tried to move, jolts of pain rocketed through me from the crown of my head to the back of my eyes. Inside my skull bells rang like the ones at St. Vitus Church on Easter morning announcing that Christ has risen. My nose hurt from where it had banged the steering wheel, and I could feel where blood had trickled down from behind my ear into my collar, almost dried now and feeling tacky. There seemed to be a mushy cantaloupe where my right ear used to be.

All things considered, it just seemed easier to lie there quietly and drift.

At one point I turned my head slightly; about six inches from my nose was the crumpled wrapper from a Reese's Peanut Butter Cup. I remembered eating the candy while waiting for Terry Yagemann, and throwing the wrapper into the back onto the floor. It was my car, all right.

The radio was playing loudly—rap, no less—and the *BOOM-CHAKA-BOOM-CHAKA-BOOM* coming from the rear speakers was getting on my nerves. Whoever had abducted me in my own car had had the audacity to change the radio station!

We must be on a freeway, I thought, because the car had neither stopped nor slowed for about ten minutes. At least it *seemed* like ten minutes. Groggy and disoriented, I had little sense of time.

Rabbitlike, I wiggled my nose. It hurt, but it didn't seem to be broken. At least there was *something* to be thankful for.

Assuming, of course, that I would even survive after we reached our destination, and that seemed rather iffy under the circumstances.

After a time I began thinking of how I could get myself loose. My wrists and ankles were taped very tightly, and any struggling or straining just made things worse. And as big as I am, practically wedged between the front and back seats, I had very little wiggle room.

So I just stayed where I was, drifting in and out of consciousness, and wondering during the waking moments where

I was going and hoping I wasn't injured too badly.

"Look back there," came a now familiar voice from the front seat, "an' see how he doin'."

Someone shifted in the front passenger seat, and I held very still. Not that I had much choice.

"Still out," a new voice said. The way he pronounced "out," as if the word had two *o*'s, suggested that the speaker had grown up in rural West Virginia.

"Hope I didn't conk him *too* bad."

"He looks like he got a hard head." The second speaker wheezed adenoidally at his own joke; evidently, he was easily amused.

Good, I thought, I had them fooled. A fat lot of good it was going to do me, though.

The car slowed and then stopped for a moment, and I figured we had exited the freeway and were at the bottom of an off-ramp. I rolled slightly with a left turn, and then we were moving along in another direction, not as fast as before. In about ten more minutes it became stop-and-go, with more turns. Finally the ride ended and the motor was shut off.

I would have been very surprised to discover that I was not in Sherman, Ohio.

I heard both front doors open, then shut hard. The back door swung open and I felt cold air on my head before rough hands were laid upon me, dragging me out and setting me unsteadily on my feet. I still couldn't see my companions because it was pitch-black and they were a little behind and on either side of me, each holding an elbow.

When I was more or less upright, a pistol was shoved hard under my chin, pushing my head back and starting up the Angelus inside my skull again.

"Reeeal quiet," the African American voice said, "or you lose your lower jaw."

We seemed to be in a dark alley behind a house. Another

car turned into the mouth of the alley, its headlights blinding me. I was guided through a door and down a set of wooden stairs into a basement. With my bound ankles restricting my movements to baby steps, it was not a pleasant trip, and if my captors hadn't been holding on to me tight, I would surely have tumbled down the steps.

Inside, a lone forty-watt bulb hung suspended from a ceiling on a swaying cord, the moving shadows in its yellowish light making me dizzy. The basement room was rectangular. Against one wall were a washer, a dryer, and double sink, and in the corner, a hot-water heater. At the other end of the room was the furnace, an old-fashioned gas boiler type. Three piano-wire clotheslines stretched nearly from one end of the room to the other.

Another set of wooden stairs led up to the rest of the house, and a door at the far end probably opened onto what used to be a coal storage bin before the heat source had been converted to gas and steam. Next to the door was a large Igloo cooler, the kind you'd take on a picnic, and several empty blue-and-white plastic milk crates. Two heavy wooden columns, equidistant from the walls, seemed to be holding the house up above our heads.

A canvas cot hugged the back wall, and it was there I was tossed like a sack of garbage. My spine hit the cinderblock wall of the basement as I landed, exacerbating the pain inside my head and creating a whole set of new ones in my back.

I looked up at the two men standing over me, one white and one black, and after a moment, recognition kicked in. I had seen them before, sitting outside the house where Jason Crowell had lived—maybe this house?—talking to Derrick Coombes.

The white one had a bad complexion and lank brown hair cut very short on the sides, as if someone had put a bowl over his head and electric-shaved everything that showed. He wore a baseball cap with the brim toward the rear, and through the snap opening at his forehead, spiky wisps of hair stuck out almost obscenely.

If I ever become emperor, woe betide those who wear their baseball caps backward—unless they happen to be catchers.

The kid had cheap, pewter-colored rings on almost every finger, and his stubby, bitten-down fingernails had been painted with a dull black polish. He had three earrings in each lobe, and a couple more through the cartilage on the curve atop his right ear. A thin gold hoop was laced through his right eyebrow. He must have had a pretty high threshold for pain.

His eyes were a little glazed, and he breathed mostly through his mouth. It was too dim in there to see whether or not his pupils were dilated, but it was my considered opinion that he was as high as the Dow Jones on a record bullish day. A blue Saturday night special was tucked in the pocket of baggy khakis, worn low on his hips with his striped boxer shorts extending a good three inches above the waistband—a redneck white kid from a small Ohio town in inner-city hip-hop drag.

Not exactly a rocket scientist, I thought. Putting a cheap pistol in your pants pocket is a splendid way to chance blowing off some vital equipment.

His companion, though he moved with the rubber-jointed ease of a born rapper, had quick, intelligent eyes and a more serious demeanor. The black-and-red nylon Starter jacket he was wearing had a cursive *Tyrone* stitched on the breast. I guess no one had told him that when you're pulling off a kidnapping, it's best not to wear your name on the outside of your clothes.

My own .38 police special was in his hand, pointed at me even though I was almost immobile from the duct-tape bindings. He was taking no chances.

"This is dumb, gentlemen," I managed to say. "You're just

getting yourself into deeper, hotter water." My thickened tongue slurred the words, and I sounded as though I'd had too much to drink. I wondered if I had a concussion. It wouldn't be the first time, and worry flickered across my mind. One can only take so many shots to the head before the damage becomes permanent.

"Just let me go, and I'll make sure the police know about your cooperation. Don't make it worse on yourselves."

"You jus' worry about *you*," Tyrone said.

"I am. That's why I'm trying to talk sense into you."

The arm with my .38 at the end of it straightened. "I show you sense, man."

I sighed, deciding to remain quiet for a moment. But I knew if I was ever going to get out of here, I'd have to talk my way out. The duct tape digging into my wrists and ankles made physical heroics an improbability.

The upstairs door opened, and a woman in a floral-patterned housedress and an apron descended the rickety stairs, looking as though she'd just come from the Betty Crocker Bake-Off. About fifty, she was plump and sour-faced, the kind of woman who angrily chases the neighborhood kids off her lawn. She seemed familiar, and I had to think for a moment before I recalled where I'd seen her: She was the one in the cloth coat at Dorothy Strassky's funeral.

"Mrs. Coombes, is it?" I said, hazarding a guess.

She looked at me dispassionately as if I were a package the UPS driver had delivered to her home in error. Then she turned to Tyrone.

"I don't like it—bringing him into the house like this."

"It only be for a little while," Tyrone said.

"Well, you see that it is. Whatever you boys are going to do, I don't want you doing here."

That confirmed my suspicion; I was indeed in the basement of the Coombes house, the one where Jason Crowell had lived, the one where they'd found the heroin in his toilet tank. It was coming together in my mind now, and it would have been nice if I hadn't been trussed hand-and-foot so I could do something about it.

"Mrs. Coombes," I said, "you seem like a sensible woman"— which wasn't true at all. "Can't you explain to these guys that they're just getting in deeper by doing this?"

She stared at me and blinked placidly like a ruminant.

"Don't you get yourself any more involved in this than you already are."

She finally chose to regard me as a living, sentient human being, and pointed a thick, blunt-nailed finger at me. "You don't tell *me*!" she said. "It's your own fault you're here, not mine. If you'd minded your own beeswax, this never would've happened."

I shrugged as best I could; after all, I make my living *not* minding my own beeswax. Nonetheless, she had a point.

"I can't let you threaten my boy. He done some wrong things, I admit. But he's all I got, and I can't let you take him away from me." She pronounced it "cain't."

"He's a good boy," she went on. "He gives me money. He takes keer of his mom just fine."

"Does it bother you that to get the money he kills people?"

She reacted as if I'd slapped her. Apparently that was one of her little baby boy's peccadillos she didn't want to confront. Then she took one threatening step toward me, her arm raised as if to clout me with the back of her hand.

But she must have changed her mind, because she lowered her arm. "You just shut up now. Hear me?"

She turned to Tyrone. "He'll be down in a minute," she said, and there seemed little question as to who she meant by "he." She pivoted on her heel and stalked back up the stairs, wiping her hands, Pilatelike, on her apron.

Tyrone followed her progress with his eyes, whistling tonelessly through his teeth. Because of the pronounced space between my own two front teeth, I've never been able to get the hang of that; then again, my dental deformity allows me to smile while simultaneously spitting in someone's eye.

"Loyal, my man," Tyrone said to the white kid, "whyn't you break out a coupla brews for us while we waitin'?"

Loyal. Some monicker, I thought, as I watched the kid's slack mouth working—a redneck name I'm certain his mother hadn't known was right out of Molière. It suited him, though, because he bobbed his head in assent and almost leaped to follow instructions, going to the Igloo cooler and extracting two large dripping cans of malt liquor. Loyal was a good little soldier in this mini-army of pushers and punks.

Tyrone accepted his can with the noblessse oblige of a fifteenth-century doge, opening it with a hiss. He took a long draught and wiped his mouth with the back of his hand.

"Tyrone, you look like a smart guy," I said.

"Smarter'n you," he agreed amiably. "I'm the one sittin' here with your piece, drinkin' a brew, an' you the one all taped up."

"Listen to reason. You're going to be in deep shit if you don't cut me loose."

"There *ain'* no deeper shit than what you in, man."

"Spending the rest of your life in the joint while some lawyer spends your money appealing a murder conviction comes close."

"Cain' you see how scared I am?" Tyrone was hanging tough.

I tried to sit up straighter but the effort made my head hurt, the pain coming in fast, rolling waves. "How many people are you going to kill before this is over?"

"I ain' killed nobody," he said. "Yet. But that c'd change anytime now, you keep runnin' you mouth. You know what I'm sayin'?" He showed me my own weapon as if to remind me who was currently running the show.

I looked over at Loyal. He was deeply engrossed in drinking

his malt liquor, as if he were taking a math test, his eyes unfocused and his brow furrowed, not really with us. Inside his head I believe he was watching an old rerun of *The Dukes of Hazzard*.

Tyrone snickered. "You gonna try an' make ol' Loyal listen to reason?"

"That would make him smarter than you, then, Tyrone. And I don't think that's the case."

Loyal came out of his reverie. "Hey, shut up, man!" he said. I think Luke and Bo had broken for a commercial.

"He's right," Tyrone said. "You sh'd to save your breath. You ain' got that many of 'em left."

I leaned back against the cold wall, feeling the cold cinderblock through my jacket. My ear was throbbing. Trying not to let them catch me at it, I wriggled my fingers and toes with a kind of desperation to get the blood moving in them again. They were beginning to prickle. A small child might have said they were going to sleep.

But the painful little needlepoints let me know that I was at least still alive—and while I was still able, I was trying to fit all the puzzle-pieces together in my head. Trying to figure an out-clause.

I was worried about Jason Crowell, too. Worried that the Cleveland police would find him and that some urban John Wayne with a badge and an itchy trigger finger would get carried away. Worried that I wouldn't live long enough to prevent that.

Then the upstairs door opened and Derrick Coombes came down the steps, wearing the top hat again and looking ready to boom out "Merry Christmas, Uncle Scrooge!"

Except he wasn't very merry. Maybe it was the .9-mm Glock automatic that he wore stuck in the waistband of his jeans.

He came over to the cot and stood looking down on me without saying anything, a hard-guy sneer on his face. A cigarette bobbed limply from the corner of his mouth; I'm sure he thought it made him look tough. But the movie legends of the past who held the patent on that one—Raft and Cagney and Bogart—never wore Victorian toppers with neckties for hatbands, always cut their hair, and didn't have acne. It sort of ruined the effect.

For almost a full minute he didn't speak. Then he said, "You nosy fuck!" and, not as circumspect as his mother, backhanded me across the face, snapping my head back against the wall. The impact didn't do much for my headache, and the effort knocked his top hat somewhat askew; he made no effort to straighten it. Maybe he didn't notice.

The coppery taste of blood filled one side of my mouth. I didn't get rid of it, but swallowed instead; some last vestige of my mother's stern upbringing kept me from spitting it onto Mrs. Coombes' floor.

"Hey, man," Tyrone protested mildly; I think he had even winced when the blow landed.

Loyal, on the other hand, seemed to enjoy watching me get slapped, because he was grinning sappily. "What're we gonna do with him, Derrick?"

"We're gonna wait," Derrick intoned. He grabbed a milk crate from against the wall and turned it on end with great ceremony, like a climber laying claim to the summit of Everest. Then he plunked his skinny butt down on it and got comfortable, as if he was planning on staying there for a while. Taking a fresh Camel from a pack in his shirt pocket, he lit it from the glowing end of the one he'd been smoking, then flipped the old butt carelessly into the sink. He had all the pale-carbon-copy cheap hood moves down to an art.

"Get me a malt, Loyal," he ordered.

It all seemed so casual, so leisurely paced. They were obviously going to kill me—I don't think Derrick would have had the guts to hit me if he thought I'd ever again get my hands loose—but I couldn't figure out what they were waiting for.

Not the courage to do it; they'd killed before. They were probably getting fairly adept at it.

Then I reasoned they must be waiting for some*one*. The Man. The guy who was running the show. It was only logical. Derrick and his pals had neither the smarts nor the experience to orchestrate a sophisticated drug operation. Mozart had written symphonies long before he was Derrick's age, and Billy the Kid had killed twenty-one men, but I doubted Derrick was in their league, prodigywise.

No question in my mind, they were hanging around until their head man showed up with marching orders. Their drug supplier, the one who was importing heroin from somewhere else and giving it to muscle-brained, testosterone-poisoned punks like Derrick to sell on the street. The one Special Agent Richard J. McAleese couldn't wait to get his hands on.

"You're a pretty tough guy, Derrick, right?" I said. "Taking a swing at me while I'm taped up. Took a lot of guts."

He narrowed his little pig-eyes at me. "How'd you like to see me do it again?"

"Oh, I know you're bad, Derrick. Brave. Like when you took that little girl out in your car and raped her."

One corner of his mouth twitched in an incipient smile. "Shouldn't a done that," he said. "She was a lousy fuck."

"How could she be anything else, with you? She was probably trying too hard not to puke."

The smile died aborning. "Go ahead," he said. "The more shit you talk, the slower you're gonna die."

Dying slowly wasn't something I was anxious to experience. But in this case it beat the hell out of dying quickly, because as long as I was breathing, I had a shot.

I decided to keep talking.

"Of course you didn't tell her your real name," I went on.

"Cowards never do. So you used the first name that popped into your head—your mother's upstairs tenant. Because you're too fucking stupid to make one up."

He flushed darkly as my arrow hit home.

"You were right about her, though, Derrick. You figured she'd be too ashamed to go to the cops and tell them. But she's a tough little girl—tougher than you thought. She wasn't going to just let it go without doing something about it. So she went and told Women Warriors instead, and all of a sudden it wasn't such a secret anymore. It was all over campus, all over town— only with somebody else's name on it."

A nascent idea flickered behind his mean little eyes, and he stood up and walked toward me, easily but with great purpose, one hand holding his cigarette and the other, the malt can. For a moment I thought he was going to hit me again.

"All that talkin' you're doin'," he said. "You must be getting thirsty. Have a brew." He swigged a big mouthful of the malt liquor and spit it into my face.

I wished he'd have hit me instead; that would have just hurt. Instead I felt dirty. Degraded. No wonder they made such a big deal a few years ago when a major-league ballplayer had deliberately spit on an umpire.

From where he'd been sitting on the steps, Loyal laughed. He was easily amused.

Tyrone didn't seem to think it was funny, though. His expression was one of disapproval, and he started to say something, then merely shook his head.

I could feel the loathsome mixture of alcohol and saliva drying on my face. "That was pretty impressive, Derrick," I said through tightly clenched teeth. "You're showing more guts all the time—spitting in the face of a man who's all trussed up. Probably took more nerve than to beat a woman to death with a log."

He glared at me for a while, then wiped his mouth with the back of his hand and went back to his milk crate. "Keep flappin' your mouth," he said over his shoulder.

"Gotta learn to control those gonads a little more," I told him, and from his puzzled expression I could tell Derrick didn't have the slightest idea of what gonads were. "Raping Joyce Hallen was a dumb thing to do. Especially since you have so much else you don't want getting spread around."

He stuck the cigarette back between his nearly invisible lips.

"Dorothy Strassky did some investigating of her own and found out that Jason Crowell wasn't the rapist. Isn't that right? Maybe she found out who was, I don't know. Either way, you couldn't afford to have her come sniffing around trying to find out the truth. Not only put you in jail for rape, but it would have put quite a crimp in your lucrative little drug hustle. You know what 'lucrative' means, Derrick? Probably not—it's got more than two syllables."

He didn't say anything, but his eyes were hooded, the smoke from the cigarette curling up into them so I couldn't read his expression.

I was still slurring my words like a wino on a two-day bender, and the blood I'd swallowed was making me nauseous, but I kept talking. I had to get it out while I still could, had to find out if I'd pieced it together properly.

"So you followed Strassky home, or maybe you looked her up in the phone book and were there waiting for her. And you beat her to death with a hunk of wood. Then you riffled through her briefcase to see if there was anything in it about you. That's just one of the ways you played it stupid, Derrick. If you'd taken her money, the police would have thought it was a robbery gone bad. Or if you'd raped *her*, too . . ."

"That old skanky dyke?" he sneered. "I wouldn't of fucked her with somebody else's dick."

Tyrone stirred uncomfortably and glowered at Derrick. "Shit, man," he protested, "that's—inappropriate."

Derrick silenced him with a look.

"So you fixed it that Jason would take the heat for both the rape and the killing," I said. "But that wasn't enough for you. You still had to make sure nobody caught on you were dealing. So you figured you'd send the police looking his way on that, too, as long as you were at it. You went up and planted that smack in his toilet tank after he'd moved out, and then dropped a dime on him. Easy, wasn't it? You had a key—it's your mother's house.

"I should have doped that one out a long time ago," I went on, "but to me you were just a weird-looking punk in a funny hat, hanging out on the sidewalk because you had nothing better to do, and it never occurred to me. I was looking somewhere else."

"At Yagemann," Tyrone said.

I swiveled my hear around to look at him. "Good guess, Tyrone. Shot in the dark?"

He shrugged.

He wasn't a good enough actor. I could tell I was getting to him. I could see that behind his eyes, he was worrying that if I had figured it out, someone else might, too.

I liked that. The more rattled he got, the better my chances for ever collecting Social Security.

"Yagemann could have made an extra key before he left. And the woman said he had smoker's breath, and Yagemann smoked. So I went after him for the rape, and the murder, too. And that's when I found out he was a junkie."

Derrick scraped his feet on the floor, dirt making a scratching sound on the soles of his shoes.

"And you were selling it to him, Derrick, right? Probably the one who got him hooked in the first place."

"Gimme a break," Derrick whined. "He had a habit before I ever saw him."

"Well, good for you—a gold star next to your name in the Book of Life. You're going to need all of them you can get. Because when I braced him in his apartment about using, I thought he was trying to call his father on the phone, but he was calling you instead, wasn't he? So you could bail him out, tell him what to do. His friend, his candy man."

Tyrone cleared his throat. "Whyn't you give it a rest, man?"

Derrick didn't look at him this time; he was too busy staring holes through me. "Let him talk," he murmured.

"You knew Terry was a spoiled rich kid," I said, "and that if the cops leaned on him even a little bit, he'd roll over on you like an old man who wakes himself up with his own snoring. So you counseled him, wise and good pal that you are, to clear out of his apartment and come to you, and you'd protect him and let him hole up here in the house for a while. Am I right so far?"

Derrick blinked like a lizard sunning itself on a rock.

"You had to make sure he didn't blow the whistle on you, though. So when he came over here, you and your pals took him for a ride in the country, blew off the back of his head, and threw him in a ditch."

Tyrone moved his head nervously and folded his arms across his chest.

"And that was the dumbest thing of all, Derrick," I continued, fighting down the bile that was twisting my stomach and banging away at the back of my throat. "It automatically took the heat off him for everything, which was where everybody was looking. Now they're going to look someplace else. Eventually at you."

"Bite my dick," he said.

"You must have figured, after you thought it over—after it was too late—that with Terry gone I'd eventually get around to you, too. That's why you brought me here. That's why you're going to kill me."

"I'm gonna like killing you," he said.

"Maybe, but it's a waste of time. The cops aren't going to quit. Not the Sherman cops, not the Cleveland cops, and for sure not the feds who want to know who's pushing heroin on campus. They'll eliminate everybody else and start looking at you and your buddies here, and you're all going down for it. Hard."

He drew deeply on the cigarette, and I thought I saw a little flicker of uncertainty behind his eyes. He blew the smoke out, in my direction, with a little bit too much bravado to be convincing.

I was getting to him now, I could tell. I pushed hard. "Ever been in the joint, Derrick? Any of you? Not the local jail, which is Disney World compared to a hard-core maximum-security pen. Ever have a cellmate who outweighs you by fifty pounds and likes to call you Momma?"

Tyrone looked away from me. Loyal didn't because he hadn't been looking at me in the first place; he hadn't been looking anywhere.

"Those cons at Mansfield are gonna love you, Derrick. A young, skinny kid like you, and a sex offender, at that. You think you're a mean mother because you smacked some little girl around and made her have sex with you. Because you beat an unarmed woman to death. Because it took three of you to kill Terry Yagemann."

"Hey, I's jus drivin' the car," Tyrone protested, and Derrick shot him a poisonous look.

I looked at him too. "Well, it might go a little easier for you when you get to prison, Tyrone. But Derrick here—he won't be such a hard guy after a while. He's going to find out what it's like to get raped."

Derrick jumped to his feet so quickly that his top hat fell off. He came over to me, taking the half-smoked Camel out of his mouth. But he didn't light another one with it.

Instead he stubbed it out on my cheek.

CHAPTER TWENTY-TWO

I wasn't going to give him the satisfaction of screaming, but I couldn't stifle the involuntary groan that sneaked out from between my clenched teeth. I could actually hear the flesh crisping, smell the sick-sweet odor of it. I fought down a gag reflex and tried not to black out.

Loyal returned from the twilight zone for a few minutes to cheerlead. "Yeah, Derrick!" he urged. "Burn the sumbitch! Burn him!"

Tyrone, who had been leaning against the wall, pushed himself off and was at Derrick's side in an instant, his arm blocking the other boy from coming at me again.

"Hey, knock it off! I mean it." Derrick looked at him, but Tyrone stared him down. "I ain't into that shit, an' I ain't gonna stand here an' watch you do it! So you jus' quit it, Derrick! I mean it!"

Well. There was at least some humanity in the room, a scintilla of decency hitherto unexpected. I blinked back tears of pain and a red rage that had enveloped me like fog rolling in off the lake. "But Derrick has to prove what a hard-ass he is, Tyrone. I wonder how brave he'd be if I wasn't tied up and he didn't have two guns to back him."

"Shut your hole, old man," Derrick warned.

"Right. I am old. You could take me easy. You're twenty-five years younger than me, you have youth on your side. Besides, my hands and feet are practically numb. Hell, give it a try, why don't you? One on one."

I knew I was skating on pretty thin ice, but I wanted to goad him now; dizzying pain had made me reckless. Besides, maybe he was stupid enough to bite. "Come on, Derrick," I said. "Cut me loose, if you have the guts. Just you and me. Show your buddies what a hard guy you are. Big shot—dot the *i*."

The little bastard was actually thinking about it. I could see the wheels turning—slowly, I admit, but turning.

"But no guns," I said. "And no fair your pals helping you. I lose, you kill me. I win, I walk out of here. You're such a macho guy, a beat-up old fart like me shouldn't give you any trouble."

Tyrone moved closer to me and lowered his voice; little beads of sweat decorated his forehead and upper lip like fake jewels on a Halloween costume. "Be cool, man. I'm tryin' to keep him offa you, but you keep talkin' trashmouth an' I won't be responsible."

"You're already responsible for two people dead," I reminded him, matching his muffled tone. "Directly or indirectly. Want to try for three?"

He shrugged elaborately. "Don' matter no more now, then. I jus' don' think you needs to be mistreated."

I raised my voice to make sure Derrick could hear. "It's all talk, Tyrone. He won't try me because he knows I'll clean his clock for him. Because I was fighting dirty when he was still sitting in his own shit."

Derrick rose to the bait. "You old bag of crap! You wouldn't last ten fucking seconds."

"Sure I would. Because in ten seconds I'd have kicked your balls clear up to the top of your head and gouged out an eye with my thumb. After that I could take my time—maybe rip off an ear. Or knock all your teeth out, one by one. Then you'd look like an old man, too."

Derrick's face was pale and drawn. He lit another cigarette, and it quivered between his lips.

"So that's why you won't cut me loose and fight, Derrick. Because you're nothing but a gutless pussy!"

Derrick's eyes got crazy, almost crossing, and he pulled the Glock from his waistband and leveled it at my face at the end of a straight, trembling arm. The bore was about three inches from my eye. He couldn't miss.

Tyrone slapped his arm away. "Damn foo'!"

"I'll cap the motherfucker right here!" Derrick foamed.

"No you won'!" Tyrone got between us and held Derrick's gun hand with both of his. "You gonna wait, man, jus like you 'sposed to. Be cool."

Nose-to-nose with Tyrone, who was several inches shorter, but solidly built and, when all was said and done, a whole lot more imposing, Derrick made a herculean effort to calm himself. Finally he dropped his gaze and took a couple of steps backward. "Make him shut his hole, then," he murmured, and went back to sit down on the milk crate, staring down at the floor between his dirty white sneakers.

Tyrone regarded me with a mixture of sympathy and what might have been admiration. He didn't realize that if I ever got loose, I would try to take out all three of them. I might have done it, too.

"Jus' keep your mouth quiet," he urged. "Don' make it no harder on yourself than it already is."

Our eyes locked for a few seconds, and finally I nodded. Tyrone went back to his job of holding up the wall, and I slumped down on my cot again, my cheek throbbing horribly. I was still in a towering rage, and felt fully capable of doing to Derrick exactly what I'd threatened.

I wanted to. And that bothered me.

I had one thing going for me—I knew they weren't going to kill me right then. The Happiness Boys were obviously under orders from a higher authority to keep me around for a while.

The basement was cold and dank, the kind of damp cold that sneaks its way into your bones, and after a few minutes I heard the furnace kick on across the room. It clanked almost as noisily as the one in the basement of my office building.

After a while Tyrone pushed himself away from the wall again and looked nervously at his watch. It was heavy gold, obviously very expensive. The drug business must be good.

In another ten minutes or so, I heard the muscular hum of a powerful car engine, and the glare of headlights illuminated the dirty streaks on the basement window; then they went out, the engine stopped, and a car door slammed. Footsteps on the gravel outside seemed to be coming toward the house.

The rapping on the pane of glass in the basement door was sharp, as if it had been done with a hard object like a car key instead of a knuckle. Derrick turned and stared at Loyal, who hastened to scamper obediently up the steps and unlock it.

I'd pretty much figured it out already, but when I saw the tan tassled loafers and the brushed cotton Dockers descending the stairs, I knew for sure. I waited until I saw the sweater— a vivid yellow cashmere this evening—before I said, "Hello there, Schuyler the Third. We've been waiting for you."

Trey Dotson came all the way into the basement, Loyal following him at a respectful distance. He stood under the dim 40-watt bulb and looked at me, seemingly amused. He took a few more steps toward me and his hand reached out and hovered near the cigarette burn on my face, not touching it.

"The surgeon general is right. Smoking can be hazardous to your health," he said.

He was a comedian, Trey.

"So who's 'in play' now, Mr. Jacovich?"

Loyal went to the Igloo cooler and fished out a dripping can. "Wanna brew, Mr. Dotson?"

Trey regarded it as if it was a vial of untreated riverwater. "I don't think so," he said.

Loyal seemed disappointed, but not so much so that he didn't open the can and drink some himself.

Trey turned his attention back to me. "You couldn't leave it alone, could you? You had to be a smart guy and force our hand. It was foolish of you. And costly. To you, to us, and to poor Terry Yagemann."

"Are you actually blaming me?" I said. "I didn't rape anybody, Dotson. It was your buttboy Derrick who did that, and stirred everything up. If it wasn't for him, your little cash register would still be going *ka-ching!*"

"Not so little," he said, smiling easily. "Would it surprise you to know we've been grossing about two hundred and fifty thousand a month?"

I shook my head. "Nothing surprises me anymore. Not even your being the big kahuna in all of this."

"Oh?"

"Yeah." I shifted to a marginally more comfortable position on the cot. "None of these guys here have the smarts to run an operation like this. Takes someone with smarts. Like an associate professor. Where do you import the stuff from? Colombia?"

"Mexico," he said. "It's cheaper. Looks better on the P and L statement."

"For an academic, you're quite the businessman."

He ducked his head modestly. "I do my homework."

"Aren't you scared of getting caught?"

"Every business—especially one with big profits—has its risks. You just have to learn how to minimize them."

"Like you minimized Dorothy Strassky and Terry Yagemann?"

His eyes got flinty. "And how we're going to minimize you."

"And the girl?"

"If we have to. And if we do, it's because of you."

"No, Dotson. She's a gutsy kid. She just needed a little nudge."

"Well," he said, "we'll deal with that when and if the time comes."

My stomach roiled and flipped, and it wasn't from the pain or the blood I'd swallowed. I knew Joyce Hallen was in jeopardy, too, and I couldn't stand the thought of her being hurt anymore. I wondered how far these clowns were prepared to go—and what I could possibly do to stop them.

They'd probably take it to the limit. Three million a year is an impressive payday.

"You aren't as smart as you think, Dotson," I said. "Your mules here aren't exactly rocket scientists to begin with, but you've made your mistakes, too."

He put his hands on his hips, the pose one of well-turned-out insouciance. "I'd be fascinated to hear which ones."

"You blew it when you came to my place, all the way from Sherman, ostensibly to help Jason and wound up trying to scare him into confessing to crimes he didn't commit. Not exactly standard operating procedure for a faculty advisor. That's when I started wondering about you. And," I added, "that cherry-red 'Vette didn't come on an associate professor's pay."

"My family has a little money, so that wasn't really a factor. The thing is . . ." He took a deep breath preparatory to revealing to me what the thing was. "You didn't do anything about your suspicions." He smiled and cocked his head like a sparrow listening for the whir of the hawk's wings. "So now what does that tell us?"

"Don't treat me like some freshman in your Poly Sci 101."

He threw back his head and laughed, white teeth gleaming. Golden boy.

"Sorry, I didn't mean to be pedantic. Old habits die hard. What I meant was, you didn't follow up on what you suspected because you didn't have any proof." He raised a supercilious, perfectly sculpted eyebrow. "And no one ever went to prison for having a lousy attitude."

"Nobody with a Roman numeral three after their name, anyway."

Like an exotic dancer's last remaining veil, the affability fell away from him. "Here's the thing, Jacovich . . ."

Another thing. I waited to hear what this new thing was.

Clearing his throat ostentatiously, he sat down next to me on the cot as if we were two kids sharing a summer-camp confidence after lights-out. "We have to know what the police know." He watched me keen-eyed. "What you've told them."

I didn't speak.

"About us, I mean. About Derrick. I don't like surprises—what can we expect?"

"To spend the rest of your life with a number across your chest."

He sat back easily. "You're lying. I can tell by your eyes."

I was, so I didn't answer him.

"Even if Jason gets out from under the rape charge—and I expect he will, eventually—there's still the heroin in his apartment. And while he had no reason to kill the Strassky woman, they might look very closely at him for Terry Yagemann's death. They'll figure Jason killed him to shut him up about the drugs." He crossed one ankle carefully over his other knee. "The police have no reason in the world to look this way. As far as I know, you're the only one who can point them here, and with you out of the picture, I doubt we'll ever hear from them."

"How many other people are you going to put out of the picture, Dotson?"

His eyes were obsidian, fathomless. "For three million a year? As many as we have to."

"Hey, what're we fucking around for, Mr. Dotson?" Derrick whined. "Let's get it rolling here."

Mr. Dotson. Nice, respectful kid, Derrick.

"Learn some patience, Derrick." Trey got up from the cot; the jostling made my head hurt. "First we have to find out exactly how much Mr. Jacovich here has told the police."

Derrick went over to the boiler, which was now clanking merrily away. He turned the handle on the purge spigot and a stream of boiling water jetted into the bucket on the floor, sending up a rising cloud of steam. "Stick his hand in this for a while," he suggested, "and he'll sing any tune we want him to."

Suddenly my armpits were wet, and my shirt was sticking to the base of my spine.

Tyrone took a step toward Derrick; he moved fast, like a jungle cat. "None o' that shit, I tol' you ! You hear me?"

Dotson raised a cautionary hand to him, but addressed his number one mule. "You really are a barbarian, Derrick." He lifted a snide eyebrow, amused and contemptuous at once. "It's why I keep you around."

Derrick sulked. "I just wanna get this over with."

Trey Dotson's head jerked up suddenly, all senses on alert, like a deer disturbed at a watering hole. "What was that?" he said in a tense whisper.

Derrick looked puzzled. "What?"

"I heard a noise outside."

I thought I'd heard it, too. Like gravel being kicked ever so softly against the pane of the basement window.

"I didn't hear nothin'," Derrick said.

"I did, man," Tyrone put in.

"Go up and see what it was, Loyal."

Loyal jerked out of his stupor, rose, and started up the basement steps.

"Loyal," Dotson said.

The boy stopped halfway up and looked around.

"Leave the beer can here."

Embarrassed, Loyal put the beer can down, ducking his head, and continued up the steps.

Dotson sighed wearily. "Take your piece out of your pocket, Loyal, and hold it in your hand."

"Oh," Loyal said. "Yeah." He drew the Saturday night special from his pocket; it caught for a brief moment on the material. Then, yanking it free, he went up through the cellar door. Dotson shook his head almost sadly.

"Just who was it killed Dorothy Strassky, Dotson?" I said. "Derrick? On your orders?"

"In every operation," he explained patiently, "there are generals and there are combat infantrymen. Foot soldiers don't make policy decisions, and generals don't crawl through the mud on their bellies." He smiled self-deprecatingly. "Rank has its privileges."

"Hey!" Derrick protested, but it was pro forma.

I pulled my wrists against the duct tape some more. There was a little give in it, maybe about a sixteenth of an inch. Not enough. "Things are getting out of hand, Trey. Rapidly. How are you going to cover your ass for all of this?"

"I'll figure a way," he said. "I always do."

I could believe that—spoiled rich kid, and everything he touches turns to gold. "And more people will die if they get in your way."

"They shouldn't get in my way, then." He glanced up at the cellar door. "Where is that fucking Loyal?"

Tyrone said, "You want me to go up an' find him?"

Trey shook his head. "Give him another minute or two."

Well, that was another minute or two I had left alive. It wasn't nearly enough. I needed more time than that. Time to think about my sons, about Connie. About my life.

"Come on, Jacovich," Trey said. "Make this easy on everybody. I know that black policewoman came to see you tonight. The boys saw her. Just tell me what you told her."

"I think I'd rather watch you sweat," I said.

"You'll be the one to sweat. Look, I don't want to hurt you—but Derrick has no such compunctions. Do you, Derrick?"

"Huh?" Derrick said as another ten-dollar word flew over his head like incoming mortar fire.

"If you're going to use words like compunction to Derrick, Dotson, you'd better talk real slow."

Derrick crossed the basement in a bound, waving the gun. I don't think he would have shot me, but he would have smashed my face in if Dotson hadn't stopped him.

"Damn it, Derrick, go over and sit down! I don't want to have to tell you again!"

Derrick wet his skinny lips and started back to his milk crate, still holding the gun, when a horrendous crash shattered the silence and what was left of the cellar door came tumbling down the steps, closely followed by Reginald Parker, Ph.D., holding Loyal's Saturday night special in his meaty brown fist.

"Nobody moves!" he barked.

More from surprise than anything else, Derrick lifted the hand with the gun in it. He didn't get it much higher than his belt before Reggie drilled him through the heart, the roar of the shot reverberating off the cinderblock walls and cement floor. The Saturday night special wasn't much of a weapon, but it got the job done.

Derrick slammed back against the wall—a look of complete surprise on his sagging features—then bounced off and fell forward on his face.

There was a moment of complete stillness, like a videotape that had frozen on a single frame.

"Jesus," Trey Dotson breathed, drawing out the first syllable, and lifted both hands shoulder-high. His face was as colorless as meringue.

Tyrone was motionless, his hand hovering near the butt of

the pistol sticking out of his belt. Reggie moved his own weapon to point at him.

"This is Black History Month for you, bro," Reggie said. "You're black, and if you even *think* about going near that piece—you're *history*."

Tyrone laced his fingers behind his head. "Don' get nervous, bro. No problem."

"Big problem, kiddo," Reggie corrected him. He spoke to me without looking at me. "Are you all right, Milan?"

"Define your terms," I said.

Reggie gestured at Dotson with his weapon. "Cut him loose."

Trey brought his arms down very slowly. "He's taped. I have a knife in my pocket, but you'll have to let me get it out."

"Do it in slow motion," Reggie warned him. "Or you'll never move again."

Trey Dotson came toward me, putting one foot in front of the other almost daintily, as if he were traversing a mine field. He kept his body turned toward Reggie as his left hand moved slowly to his pocket.

"Careful," Reggie warned.

Trey opened his hand, fingers splayed out, to show he had no ill intent, then extracted from the pocket of his Dockers a Swiss Army knife which was attached to his key chain, and showed it respectfully to Reggie.

"Okay?" he said.

"Use the little blade."

Trey did as he was told. When he'd opened the small blade with his fingernails, he knelt at my feet and carefully sliced the duct tape from my ankles. It hurt like hell as the blood came rushing back into my feet, and I winced as I wriggled my toes in hopes of increasing the circulation.

"Have the local police been notified?" I asked Reggie.

"Coming."

"Good. Thought you were doing another one of your famous one-man shows."

Reggie allowed himself a small smile. "Now the hands," he said to Dotson.

I turned my body around so he could get to my hands, taped behind my back. It gave me a moment's pause knowing that Trey Dotson was behind me with a knife—even a little one. But he must have realized that before he could do much damage to me, he'd be dead. Reggie, standing on the steps, wearing his glasses and a corduroy sport coat over an argyle sweater and brandishing that Saturday night special, must have looked to him like the embodiment of Genghis Khan.

I felt the blade sawing through the thick tape on my wrists. Then, a release of the pressure and I was free, my hands prickling from the points of a thousand needles. I stood up, staggering a little on my ankles, and flapped my hands around, flexing the fingers. It was sweet pain I was feeling.

"Drop the knife on the floor and kick it over here," Reggie ordered.

Trey did.

"Frisk him, Milan."

Through all my aches and pains I had to smile. The only cop in history who had ever said, "Frisk him!" was played by the old character actor, Barton MacLane, in countless Warner Bros. black-and-white movies.

"Assume the position," I said gruffly. I shoved Trey's legs against the edge of the cot and pushed the top half of his body forward so both his hands were on the wall, a technique still remembered from my days on the police force. It's like riding a bicycle—you never really forget how.

"He's clean," I said, after patting Trey down thoroughly. I wasn't surprised. People like Trey Dotson didn't carry concealed—they left the dirty work to the other guys.

Which made me wonder just how hard Trey would take the

fall. For the drugs, yes, certainly. But for the murders of Dorothy Strassky and Terry Yagemann? It would be Derrick Coombes' word against his in court. And if you were on the jury, which one would *you* believe?

That troubled me.

I turned him around roughly to face me, and pushed him down on the cot. Hard.

"Where's Loyal?" I said to Reggie.

"Who?"

"The kid who went outside a few minutes ago. The kid whose weapon you—borrowed."

"Oh. He's taking a nap."

Reggie came the rest of the way down the steps and turned his attention and his gun on Tyrone. "Okay, junior. With the thumb and forefinger of your left hand, take that piece out of your pants—*oh* so slowly—and set it down on the floor."

"Okay, man. I will. You jus' be cool now." Tyrone followed instructions well.

"Now kick it over toward Mr. Jacovich. An on-side kick, nice and easy."

The .9-mm skittered across the floor to me like a scampering rat, and I bent down and scooped it up while it was still moving. I would have made a great shortstop.

I checked to make sure it was still loaded. It was.

More silence, except that the cold air rushing through the demolished doorway made the furnace clank again. And then the sound of distant sirens—usually a cold, frightening, eerie sound, but tonight it sounded to me like Beethoven.

"It's about time," I said.

And then the door to the house at the top of the second set of stairs slammed open and the barrel of a shotgun came poking through it, followed by a distraught-looking Mrs. Coombes, still in her Betty Crocker drag. She took in the scene and her eyes fastened on Derrick's lifeless body, what little color she had draining from her doughy face.

"What-all you done to my boy?" she wailed, and swiveled the shotgun in Reggie's direction.

"Wait!" Trey cried, springing up from the cot and moving toward her.

I saw her knuckle whitening as her finger tightened on the trigger. It must have been a tight pull, because it took her a second. I raised up Tyrone's .9-mm and shot her in the shoulder.

She half turned toward me, and the impact of the slug twisted her around a little farther; the pain must have caused her finger to tighten involuntarily, because the shotgun's roar filled the basement just before she fell.

And the left half of Trey Dotson's face went away in a red mist.

The sirens came closer, got louder, painfully assaulting our eardrums. Outside, brakes squealed, car doors slammed, running feet crunched over gravel. Khaki-clad legs appeared at the top of the outside stairs.

"Drop your piece, Milan," Reggie yelled, suiting his own action to his words, and raised his hands. I threw the .9-mm away from me onto the cot, stepped over what was left of Trey Dotson, and did the same.

Two state troopers, one of them fortyish and black, the other a pink-faced kid, clattered down, service weapons drawn. They took a millisecond to look at the carnage.

"Highway Patrol!" the older one announced, as if there was any question.

"Oh, sure," I said. "*Now.*"

CHAPTER TWENTY-THREE

It was morning. Finally.

Midmorning, actually, after a long night. Reggie and I had spent about ten hours at the state police barracks in Elyria, telling our stories in separate interview rooms, to separate officers, several times, and finally, each giving formal statements that took forever to transcribe. Luckily for me, the troopers seemed to have a limitless supply of Tylenol, which I'd been popping every few hours for my various hurts. But my head still ached, my cheek was throbbing and blistered, and I was wired to the eyeballs on at least an entire pot of cop-shop coffee.

And now we were sitting in a little eatery just off 1-90 in Sheffield, halfway between Sherman and Cleveland, the kind of place that styles itself a "family restaurant," drinking even more bad coffee. Our fellow diners—a couple of long-haul truckers taking an early lunch and several senior citizens enjoying a late breakfast—never would have guessed that we were within hours of having witnessed two violent deaths.

We were talking it over.

When shots are fired and when one person saves another's life, there are things to be talked about.

Even though we had shared much, Reggie and I, things were strangely stiff between us at first. Almost the way it is after the first time you've made love with someone who's previously been just a friend or a coworker, and you're not a hundred percent sure it was such a terrific idea after all.

The sun had finally remembered where northeast Ohio is, and we were both squinting out the big window next to our table, watching the world go about its business—mostly people who hadn't shot anybody within the last twenty-four hours.

Reggie was stirring two packets of Equal into his coffee, and the sound of the spoon against the side of the cup was vaguely irritating. Finally he said, "You should see a doctor about your head, Milan. I think you were concussed."

"I've been concussed before. I know how to take care of it."

"Yes, I've seen the way you take care of yourself."

"It comes with the license."

I took a deep breath and met his eyes directly. "So do friends like you, I guess. If you hadn't saved my ass, I'd be fertilizing a cornfield by now. How the hell did you manage to show up in Sherman when we were supposed to be having dinner in Cleveland Heights?"

"I was just pulling into the parking lot next to Nighttown when I saw your car going out," he said, "but I couldn't see you in it. The black kid was driving and the dorky white boy was in the passenger seat, and neither of them looked like they might be friends of yours who were borrowing a ride. Then I noticed another car right on their tail—I couldn't make out the driver, but he seemed to be wearing a top hat. I thought there was something funny going on, but I just figured they were stealing your car. So I followed them."

"Clear out to Sherman?"

He nodded. "I imagined they'd head directly to some chop shop on the east side and I could call the cops in then. Bust the carjackers and the chop-shop guys in one fell swoop. By the time I realized they were taking a long freeway trip, it was too late."

"Why didn't you call the law from your car phone?"

"I didn't know exactly what was going on. What if you *had* loaned them your car? And I didn't want to risk a high-speed highway chase. Innocent people get hurt when cops are in hot pursuit at a hundred miles an hour. Don't you watch those car-chase reality shows on Fox?"

"No. And I'm amazed that you do."

"I have lots of vices you don't know about, Milan." He gulped down some coffee and evidently, like Goldilocks, found it too hot, because he grimaced and took a quick sip of ice water. "Anyway, I thought I'd wait till they stopped, if for no other reason than I didn't want your car getting totaled." He grinned wryly. "Even though it's time you got a new one. Been driving that one six or seven years, haven't you?"

"Nine," I said, "but who's counting?"

"Anyway—when I finally realized they were heading for Sherman, under the circumstances of the Jason Crowell thing it kind of piqued my interest. So I followed then right to the mouth of that alley that runs behind the house."

"And?"

"And I parked out of sight around the corner, walked back into that alley, and saw them haul you out of the backseat and stick a gun under your chin."

"Why didn't you do something about it then?" I said, my fingers fluttering around the angry red blister on my cheek. "You would have saved me some pain."

"I wasn't armed, Milan. I'm a high-school principal; I don't pack a gun to go out to dinner!"

"Oh," I grumbled. "Right."

"Besides, then the Coombes kid drove up and went around the front of the house. I peeked into the basement window. I could see you were in bad shape, but I didn't figure them to kill you right there. Even Coombes wasn't stupid enough to foul his own nest. And that wasn't their MO anyway—remember Terry Yagemann in the culvert?"

I suppressed a shudder. I remembered Terry Yagemann in the culvert all too well—and whose fault it was that he'd wound up there.

"Anyway," Reggie said, "that's when I went back to my car and called Highway Patrol."

"How come not the Sherman police?"

He shrugged. "It's a small department, Milan, in a quiet college town. Small town cops like that, I don't think any one of them has ever unholstered his weapon except to clean it." He looked sheepish. "I explained what was going on to a trooper over the phone, and he put in a radio call. Unfortunately, that meant it took them a little longer to get there."

"Unfortunately," I said. Every part of me was hurting.

"So I went back to watch some more and saw the Coombes kid burn you. I decided not to wait for the cops anymore. Except that's when Dotson showed up. He almost saw me. I had to do a Fosbury flop over the fence into the neighbor's yard. Tore my pants and risked my ass doing it."

"Risked your ass?"

He grinned. "A small-town rural Ohio homeowner looks out his window and sees a black guy in his backyard, he grabs his deer rifle first and asks questions later."

I sighed, and winced as I slurped at my own burning coffee. The inside of my mouth was cut, too.

"So," Reggie said, "after Dotson went inside, I figured if I made just a little noise back there, someone would come out and see what was going on. That big dumb kid, he comes out waving that popgun around like he was in an old John Wayne movie. I sneaked up behind him and hit him in back of the ear with the edge of my hand. He never knew what hit him; he went down like a dead red bird."

"And you took his gun."

"He wasn't using it at the moment. Piece of crap it was, too."

"It got the job done."

Some lambent light behind his eyes, some spark, flickered uncertainly and then went out. He stopped and pushed his cup away, staring out the window. But he was looking inward and I could see the pain in him.

"The Coombes kid," I said.

The kid he'd killed.

I knew where he was coming from. I'd ridden that same horse myself. The self-loathing, the torment . . . We're so inured to mindless violence on TV and in the movies, we really don't comprehend what it's like to take a human life.

Until we do.

And then we live with it every waking moment. The circumstances might justify it, but that doesn't really matter when you wake up shaking in the middle of the night, soaked with the sweat of remorse and guilt and what-might-have-beens.

"You had no choice, Reg," I said.

"I know." He spoke softly, not looking at me. "But, Jesus, Milan! He was just a kid!"

"Just a kid who'd already killed two people and was going to make me his third-time lucky charm." I was trying to make him feel better, but deep down I knew it wouldn't work.

He nodded. He filled his lungs with air and held it a few seconds too long before expelling it wearily; it sounded like a ghostly wind sighing through a pine barren. His deeply shadowed eyes were sunken in their sockets, and his mouth was an inverted bow like a theatrical tragedy mask. He cleared his throat too loudly. "You know what's been pecking at my liver, Milan?"

"What?"

"I've been thinking, what if Derrick Coombes had been one of my kids? At St. Clair High, I mean. If I could've gotten hold of him three, four years ago—worked with him—maybe I could have turned him around."

"Don't even go there, Reggie."

"No really. Look. A kid is born on the east side of Cleveland. Say your kid. Milan Junior, okay?"

"Okay," I said.

"His family loves and nurtures him, even though his father is sometimes too dumb to tie his own shoes. . . ." He glanced at me apologetically. "Well, sometimes you are, Milan. Anyway, he's taught values and respect. He goes to a school where the teachers give a damn. He winds up at Kent State on a football scholarship."

"Partial scholarship." I reached for a cigarette, then remembered, when we'd come in Reggie had asked for a seat in the nonsmoking section. With more regret than you could imagine, I dropped my hand back onto the table.

"Now there's another kid, same age. Born in Sherman or wherever. Father, address unknown right now. Mother, a greedy, grubbing Ma Barker of a harridan who teaches him nothing except how to get away with it. Falls into the clutches of somebody like Trey Dotson, who thinks he can use him. He winds up dead on the floor of a dirty basement." He drummed a piano riff on the edge of the table. "I guess I just don't understand how that happens."

"Luck of the draw, Reggie. Your family are black Baptists; mine, Slovenian Catholics. You turned out smart and tough, I turned out big and dumb. Who knows why? It's not the cards you draw, it's how well you play them."

He took off his glasses and rubbed his eyes. "I'll never forget him lying there on his face with the blood spreading out underneath him—"

"Forget it!"

"Easy for you to say."

"It's not easy for me to say! I've been there, too. Besides, you were a Green Beret, you've killed people before. . . ."

"Yeah, but the army gave me a Bronze Star for it."

"Keeping the world safe for democracy. That's what they told us, anyway. . . ."

He snorted.

"Isn't that what we all do, Reg?" I said, leaning forward. "In our own small, bumbling, sometimes pitiful way? Try to make the world a little better?"

"Did I make the world better for the Coombes kid?"

"You made it better for me, because he would've killed me. You made it better for Joyce Hallen because he would've killed her, too. That's the catch, Reg, we've got to make choices."

"Choices . . ." he murmured.

"Derrick had choices, too, just like the rest of us. He made bad ones."

Reggie didn't say anything. He picked up his coffee mug, and it was evidently cool enough to drink now, because he gulped most of it down as if he was thirsty.

"Marko Meglich said something to me a few days before he died," I went on. "Now Marko was a cop, he'd dedicated his life to law and order. Think about those words, Reg. Law and order. He was upholding the law and keeping the order, keeping things neat and in line so the rest of us could function productively. But even he told me he couldn't be a cop for the whole world. He couldn't get his knickers in a twist because somebody was breaking the law in Kansas City or Chicago, because that way he'd go nuts. He just did the best he could."

My chest burned with old sorrow.

"Yeah," Reggie said. "And when Marko stepped out from between the lines, he died."

"And when you stepped out, somebody else died. It wasn't your fault—you just did what you could do." I took a gulp of ice water to cool down the heat inside me. "A lot of kids that come through your school might turn out like Derrick Coombes if not for you. You make a difference, Reg, a hell of a difference. Be proud of that and feel good about it, instead of eating yourself alive because you can't save the whole world."

He remained silent for a long moment, staring out the window some more, and then he snapped out of it, almost shaking himself the way a Labrador retriever does when he first comes out of the water with a duck in his mouth.

"You son of a bitch," I said.

"Me?"

"Yes, you. I only got involved with the Jason Crowell business because you saved my life a few years ago. Because I couldn't very well say no to you."

He leaned back against the cushion of the booth.

"And now you saved my life for the second time."

"And that makes me a son of a bitch?"

"Damn right it does. Because now I owe you—"

The smile only reached one corner of his mouth, but it was there, all right, because he knew where I was going, and he was loving it.

"—again," I said.

Mrs. June Coombes—it didn't help me to learn the first name of the woman I had shot—got fifteen years for conspiracy to commit a crime, drug trafficking, and attempted murder. They didn't nail her for Trey Dotson—the coroner ruled that "accidental."

Tyrone got thirty years to life. He'll probably be out on parole in another twenty.

Joyce Hallen went on with her life, got her degree, and moved to New York City.

Jason Crowell couldn't very well stay at Sherman. There were too many bad memories, and even though he was publicly cleared of the accusation leveled at him by Women Warriors, people still looked at him strangely on the campus and whispered behind their hands. He took a large chunk of the enormous settlement Jeremiah Locke squeezed out of the college and moved to San Francisco to continue his art studies—and to get away from his father.

It was probably the best thing he could have done under the circumstances, but it didn't keep me from feeling tremendously sad that a parent could be so single-minded and righteous, that Jim Crowell could reject his son for being who he was. I was glad my own sons had no such problems to deal with, but I knew without doubt that if they had, it would make no difference at all in my love or caring for them.

But Jason, like all of us, had to learn to play the cards he'd been dealt.

Women Warriors—both of them—I don't know about. I think Judy Naft might have learned her lesson, because she spent the rest of her college career keeping a fairly low profile. But Diana Flaster remained as angry and militant as ever, and never really admitted her mistake, at least not to me, and didn't even bother apologizing to Jason for sending his life spinning out of control. She was one of those people whose agenda, however worthy, blinds them to everything else around them, including even the truth.

Of course, I didn't know any of this when I said good-bye to Reggie Parker at that little family restaurant in Sheffield, climbed wearily into my reclaimed nine-year-old car, and started back to Cleveland. All I knew was that I'd ventured pretty close to the edge, I'd almost reached the abyss, and that I'd probably never come any closer without going over.

I drove east, the sun burning an image on my retinas as I squinted through the windshield, and I realized that I hadn't eaten in a long while. I'd missed my dinner at Nighttown, spent breakfast time giving a statement to the police, and had been too upset to eat anything when Reggie and I were doing our "recap."

And there I was, on the freeway that cut through Cleveland's western suburbs, perhaps four minutes away from the White Magnolia.

And I wanted to see Connie.

More than I ever imagined I would.

I wanted to sit at the Magnolia bar and eat three or four of Sean's roast-beef sandwiches, and to look at her eyes and her mouth and her dimples, to touch her hand, her face, to put my arms around her and feel the softness against me, breathe the fresh shampoo-smell of her hair, and somehow let her know, without being too specific and frightening her away, that when I had thought I was done for, one of my last thoughts had been of her.

I made a decision quickly, cut across three lanes of freeway traffic, and headed up the off-ramp.

What the hell, I had to eat anyway.